**I couldn't believe I had let n
was in danger too…**

D1111205

I had just started to head l
stepped into my way. Bone-chilling fear rattled me as my
eyes locked with his sinister stare. "Laken," he said with an
evil smile. "It's time for you to come with me."

An icy blast of panic shot through me. I looked around
him, searching for an escape route. But it was hopeless. I
was trapped between him and the Explorer, and I had no
doubt that he'd catch me if I tried to run. My nerves on edge
and my heart nearly jumping out of my chest, I forced myself to remain calm. "But you don't want me. You told me
that."

"That's right. I want your boyfriend. But he had twenty-
four hours to show up, and yet he's nowhere to be found. So
it's time for plan B. If he won't come for his father, perhaps
he'll come for you." Efren grabbed my arm and, as I opened
my mouth to scream, he darted behind me, covering my
mouth with his free hand. "You really don't want to do
that," he whispered in my ear. "Let your parents sleep. I
don't want to have to hurt them."

Tears burst from my eyes. I couldn't believe this was
happening. How could I have been so stupid to leave my
phone in the truck? Dakota wasn't even around to protect
me. Left with no choice but to obey, I held still as his hand
dropped from my mouth to my ribs, anchoring my body
against him.

"There, now. It's much easier to cooperate, isn't it?" he
asked. One of his arms released me and a strange pop
sounded, like that of a cap coming off a container. Then a
needle pierced my upper arm through my sleeve and something cold was pumped into me. As the liquid circulated
through my veins, the dim light from the single bulb outside
the house blurred. I fought to stay awake, but I lost that battle, watching the shadows whip around me for a split second
before my world went black.

On her own since Noah walked away, Laken finds her resistance to Xander crumbling. As she turns to him for comfort, the stranger in the woods reappears, threatening Xander and his father, Caleb.

When Caleb reveals the secrets he and Xander have been protecting, Laken realizes she must stop at nothing to help them defeat the stranger. But Xander eludes him, and Laken is captured instead. Facing an unknown fate at the hands of a mad man driven by greed and jealousy, she resolves to fight to the bitter end for her life and her love.

The stakes are high, and no one, including Dakota, is safe. Will Laken survive, or will the curse she tossed aside as a fairy tale prove to be true?

(Twenty-five cents for every print and ebook copy sold will be donated to the Ian Somerhalder Foundation.)

KUDOS for *Surrender at Sunrise*

In *Surrender at Sunrise* by Tonya Royston, we get the third installment of Laken, Xander, and Noah. In this version, we discover why Noah has been acting so strangely, and what Xander and his dad have been hiding. You just can't help feeling for Laken as she uncovers one dark secret after another. Is there anyone who hasn't been lying to her? She has to grow up in a hurry, while protecting herself and those she loves from danger. A hard row to hoe when you are only 18. Like the first two books in the trilogy, this one is well written with a number of twists and turns that keep you guessing—and turning pages—from beginning to end. ~ *Taylor Jones, Reviewer*

Surrender at Sunset by Tonya Royston is a worthy addition and a satisfying conclusion to the *Sunset Trilogy*. Our heroine, Laken Sumner, is mourning her breakup with Noah, the sheriff's deputy, who left her with no explanation. But she can't be too down as Xander is still making his interest known. Laken finds herself drawn to Xander for reasons she can't explain, but she doesn't completely trust him. And why should she? She knows he's hiding something, but then so is Noah. Men! It seems the only one she can trust is Dakota, and he's a wolf. As Laken struggles to discover what Noah and Xander are hiding, and who the stranger is who seems to be stalking her, she uncovers some dark secrets that shake her faith in what she believes. Now she is fighting for her life and the lives of those she loves, including Dakota. Royston's love of animals, especially wolves, comes through clearly in this exciting tale of love, loss, courage, and forgiveness. The *Sunset Trilogy* is a page-turner that will appeal to animal lovers, romantics, and suspense fans of all ages, easily crossing the YA, NA, and adult genres. ~ *Regan Murphy, Reviewer*

Surrender at Sunrise

Book Three of the Sunset Trilogy

Tonya Royston

A Black Opal Books Publication

Black Opal Books

BECAUSE SOME STORIES JUST HAVE TO BE TOLD

GENRE: PARANORMAL THRILLER/YA/PARANORMAL ROMANCE

This is a work of fiction. Names, places, characters and incidents are either the product of the author's imagination or are used fictitiously, and any resemblance to any actual persons, living or dead, businesses, organizations, events or locales is entirely coincidental. All trademarks, service marks, registered trademarks, and registered service marks are the property of their respective owners and are used herein for identification purposes only. The publisher does not have any control over or assume any responsibility for author or third-party websites or their contents.

SURRENDER AT SUNRISE ~ Book Three of the Sunset Trilogy
Copyright © 2016 by Tonya Royston
Cover Design by Jennifer Gibson
All cover art copyright © 2016
All Rights Reserved
Print ISBN: 978-1-626944-93-0

First Publication: JULY 2016

All rights reserved under the International and Pan-American Copyright Conventions. No part of this book may be reproduced or transmitted in any form or by any means, electronic or mechanical, including photocopying, recording, or by any information storage and retrieval system, without permission in writing from the publisher.

WARNING: The unauthorized reproduction or distribution of this copyrighted work is illegal. Criminal copyright infringement, including infringement without monetary gain, is investigated by the FBI and is punishable by up to 5 years in federal prison and a fine of $250,000. Anyone pirating our ebooks will be prosecuted to the fullest extent of the law and may be liable for each individual download resulting therefrom.

ABOUT THE PRINT VERSION: If you purchased a print version of this book without a cover, you should be aware that the book is stolen property. It was reported as "unsold and destroyed" to the publisher, and neither the author nor the publisher has received any payment for this "stripped book."

IF YOU FIND AN EBOOK OR PRINT VERSION OF THIS BOOK BEING SOLD OR SHARED ILLEGALLY, PLEASE REPORT IT TO: lpn@blackopalbooks.com

Published by Black Opal Books **http://www.blackopalbooks.com**

DEDICATION

For Wolves Everywhere…

*I hope this world will someday
be a better place for all wildlife.*

Chapter 1

My world was falling apart. The morning after the stranger appeared in my backyard, I woke up wishing that the night had been a bad dream. But the man, his threats directed at Xander and his father, and Noah's confession that there was someone else were all very real. I was living my worst nightmare, and I didn't know where to turn.

I tried to use my calculus problems and the English essay due on Monday to distract me, but it was hopeless. Giving up on my homework, I called Brooke and relayed everything that happened with Noah after she and Ethan left. It helped to hear her voice, though she offered me little reassurance that Noah would be back soon, as she had over the last few weeks.

Later that evening after a long day of wondering what else would go wrong in my life, I returned to my homework. As I stared at the empty computer screen, the cursor blinking in the top left corner, my mind drew a blank. I lifted my eyes to the gray sky looming outside the window. Despite my leggings and sweatshirt, a chill raced through me. I felt as though the world was closing in on me. So much had happened in a short period of time. I had met Noah, fallen for him, and then lost him. I had learned that my mother wasn't my birth mother, and I had discovered that I'd been used as bait to lure Xander and his father to our sleepy town, although I still wasn't quite sure why. The last thing I could think about today was my homework.

I pondered over every word the stranger had said, trying to piece the clues together. The only thing that made sense was knowing that Ryder's disappearance had been carefully planned. It was somewhat of a relief to know his abduction hadn't been random, but it weighed on my shoulders now that I knew it had to do with me.

Something else nagged at me. The stranger said he'd watched Ivy from a distance. I wondered if she had known who he was and what he wanted. There was only one way to find out. I tore my eyes away from the computer to glance across the room at my dresser.

I jumped up and rushed over to it, pulling the top drawer open. After grabbing the shoebox containing memorabilia of my birth mother, I carried it back to the bed and sat on the edge. I held my breath as I removed the ragged lid, wondering what answers I might find.

Rummaging through the photographs, I paid no attention to Dakota, who watched me from his bed, a curious expression in his amber eyes. Finding the envelope that held Ivy's letter, I lifted it out from under the pictures. Then I set the box down beside me, forgetting about it as I ripped open the envelope and pulled out a handwritten letter.

After unfolding it, I began to read.

> *Laken,*
> *I trust that by the time you receive this, you are grown up and your father has explained why I had to give you up. I won't go into those details except to tell you that I loved you very much from the moment I felt you growing inside me until you*

were born. I also loved your father. He was every-thing to me. When I found out I was sick, I couldn't watch him suffer as I slipped away from this world. So I made the very difficult decision to leave. I know what it feels like to lose someone you love. I lost my mother to cancer when I was five years old. I remember the unbearable pain and sorrow it put me through, but I also remember the torment my father endured as he watched her fight a losing battle. I couldn't put you both through that. Gwen was an angel to take you into her arms as if she had given birth to you herself. I'm sure you would agree that she was the perfect woman to raise you as her own. I believed that she would care for you and love you as only a mother can.

Now that you are older, you may have noticed that you have a very special talent to communicate with animals. Don't be frightened of this. I, too, could talk to them, and they understood my thoughts. It was a gift my mother had, that she in-herited from her mother. I'm not sure how it all started or when, but I believe that this ability was bestowed upon our bloodline centuries ago. It has been passed on from mother to daughter, and you will pass it on to your daughter. Perhaps by the time you read this letter, you already have a little girl of your own.

I paused, lifting my tear-filled eyes to glance at Dakota. I wondered what my birth mother would have thought if she knew that her love of wolves lived on in me. Dakota raised his head, his ears up and pointed at me. He watched me, as if listening to me read the letter. My eyes met his for a brief moment before I dropped my gaze back down to finish reading.

I hope this helps you understand where you

came from and how you can talk to animals. At least you know that it's not just you, and I'm sure that's reassuring. I wish I could be there for you, to talk about all the wonderful things you can do with this gift, and to tell you some of what I experienced because of it. But life has dealt me a bad hand, and I will soon move on in death. I will watch over you from the stars above and, perhaps someday, only after you've had a lifetime of love and happiness with your own family, we will be reunited.

She had signed the letter, *All my love, your mother, Ivy.*

Nowhere had Ivy mentioned that a stranger would use me to find two people I had never known. If she hadn't warned me, then she must not have known anything about him. At least the letter reinforced what my father had already told me. There was no doubt in my mind that she had wanted me, but had made her decisions based on what was best for those she loved.

I carefully folded the letter back into place and slid it into the envelope. Someday, I would read it again. But for tonight, it was time to return the shoebox along with all my questions to the dresser and attempt to write the essay due tomorrow.

ᕮᔕᕮᔓ

I expected Xander to ambush me at my locker the next morning before homeroom but, to my surprise, he never appeared. His absence meant I would be spared his sarcasm and condescending remarks about Noah or anything else that came up in conversation. It also meant that I couldn't warn him about the stranger before the first class of the day as I had planned.

I tried calling him, but got his voice mail. Then I sent

him a quick text. *Where R U? We need to talk.* But he never answered me. Several times, I debated telling him about the stranger in a text. More than once, I worried that the stranger had already found him and my warning would be too late.

I was tempted to leave school and drive up to his house, but fear held me back. I finally decided that if I didn't hear from him by the end of the day, I would tell my father everything and let him and Noah take it from there.

I trudged through my classes as best as I could, turning in my essay with little confidence that I would get anything higher than a B minus grade, if even that. The day passed by slowly, and I caught myself dozing off in class several times due to my last two restless nights of little to no sleep. By the time the final bell rang, I still hadn't heard from Xander. I quickly rounded up Ethan for the ride home, reminding myself to act as if nothing was wrong. The less he knew, the better.

I said little on the way home. Instead of talking, we listened to the radio as a comfortable silence hung between us. When my house came into view in the distance, I immediately recognized Xander's black pick-up parked next to our mailbox. Relief settled over me. He was safe. But as I sighed with a silent thank you, I frowned. Why hadn't he responded to my text?

When I pulled into the driveway, Ethan asked, "Isn't that Xander's truck?" He turned to stare at it as I eased the Explorer to a stop facing the garage.

"Yes," I said, shutting off the engine and not bothering to give the pick-up another glance. I was exhausted and overwhelmed with conflicting emotions after such a long day. I'd been prepared to tell Xander about the man this morning after rehearsing what to say all night. But my carefully crafted speech suddenly escaped me, and all I wanted to do was rest.

"I wonder what he's doing here when he didn't show up for school today," Ethan mused.

"He probably wants me to give him my class notes from Friday and today."

"Or maybe he wants to ask you to the Halloween dance again," Ethan suggested with a teasing grin.

"If that's it, then he's wasting his time," I declared before hopping out of the SUV. I closed the door and grabbed my book bag from the back seat as Ethan jumped out on the other side.

When I turned away from the Explorer with my bag hanging from my shoulder, Ethan stood before me in the late afternoon sunshine. I squinted up at him, the descending sun behind him nearly blinding me as it hovered above the mountain.

With all the distractions from the weekend muddling my thoughts, I had left my sunglasses on my dresser this morning.

"Do you want me to stick around?" he asked.

"No. I can handle this. But thanks for the offer."

"Anytime. See you tomorrow for another fun day at school." Ethan smiled and raised his eyebrows for a moment before turning. His backpack hoisted over his black jacket, he headed across the lawn. I watched him stop at Xander's truck to look in the window. "He's not here," Ethan called over to me.

"He must be out back. I'll find him," I said before hurrying up the sidewalk to the front door, my keys jingling in my hand.

As soon as I let myself into the house, I locked the door and wandered into the kitchen where I dropped my things on the table. The house was warm, but I kept my parka on and went straight to the back door.

I stepped outside to find Xander sitting on the patio steps. His back was turned to me, his dark hair shining in the slanted afternoon light. Dakota lay beside him, basking in the sun as Xander rubbed the fur between his ears.

Hearing the door, Xander stood and turned, his black trench coat falling to his knees. His clear blue eyes met my curious gaze, and he smiled. "I hope you don't mind me waiting out here."

I stood a few feet away from the house and glanced at the patio table where a big silver box with a red ribbon tied around it had been placed. Then I looked back at Xander, noticing that Dakota lingered beside him, seeming hesitant to leave his side. "No, I guess not. I mean, if Dakota's okay with it, then I am, too." I didn't know what else to say since our last conversation had ended so abruptly when he'd told me I was naïve for believing that Noah would come back to me. But I could hardly stay mad at him. Not only had he been right, but now I was worried about him. I just hoped that my warning would keep him and his father out of harm's reach. "Come on in. It's pretty cold out here. I want to hear about your trip."

I gestured to the house before turning to lead the way. Dakota trotted across the patio and slipped inside while Xander went to the table to pick up the box. I held the door open for him as he carried the package into the house, our eyes meeting for a quick moment when he walked past me.

Once inside, I shut and locked the door. Leaning against it, I watched him set the box next to my book bag on the table. He slipped off his coat and hung it on the back of a chair.

Then he smiled across the kitchen at me. Even against his black shirt, his skin seemed darker than I remembered, kissed by the California sun from his weekend trip. "Don't you want to take your coat off?" he asked, breaking me out of my trance as I studied him.

"I guess so," I said, removing my parka to reveal the burgundy sweater I wore with jeans and tall black boots. I folded the parka over my arms as I lingered by the door. "You look like you got some sun. Did you have a nice time?"

"Aside from missing you?" he asked with a sly grin that faded into a wistful look when he continued. "Yeah, it was awesome to be home. A storm churned up the ocean and the waves were huge. I didn't realize how much I missed it until I got out there in the water."

"Well, maybe now that you've been on good behavior, your dad will move you back." The farther he and his father got from here and the man searching for them, the better.

Xander flashed a smile, choking out a laugh. "Not a chance. I hope that's not what you want."

"Well, no, I guess not. At least not until we're done with the History project."

"At least you're honest," he said.

I sighed with an awkward smile as I approached the table, dropping my coat on a chair. "What happened to you today? I thought you'd be at school."

"We flew back on the red-eye and didn't get home until about nine this morning. I went straight to bed."

I continued standing, hesitant to sit down and get too comfortable. "Is that why you didn't answer my text?"

"Sorry about that. I only saw it an hour ago, so I figured I'd meet you here." He paused then changed the subject. "I suppose you're wondering what this box is. It's a gift for you." He pushed it across the table until it reached the edge closest to me.

I glanced at him, not quite sure what to say or whether or not to accept it. "Xander, this is too much. I'm not sure I can take this from you." I looked down at the box, admiring the huge bow tied in the center.

"I can't return it. I picked it up in LA. It wasn't something I planned, trust me. I just stumbled upon something that reminded me of you. It's perfect for you, you'll see. You can open it later if you'd like."

I mustered up a weak smile. "Yes, I'd feel more comfortable waiting. You don't mind?" As curious as I was to know what he had brought back for me, I couldn't open it now, not when I needed to tell him about the stranger.

"No, not at all. I kind of figured you'd prefer to do that. Consider it a peace offering after the way we left things last week. Speaking of which, how's it going with Noah?"

"It's not," I blurted out. "And I'd rather not talk about that."

"Got it." Xander studied me for a minute, his eyes holding a mixture of sympathy and satisfaction. In the end, his satisfaction won out. "Maybe now you'll reconsider my invitation to the Halloween dance?" he asked, his voice hesitant.

"No," I replied flatly.

Xander nodded with a thoughtful smile. "Well, I still have four days to try to change your mind."

"I'm not going to change my mind." I shook my head, trying desperately to figure out the best way to change the subject and tell him about the stranger. "Can I get you something to drink?"

"Sure. I'll have whatever you're having."

"Diet Coke?"

"Works for me."

Without another word, I walked across the kitchen to get two glasses from the cabinet. After filling them with ice, I retrieved two Diet Cokes from the refrigerator. Wrapping my hands around the glasses and cans, I carried them all together to the table.

Halfway across the kitchen, the glasses shifted in my grasp. Before I could rebalance them, everything I was holding fell to the floor in an explosive crash. On impact, the cans rolled across the tile until they hit the wall, but the glasses shattered and sharp fragments scattered everywhere.

"Damn it!" I swore, kneeling down to pick up a piece of broken glass, careful not to touch the jagged edge.

Tears of frustration filled my eyes, and I nearly forgot about Xander as I scanned the mess of broken glass and ice littering the kitchen floor. Out of the corner of my eye, I spotted Dakota who had been standing near Xander this whole time. "Dakota, upstairs before you cut your paws."

He promptly turned and trotted up the stairs, the familiar clicking of his nails on the wooden steps growing softer as he reached the top.

"Here, let me help you," Xander offered as he approached me, stooping down to collect a few of the big pieces of glass.

My attention shifting for a moment, I felt a sharp broken edge nick my palm. "Ouch!" I winced as blood pooled on my skin. Tears finally burst from my eyes, and my pulse quickened with anxiety.

"Laken," Xander said, looking at my cut. "You need to be more careful." He reached over and gently touched my injured hand. "Here, let me—" He stopped when he noticed my tears. "Hey," he said softly. "It's okay. It's just some broken glass. We'll get it cleaned up. No big deal."

"It's not about the glass!" I cried. "And it's not about my hand. A guy showed up here Saturday night looking for you and your father. I think you're in some kind of trouble and I didn't know how to tell you." I watched him, wondering how he would react.

Xander's face paled as he stared at me in shock, seeming to forget about the broken glass scattered all over the floor and the cut on my hand. "What?" For once, he didn't have a snappy comeback. In fact, he didn't seem to have any words at all.

"You heard me. Someone was looking for you. That's what I wanted to talk to you about today. I didn't know how to put that into a text. And then I was so worried all day that he already found you. If you hadn't shown up here this afternoon, I was going to tell my dad." I paused, gazing at him as I applied pressure on my palm, hoping the bleeding would stop. "Who is that man? What does he want with you and your dad?"

Xander took a deep breath, his brow furrowed in thought. "I'm not sure. My father has been a little on edge lately, but he hasn't told me what's been bothering him."

"Well, the man told me he used me to lure you and your dad here. What is going on?" I felt like there was so much that Xander wasn't telling me. And now that he and his father were in danger, it was about time he started explaining.

"Nothing you need to worry about."

As Xander rose to his feet, I stood up beside him, the broken glass suddenly the farthest thing from my mind. "Like hell," I gritted out. "Clearly, I have something to do with this. And if I'm involved, I think I should know how and why."

Xander gazed at me thoughtfully. "I've already told you, it will be revealed soon enough. But right now, I don't have time for a history lesson. I need you to tell me everything about this guy. Did you know him or recognize him? What exactly did he say?"

"I don't know who he is but, yes, I've seen him before. Remember the night you gave me a ride home from the restaurant when Noah had to take Mark and Eric to the station?"

"Of course, I remember. Go on."

"There was a man at the bar who helped. Noah was outnumbered, and a guy, the man who is now apparently after you and your dad, jumped right in without hesitating. I remember how calm he was about the whole thing when he held one of the boys back from taking a swing at Noah."

"Had you ever seen him before that night?"

I shook my head. "No, never."

"What does he look like?"

I described the man to Xander, cringing as a vivid image of him flashed through my mind. "Even though he was helpful that night at the restaurant, I remember he sent shivers down my spine. Now I know why."

"Did he tell you why he was looking for us in your backyard?"

"I don't think he was. I think he's playing with all of us by scaring me. But here's the really weird part. He thanked me for finding Ryder. He set up Ryder's abduction. It was a trap. He said he had Ryder taken so that I would find him and bring you and your dad to town. Is that true? Did you and your dad move here because of me?"

"Yes, we did," Xander replied steadily.

"Why? What do you want from me?"

A knowing grin swept over Xander's face for a brief moment. "A date. What else would I want from you?"

"I don't know. You tell me."

An awkward silence fell between us before Xander's apprehension returned. "We're digressing here. We'll have plenty of time to talk about that later."

"Maybe you and your dad should leave town."

"That's not an option," he said, without giving it a thought.

"Why not?"

"Because we just found you. We can't leave now."

"Funny. That's what he said."

Xander frowned, averting his gaze away from me. "Well, I need to get home to talk to my dad. I'm afraid I can't help you clean up. Sorry."

"That's okay."

He walked over to the table, stepping gingerly in between the pieces of broken glass. He reached for his coat and slipped it on, wrapping the long sides around his muscular frame. Then he returned to me, sidestepping around the glass again. "How's your hand?" he asked, glancing down.

I held it up. Blood still seeped from the cut. "The bleeding is starting to slow down. I just need a Band-Aid. I'll be fine."

Xander reached for my wrist, lifting my hand to inspect it. His touch sent electricity up my arm, the shockwaves reaching my toes. He stood so close and, when I looked up, his gaze locked with mine.

The moment ended when a dark frown swept across his face and he let go of me. He looked around as if noticing the kitchen for the first time since he had arrived. A haunting silence loomed throughout the house. "Where are your parents?"

"At work, where they always are at this time of the day. My mom should be home within an hour or so. Why?"

"Because I'm not sure I should leave you here alone."

"I'm not alone. Dakota's upstairs."

"And where was Dakota when the man showed up?"

"He—he took off after something in the woods. One of the other wolves, I think. But I won't let him out this afternoon."

"Hmmm," Xander huffed.

"If you're worried about leaving me alone for an hour, don't be. That guy doesn't want me."

"I wish I could be sure of that. But I doubt he's going to show up here in broad daylight when your parents will be home any minute. If he's been in town for a few months, he knows your parents' schedules by now."

"Okay, that's just creepy." I shuddered to think that someone had been watching me and my parents for months, studying our daily routines.

"You sure you'll be okay? I'll stay until your mom gets home if you've changed your mind."

I shook my head adamantly. "No. Like I said before, I have Dakota. I'm not going to let this guy scare me to the point that I need a babysitter in the middle of the afternoon. Go home to your dad. I know you want to fill him in as soon as you can."

"For what it's worth, I'd rather stay here with you," he said with a faint smile. "Walk me out?"

I nodded and followed him out of the kitchen to the front door. Tiny shards of glass reached as far as the edge of the hallway, gleaming in the light. Xander unlocked the front door and stepped outside into the brisk fall afternoon. The light had softened from the setting sun, turning the sky to dusky purple.

"I'll talk to you soon," was all he said, his eyes meeting mine for a moment before he hurried down the sidewalk and disappeared around the corner.

As I closed the door and clicked the lock into place, I pushed my questions out of my thoughts. Then I returned to the kitchen to clean up the broken glass before my mother arrived home. I knew she wouldn't be angry about an accident, but I didn't want to have to explain why I was so jittery. I couldn't exactly tell her the glasses had slipped out of my hands because a stranger lurking in our backyard Saturday night had frazzled my nerves.

After I dumped the last pieces of broken glass into the garbage can and wiped up the melted ice, I turned my attention to the silver box on the table. Hesitantly, I reached for it, not sure if I wanted to accept what I expected would be a lavish gift. But I had no choice. I picked it up, noting the medium weight. The contents seemed to fit securely within the box, not shifting from one side to another as I tilted it. Curious, I carried it up to my bedroom and placed it on my bed. Dakota paced in the room, as if he'd been locked in and not allowed to leave. I ran a hand along his head and neck, telling him he could return to the kitchen now that the broken glass had been cleaned up. He charged out into the hallway as I stared at the box, daring myself to untie the exquisite red bow.

Finally, my curiosity got the best of me. I slid the ribbon off the box, removing it without untying the bow. After discarding it, I lifted the lid and placed it on the bed. Then I unfolded the tissue paper to reveal red velvet material with sparkling rhinestones scattered along the edge. A small envelope poked out of the folds. I reached for it, ripped it open and pulled out a notecard.

> *I can't think of a more perfect costume for you than Red Riding Hood. I hope you'll wear this to the Halloween dance. And if I can't convince you to be my date, perhaps you'll at least save me a dance.*

It was signed *Xander*.

I sighed thoughtfully, tucking the notecard back into the envelope. Then I covered the material up with the tissue paper, laid the envelope on it, and replaced the lid on top of the box. The costume was beautiful, at least what I could see of it without removing it. As much as I wanted to pull it out and admire every detail, it reminded me that Noah wouldn't be going to the dance with me. Perhaps I would be ready to try it on in a few days. But for now, it had to stay in the box, at least until I decided whether or not to accept Xander's invitation to be his date.

Chapter 2

"Did you open your present?" Xander asked, approaching me from behind the next morning at school.

I finished hanging my parka on my locker hook as he leaned against the locker next to mine. His charming smile made me wonder if he had forgotten about the man and his threats. "Well?" Xander mused, his hands shoved into his jeans pockets under his loose navy shirttails.

I tilted my head, my eyes narrowing in astonishment. "Aren't you forgetting what I told you yesterday?"

"What's that?"

"The guy. The stranger who's looking for you." I shook my head, my hair swaying against my pink sweater. "Did you even talk to your dad yesterday?"

Xander's grin faded as he studied me. "You just had to remind me about that, didn't you?" He sighed, not waiting for me to answer. "Of course, I did."

"What did he say? Does he know who that guy is and what he wants?"

Glancing nervously out into the hallway, Xander

watched the students milling about in groups, their steady chatter humming in the background. After a moment, he returned his gaze to me. "My father doesn't know who the man is, at least that's what he told me. But we both have a pretty good idea of what he wants."

"And that is?"

Xander frowned. "Money. Wealth. Laken, my dad has made a fortune on his jewelry. And when you have as much as we do, someone's bound to come after it sooner or later."

I shook my head, unconvinced. There were still too many unanswered questions. "But how does this guy know about you? Your dad seems to keep a pretty low profile. And it doesn't explain why he used me to find you two. Apparently, he really didn't know either one of you until you moved here." I watched his reaction to my questions, expecting answers. As I met his blue eyes, my bag rested on the floor by my feet, my books and classes completely forgotten.

"You're giving this way too much thought. It's not your problem, so let my dad and I worry about it."

"It's not my problem?" I repeated, my jaw dropping open. "The guy showed up in my backyard and, clearly, it's not the first time he's been lurking around my house. Not to mention his wolves are running around doing who knows what. So I think I'm in this just as much as you and your dad are."

"My father and I are monitoring the situation. We'll protect you if, or when, we believe you're in danger."

"But what about the two of you? You took off in a hurry yesterday, so I know you're worried about this, despite your tough guy act."

Xander smiled subtly. "We'll be prepared. We won't be caught off guard."

"What does that mean?" I asked with a huff. Calming down, I softened my tone. "Are you going to report this to my dad?"

"There's really nothing to tell him right now. No one has

done anything except trespass in your yard." Xander paused before changing the subject. "You haven't answered my question."

When I looked at him with my eyebrows raised, he explained, "The present. Did you open it?"

Although I wanted to continue pressing him for answers, I decided to let it go for now. "Yes. It's beautiful. You shouldn't have."

"Why not? What good is being rich if you can't spoil someone you care about? Now will you be my date for the Halloween dance?"

"Aren't you going with Marlena?"

Xander groaned and tapped his head against the locker. "Not if you agree to be my date."

"So that means the two of you are still an item?"

Xander avoided my stare, glancing to the side. "We haven't officially broken up if that's what you mean."

"You really are trying to get me killed, aren't you?"

"I'll take care of her. I already told you that."

"How?"

"I haven't figured it out yet, but I will. She's been a fun distraction, but it's getting kind of old."

"Oh, no," I said, shaking my head. "You need to finish what you started there. And even then, I probably shouldn't go out with you." Noah suddenly crept into my thoughts. Perhaps by the time Xander figured out how to let go of Marlena without her retaliating, I would be back together with Noah.

"You're not still waiting for him, are you?" Xander asked, practically reading my mind.

I glared at him in surprise, but forced myself to stay calm. "What difference does it make? No girl in her right mind would go out with you until you've ended things with Marlena. And maybe not even then. If you break up with her, she's bound to go after anyone you touch, whether or not you're free. There's no such thing as a clean break from her."

Xander smiled as if he hadn't even heard me. "But you'll wear the costume to the dance, right?"

I groaned, wishing he would take this seriously. But I had a feeling I could be waiting forever. "Yes," I said with a sigh.

"Good. Because I can't wait to see you in it."

"Just don't be too obvious."

"What's that supposed to mean?"

"You know," I said, rolling my eyes. "I don't need Marlena breathing down my neck again. First it was Noah, and now you."

"Oh God, Laken. You are way too paranoid about this. I told you not to worry. I'll take care of her. Speaking of which..." Xander glanced across the hallway out at the sea of students. "I need to run. See you in homeroom."

Before I could say another word, he jumped away from the locker and disappeared into the crowd. Without even watching, I knew what had caught his attention. Marlena. He was in deep with her, and he would have an awful time breaking up with her if that was what he really wanted. No boy dared to break up with Marlena. Marlena broke up with them.

Shaking both of them from my thoughts, I reached down for my book bag. It was time to focus on my classes for the day, or at least try.

ജ

Saturday night, Brooke came over to my house to get ready for the Halloween dance. Her nurse's costume consisted of a short skirt, crisp white top, and a cap pinned to her red hair. When I showed her the costume Xander had given me, she gushed over every detail from the cape's red velvety folds to the gold band that circled my forehead. I curled each lock of hair then pulled them to the side to hang in ringlets over my right shoulder. Two tendrils framed my face, and the hood glittered with rhinestones along the edge. The costume even included lace-up shoes that fit me perfectly. How Xander had gotten my size right, I would never know.

Ethan was a good match for Brooke that night in his light blue scrubs, a hospital mask hanging around his neck. After driving us to the dance in his parents' car, he ushered us into the crowded dark gym. Loud music blared over the muffled voices and speckled lights passed over the students dressed as skeletons, dismembered victims, and other creepy characters. I didn't recognize a single soul as I pushed my way through them, trying to keep up with Brooke and Ethan. The masked faces seemed to stare at me, unnerving me. I wondered if Xander hid behind one of them, but I tossed that thought away as quickly as it had come to mind. I would find him wherever I found Marlena, and she would never hide her face behind a mask.

When we located some space near the bleachers, we sat on the bench, looking out at the mob scene. I sighed, wondering why I had even come tonight other than to wear the costume Xander had given me.

"Well, this is fun," I muttered sarcastically, staring at the crowd dancing in the dark. I sat between Brooke and Ethan, suspecting that they'd deliberately stuck me in the middle so I wouldn't feel alone.

"I'm not going to let you feel sorry for yourself," Brooke scolded. "You look amazing. Noah doesn't know what he's missing. And Xander is here." She gestured to the crowd. "Somewhere. He obviously likes you. A lot."

I frowned even more. "Like that's going to do me any good tonight. You know he's here with Marlena."

"From what you told me and, knowing he bought you that costume, it sounds like he's had enough of her."

"Brooke," Ethan said, his eyebrows raised. "We promised Laken a fun night with no boy talk."

"I know," Brooke groaned before flashing him a brilliant smile. "I can't help it. I want her to be as happy as I am."

The music slowed, the deafening beat softening to a muffled ballad. Students shuffled about the dance floor as they paired up into couples. The dateless ones trickled away from the crowd toward the edge of the gym. "And I want you two to remain blissfully happy. So why don't you get out there?" I turned to Ethan. "What do you say, doctor?"

"Only if you're okay hanging out here alone."

"I'm fine. Stop worrying about me. I'm going to get some punch."

"Okay." Ethan stood up, passing by me to where Brooke sat and extending his hand out to her. "You heard her, Nurse Carson. May I have this dance?"

Before accepting it, Brooke offered me a grateful smile. Then she placed her hand in his and he pulled her to her feet, her white costume practically glowing in the dark. Within seconds, they disappeared into the crowd.

Not wanting to linger on the bench alone, I stood and started to make my way to the far corner where a punch bowl had been set up on a table. The floor-length cape swayed around my ankles and the hood blocked my peripheral vision. I barely managed to cross the gym unscathed. The other students bumped into me, or was it me who knocked into them? I couldn't be sure with the hood draped over my head, shielding the sides of my face.

When I reached the table and picked up a paper cup, someone slammed against my back. The cup fell from my hand, bouncing on the table as I was pushed into the edge. Then a piece of paper was shoved into my hand.

I whipped around, searching the crowd for the person who had given me the paper, but no one stood out amongst the students who gathered nearby. The punch forgotten, I moved away from the table and squinted as I read the note in the dim light.

Meet me behind the school. Xander. I glanced up, scanning the crowded gym for any sign of him. Either he had disguised himself well or he wasn't close enough for me to spot him in the crowd. Without another thought, I clutched the note and hurried through the mob until I reached the gym entrance. Escaping the darkness, I gathered up my gown and rushed down the bright hallway. At the end, I turned right and passed through another corridor until I reached the back exit. I pushed on the lever, hoping it was unlocked.

The door opened at once and I stormed outside into the dark. It slammed shut with a loud bang as I followed the sidewalk to the steps leading down to the back schoolyard. Slowly, my eyes adjusted to the pitch black lit only by the full moon.

I shivered, pulling the cloak around me as a cloud puffed out from my mouth with every breath. The night was silent and still, and I didn't see Xander anywhere. I stopped at the top of the steps, debating how long I should wait for him. As much as I wanted a distraction from my lonely night, I wouldn't wait out here in the cold for long.

After a few minutes that seemed to last forever, I turned, planning to go back to the dance. But the stranger who had approached me in my backyard last weekend stood in my way. He wore all black again, making his broad frame almost impossible to see in the shadows.

"You!" I hissed.

"Hello, my dear," he said, a sinister smile curving upon his thin lips. His black eyes scanned over me, sending panic through me. "We meet again, Laken."

"What are you doing here?"

"Just making sure my insurance policy is still safe and sound."

"What's that supposed to mean?"

"That you, my dear, hold the key to getting what I want."

"If it's money you want, I'm sure Xander and his father will give it to you if you leave town and never come back."

He smiled as one would smile at a child. "Laken, you have so much to learn about your new friends. It's not their money I want, it's their power."

"Power?"

"I suspect by your expression they haven't told you who they are and what they can do. Well, unfortunately, it's not my secret to tell."

I shook my head. "I'm sure they would have told me if I needed to know."

"One would think so." He tilted his head, his eyes running down the length of my gown and back up to meet my stare. "You look absolutely stunning tonight. That costume is exquisite. Was it a gift from Caleb's son?"

"What does that matter to you?" I shot back, hoping he couldn't sense my fear.

He laughed, making my skin crawl. "You are a feisty one. But I don't need you to answer me. That's not something you can buy in this God-forsaken town."

"If you don't like it here, then why don't you leave?"

"Not until I get what I want." The man inched closer to me and I took a step backward. "Tell Caleb and Xander that if they run, I'll go after the one person they'll do anything to protect. You."

Panic shot through me, and I fought the urge to run, forcing myself to stay strong, to be brave. "Why me?" I asked, my voice barely a whisper.

"Because you're the one just like your mother was the one. Years ago, Caleb searched for her. But he never found her, so he took a wife and she gave him a son before she died."

"Why was he looking for my mother? Did he know her?"

"No. That's just it. He needed to find the girl who could talk to animals. The only problem was that it was like trying to find a needle in a haystack. But I found her and, when she died, I followed you until the timing was right." He clasped his hands together, his black leather gloves reflecting the moonlight. "It's all coming together. It won't be long now. Their power will soon be mine."

"Whatever that is, how can you take it from them?"

"It's simple. Caleb has it now because he's the oldest living male in his line. When he dies, his firstborn son will inherit it. When that son dies, the next one will inherit it. And since I control him, I will control his gift. I'll be rich beyond my wildest imagination."

"Wait a minute," I said, shaking my head. "Xander doesn't have a brother. He told me his mother died right after he was born."

"That's correct. She did die. But she left behind a lonely man who turned to the first woman who showed an interest in him." Pausing, the stranger whipped his gaze away from me as if something in the woods across the lawn had caught his attention. After a moment, he looked back at me. "Well, I've said enough. I must go now. I'll see you soon, Laken." He flashed an evil smile before brushing past me.

By the time I spun around, he was gone. My heart accelerated, pumping adrenaline through my veins as I stared out into darkness. My legs felt paralyzed, and I was barely able to breathe. Questions raced through my mind. What did he mean by powers? Were Caleb and Xander like me in some way? Could they talk to animals? I shook my head at the absurdity of that idea. It made no sense at all. How could an ability like mine make someone rich? It had to be something else.

My trembling subsided, and I pulled the cloak tighter around my body, realizing how cold I was. My fingers and toes were becoming numb. I started to head toward the school when a sudden movement behind me pushed a breeze across my cheek. I stopped, lowering my hood so that I could see to the side. I turned my head, afraid that the man had returned.

Without any warning, someone grabbed me from behind. Arms wrapped around my chest, clamping my hands against my sides and holding me still. Panic surged through me as I struggled to break free.

"Shh," a familiar voice whispered. "It's just me, Laken."

I immediately recognized Xander's voice. My pulse quickened, but this time from my undeniable attraction to him. He was so close, his breath grazing my ear as he spoke.

"Let go of me," I whispered with as much force as I could muster.

But my voice was weak. I wasn't sure that I wanted him to release me. He felt warm against my back as he lowered his face to my neck. His breath tickled me, sending me into a dizzy head spin. The scruff of his five o'clock shadow scratched my skin, flustering me.

"Not yet," he murmured. He paused until I stopped struggling against him. "You look irresistible in this costume. It suits you. If only Little Red Riding Hood could talk to the wolf like you can."

I gasped and started to turn around, but he tightened his grip on me. "I don't know what you're talking about."

"Of course, you do. Don't play dumb with me, Laken. I've known about you all along. Ever since my dad and I heard about the girl who rescued a little boy lost in the New Hampshire wilderness, we knew you were different."

"You knew all this time?" I asked. Why hadn't he told me? "That day on the hike, when the bear approached you. You knew then?"

Xander laughed softly. "Yes, and it's a good thing. If I hadn't, I probably would have pissed my pants and that would have been awfully embarrassing. You need to be more careful with your talents."

"Why didn't you tell me?"

"There was never a good time."

"Then why now?"

"Because it was getting too hard to keep pretending that I didn't know." He loosened his hold on me, dropping his right arm to my waist and sliding it under the cape. I felt the heat of his touch through the thick gown, and butterflies stirred in the pit of my stomach.

I swallowed as he reached his other hand up, grazing my cheek with his fingers. Even if I wanted to move, his voice mesmerized me and his touch paralyzed me. I felt like lead weights had been attached to my feet and it was all I could do to remember to breathe. "So you know. It doesn't change anything."

"I wouldn't expect it to."

"Then can you let go of me now? I presume that's why you wanted to meet me out here."

"I'm barely holding on to you. You can move away if you want."

I held my breath as he lowered his lips to my neck, hovering just above my skin. His left hand slowly trailed down my side, leaving a line of tingling sensations under my arm and along the curve of my hip. When he stopped, his hand rested just above my thigh. "But first, there's something I want to try."

I sucked in a quick breath as he kissed my neck, his lips soft and his stubble prickling me. I trembled from his touch, not sure that I was ready for this. My nerves on edge, Noah flashed through my thoughts for a moment. How could I let Xander sweep me off my feet so soon after Noah had stolen my heart only to break it?

Easy, a voice rattled off in my head. *Forget about Noah. Even if he comes back, do you honestly think you'll ever be able to trust him again? Xander has been pretty clear that he wanted you since he arrived in town. Maybe it's time for you to stop fighting your feelings for him and give him a chance.*

My heart raced faster than it had when the stranger flashed an evil grin at me. But this fear was different. It was filled with excitement and anticipation.

As Xander nuzzled my neck, the arm he had wrapped around my stomach pulled me toward him, pressing my back against his chest. His lips trailed kisses up to my earlobe, avoiding the dangling earring. The night blurred in front of me as my resistance crumbled. I raised a hand, placing it on Xander's. As soon as he felt my touch, he lifted away from my ear and twirled me around in his arms.

He held me close, his embrace locking me against his

broad chest. I looked up at him, his smoldering blue eyes dark. As I reached up around his shoulders, I barely glimpsed his black costume. I had no idea what he had dressed up as, nor did I care at this moment. My breath hitched as he gazed down at me, his sultry eyes meeting mine.

Xander slowly brushed his mouth over mine. My eyelids fell shut as fire erupted along my lips, traveling down to the pit of my stomach. The world spun around me as I waited for him to deepen his kiss. But he never did, teasing me with his feather-light touch instead.

His arms tightening around me, he abruptly jerked his head up. I whipped my eyes open to see him intently watching the woods. "What is it?" I whispered, realizing I hadn't told him about the stranger's visit minutes ago. I wondered if the man lurked nearby.

"Shh," he said in a hushed voice, his eyes locked in on the darkness. "I heard something."

After a few moments, Xander took a deep breath and looked back down at me. "I guess it was nothing." He smiled, bending his head toward my lips. "Now where were we?"

"He was here," I whispered, tearing my eyes away from him to gaze across the yard, searching for any sign of the man. But all was still and quiet under the moon.

Xander straightened up, the desire lurking in his eyes gone. "What?" he demanded with a worried frown.

"The man. He was out here a few minutes ago. Right before you found me."

"Laken," Xander gasped. "I asked you to tell me the moment you saw him again."

"You didn't exactly give me a chance."

"Point taken," he said with a sigh, loosening his hold on me without breaking away. "Now tell me what happened."

I shivered from the cold slipping in between our bodies. "He wants what you have," I said calmly, staring at Xander as though he owed me an explanation. If he knew my secret, it was only fair that he told me his. "What is that?"

"I don't know. I have a lot of stuff. That could mean anything."

"No," I said, shaking my head. "It's not money or stuff that he wants. He said he wants your power and, if you and your father don't give it to him, he's coming after me. I'm his insurance policy."

Fury burned in Xander's eyes as I spoke. "He's crazy. We can't give him our power like it's a bouquet of roses. It's like your gift. You could only talk to animals once your birth mother died. Well, I can't do what my father can do, and I won't be able to until he dies. I'm not sure about him, but I know I'm not ready for that."

A lump formed in my throat and tears welled up in my eyes. "What did you say?" At that moment, I forgot that I didn't know his secret because suddenly, I didn't care. Only one thing mattered right now.

He looked at me, confused. "About what?"

"About my birth mother," I whispered, my voice threatening to break down into sobs.

"That she passed on her gift to you when she died?"

I nodded, biting down on my lip to keep my composure.

"Laken, you didn't know that?"

I stared at him, my vision blurry. "How could I have known that? I never knew my real mother, and I didn't even know who she was until a few weeks ago. If she had to die before animals could understand me, then she didn't die until I was almost seven years old. I could have known her. If she lived that long, why didn't she come back for me?"

Sympathy flashed through Xander's eyes. "I'm sorry, Laken. You're right. Sometimes I forget that you haven't been exposed to what you are the way that I've been." He started to pull me close to him again, but I wrenched away from him and stepped back.

"No, I haven't. But tell me, what are you? What power does your father have that this man wants? Maybe it's time you're honest with me for a change."

"I've never lied to you, Laken."

"No, you've just been hiding things from me. Things that obviously involve me and, now, could get me hurt, or worse, killed."

"We didn't know how to tell you."

I shook my head in frustration. "Tell me what? None of this makes any sense."

"I know. There are a lot of pieces to the story. You'll see how they fit together, I promise."

I huffed, about to respond, when the back door to the school was flung open and several students barged out into the night. As the door slammed shut, one of the kids said, "Who has a lighter? Mine's all out, man!"

I looked at Xander, worried that we would be seen together and someone would tell Marlena. He must have read my mind because he grabbed my wrist and pulled me down the stairs behind him. I gathered up my gown before I could trip on it and hurried to keep up with him. At the bottom, Xander turned the corner, leading me across the lawn and around the school.

"Where are we going?" I choked out, gasping for breath as I ran with him.

"To see my father."

Chapter 3

The drive from the school to Xander's house was a quiet one. Before we left, Xander sent his father a text to let him know we needed to see him and we would be there soon. Along the ride through the dark winding roads, I dug my phone out from the inside pocket of the cloak and sent Ethan a message to tell him I was leaving with Xander who would take me home. My message was short and simple, omitting the part about the stranger outside the school. There was no doubt in my mind that Brooke would grill me with questions tomorrow and, as long as they were only about Xander, I could handle them.

The outside lights of the log mansion shone like beacons in the night when Xander pulled the truck up to the garage. As he jumped down from the driver's seat, I opened my door. Cold air blasted into the truck cab, burning my throat and lungs with every breath I took. I gathered up the folds of my costume, studying the drop to the pavement. Getting out of the truck in a long gown posed a new challenge. I hesitated, grateful when Xander appeared, his hand extended to me. I took it and carefully stepped down. After shutting the door, he wrapped his arm around my shoulders and whisked me across the driveway to the brightly lit front porch.

We climbed the steps, meeting Caleb at the door, a serious frown etched on his face. He smiled faintly, his warm brown eyes softening for a moment before worry returned to them. He wore jeans and a dark green shirt, his graying hair disheveled as though he'd run his hands through it hundreds of times. "Laken, my dear. You look lovely tonight," he said before giving me a quick hug.

"Thank you." I flashed him a weary smile and walked into the entry hall, thankful for the warmth. The house was even brighter on the inside than it was outside, and a fire flickered in the stone fireplace, crackling over split logs.

"You're quite welcome," he said before turning to Xander and placing a hand on his shoulder. "Good work, son. I'm glad you brought Laken over tonight. We need to talk."

Xander nodded then slipped away from his father to shut the door. For the first time that night, I noticed his black medieval costume. His shirt was buttoned about halfway up his chest, his exposed skin smooth and kissed by the sun. His eyes shifted, meeting my gaze, and I looked away, blushing from being caught staring.

"I made some tea. Who would like some?" Caleb offered, breaking the awkward moment between me and Xander as he led us into the living room.

"I'd love some," I said.

"Make yourself comfortable," he said, gesturing to the couch. "I'll be right back. Xander, shall I bring a third cup?"

"No thanks, Dad. I'm good."

I walked around the couch and sat at one end as Caleb disappeared into the kitchen. Xander followed me, sitting so close that our legs almost touched. He reached for my hand.

"I love your fireplace," I gushed, wanting to avoid the real reason we were here. I longed to be at the dance with Noah, living out a normal teenage life. Instead, here I sat waiting for Xander and his father to explain why someone wanted to kill them and what I had to do with it. I stared at the fire, watching the flames dance over the crackling wood, orange reflecting in the black window along the wall.

"We do, too. It was one of the things that sold us on this house." He paused, letting go of my hand when I refused to look at him. "How are you holding up?"

I shook my head and shrugged. "As best as I can, I guess," I replied, tearing my gaze away from the fire to meet his eyes.

"I never wanted you to find out about us this way. I'm sorry it was so sudden," Xander said softly.

"It's not your fault some guy wants you dead and is using me to get to you. But it would have been nice if you'd been up front with me from the beginning." I looked away from him again to stare at the fire.

"If I'd known things were going to turn out this way, I would have told you a lot sooner."

I wasn't sure if I believed him, but I nodded anyway.

Caleb returned from the kitchen and placed a silver serving tray on the coffee table in front of the couch. Steam rose up from two white cups on saucers, tea bag strings hanging over their sides. He lifted one of them and handed it to me. The tea smelled minty and the heat of the cup warmed my hand. "Thank you," I said, bobbing the tea bag up and down in the water.

He carried the remaining teacup and saucer to the chair facing the couch and sat down. His eyes swept over both of us. "What happened tonight?" he asked.

"The man found Laken again outside the school." As Xander spoke, he shifted his gaze from his father to me. "Wait a minute. What were you doing outside in the dark all alone to begin with?"

I wrinkled my eyebrows in confusion. "You asked me to meet you there."

"No, I didn't."

"Yes, you did. Someone passed me a note from you. It said to meet you out back." I placed my tea on the coffee table and pulled the crumpled note out of my inside cloak pocket. I opened it, smoothing out the wrinkles. "Here." I handed it to him.

Xander grabbed it, reading it quickly. "This isn't my handwriting. Who gave this to you?"

"I don't know. Someone bumped into me from behind and put it in my hand while I was at the punch table. By the time I turned around, they were gone, or at least I thought they were. It was really hard to tell who was who between all the costumes and dim light. I thought it was you, but that you didn't want to be seen near me because of Marlena."

Xander frowned. "I can't blame you for thinking that."

Caleb leaned forward, resting his elbows on his knees. "Laken, I don't think we need to tell you that this is pretty serious. We don't know who this man is or what he wants. You have to be more careful from now on. If you go out, stay where the crowd is, whether you're at a dance or a football game or anywhere else. If you get another note like that, don't go. Xander won't ask you to meet him in a dark secluded place, so don't believe it."

"Well, I'm not so sure about that," Xander piped up with a sly smile that disappeared the moment his father shot him a warning look. "But if I want you to meet me somewhere, I'll send you a text. That way, you'll know it's me."

I nodded, glancing at Caleb. "I know what the man wants. He wants your power. What is he talking about?"

"Remember the story I told you about your necklace?" Caleb asked.

"Yes. Of course."

"I know you didn't want to believe it at the time, but the curse is real. Only there's a lot more to it than that."

I took a deep breath, my composure starting to crumble. Caleb and Xander stared at me, flustering me. "Okay," I said slowly. "I'm not sure if I'm ready for this, but I guess I don't have a choice."

Caleb offered me a faint smile. "It's not that bad. It's actually a fascinating story. Might even make a good movie someday," he began, pausing when Xander cleared his throat. "Sorry. I'm going off on a tangent here." He stopped again, continuing only once his eyes met mine. "It started in ancient Rome during the time before Christ with two best friends, one rich and one poor, who fell in love with the same woman. Her name was Anastasia, and she chose the wealthy one. After they went off to get married, the poor man spent the next two years saving every penny he could. Then he took it to a powerful sorcerer. He asked, no, more like begged, the sorcerer to give him any means to be rich. Because then, just maybe, he could steal Anastasia from her husband. Before the sorcerer granted his wish, he warned that any spell he cast would come with a price. Only he never knew what that was until it was too late. The man agreed, and so the sorcerer worked his magic and gave him a unique power." Caleb stopped for a moment to sip his tea.

"What kind of power?" I asked, my attention captivated by the story.

Xander smiled at me, but remained silent as his father continued. "The ability to turn raw materials into precious gems and transform them into beautiful jewelry."

I gasped, my jaw dropping open as I raised my eyebrows. "That's what you do..."

"That's right," Caleb confirmed, nodding. "We, Xander and I, are the living descendants of that man."

"But you said there would be a price. Was there?"

Caleb nodded, a serious look in his eyes. "Yes. Our bloodline was cursed. But before I explain that part, let me get back to the story. The young man used his new gift to make a special necklace for Anastasia. But when he tried to find her to give it to her, he learned that she had died."

"How?"

Caleb frowned, his eyes full of sadness as if he'd known her. "Unfortunately, her death was violent and gruesome. You see, Anastasia was a very beautiful woman with long blonde hair and emerald green eyes. She was desired by many men, not just the two friends. And because of it, she was hated by the women who knew her. One jealous woman accused her of having an affair with her husband. By this time, Anastasia had been married for almost two years and had just given birth to a baby girl. She hadn't gone anywhere near the man she was accused of sleeping with, but the facts were of little concern back then. She was locked up without a fair trial, and then her fate was sealed."

"What was her fate?" I asked, almost afraid of the answer.

"Gladiator," Xander said as his father took another sip of his tea.

"Gladiator?" I repeated, not sure if I believed it. It really did sound more like a movie than something real. But then again, everything from the curses, to being able to make gems out of dirt, to my ability to communicate with animals, was much more like a movie than real life.

"He's right," Caleb said. "That's what they did to prisoners back then. They fought for their lives as entertainment for the crowds. She was weak from having a baby and didn't last long. She met her demise in the ring with a lion. Her husband was forced to watch as it tore her limbs from her body."

My jaw fell open as the grisly scene of a woman being mutilated by a lion while the crowd cheered from the coliseum stands turned my stomach. "That's horrible. Why did people do things like that?"

"I don't think people had much of a conscience back then. It was a brutal time in history."

"What happened to the baby? Did she survive?"

"Yes. Her father raised her on his own, but his former friend gave the baby the necklace intended for Anastasia. And he told him about the sorcerer. So the distraught man took his baby daughter to him."

"Why? What did he want?"

"To make sure that his daughter would never meet the same fate that had befallen her mother. So, for a hefty price, the sorcerer cast a spell on the baby, giving her the gift to talk to animals. He warned her father that, just like his friend's power, hers would come with a price. That baby was your ancestor. And the price for her gift was that she was cursed to die young. Every girl in her line had the ability to communicate with wild animals, and every one of them met an untimely death."

I thought of Ivy, her mother, and Josephine Kramer. All of them had died at a young age. "How can the curse be broken?"

"We already told you," Xander said. "By finding your soul mate."

"Great," I huffed, throwing my hands up in the air. "That's just great. How do I know who that is?"

Xander and Caleb started at me incredulously, as if I should know the answer. "I think I need to back up," Caleb said. "I told you the first friend who was given the gift to make jewelry would also have a price to pay. His price, or curse rather, was that any woman he fell in love with would die, leaving him alone until he found his soul mate, or his descendants found her descendants."

"What are you saying?"

"Xander and I are his descendants. You are hers. My son is the key to break the curse on your bloodline so that you and all of your descendants can live a long life. You are the key to break our curse and let Xander be the first male in our family in centuries to escape a lonely life."

Silence filled the room, broken only by the crackling fire as I absorbed every word. A part of me didn't want to believe any of it, but everything made sense now. Everything except for one detail. "But who is the man looking for you?"

"We don't know," Xander replied quickly.

"He's right," Caleb said. "We have no idea. There's no prophecy or indication in all the research I've done on our ancestors that a man will come after us. But I'm most worried about you. Until you break the curse, you aren't safe."

"You said it would be broken once I found Xander."

Xander suddenly grinned from ear to ear as Caleb explained, "Simply finding him won't break it. You have to fall in love with him and consummate your love. Only then will you be safe."

I raised my eyebrows, not quite sure what to say or think.

Xander wore a smug, teasing grin on his face, and his eyes twinkled as they met mine. "Sounds great. I'm ready when you are."

I groaned, rolling my eyes. It figured he would find a silver lining in the dark cloud hanging over us. Before I could respond, Caleb spoke again. "Xander, you know it can't be like that. It has to be pure. This isn't about sex."

"I know," Xander agreed. He grinned at me, his blue eyes lit up in anticipation. "But that won't stop me from thinking about it."

I shook my head, turning my attention to the fire. "I can't think about this right now. It's a lot to process."

"I'm sure it is," Caleb said gently.

"How do you know all this?" I asked him.

"My father had a book that was passed on to every generation. It explained the story in great detail."

"May I see it? I'd like to read it."

Caleb sighed. "If I had it, yes, I would let you borrow it. But unfortunately, it went missing many years ago before my father passed away."

"Or it was stolen," Xander mused.

"Well, yes, that's possible," Caleb agreed. After a brief silence, he continued. "Laken, is there anything else you remember about the man? Anything else he said that you think you should tell us?"

"Yes," I said, staring at the fire as if in a trance. "He said the next in line would inherit your power once you and Xander are gone. Is that possible?"

"It would only be possible if I had another son. One younger than Xander. But I don't, so it can't be," Caleb explained.

"He seemed really sure of this," I countered.

"He's mistaken," Xander said matter-of-factly. "He obviously doesn't know what he's talking about."

"So what are you going to do?" I asked.

"There isn't much we can do," Caleb answered.

"Wouldn't it be safer if the two of you left and went somewhere he couldn't find you?"

Xander shook his head. "No way. We're not leaving you behind. He would use you to get us back, and we're not risking your safety to protect ourselves."

"He's right," Caleb said. "Either we all leave together, or we stay here and fight." He looked directly at me. "Laken, are you prepared to leave town? You'd have to leave your parents behind and you wouldn't be able to contact them."

I shook my head. "I can't do that. What if he hurts them or my friends in retaliation? I'm not willing to take that risk."

"That's what I was thinking. Your father would launch a huge manhunt for you, anyway."

"So we stay," Xander concluded. "And fight."

I glanced nervously at Xander then back at Caleb. "You're just going to wait for him to make a move?"

"We have no choice. But we'll be ready when he does," Xander replied with a smooth confidence in his voice.

"That's crazy. He'll have the element of surprise on his side," I said.

"Your lack of confidence in us isn't helping my ego," Xander stated.

I stared at him. "You don't need any help in that department. It's already too big."

He shot a sarcastic smile my way before looking back at his father.

"What about Laken?" Xander asked. "Where do you think she'll be the safest?"

Caleb pursed his lips in thought. "I know you're thinking she'll be better off here with us, but we can't do that." He turned his attention to me. "You won't be any less safe at home with your parents and your wolf. Xander told me about Dakota, and don't worry, your secret is safe with me. But back to the situation at hand. You have to be vigilant. I know this is a town where no one locks their doors, or at least they didn't before the little boy was taken. Unfortunately, times have changed. Keep your doors locked and, whatever you do, don't go outside after dark. Stay with Dakota at all times. He'll protect you."

"Okay. I'll make sure I'm careful."

"Good. And most importantly, call us if you see anything suspicious. I mean anything at all, even if you're not sure."

"I will, I promise. What about my dad? Should I tell him anything?"

"I don't think that's a good idea just yet. It could put him in danger and the fewer people involved, the better," Caleb answered.

"I hate hiding this from him, but he might freak out if he knew about any of it."

"There's that, too," Caleb agreed. "I'm sorry you had to be dragged into all of this."

I shrugged with a sigh. "I don't blame either one of you for this. But you moved here to find me and I wish you'd told me everything sooner, at least about the magic and how it's passed on."

"We couldn't," Caleb stated. "You didn't know about your real mother when we first got here. It would have been very difficult if we had to tell you that you were adopted, even if only by your mother. I'd like to know about Ivy someday, when all of this is over. I looked for her years ago, but I never came across any leads. I didn't even know where to begin."

I smiled softly, noticing a deep sadness in his eyes. "I wish you had found her, too. Maybe then she'd still be alive and I would have had a chance to get to know her."

He nodded wistfully. "That would have been nice. I'm just glad Xander won't have to go through life alone like I have."

"You miss his mom, don't you?"

Caleb took a deep breath. "I went through a phase of denial, even though my father told me any woman I married who wasn't in your bloodline would die young. He tried to convince me that the curse was real, but I was too stubborn to listen."

"I'm sorry. Xander told me what happened to her."

"Thank you, dear. Not a day goes by that I don't think of her."

"I don't mean to pry, but did they ever catch the driver who caused the accident?"

"Yes, and he was prosecuted. But I found it in my heart to forgive him. Hating him and holding onto my anger would have eaten me up long ago. It's all in the past now."

I nodded without saying a word. Instead, I reached for my tea on the coffee table and took another sip.

"Have I answered all of your questions, Laken?" Caleb asked.

"I think so, but I'm sure I'll have more once all of this sinks in."

"Of course. That's only normal." Caleb smiled at both of us. "Well, I've got some work to finish up in the den. Xander, I trust you'll see that Laken gets home safely."

"Yes." Xander watched me as his father stood up.

"Goodnight, Laken. It is always a pleasure to see you, my dear, but hopefully next time, it'll be under better circumstances."

"I hope so, too," I said with a smile. "Goodnight, Caleb." He carried his tea into the kitchen, leaving the silver tray on the coffee table. I turned to Xander. "Will you take me home now?" I asked. I suddenly longed for the familiar surroundings of my room and Dakota's silent company.

"I was going to ask if you wanted to stay and hang out for a while, and not to work on our History project," Xander said slowly, his voice hopeful.

I shook my head. "Thanks, but can I get a rain check? I'm dying to get out of this costume. It's kind of heavy and awkward."

Xander grinned, and I immediately knew that I'd said the wrong thing. "I'll be happy to help you with that here."

I felt a blush creep over my face as I met his stare. "I guess I walked into that."

"Yes, you did." He nodded, still smiling. After a brief silence, the hopeful look in his eyes faded. "Okay, come on. I'll take you home." He stood and extended his hand to me.

I set the teacup back on the tray. "Is it okay to leave this here?"

"Of course. One of us will get that later."

"Thanks." I took his hand and rose to my feet, the cloak and dress unfolding around my feet. Without another word, he walked me outside into the cold darkness and across the driveway to his truck. Once we were both seated in it, he turned the key in the ignition and the engine roared to life. Shivering, I pulled my seatbelt across my shoulder and clicked it into the lock.

"Aren't you freezing?" I asked Xander, noticing that he hadn't bothered to grab a coat on our way out.

He shrugged as he backed the truck around and guided it down the driveway. "The cold doesn't really bother me. I've always been able to handle extreme temperatures whether it's hot or cold."

"Not me. I don't mind winter as long as I have the right clothes and shoes. As for the summer, it doesn't get too hot around here. But when we get a heat wave, there are some fun places to go swimming."

"Really? There are pools around here?"

"No. Just lakes and rivers. There are a couple of water-parks around, but that's where the tourists go."

"Hmmm," Xander mused, smiling as the dark shadows from the tree branches overhead danced across his face. "So, are you a bikini girl or a one-piece girl?"

"Neither," I answered. "We swim naked up here." I laughed at the shock and anticipation racing through his eyes.

"Damn! How many months until summer?"

"I'm only kidding. Even on a hot day up here, the water can be really cold. I'd prefer a wetsuit. But in answer to your question, I'm a bikini girl." I'd never had a problem wearing a two piece bathing suit as long as it provided enough coverage in the right places.

Xander nodded appreciatively. "Good to know. Now I have something to look forward to."

As soon as he said it, my thoughts reverted back to the stranger and his threats. I hoped that Xander and I had a long future to enjoy, whether or not it was together. Staring straight ahead, I said, "Don't get too excited. It doesn't get hot enough to swim around here every summer."

"Then I'll just have to take you to California or Hawaii someday. I'd love to teach you to surf, and maybe you can explain to all the sharks that surfers aren't dinner."

"Hmmm. I don't know if I can talk to fish. I never tried that before."

"Well, I guess we'll have to find out, won't we?"

"Xander, we're not even a couple. I can't think that far ahead right now. There's too much going on."

"That's precisely why we have to think about the future. To distract us from reality."

I whipped my eyes to the side to study him. I knew what he meant, that we needed something to look forward to, something to lift the dark shadows threatening us. But I couldn't agree with needing a distraction. "I'm afraid if we let ourselves get distracted right now, we could all end up hurt, or worse, killed."

"Let my dad and I worry about that. You just stay behind locked doors and don't go outside alone, day or night. I'm sure you'll be fine. It's us he wants, not you."

"I know. But I'm really scared," I admitted. "For all of us."

Xander reached over and gently squeezed my hand. "We'll be fine. We're going to get through this."

I smiled at him before returning my gaze to the dark woods passing by. Neither one of us spoke again for the remainder of the ride home. An occasional car passed, its headlights blinding us in the darkness. Xander carefully guided the truck around the tight turns and up and down the steep slopes until we reached my house.

When we pulled into the driveway, an unsettled feeling came over me. With only a single light on beside the front door, my house blended into the dark shadows as midnight approached. It was unreasonable to expect my parents to keep any other lights on. They had no idea that a dangerous man was stalking Xander, his father, and perhaps even myself.

Xander stopped the truck next to the Explorer, and the bright headlight beams reflected against the garage door.

I turned to him. "Thanks for the ride home."

"No problem."

When I tugged at the door handle, Xander said quickly, "Wait here. I'll help you down and walk you to the door." Leaving the truck running, he rushed around the front of it through the headlight beams. Once on my side, he held his arms out to me.

Confused, I reached for one, but he put both hands on my waist and lifted me out of the truck. I reached up for his shoulders as he lowered me to the ground. When my feet touched the pavement, Xander kept his hold on me and shifted his gaze to meet mine.

My heart pounded as he pulled me closer to him, pressing against me. He released my waist and ran his hands up my back. "Xander," I murmured. "Don't do this, please."

"Don't do what?" he whispered, lowering his mouth to mine. Electricity raced down my spine when his lips brushed against mine, gently tickling me. His kiss was light and soft, leaving me breathless and longing for more.

In spite of the desire shooting through me, I slid my hands down from his shoulders, placing my palms on his chest. I whipped my head back, breaking away from his kiss. "What are you doing?" I demanded.

"Just picking up where we left off when we were behind

the school. Why are you pushing me away? I know you want to be with me. I can feel it," he whispered arrogantly.

I huffed, shaking my head. "Aren't you forgetting something? Or should I say someone?" When he raised his eyebrows, looking at me with a questioning stare, I stated, "Marlena."

"Oh, her. Why are you so obsessed with that?"

"Because if she finds out we're messing around behind her back, I'm dead. Have you broken up with her?"

"I'm working on it."

I reached around my back, grabbing his arms and loosening his grip on me. As soon as he released me, I backed up until my legs hit the running board. "That's not good enough. You can't date her and have me on the side. It's not fair to either one of us."

"I only went out with her in the first place so that she'd leave you alone after your date with Noah," he admitted. "She was never the one I really wanted. I hope you know that."

"How noble of you. Well, thank you. Your master plan worked like a charm, and I certainly appreciated it. But now it's about to backfire."

"Yeah. I guess I never thought about breaking up with her once you finally came around."

"Don't you mean *if* I came around?"

"No. You heard my dad. We're meant for each other. You can't deny the attraction pulling us together. And you can't tell me you're not worried about the curse. You need me."

"Your dad also said it has to be pure. I'm not going to do something impulsively on a whim just to break a curse that I'm not sure I believe is real. Besides, if something happens between us before you've made a clean break from Marlena, she's liable to kill me even if the curse is broken. So what are you planning to do about her?"

Xander averted his gaze away from me as he took a deep breath. "I'm not sure yet," he admitted.

"Why doesn't that surprise me?" I sighed, wondering why it seemed that every time we crossed paths, things ended badly. "I'd better get inside," I muttered. I brushed past him, holding up the long gown as I ran around the front of the truck and through the headlight beams. I hurried down the sidewalk to the front door where I came to a crushing halt.

Trying to catch my breath, I fumbled with the cloak to find my keys in one of the pockets. As I slid the key into the lock, Xander approached behind me. "Laken, please don't be upset. Breaking up with her is going to be tricky. I have to be careful with this."

I reached for the door handle, not wanting to turn around and let him see the disappointment that surely lurked in my eyes. "All I ask is that you don't touch me again until you break it off with her. I just got dumped two weeks ago, and I don't need to be jerked around again." I flung the door open and stepped into the warm house. Pulling my key out of the lock, I turned to him. "Goodnight, Xander," I said before shutting the door and locking the deadbolt.

Chapter 4

As if I didn't have enough to worry about between the curse and the stranger, Brooke's call at nine o'clock the next morning brought another threat to light. "It's too early," I grumbled, my voice husky from sleep when my phone woke me up from where I had left it on the nightstand.

"You have some explaining to do," Brooke said without offering a quick "Hello" or "Good Morning." Instead, she huffed. "What happened last night?"

"I…had to take care of something," I explained lamely.

I hadn't come up with a good story for leaving the dance last night, but I'd better think fast. I couldn't tell Brooke the truth.

"With Xander? Ethan told me you left with him. What's going on between you two?" She sounded hurt, as though she shouldn't need to ask. And normally, she didn't. I would have already told her everything if it wasn't so dangerous, not to mention unbelievable.

"I assure you nothing happened with him. If it does, you'll be the first to know."

"I'd better be," she said, her voice more upbeat. "And I'll want details. You owe me after leaving us high and dry last night."

I couldn't help smiling. "When—I mean if—anything happens, you can count on it."

"When?" She wasn't about to let that go. "You sound pretty sure of this now."

"Well, I'm not. Things are complicated, to say the least."

"You're not kidding. I didn't want to tell you this, but Marlena spent most of the dance boiling with anger when she found out her date ditched her. She even went out to look for his truck. When she found it missing, she looked like she could kill someone."

"I'm not surprised," I murmured. My worst nightmare appeared as though it was about to come true. "Did she ever calm down?"

"Not as far as I could tell. She isn't accustomed to being left at a dance like that. Xander's got some guts, I'll give him that."

"Only problem is he's putting me in the middle. She'll come after me before she dares to go after him." I sighed, my heart heavy as I realized that I might not make it through the next week alive. *You might as well forget about the stranger because Marlena will kill you first,* a voice in my head insisted.

"What was so important that you two had to leave?"

"Um…his dad needed some help with something. I just happened to be with Xander when he got the call, so when he asked if I wanted to go with him, I said yes. I mean, my only other choice was to stay at the dance and wallow in my self-pity watching all the happy couples. It seemed like a good idea at the time."

"Hmmm," Brooke mused. "I'm not sure Marlena's going to buy that."

"Well, it's true." *At least close enough,* I thought with a frown.

"Hold on," Brooke said before hollering away from the

phone. "In a minute!" Then she lowered her voice. "I have to go. My parents are dragging me to my grandparents' house in Concord for brunch. See you tomorrow?"

"Of course," I replied, wondering if I should conveniently wake up with a massive headache in the morning and skip school. "Have fun today."

"Yeah, right. I'll text you later just to tell you just how boring it is." We both laughed. "Okay. Time to go before my mom comes up here to find out what's taking me so long."

"All right. See you tomorrow." I hung up the call and put my phone back on the nightstand. As much as I wanted to hide in bed all day, I forced myself to get up. My homework waited and, in spite of everything going on, I was determined to keep up with my classes.

I received several text messages from Xander that day, most of which I didn't answer. It wasn't until he threatened to drive over to my house and check on me that I responded. *I'm fine. No sign of anyone today. Dakota's here with me. See you tomorrow.* My message must have appeased him because he left me alone for the rest of the evening.

The next day, I steered clear of Xander and Marlena. Xander watched me everywhere I went, our eyes meeting frequently when we passed each other in the hallway. I caught sight of him with Marlena once, and sparks flew between them in a heated discussion. Trying to be discreet, I escaped into the crowded hallway, leaving them far behind.

When the final bell rang, I rushed through the sea of students to my locker. As I reached up to grab my Calculus book from the shelf, something sharp poked me in the back. It felt pointed, like the tip of a pocketknife. Confused, I dropped my arm and turned my head far enough to see Carrie out of the corner of my eye. Any hope I'd had of getting home without being confronted by Marlena was shattered in that moment.

"Laken," Carrie hissed. "You're wanted behind the school."

"I can't. I'm meeting Ethan at my car in a few minutes," I said, staring at my parka that still hung from the locker hook.

"Ethan can wait. This can't. Come with me. Now." She jabbed the knife against me, and I winced from the pain, hoping she hadn't drawn any blood.

I inched toward my locker, away from the knife's pressure, a sigh of defeat escaping my lips. Reaching down, I shoved my book bag into the bottom of the locker and shut the door, not daring to ask if there was time to put my coat on. "Fine," I grumbled.

Carrie pushed me through the crowded hall, the blade poking into my back when I had to stop suddenly to avoid running into another student. She stayed close behind me, keeping the knife hidden from sight. "Smile, Laken," she whispered. "We don't need to make this any worse than it already is."

"It's kind of hard to smile when you're hurting me," I muttered.

"Then keep moving unless you want it to hurt more."

"Do you mind telling me what this is all about?" I asked.

"Yes, I do. You'll find out soon enough."

I frowned as she guided me to the back exit of the school. We barged outside to the spot where I'd seen the stranger Saturday night, but I didn't feel any less threatened being able to see the faded lawn and the gray clouds hovering over the bare trees. The chill in the air was the last thing on my mind as Carrie pushed me down the stairs to the schoolyard.

At the bottom, Marlena stood tall with her hands on her hips, her blonde hair spilling over her brown shearling coat that reached her jean-clad knees. Three other girls gathered beside her. Angry sparks shot from her blue eyes, rattling my composure. But I stood tall, refusing to let her get to me.

When we stopped several feet away from them, Carrie withdrew the knife from my back and I heard a click that sounded like a retracting switchblade.

"Good job, Carrie. Did anyone follow you guys out here?" Marlena asked.

"Not that I can tell," Carrie told her.

Marlena smiled wickedly. "Perfect."

"What do you want with me?" I demanded, staring at her, challenging her.

"I want to know what you were doing out here with Xander Saturday night," Marlena said in a suspicious voice.

"I—we—were just talking. He's my History partner."

"You expect me to believe that you were discussing a History project during a dance on a Saturday night? How stupid do you think I am?"

I took a deep breath, my mind racing to come up with a believable explanation. But I came up empty. And I couldn't tell her the truth. "Why don't you ask him? He is your boyfriend, isn't he?"

"I tried, but he's hiding something. I want to know what it is, and you're going to tell me."

"I don't know what you're talking about," I lied, praying that she'd let it go. But I knew better than to think Marlena would give up that easily.

"Yes, you do," she hissed, approaching me. When she stopped less than a foot away, she continued. "Mark saw you two making out. You didn't really think you were going to get away with this, did you?"

I backed away from her, wondering if Mark had been in the woods when Xander had looked up from me. But I didn't get very far. I bumped into Carrie who lingered behind me, trapping me between them.

"Let me get something perfectly clear, Laken," Marlena said. "Xander is off-limits. I gave you Noah because of him. I don't know what happened between you and Noah, but—"

"She probably couldn't keep up with an older guy," Allison, the brunette with a short pixie haircut, interrupted before turning her attention to me. "You need to put out if you're going to keep a guy like that interested."

Marlena laughed as I fought to keep the tears from filling

my eyes. "Allison's right. And if you couldn't hold on to Noah, how in the world do you think you can steal Xander from me? I'm a hard act to follow."

"Then keep him," I said. "I don't want him."

"Yeah, right," Carrie said from behind me.

"It's true," I insisted. "Xander caught me off-guard. I wasn't prepared to deal with him, and I told him to leave me alone."

Marlena smiled accusingly. "When? Before or after you took off with him for the rest of the night? Did he mention that he brought me to the dance? That he left me and I had to find a ride home? I've never been so humiliated."

"Then take it up with him. Leave me out of this," I begged.

"Oh, don't pretend to be so innocent. I see the way you act around him. You're constantly giving him that adoring puppy-dog look. Don't deny it. You're in love with him."

My jaw dropped, and I shook my head. "No, no, no," I repeated in shock. "That's crazy. You don't know what you're talking about. The only guy I want is Noah."

"Good try," Marlena said. "You're not a very good liar, Laken." She shot a knowing look at Allison and nodded.

Before I realized what was happening, Carrie grabbed my upper arms from behind as Allison approached me. She drew up a fist and slammed it into my stomach, sending a shooting pain through me. I nearly doubled over, but Carrie held me up as Allison raised her hand and curled her fingers into another fist.

Before she could hit me again, Marlena placed a hand on her shoulder. "Wait," she told Allison, her narrowed eyes focusing on me. "Maybe now you'd like to tell us the truth."

"I already did," I choked out.

Marlena laughed, removing her hand from Allison. "Do it," she instructed.

As Allison prepared to strike me again, a dark shadow moved within the trees surrounding the yard. When the black shape emerged from the woods, my heart dropped into the pit of my stomach. Dakota stood in plain sight. *'No, Dakota!'* I thought. *'Go back before they see you!'* But he ignored my thoughts as he stared at the girls. Their backs were to him except for Carrie who released my arms at once.

"Marlena, Allison," she whispered, her voice trembling. "Turn around slowly."

Allison dropped her fist. "What the hell?" She gaped at Carrie before she, Marlena and the other two girls followed her gaze.

As soon as they saw Dakota, they stiffened with sudden fear. Dakota's black fur stood straight up along his back. He emitted a loud growl, his lip curling up to expose sharp fangs. In a flash, he charged across the field, heading directly for the girls.

"Dakota! No!" I screamed. He knew better than to expose himself, and I shuddered at the thought of what this would mean for his future.

He paid me no attention as he skidded to a halt in front of Marlena, his growl rumbling deep in his throat and his eyes glaring at her. She took a step back, her eyes locked on him. When Dakota didn't come any closer, she and her friends backed farther away. "Let's get out of here," Allison mumbled before taking off with the other two girls. Marlena and Carrie remained, their expressions frozen as though they had seen a ghost.

Then Carrie slipped around me and jogged backward, her fearful eyes never leaving Dakota. "Come on, Marlena. Let it go. Don't do anything reckless."

Marlena glanced at Carrie before moving toward her with long strides. Stopping beside Carrie, Marlena shifted her eyes from Dakota to me. "This isn't over, you little bitch. You're going to be sorry for the mess you created," she warned before she and Carrie spun on their heels and fled.

As soon as they disappeared around the corner, I gaped at Dakota with disappointment and sadness, fearing what could happen now that he had been seen. I wasn't sure what to say to him.

I knew he'd only meant to protect me, but the risk he had just taken was unforgivable.

Dakota's fur flattened onto his back and his lips lowered over his fangs when footsteps sounded on the cement steps behind me. Dakota took one look beyond me before darting across the lawn and escaping into the woods.

I spun around only to have the wind knocked out of me as Xander pulled me into a crushing embrace.

"Ow!" I said, wincing from the pain in my abdomen where Allison had punched me.

He ran a finger along my cheek, wiping at a stray tear. "Laken! What happened? Are you all right?"

"Do I look all right?" I asked quietly, shuddering. "No, I'm not. This never should have happened. It's all over now."

A breeze rippled through his dark hair and his eyes searched my expression for answers. "What are you talking about?"

I broke out of his arms and backed up, taking a deep breath. "He was here. Marlena, Carrie, Allison, they all saw him. It's over."

"Who was here? Laken, you're not making any sense."

"Dakota," I whispered.

Xander drew in a sharp breath, seeming to understand my concern right away. "Oh, no, I'm sorry." He stepped closer, pulling me back into his arms. "It's okay. No one will believe them."

"There were five of them, and they all saw him. It's only a matter of time now. He'll be taken from me, I'm sure of it."

Leaning my cheek against his shoulder, I closed my eyes as if I could shut out the future. Even though I wanted to blame him for Marlena's fury, it wouldn't do any good.

The damage had been done, and nothing could turn back time. So instead of being angry with him, I accepted his support, allowing him to comfort me.

"But why? He didn't do anything. I'll attest to that."

I lifted my head to look up at Xander. "It won't matter. This is a small town. Once word gets around that a wolf nearly attacked the mayor's daughter, Dakota won't be safe."

"Then bring him to my house. He can stay with us until this blows over."

I shook my head. "It won't be forgotten anytime soon. You have no idea what this is going to lead to."

"Neither do you. And he can stay as long as it takes."

I swallowed the lump forming in my throat. "Really? You'd do that for me?"

"Of course. Besides, he loves me," Xander said with a sly smile. "It'll be kind of cool to hang out with a wolf for a while." When he paused, his grin faded. "Laken, where's your coat?"

"I didn't have time to get it."

"Why?" he gritted out, a scowl forming on his face.

"Because…" My voice trailed off and I tried to think of something to tell him other than the truth. But nothing came to mind. "Because Carrie dragged me out here. Getting my coat wasn't an option."

"Damn it! I knew it. What did they do to you? Why did Dakota rush out here?"

"Nothing. It's nothing, okay?"

"If that's what you want to tell your dad or the principal, that's fine. But I need you to tell me the truth. Did they hurt you?"

I nodded slowly. "Yes," I whispered. "Carrie shoved a knife in my back to get me out here, and Allison took a swing at me. But I'm okay, really. Turning this into a bigger deal than it is will just make things worse. All I care about right now is Dakota."

Xander sucked in a deep breath, trying to calm down. Anger was etched in his expression, burning in his eyes. "Speak for yourself. Dakota should have attacked them when he had the chance. Now I'll have to do what he didn't."

"Xander, no," I begged. "I'll be fine. I think they hurt my pride more than anything."

"You're in pain. I can see it in your eyes. They're going to pay for this," he vowed. "But not today. Right now, let's get back inside so you can get your coat."

"Okay," I said, hoping that Marlena and her friends had already left the school. The last thing I wanted was to run into them again this afternoon, especially with Xander by my side. That would only prove their case.

A cold wind blasted across the lawn as Xander wrapped his arm around my shoulders. Then he led me up the stairs and toward the school, the heat from his body warming me in the few seconds it took to reach the door.

Bang! Bang! Bang! Someone pounded on our front door as I sat down to dinner with my parents.

"What the hell?" my father muttered, pushing his chair back as he rose to his feet. Still wearing jeans and a light blue button down shirt from a long day at the station, he shook his head, clearly annoyed. Without another word, he rushed across the kitchen and into the entry hall.

"Sheriff Sumner! Open up!" a man's muffled voice hollered from outside the front door.

I glanced at my mother who sat next to me. She raised her eyebrows, remaining calm as she reached for the bowl of spaghetti. "Let your father handle it, whatever it is," she told me.

"Mom, someone's practically breaking down our door."

Before she could protest, I scooted my chair out behind me and stood, tossing the napkin from my lap onto the table. I hurried around the table and across the kitchen to the entry hall, stopping when the mayor walked in. Feeling the blood rush out of my cheeks, I hoped neither he nor my father would sense the anxiety taking a hold of me.

"Mayor. What can I do for you?" my father asked, his tone respectful. In spite of his calm voice, a nervous shadow lurked in his eyes.

"Sheriff, I'd like a word with you."

My father frowned. "Okay." He seemed to realize that this was no social visit. Something was wrong. Very, very wrong.

"Would you mind telling me what your daughter is doing with a wolf?" the mayor demanded.

My father's face went white as he averted his gaze to me. But he quickly composed himself, returning his attention to the mayor. "What is this really about?"

"It's about a wolf that nearly attacked my daughter behind the school today. You have some explaining to do."

"Mayor," my father said calmly. "I don't know what happened, but I do know that your daughter was in no danger."

"So you admit that you knew there was a wolf running around?"

My father dropped his head for a moment before raising his eyes to meet the mayor's cold stare. "Sort of. He's been in the area for a few years."

"What? You've been harboring a wild, not to mention illegal, animal for years?"

"No, absolutely not. He just lives around here. I only know about him because he took to Laken a few years back. They're...friends, if you will."

"What kind of girl befriends a wolf?"

My father didn't miss a beat. "A very special one." He glanced at me as he spoke, a mixture of disappointment and pride in his eyes.

"No, a very stupid one. Now you listen to me, Sheriff. As mayor of this town, I won't allow a wolf that shouldn't be around these parts in the first place to terrorize innocent people."

I nearly choked when he referred to Marlena and her

friends as innocent. But I remained quiet, afraid that my worst fears were about to come true.

"Tomorrow morning, I'm meeting with the town council to organize a hunt."

A lump formed in my throat and I shuddered as a tear rolled down my cheek. I couldn't believe this was happening. But it was no surprise, either. Wolves invoked an irrational fear in people for no good reason. Perhaps it stemmed from folklore filled with tales of man-eating wolves. Whatever it was, there was no way to change an attitude that had been ingrained in people for centuries.

Nothing my father or I could say right now would change the mayor's mind.

"Mayor, be reasonable," my father said. "No one's been hurt. He didn't do anything."

"And thank God for that. But I'm not about to wait around for that to change. People live here because it's a safe place where their children can play in their backyards. It's our job to keep it that way."

"What are you really afraid of, Mayor? That the rumor of an alleged wolf will ruin your chance of being reelected? Maybe you should ask your daughter why it threatened her. Perhaps you need to understand the circumstances before taking drastic measures."

"It's a wolf, Sheriff, not a human. It's not innocent until proven guilty. A wolf is a threat to the people of this town, their children, and even their pets and livestock. Come tomorrow morning, I'm going to ask the town council to set a reward for anyone who brings it in, dead or alive. But preferably dead."

"No!" I cried, stepping into the entry hall, tears filling my eyes. "Mayor, please, he was only trying to protect me. I didn't want to tell anyone, but Allison hit me. And Marlena might not have touched me, but she was there. Please, don't have him killed. He won't hurt anyone, I promise."

"You can't be sure of that, Laken," the mayor said.

"But I am sure of it. That wolf is the only reason I found

Ryder. He's a hero, not a threat. Without him, Ryder could have died that night."

"Then he will be remembered as a hero, not the monster he could become tomorrow." The mayor shifted his gaze back to my father. "My mind is made up. I expect you'll respect my decision. The wolf will be caught and our town will be safe again."

I couldn't bear to listen to another word. When I ran back to the kitchen, my mother had stood up, the food forgotten as moisture glistened in her eyes. She caught me right away, pulling me into her arms. "Laken. It'll be okay," she said, but her words failed to comfort me.

The idea of losing Dakota was unbearable and sent shockwaves of despair through me. I took a deep breath, quivering as I exhaled. Grateful for my mother's support, I leaned against her and listened to the rest of my father's conversation with the mayor.

"I trust I'll see you at the council meeting in the morning," the mayor said to my father.

"I'm not sure if I can make it."

"Be there, or the town will know that the sheriff they've put their trust in for years has been hiding this beast in his own backyard. And if that happens, well, we'll see if you still have a job by the end of the day. I hear Noah's doing a fine job and could easily take over. Is that what you want?"

"No, sir," my father answered quietly.

"Then it's settled. Goodnight, Sheriff."

As soon as the mayor left, my father clicked the deadbolt into place and took a deep breath. He crossed the entry hall to where my mother and I stood.

"Laken," he said, folding his arms across his chest. "Why didn't you tell us what happened today?"

I lifted my face away from my mother's shoulder. "I didn't want you to know they hurt me."

My father nodded with a look of sympathy. "Damn," he swore under his breath. "I never thought anything like this would happen. Dakota has never taken a chance like this.

He's too smart. How could he do this?"

"It's too late to think about that now. What's done is done. But Dad, you have to stop this. You can't let them hunt him down. He doesn't deserve that."

"I know he doesn't. And I wish I had another choice, but I don't. You heard the mayor. It's either Dakota or my job."

"Please," I begged. "There has to be something you can do."

"Tom, honey, Laken's right," my mother said. "Those girls hurt her. Can't you arrest them or something?"

He looked at me, his eyebrows raised. "Only if that's what Laken wants."

I shook my head. Pressing charges against Marlena and her friends would only give them a reason to make my life more miserable than it was about to become. "I'm fine now, and I just want to forget about it."

"There you have it," my father said. "My back's up against a wall. There's nothing I can do."

As the tears rolled down my cheeks, I backed out of my mother's arms. The three of us stood in silence, our dinner waiting in the kitchen. My appetite had disappeared completely, even though I hadn't eaten a single bite before the mayor showed up.

"If we can't get the mayor to change his mind, how can we protect Dakota?" I asked.

"Well, for starters, he can't stay here anymore. And you'll have to get rid of any evidence that he ever came into this house, meaning his bed upstairs," my father told me.

"Okay. But what about him?"

"You're going to have to see to it that he runs as far away from here as he can. He may not be safe until he reaches Canada, and maybe not even then."

My eyes shot up to look at my father as I wondered how he thought I could do that. His gaze met mine for a brief moment, but I quickly looked away.

"Let's get back to dinner before it gets cold," he said, passing me and my mother on his way into the table.

My mother glanced at me. "Are you going to eat?" she asked.

I shook my head. "I lost my appetite," I whispered.

"Well, there will be plenty of leftovers if you get it back," she said softly before sitting down at the table with my father and leaving me to contemplate my next move.

Chapter 5

Numb from the mayor's threat, I rushed over to the coat closet, not quite sure what I intended to do. I grabbed my parka and put it on, zipping it up as I hurried through the kitchen on my way to the back door.

"Where are you going?" my father asked.

"Out to look for Dakota. I need to see him. I'll be back." Before my parents could protest, I flipped on the outside light and hurried out onto the patio. The night was still, the early November air cold. But I barely felt it. Even the fog from my breath went unnoticed.

In the darkness, I crossed the patio, my eyes searching the yard and woods for any sign of Dakota. I briefly worried that the stranger might be nearby, but it was far more important that I found Dakota, even if it meant encountering the man again. Xander would probably scold me if he knew I'd gone outside alone after dark, even with my parents in the house, but I would risk anything to find Dakota. No price was too big to try to protect him from the imminent danger lurking in his future.

Shaking thoughts of Xander and the stranger from my

mind, I walked down the patio steps and through the grass to the center of the yard where I stopped. Scanning the perimeter, I spotted a pair of familiar amber eyes at the side of the yard. Dakota. The sight of him in the shadows shattered my heart into pieces. This could be the last time I ever saw him.

I rushed over to him and kneeled beside him. The idea that anyone could look at him as a monster was beyond belief. He had been nothing but a guardian angel to me. "Dakota!" I whispered, my lips trembling. I couldn't stop the tears from spilling as I rubbed the side of his face. He leaned toward me, welcoming my touch. "What were you thinking today? We're all in big trouble, but mostly you. They're going to put a bounty on your head tomorrow."

Dakota tilted his head, his expression serious and somber.

"They're going to hunt you down. You have to run as far from here as you can," I told him through my sobs. The realization that this was my final goodbye to him struck me like a knife in my heart. I swallowed again. "You have to leave and never come back. It's the only way."

Dakota whined, nudging my neck. Sadness and despair lurked in his eyes. I wrapped my arms around his neck and buried my face in his fur, clinging to him, causing my sorrow to deepen. I recalled our time together—the mountain hikes and the countless times he had comforted me just by being there. I couldn't imagine life without him.

I wasn't sure how long I held him before I let go. Tears clouded my vision as I rose to my feet. "Goodbye, Dakota," I said. I turned and walked across the lawn to the steps. As I approached the back door, Dakota's nails clicked on the patio behind me. I whirled around in frustration.

Dakota stopped several feet away, a forlorn look in his eyes. When he took another step closer to me, I shook my head. "No. You can't come in and you can't stay. You have to leave and never come back!"

Not moving, he took a deep breath, his chest expanding.

Desperate to get this over with, I ran at him, waving my arms to shoo him away. "Go! Get out of here! Go on!" I cried, my tears flowing again.

Instantly, his eyes met mine with understanding and sorrow. Then he spun around and, with a swish of his tail, darted down the patio steps, across the grass, and into the woods.

Alone in the silence, I shivered. I couldn't believe Dakota was really gone. Only quiet and pitch black loomed around me. And this time, it was permanent. This time, he wouldn't return.

The last of Dakota. My final goodbye. The realization of what was happening struck me hard and fast. I dropped to my knees and fell to a crumpled heap on the cold patio as sobs wrenched through me. My life would never be the same without him. No more mountain hikes. No more silent looks from him when he read my mind. How would I get through the future without him?

I lay on the cold cement and cried for what seemed like forever. When my parents came outside to find me, they urged me to my feet. At their insistence, I retreated back into the house for the night. Turning my nose up at the thought of dinner, I escaped to my room with an empty stomach. And later, after hours of tossing and turning, I cried myself to sleep.

ᥱ᳗ᥱ᳗

I felt like a zombie the next day, going through the motions of getting ready for school. Several times, my gaze drifted to Dakota's empty bed in the corner. Tears welled up in my eyes as I pulled on a pair of jeans, a black hoodie, and sneakers. After brushing my hair, I lifted the hood, hoping it would hide me from Marlena and her horrible friends. I knew it probably wouldn't, but at least I felt hidden from the world.

The ride to school that morning was painfully quiet. Ethan attempted to draw me out of my shell into a conversation, but after I explained the mayor's plan to organize a wolf hunt, he fell silent.

When I pulled the Explorer into the school parking lot and turned off the engine, Ethan turned to me, his eyes soft and caring. He placed his hand on mine, squeezing it gently. "Are you going to be okay?" he asked.

I nodded slowly, scared that the tears I held bottled up inside would run down my face again if I tried to talk.

"Because I'm supposed to meet Brooke, but I'll stay with you if you need me to."

I shook my head, hoping that I could convince him I'd be okay even though I wasn't sure of it myself.

Ethan's gaze shifted to look beyond me. "Looks like you won't be alone after all. Someone's waiting for you."

Curious, I whipped around to see Xander out my window. His pick-up was parked two spaces away, and he leaned against the passenger side door, his leather jacket blending into the black finish on his truck.

I turned back to Ethan and mustered up a weak smile. "Go meet Brooke. I'll be fine."

Ethan nodded. "All right. See you in homeroom." With that, he reached for the book bag at his feet and jumped out.

I slid out of the driver's seat, shivering in the cold. As soon as I shut the door and turned, Xander stood in front of me. My eyes meeting his, I shoved my freezing hands into my jacket pockets and took a deep breath, afraid that I would start crying again if I tried to tell him what happened last night.

"Hey," he said softly. "You look awful."

"Gee, thanks," I muttered. "You sure know how to make a girl's morning."

"You know I think you're beautiful, but it's pretty obvious you had a hard night. I know yesterday was rough, but this will all blow over soon."

I shook my head against the black hood. "No. It got a lot

worse last night. He's gone now. For good." A tear rolled down my face.

"Who?"

"Dakota."

"What are you trying to say?"

I sniffed, fighting to reign in my tears long enough to explain. Hesitating, I drew in a long breath and found the courage to relay the events of the night.

"The mayor stopped by. He was pretty mad that a wolf threatened Marlena, especially a wolf kept by the sheriff's daughter. He's organizing a hunt and offering a reward to anyone who catches Dakota. He wants him dead or alive, but I know no one's going to bring him in alive. I told Dakota to leave. To run as far from town as he can go."

Anger raced across Xander's face. "This is ridiculous. No one got hurt. Dakota was only protecting you. They were beating you up. This is just wrong."

"I know, but there's nothing we can do other than hope Dakota makes it out of the country alive."

"Dakota is family to you. How can your father accept this? He shouldn't just lie there and let them walk all over you."

"Then tell me what he's supposed to do!" I cried exasperatedly. "The mayor threatened his job. If he gets fired for allowing me to keep a wild animal in our backyard, which, by the way, is illegal, he'll never work again. I can't let my father's career be ruined because of this."

"They can't prove that Dakota was your pet. He could have been a stray wolf that someone dumped up here. And what about the little boy? Did your father tell the mayor that Dakota was the one who led you to him?"

"I told him that," I whispered, wishing Xander would calm down. "He didn't care. It's over. There's nothing else we can do." As I admitted defeat, tears leaked from my eyes.

Xander slid an arm around my waist and drew me toward him. I leaned my cheek against his chest in between the sides of his jacket, feeling his strong hold on me through my thick parka. He smelled like leather and spicy after-shave.

"I'm so sorry, Laken. I never wanted this. It's killing me to watch them do this to you. And it's all my fault. Damn it! If only I hadn't dated Marlena."

I lifted my face away from his chest and looked up at him. "No, you can't blame yourself. I didn't exactly push you away the night of the dance. I knew you were still with Marlena, and yet, I got carried away in the moment. Besides, Dakota should have known better."

"He was only trying to protect you," Xander reminded me. "I'm guessing he would do it over again if he had to. You're his pack, remember? And wolves are very loyal to their pack."

"Yes, they are," I agreed quietly.

"He obviously cares about you. I would never blame him for that." Xander paused, smiling coyly, despite the dark situation hanging over us. "But back to what you said about getting carried away with me. Does this mean I have a chance with you? It's pretty safe to say that it's over with Marlena. Good riddance if you ask me."

I sighed, not sure what to say. The truth was, he did have a chance. I couldn't deny my feelings for him any longer since it was obvious Noah wasn't coming back to me, and now I couldn't keep using Marlena as an excuse to turn him down. But how could I allow myself a sliver of happiness with Dakota's life on the line? Xander would just have to wait.

After a moment, Xander asked, "Are you going to answer my question?"

I glanced up at him, meeting his blue eyes. "I don't know. It's hard to think about something like that at a time like this. All I can think about is Dakota." I sighed with worry, looking down as I leaned against him again.

"Fair enough," he whispered.

We stood together for another minute before Xander

broke the silence. "We'd better get to homeroom before we're late."

I slowly drew out of his arms, nodding. I felt numb all over, knowing that the hunt for Dakota would begin before school ended today. A part of me wanted to ditch my morning classes and bust in on the town meeting to tell the council that it was absurd to spend the taxpayers' money to hunt down an animal that had never hurt anyone. But I knew my efforts would be wasted. "Okay," I said. "Just let me get my book bag."

After I retrieved my bag from the back seat and locked the truck, Xander wrapped his arm around my shoulders. We walked across the parking lot and up the steps to the school. Before we made it to the entrance, Marlena stepped into our path, blocking our way. Her blonde hair fell below the fur-lined collar of her coat and sparks flew from her icy blue eyes.

"If it isn't the happy couple," she said, sarcasm dripping from her every word. "Well, Xander, you sure didn't waste any time. But don't get your hopes up. I'm sure she won't be as easy as I was."

"Cut it out, Marlena," Xander snapped.

She shifted her cold stare toward me. "What's the matter, Laken? You look like you've been crying. Rough night?"

I stared at her, but didn't dare try to speak. Crying in front of her would only give her more satisfaction, and I refused to let her see how much pain she had caused me.

"Haven't you done enough?" Xander asked.

Marlena's mouth curled into a wicked smile for a moment. Then it vanished. "There's nothing I could do that will make up for the humiliation you put me through Saturday night. You didn't even have the courtesy to tell me you were breaking up with me. Or did you think you two could fool around behind my back?"

"I would apologize to you, but I know it wouldn't even matter," Xander said.

"No, it's too late for that. Besides, I got my revenge.

Now it's only a matter of time before that wolf is dragged back into town by a hunter. He probably won't live to see another day."

Her words cut through me like a knife, prompting a tear to leak from my eye. Xander squeezed my shoulders as if reminding me he was still there. "You're really sure that the hunters around here will be able to track down a wolf?" Xander countered. "It's not like they've done it before."

"How hard can it be? I'm sure that beast can be lured with a piece of meat. Then all one of them has to do is aim and fire."

"I find it hard to believe it will be that easy," Xander scoffed.

"Once my father sets the reward this morning, there will be hunters from all over the state up here. That wolf can run, but he can't hide forever."

"I suppose it doesn't matter to you that he was the only reason Ryder Thompson was found, does it?"

"No. Because he attacked me!" Marlena shot back. "I don't care how many children he may have saved. Yesterday, he showed his true colors. He's a wolf and we don't want one around here."

"I assume you didn't tell your father that the only reason he came out of the woods in the first place was to protect Laken from getting beat up at your command."

Marlena's eyes narrowed as she stared back at Xander. "Maybe I should tell my father how you used me. Maybe he needs to know that you forced yourself on me when I said no and begged you to stop." She choked back tears, her voice softening.

I felt Xander's body stiffen beside me. "That's a flat out lie."

"Who do you think he's going to believe? His own daughter or some kid from California who got his ass moved to our hole-in-the-earth town to keep him out of ju-vie?" Marlena watched both of us with complete satisfaction. "That wolf will die, mark my words. And when he does, I think I'll have a party to celebrate. Shall I add you two to the guest list?"

"You're going to have to wait a long time to hold that party," Xander said confidently, his eyes locking with hers.

"We'll see about that." Marlena shot us one last glare before turning on her heels and rushing into the school.

As the door slammed shut behind her, I stood with Xander at the top of the steps, hesitant to move. The schoolyard was empty now, and we were alone in the brisk morning sun.

My book bag hung from my shoulder, feeling like a ton of bricks. I tried to focus on the strap pinching my shoulder because that felt better than the hurt and pain from Marlena's spiteful words. "You okay?" Xander asked quietly, wiping at the tear rolling down my cheek.

I nodded silently.

"Then we'd better get going before we're late. Come on, let's go inside." He threaded his fingers through mine, his touch warm and comforting. Then we headed toward the school for what I knew would be a wasted day with far more time spent worrying about Dakota than listening to my teachers.

∽✄∾

The hunt for Dakota began before classes ended that day. By the time Ethan and I drove home that afternoon, reward posters hung from every telephone pole in sight. The huge signs showed a wolf's face, its lip curled up to reveal sharp fangs. Below it read "$5,000 Reward, Dead or Alive." I tried to ignore them, but even as I focused straight ahead at the road, I could see them out of the corner of my eye.

Tensions mounted that week as the hunt got underway. Students stared at me as if they'd never seen me before. Boys howled like wolves when they saw me, and then laughed as if it was the funniest thing they'd heard in years.

Others taunted me, proudly announcing that their fathers were tracking the wolf and that it would only be a matter of time before they killed him. Some kids snickered when I passed them in the hall, shouting things like "Hey, wolfgirl!" or "Look, it's Little Red Riding Hood without her cape!"

Xander rarely left my side that week, often chasing off the kids who laughed at me. Between his muscular build and the rumors circulating about his shady past of stealing cars and getting in trouble with the law, all Xander had to do was look at the students spouting off cruel words at me and they ran off immediately. I had never been so grateful to have him as an ally since he'd moved to town. Fortunately, the stranger and the story his father had told me Saturday night didn't come up in conversation. I could only handle one crisis at a time and, until the wolf hunt blew over, the last thing I wanted to think about was the stranger and the curse.

To my surprise, Noah sent me a text message Tuesday night. *I'm sorry about Dakota. He doesn't deserve to be hunted. I hope he's halfway to Canada by now.*

I smiled when I read it. Even though Noah hadn't called or stopped by, at least he was thinking about me.

As the week wore on, the excitement of the wolf hunt faded and the taunts from the other kids died down. By Thursday evening, things had calmed considerably. Rumor had it that none of the hunters had seen a trace of Dakota all week, and I was able to relax with the hope that he would survive after all.

I finally slept through the night without tossing and turning until the sun came up. The redness in my eyes disappeared and, for the first time in days, I didn't look like I'd been up all night crying. Xander met me at my locker that morning, smiling as he studied me. I wore a pink sweater with jeans, and I'd actually been able to put make-up on. Silver hoops dangled from my ears, matching my diamond necklace that I wore for the first time that week.

"No hoodie today. You look nice," he commented as I slid my French book onto my locker shelf.

I turned to him, studying the black shirt that outlined his muscular frame and the shark tooth necklace that gleamed against his tanned skin. "Thank you. You don't look so bad yourself."

He tilted his head to the side, a grin lighting up his face. "Hmmm. Are you admitting you're attracted to me?" he asked.

I groaned, realizing that after several days of his tender protectiveness, the old Xander was back. I shrugged and rolled my eyes. "I never told you I wasn't attracted to you. I just told you I wouldn't go out with you."

Xander raised his eyebrows, his smile growing. "You have an excellent point. So, it's Friday. What do you say I take you out tonight? You've had a hard week, and I don't think you should be alone tonight."

Sighing, I gazed up at him, knowing that I didn't have an excuse to refuse his offer. But more importantly, I didn't want to turn him down. "Okay," I agreed, my tone void of emotion.

"Really?" he asked with surprise.

"Sure. Why not? Now that Brooke and Ethan are a couple, I don't want to be a third wheel with them again. And you were right about Noah. That's over. Since you're done with Marlena, I guess I can't say no. Besides, I don't want to be alone tonight."

"So you're going to go out with me because you have nothing better to do?"

"Maybe?" I wasn't sure that he was right, but I had made it sound like that.

Xander smiled brightly, not seeming to mind. "Great. I'll take a yes any way I can get it."

I raised my eyebrows before turning back to my locker. "So what are we going to do tonight?"

"I'm not sure. I'll have to give this some thought. I want our first date to be special."

"Just nothing fancy, please."

"Got it." Still smiling, he leaned against the locker next to mine, quiet for longer than I could remember him being as he seemed lost in his thoughts. Relieved that I had something other than Dakota's uncertain fate to think about, I finished organizing my books.

The day progressed uneventfully until after my last class when my world came crashing down. I had just arrived back at my locker when Marlena's smug voice rose over the chatter in the hall behind me.

"Really?" she asked. "I'll spread the word. I'm glad this nightmare is finally over."

My heart skipped a beat as I whirled around to see her standing in front of me. Beyond her, the other students blurred in the background as they rushed down the hallway, excited about the weekend. I stared at Marlena, the hatred and laughter in her eyes unsettling me. But even that wasn't enough to prepare me for what she was about to say. "They killed your wolf," she announced, smiling with pure evil.

"No!" I cried, feeling as though someone had just shattered my heart into a million pieces. My breath got caught in my throat, choking me. Dizziness took a hold of me, and my legs felt weak. As I felt myself starting to fall, Xander appeared, catching me in his arms. Trembling, I clutched his shoulders, hanging on to him. He was warm and strong, and without him, I would have fallen to the floor. Tears stung my eyes, blurring everything around me. But I didn't care. Only one thing mattered and that was Dakota. I couldn't believe that he had paid with his life for protecting me.

"Was that necessary, Marlena?" Xander snapped. "She was going to find out eventually."

"I wanted to see the look on her face when she found out her wolf is dead," Marlena said with an emphasis on the word dead.

Xander held me tightly with an arm around my waist and the other one around my shoulders. "You really are a bitch, Marlena," he said. "I sized you up right the first week of school. All that matters to you is you."

"Call it what you want, Xander, but she took something of mine, so I took something of hers. Now we're even."

"We were on the verge of breaking up. You knew that. Killing an animal that didn't hurt anyone is hardly what I'd call an eye for an eye."

"Whatever. I feel better knowing that the wolf is dead and will never come after me again." She grinned with delight. "Have a nice weekend, Laken."

As sobs wrenched through me, Marlena turned on her heels, her blonde hair spinning out around her shoulders before she walked away through the crowd.

Chapter 6

I felt as though the wind had been knocked out of me, and I couldn't catch my breath. My hope that Dakota had made it up to Canada alive had been crushed. "No," I muttered, shaking my head. "This isn't happening. It can't be." Closing my eyes, I pictured Dakota, his ears pointed at me, his head tilted to the side, his amber eyes reading my thoughts. The image of him sent another wave of anguish over me as I realized that the only time I would see him again would be in my dreams.

Xander pulled me close, hugging me as I tried to calm down. "It's going to be okay," he whispered. "You're going to get through this."

"No," I said, sniffing. "I can't."

I wasn't sure how long I clung to Xander, but he seemed willing to stand there for as long as it took me to catch my breath. When I finally realized it could be hours before my tears dried up, I lifted my face away from his chest. Looking up at him, I stuttered through my tears. "I—I'm sorry. Dakota was everything to me. I can't believe he's gone."

"Shh," he whispered, his blue eyes glistening with tears.

"You have nothing to be sorry about. I'm here as long as you need me. I'm not leaving you. Not tonight, and probably not ever."

I sniffed, watching a tear roll down his face over the five o'clock shadow that sprinkled his jaw. Then I noticed a wet spot where my tears had soaked his shirt. "Your—your—shirt," I choked out between sniffles. "Look—look what I've done. I'm—s—sorry."

Xander forced out a soft smile. "That's the last thing I care about right now." He loosened his grip around my waist, raising his hand to wipe my cheek. "Can I let go now? Not that I want to let you go, but the hall is clearing out. I don't think we want to hang out here all night."

I sucked in a deep breath and nodded. "Okay." When he released me, I focused to keep my balance. The feeling was coming back to my legs and, as surreal as the last few minutes seemed, I found my bearings. At least concentrating on standing up shifted my thoughts away from Dakota.

"Why don't you get your things so we can get going?" Xander asked.

Holding up a finger, I knelt beside my book bag. My hands shook as I fumbled with the zipper to the main compartment. As soon as I opened it, I dug into it and grabbed my phone. After swiping the screen, I called my father's cell phone. I needed his confirmation that it was true. That Dakota really was dead.

The other end rang four times, and just when I expected my father's voice mail to pick up, someone answered. "Laken?" asked a familiar voice, but it wasn't my father's.

"Noah?"

"Yeah, it's me. Your father asked me to answer his phone when he saw your name. He's got his hands full over here today."

"So it's true?" I choked out, my tears returning as I stared blankly at the empty bottom half of my open locker.

When Noah didn't answer right away, I spoke again. "Noah?"

"Yes, I'm here. What have you heard?"

"That they—they got Dakota." I couldn't bring myself to use the word killed.

Silence lingered on the other end. Finally, Noah replied, "Yes. They just brought him over in a pick-up truck."

Another lump formed in my throat. I couldn't bear to hear anything more. As I struggled to find my voice, Xander knelt behind me and pried my fingers off of my phone. Sobs wrenched through me again as he put my phone up to his ear. Biting down on my lip to keep from crying, I dropped onto the hard floor and leaned my shoulder against the locker next to mine.

"Noah, it's Xander. Laken can't talk about this anymore. It's really upsetting her." He paused, listening to Noah. "I know there's nothing you could have done. There's nothing any of us could have done. Tell her dad that I'm going to take her home. But we'll have to leave her truck here at school. She's in no shape to drive."

I looked at him through my blurry tears, shaking my head. "Ethan," I whispered.

"Hold on, Noah." Xander dropped the phone down from his ear. "What was that?" he asked.

"Ethan can drive it back to my house. Don't worry about my truck."

Xander nodded in understanding and lifted the phone back up to his ear. "Strike what I said. She'll have Ethan drive the Explorer back to her house. You should have her dad call her soon." He paused, listening intently to Noah as he stared at me, his eyes softening. "You're right. She is." Without saying goodbye or giving me a chance to talk to Noah again, he hung up the call.

"What did he just say?" I asked as my tears began to subside a little.

"That you're very special."

"What?" I gasped, surprised that he would say something like that when I hadn't heard from him in weeks other than his text a few days ago. "He said that?"

"Yes. And I agreed with him. But enough about him. I should get you home."

Staring down the hall, I shook my head. "Please don't take me home."

"Where do you want to go? We could go back to my place."

"No," I said as if in a trance. "Take me to the station. I need to see Dakota."

"Laken," Xander said slowly. "I'm not sure that's a good idea. You don't need to see him like this."

I knew he meant I didn't need to see Dakota dead, but couldn't bring himself to say that. "Yes, I do," I snapped, whipping my eyes up to meet his. "That's exactly what I need. I need to see him so that I can say goodbye. I need closure."

Xander met my stare, not answering right away. "Okay. If that's what you really want, I'll take you. But I meant what I said earlier. I'm not leaving your side."

"Thank you," I whispered, staring down at the floor.

The reality was starting to set in, a reality I thought I wouldn't have to endure for at least another five years. Dakota should have lived to be at least ten, if not older, but now his life had been ended all because he had protected me.

"Laken," Xander prodded gently. "You're going to have to get your things together if we're going to make it to the police station before dark." He slipped my phone back into my hands. "Here, take this."

I nodded numbly and stuffed it into my back pocket. Then, with his hand grasping my upper arm, I rose to my feet, lifting my book bag as I stood. Xander let go of me, and I went through the motions of organizing my books. I don't know how I remembered which classes I had homework in, but somehow, I managed to pack up my things. As I reached for my jacket, Xander stepped back from me and I heard hushed voices.

After slipping into my parka, I turned and flipped my

hair out from under the collar. Brooke and Ethan stood with Xander, and both of them seemed to be holding back tears. They had known Dakota, maybe not as well as me, but they knew that he wasn't a threat to anyone and that he didn't deserve to be hunted down like some kind of monster.

"I'm so sorry," Brooke said, throwing her arms around me.

"Thank you," was all I could think of to say, swallowing back another lump in my throat.

When Brooke pulled away, Xander looked at me. "Laken, Ethan needs your keys to drive your truck back to your house."

"Oh yeah, right." I fished them out from under a text book in my book bag. "Here." They jingled as Ethan took them from me."

"Call me when you get home and I'll bring them over," Ethan said.

"Thanks." Before I could say another word, Brooke and Ethan disappeared down the hall, leaving me alone with Xander. I shut my locker and turned to him. "Do you need to get your jacket?"

"It's in the truck." He stretched his arm out over my shoulders. "Come on. Let's get this over with." Side by side, we walked down the hallway, skirting around the few students still there. All I saw were blurs beyond my tear-filled eyes. And all I could think about was seeing Dakota's dead body in the back of a hunter's pick-up truck.

I couldn't shake the feeling that going into town to say my last goodbye to Dakota would be a mistake. I barely said a word on the ride as I stared at the gloomy sky and lifeless trees. My eyes were still glazed over with tears, but my face had dried, at least until the next round of tears were unleashed. I felt numb all over. Even Xander's touch ceased to spread butterflies through me as my grief took over.

The town was particularly busy for an early November afternoon. Truck after truck, many with shotgun racks attached to the back windows of the cabs, lined the streets.

When we approached the police station, a crowd of hunters clad in flannel jackets, camouflage suits, and bright orange hats milled about on the sidewalk. They surrounded a red pick-up truck, gawking at something in the bed. Without seeing it for myself, I knew they were staring at Dakota's dead body.

As Xander drove past the crowd, I turned to watch them, craning my neck. "Stop!" I cried. "Go back. He's there, I know it."

"Take it easy. I'm just turning around. I saw an empty spot on the other side of the street." He jerked the truck around in a U-turn and eased it into a parking space across from the station and crowded sidewalk.

Before he turned off the engine, I jumped down from my seat and slammed the door. Racing around the front of the truck, I ignored the chill in the air. Intermittent raindrops stung my face as they began to fall, but I didn't care. Nothing mattered now that Dakota was gone.

I started to step into the street, but stopped when a car whizzed past me. Before I could continue after it passed, Xander approached me and reached for my hand. "Slow down. I don't want you to get hit," he said.

I glanced at him, nodding. "Me, neither," I said.

After looking both ways, Xander led me across the street. Tears filled my eyes again when we reached the other side. The excited chatter amongst the hunters grew louder as we pushed our way through them. A few of them slapped a young bearded man on the back and congratulated him. Others grumbled at the fact that they no longer had a chance to kill the wolf and claim the reward. In all the excitement, they didn't seem to notice us as we reached the back of the truck.

I halted when I saw Dakota's lifeless body in the bed of the pick-up. His head rested just before the gap where the tailgate hung open. I clasped a hand over my mouth as my heart nearly shut down from the pain that struck me. I wasn't prepared for the shock and overwhelming grief I would feel when I saw him. I stared at him, noticing how his ears fell to one side and his mouth gaped open, his blood-covered tongue hanging out over his teeth. His body was motionless. Not even the slightest rise and fall of his chest could be detected. Dried blood matted the smoky black fur around a wound in his side, presumably from a gunshot.

I felt faint, my knees weak, and my entire body numb. I would have lost my balance if Xander hadn't grabbed my waist from behind. "Laken, this is enough. You can't do this to yourself. We have to go." He started pulling me away from the truck.

"No!" I took a deep breath and, finding my courage, pried his arms away from my waist. Then I ran back to the truck, to Dakota, to say my final goodbye.

After pushing my way through the crowd, I bent over the tailgate to touch his head between the ears like I used to do. Tears filled my eyes, but I noticed something amiss. I studied him carefully. Things were different about him, like the way the fur on his neck seemed darker and how the white mark on his chest between his front legs seemed smaller.

Holding my breath, I scanned the rest of him for other oddities. Something was wrong, but I couldn't put my finger on it. When I looked at his front paws, I gasped. Dakota had a white spot just above one of his nails on his right front paw, but the right front paw on this wolf was solid black.

Glancing around me, I watched the men turn their attention toward the station when the mayor emerged from the building. As his voice lofted through the air, the hunters' banter slowly faded. "Thank you all for your valiant efforts to slay the beast who threatened our citizens," the mayor began.

Huffing at his words that didn't hold an ounce of truth, I turned my back to him and the hunters as he continued his speech. Tuning him out, I held my breath and lifted the wolf's eyelid. The sliver of gold underneath confirmed it. This wasn't Dakota! They had killed the other wolf. The mayor would never know that this wasn't the same wolf who had charged onto the school lawn Monday afternoon.

I trembled with joy, a tear of happiness rolling down my face. I couldn't believe this was happening, but it made sense. I knew Dakota was smart enough to elude the hunters, but I never expected the other black wolf to get caught in the crossfire. After thinking that Dakota was dead, I suddenly felt elated, as though I could handle another day. I may never get to see him again, but at least I knew he was alive.

In spite of the relief I felt knowing that Dakota had escaped the clutches of the hunters, sadness lingered in my heart. I may not have connected with this wolf and it may have frightened me a few times, but I wondered what had happened to it to make it feel threatened.

Ever since the stranger admitted releasing the wolves, I suspected that he hadn't treated them well when they had been in his care. I viewed this other wolf's death with a heavy heart, and I was disgusted to see a sentient being killed for no reason other than an irrational fear based on fiction.

Thank you, I thought even though the wolf couldn't hear me. *Your ultimate sacrifice will not be forgotten. Rest in peace.*

When I backed away from the truck, Xander came up behind me, placing his hands on my shoulders. "Laken," he whispered with grave concern.

I spun around to face him, thankful that the emotions flying through me at the moment kept the tears coming. Looking up at him, I started to say something when a figure beyond the hunters caught my attention.

Noah.

His brown eyes met mine, sorrow and sympathy lurking in his expression. He headed toward the crowd as if intending to cut through it on his way to me.

"Get me out of here," I said, shifting my attention back to Xander. "Please."

"Say no more." Xander draped an arm around my shoulders and guided me across the street.

I never looked back as we scooted between the parked cars to reach the sidewalk and hurried to Xander's pick-up. I took shallow breaths, concentrating as hard as I could to look like the grieving girl everyone thought I was. Raindrops continued to spit out of the dark sky, pinging us until we climbed into the truck.

As I stared straight ahead at the tail lights of the car parked in front of the truck, I bit my lip to keep from smiling. My arms and legs shook, the relief pushing pure adrenaline through my veins.

Xander slid the key into the ignition and the engine roared. Before pulling out, he glanced at me, seeming to notice a change in my mood. His blue eyes meeting mine, he raised his eyebrows. "My place or yours?" he asked, easing the truck out onto the street.

"You choose," I replied.

"Then my place. I'm not taking you home to more reminders of Dakota."

I nodded, reaching for my seatbelt. Xander flipped the windshield wipers on to a slow speed and I watched them, wondering when I should tell him that Dakota was still alive. But I remained quiet as I fastened my seatbelt, staring out his side window now streaked with rain. The crowd still gathered in front of the station as the mayor continued his speech. I watched until they disappeared from sight when Xander turned onto a side street.

"I'm not sure taking you there was a good idea. I'm sorry I did it," Xander said, guiding the truck along the road winding through the woods.

"I'm not," I replied with a bright smile. It felt so good to not have to hold in my excitement any longer.

Xander slid his gaze toward me, surprise and confusion sweeping across his face.

"That wasn't Dakota," I blurted out.

Xander's jaw dropped as he stared at me in disbelief.

"What?" In the split second that his attention was diverted away from the road ahead, the truck veered toward the woods.

"Xander!" I pointed at the trees looming in front of us. He snapped back to reality, jerking the truck just in time to avoid a collision.

"Sorry," he gasped. "Say that again. I don't understand." He shook his head, but kept his eyes on the road this time.

"I know Dakota, and that wasn't him. He has a few white markings, one of which is on his right front paw. He also has light brown eyes. That wolf had no white on its paws, and it had golden eyes. They killed another wolf. It's one of the others that I saw the night I ran off the road."

"Wow. You're kidding. I don't know what to say other than this is absolutely awesome. I'm so happy for you!" He glanced at me, smiling and shaking his head in astonishment.

My thoughts raced with possibilities for Dakota's future, and I hoped that I might see him again someday. "Do you realize what this means?"

"Laken," Xander started in a serious tone, practically reading my mind. "Just because they didn't kill Dakota doesn't mean things can go back to the way they were. I don't think it would be a good idea for him to go back to your house. If anyone suspects there's another wolf in town, you know what they'll do."

I frowned, not wanting to admit that he was right. I leaned back against the seat and stared out the window. "All I care about is that he's alive. I know he'll find me again someday. Whether that happens today or a year from now, I don't care. When he does, I'll figure out what to do then." My voice faded as I watched the wiper blades slowly thrusting up and down, mesmerizing me. I pictured Dakota's amber eyes that always seemed to see into my soul. I would miss him, but at least he had a chance to live another day.

When we arrived at Xander's house, dusk had fallen and the light rain persisted. Despite the fading sunlight and gray sky, I felt lighter than I had in days, as if a threatening shadow had been lifted from the heavens above. I felt like jumping out of the truck and leaping for joy, but when I reminded myself that Dakota wouldn't come around the corner of the house to greet me, my enthusiasm waned.

After hopping out of the truck, I followed Xander up the steps and into the house. As soon as he punched in the code to the alarm, we wandered down the hallway to the kitchen. The stainless steel appliances and granite countertop seemed even more impressive when he flipped on the light, the view out the tall windows quickly fading to black.

Silence greeted us with no sign of Xander's father. "Wait here," Xander said. "I'm just going to find my dad and let him know we're home."

I nodded before he disappeared around the corner. Alone in the kitchen, I took off my jacket and hung it on the back of a chair. Feeling warm, I pushed my sleeves up to my elbows and waited for Xander to return. The seconds ticked by, reminding me that Xander and his father were still in danger. Now that Dakota was safe, the stranger popped into my mind, and the fear that he would hurt Xander and Caleb returned to the forefront of my thoughts. I felt like I had just traded one threat for another.

After a few minutes, Xander came around the corner. His coat was gone and he had rolled his black sleeves up to his elbows. "He must have gone out to the store, so I sent him a text to let him know we're back," he explained.

"You don't think something could be wrong, do you?"

"Only if he doesn't text me in a few minutes." Xander paused, flashing a teasing grin. "Believe it or not, he goes out occasionally. So, what do you want to do? I promised you a night out, but—"

"But we can't be seen in town celebrating. I'm supposed to be in mourning right now."

"Exactly. I can make dinner. Are you hungry?"

"Starving. I can't believe what a day this has been. Talk about a rollercoaster. I feel like I've been to hell and back."

"You have." Xander approached me, stopping inches away. "And now, you're due for a little piece of heaven." He reached up to touch the sensitive skin just below my ear. Then he trailed his fingers along my jaw and tilted my chin up, gently kissing me. He moved so fast that I barely had time to catch my breath. His touch, as light as it was, sent a wave of electricity through me.

Without any warning, the image of Noah watching me from outside the station not even an hour ago rushed into my thoughts. Was it possible that he still cared? That he might come back to me? If so, what was I doing here with Xander? *Exactly,* a sarcastic voice rattled off in my mind. *It's time to make a choice. Xander or Noah? You can't have both of them.* Annoyed with my inner self, I tried to push the words in my head away, but I only ended up stiffening.

Xander seemed to sense my hesitation and lifted his lips away from mine. "What's wrong?" he murmured, his eyes searching mine for answers.

"Nothing," I lied, my heart racing. "It's just, well, I must be a wreck from crying earlier."

Xander shook his head. "You're always beautiful, so don't even worry about that." Smiling, he stepped back, putting some space between us. "But back to dinner. We'll have plenty of time for more of that later." He grinned with anticipation before he circled the island. Without a word, he pulled a bottle of sparkling water out of the refrigerator and a glass out of a cabinet. After filling the glass with ice, he handed them to me from across the island.

I caught him watching me as I opened the bottle and poured the water over the ice. "Thank you."

He scurried about the kitchen, pulling a box of spaghetti out of the pantry. He looked at me as he set it down on the island. "How about pasta and salad? I think there's some garlic bread in the freezer, too."

"Sure. That sounds great. Can I help?"

"No way. I got this." Xander grabbed a black pot from under the island, filled it with water and placed it on the stove. He turned the burner knob and, after a few clicks, a blue flame shot out from under it. After adjusting the setting, he pulled lettuce, tomatoes, and salad dressing out of the refrigerator.

I watched him, amazed. He certainly knew his way around the kitchen. "You can cook?" I asked.

He reached for a knife from the block next to the refrigerator and turned to face me. "Yes. Why do you seem so surprised?"

"I don't know. I guess I never pictured you as the domestic type."

"Yeah? Well, don't go spreading it around. I don't want it to ruin my reputation."

I laughed. "Is there anything else I should know?"

"I'm housebroken, too, but don't spread that around either."

"Seriously, when did you learn to cook?"

Xander knelt down below the island, rising with a cutting board in his hand. He set it down and unwrapped the plastic covering the lettuce. "A long time ago," he explained. "I never had a mother, remember? And my dad tends to lose track of time when he's working, so I didn't have much of a choice. It was either learn how to cook or starve."

"How did your dad feed you before you were old enough to cook for yourself?"

"He hired a nanny."

A faint buzzing sounded, and Xander dropped the knife onto the cutting board. Reaching into his back pocket, he pulled out his phone and swiped the screen. "Speak of the devil," he muttered. "Dad's fine. He just went out to the store. He's on his way back now." Xander slipped his phone back into his pocket and picked up the knife.

"That's a relief."

As he sliced the lettuce, he glanced across the island at me, his eyebrows raised. "You're not still worried about us, are you?"

"Yes, I am. And I won't stop worrying until that man is gone for good. He was pretty clear about what he wants. With everything that happened this week, we haven't talked about it much. Please tell me you're being careful."

Xander stopped chopping for a moment to look up at me. "Of course, we are. But let's not talk about that tonight, okay? I want tonight to be fun. After all, we have something to celebrate."

Xander's enthusiasm went right over my head as fear struck me. All I could think about was that the dead wolf had once belonged to the stranger. What if he got angry that one of his wolves had been killed instead? He hadn't seemed too attached to them when he mentioned them that night in my backyard, but there was no way to tell how he would react. "What about the wolf they killed?"

"I don't understand why you'd worry about that. It's dead, end of story."

"What if that guy gets really mad when he finds out the town killed one of his wolves instead of mine?"

Xander lifted his gaze from the lettuce, holding the knife in mid-air. "I never thought about that. I don't know. But something tells me that if he's ruthless enough to threaten people, he's not going to be too broken up over an animal."

Silence fell between us as our eyes locked. Before either one of us spoke again, I heard a door open and shut. Footsteps echoed from the hall before Caleb appeared in the kitchen doorway, several plastic grocery bags in his hands.

"Laken, it's good to see you again, my dear," he said, walking into the kitchen and hoisting the bags onto the counter.

He unwrapped the navy scarf around his neck, folding it over the back of a chair. His black coat glistened with rain along the shoulders and sleeves.

Grateful for the interruption, I smiled. "Hi, Mr.—I mean Caleb," I said, catching myself. "Is it still raining out there?"

"It's just sprinkling right now." Caleb pulled a block of

cheese and a box of crackers out of a bag. As he carried them across the kitchen, he stopped to see what Xander was cooking. "Hmmm. Looks good, son. But don't mind me. I'll just put my things away and get out of here. I don't want to intrude."

"That's okay, Dad. There's plenty if you'd like to eat with us."

Caleb put the cheese and crackers away before glancing at us. "Are you sure? I want you kids to have your space."

"Of course, we're sure, Dad. Right, Laken?"

"Absolutely," I agreed.

"Besides," Xander said as he dumped spaghetti into the boiling water. "Just wait until you hear what happened today."

Caleb stiffened. "Oh, no. Don't tell me Laken's been threatened again."

"No, that's not it. I haven't seen that guy since last weekend," I assured him. "What happened today is a good thing. A very good thing."

He breathed a sigh of relief. "Whew. Okay, so if that's not it, what did I miss?"

Xander explained the day's events while he continued preparing our dinner. I sat at the island, sipping my water and listening quietly.

Every now and then, he looked at me and I smiled, happy to let him do the talking. Caleb eventually took off his coat and poured a glass of red wine. Then the three of us enjoyed a comfortable dinner together, talking about school and the upcoming holidays to take our minds off the imminent danger.

After dinner, Xander drove me home through the steady rain. He pulled into my driveway just after ten o'clock. As he shut off the engine and lights, I stared at my house lit up by the single light next to the front door.

Dakota jumped into my thoughts as I realized he could never come home. It wouldn't be the same without him.

When I unfastened my seatbelt and reached for my book

bag at my feet, I remembered that Ethan had my keys. "Darn it," I whispered, searching for my phone in my bag.

"What is it?" Xander asked, shifting in his seat to face me. Raindrops beat down on the windshield and the truck roof.

"I don't have my keys." I pulled out my phone and swiped the screen. After typing a short text to my father, I continued. "I need my dad to let me in. I hate ringing the doorbell this late. Sometimes my mom goes to bed early on Friday. Do you mind waiting for a few minutes until he answers?"

Xander smiled, releasing his seatbelt and leaning across the console. "No, of course not. Whatever shall we do while we wait?" Even in the dark, I could see the twinkle in his eyes.

"Talk."

"I have something better in mind."

As he leaned toward me, I raised my hand, placing it on his chest. "Xander, please," I whispered, looking down to avoid his eyes. "This is all happening so fast, and I'm not ready. That story your dad told me last weekend kind of has me freaked out. It's like fate has decided my destiny, whether I like it or not."

Xander drew in a sharp breath. "Last weekend, you pushed me away because of Marlena. That's over now, and we just had a great evening. So what's wrong?" he asked, sounding hurt and disappointed.

I stared out the windshield at the darkness. "I'm sorry. It's not you. It's—him. I saw him right before we left the police station. I'm not sure if he still cares, but I need to find out." There. I said it. As long as I had the slightest hope that Noah would come back, I couldn't move on with Xander.

"Noah? Seriously? If he still cared, you'd be with him right now, not me," Xander said, his voice bitter.

"Maybe you're right," I said, whipping my eyes back to him. "But I guess I still care. And I don't want to start anything with you until my heart is free from him. It wouldn't be fair to any of us."

"Maybe you should have thought about that before you agreed to go out with me tonight."

"I didn't know I would see him when I agreed to tonight." My phone buzzed, the screen lighting up with a message from my father. "My dad's at the door waiting for me. I have to go." I glanced at Xander, hoping he could tell from my expression that I really was sorry. "Thank you for everything today. You were wonderful, and I appreciate you being there for me." I reached over, touching his hand. "I'll call you tomorrow, okay? Maybe all I need is a good night's sleep to clear my head."

Xander nodded, staring straight ahead, his expression cold. "Fine," he muttered.

I glanced at him one last time, realizing that there was nothing more I could say to make him feel better. I felt horrible, pushing him away like this, but I owed him the truth.

"Goodnight," I said with a sigh.

Then, holding my book bag and phone, I hopped out of the truck and shut the door behind me. I almost expected him to get out and walk me to the door, but I wasn't surprised when he didn't. As I hurried around the front of the pick-up through the intermittent raindrops, the truck engine roared to life.

By the time I reached the front door, my father held it open. I hesitated before walking in, turning to glimpse the headlights as Xander backed out of the driveway and raced away. As soon as the red tail lights disappeared into the night, I spun around to face my father.

"Hi, Dad," I said, meeting his solemn gaze.

He moved aside so that I could pass through the doorway. "Was that Xander?" he asked after shutting the door and locking it. The entry hall was dark, lit only by the light coming from the family room off to the side.

"Yes," I answered, dropping my book bag to the floor by my feet and pulling off my jacket. "He drove me to the station this afternoon when I heard about Dakota."

"I know. Ethan told me when he brought your keys over this evening." He paused, a frown burrowing in his gray eyebrows. He looked exhausted, and his wrinkled blue shirt hung untucked over the waist of his jeans. "You need to let us know when you won't be home for dinner. I tried calling you earlier, but you never answered."

I averted my gaze to the floor. "Sorry, Dad. Xander took me to his house for the evening, and I left my phone in his truck. It was a crazy day, and I guess I wasn't thinking right after we left the station."

My father ran a hand through his disheveled hair. "Yeah, well, Noah told me he saw you with Xander, so I figured you'd be out with him for a while. I was getting ready to call you again when I heard his truck. I'm glad you're here now. We need to talk."

My eyes flew up to meet his stare. "Now?"

"Yes, now. The hunters brought in a wolf today."

"Yes, Dad, I know that."

He studied me carefully for a moment before continuing. "I suppose you also know it wasn't Dakota."

I nodded, wondering why he didn't seem happier about it. "Yes. I noticed that right away."

"It was a female. Either the mayor didn't notice or he thinks we didn't know that our wolf was female. In any case, apparently, there was another wolf running around. Did you know about this?"

"I saw it once or twice. At first, I thought it was Dakota, but the eyes were different. So I knew it wasn't him."

"Why didn't you tell me about this?"

"I didn't see any reason to. I was just hoping it would move on to new territory at some point."

"As the sheriff, I would have liked to have known. But it doesn't matter now because we have another problem on our hands. Dakota."

"Dakota?" I asked with alarm.

"Yes, Laken. He may have survived, but he can never

come home. People are going to be watching us after this, and we can't afford to take any risks. If they find out about him, I could lose my job and they may actually kill him next time. You need to understand this because you need to make sure he stays away. Forever. Am I clear?"

I nodded, recognizing the warning in his voice. "Yes."

"Good. Now it's been an exhausting week. I'm going to bed. I'll see you in the morning."

"Okay, Dad. Goodnight." After he disappeared down the hall, I hung up my coat in the closet. Then I turned off the light in the family room and headed up to my room.

Chapter 7

I woke up to an empty house the next morning. By the time I wandered into the kitchen after a rough night of tossing and turning until nearly daybreak, the clock read ten-thirty. A note had been left on the table, and I reached for it, recognizing my mother's handwriting. *We didn't want to wake you up. We went out for coffee and groceries. We'll be back soon. Love, Mom.*

Dropping the note back on the table, I scanned the kitchen and realized this was the first time I'd been home alone since the Halloween dance. An unsettled feeling raced through me, and I glanced at the back door to make sure the lock was secured. Relieved that it was, I rushed into the entry hall to check the front door. It, too, was locked as my father had left it last night.

I turned, leaning against the door as I tried to relax in the silence. It wasn't my parents' absence that bothered me. What I missed the most was the comfort I felt every time I heard Dakota's nails clicking on the floor or noticed his honey-colored eyes watching me. Knowing that he was gone for good would take some getting used to.

A sudden knock behind me startled me out of my thoughts. I jumped away from the door and spun around, my eyes wide and my heart pounding. Worried that the stranger had come knocking in broad daylight, I stared at the door, hesitant to answer it.

The knock sounded again, and this time I heard a familiar voice. "Laken, are you home?"

My heart skipped a beat with excitement and surprise. "Noah?" I gasped, pulling the door open. "Hi," I said breathlessly, my eyes meeting his. "What are you doing here?" I ran a hand through my bedridden hair, feeling self-conscious in my sweatshirt and pajama pants next to Noah who wore a black button-down shirt, jeans and a fleece-lined denim jacket.

He smiled softly. "I thought I'd stop by and see how you're holding up. Can I come in?"

I took a deep breath as a strained tension filled the air between us. As much as I wanted to jump into his arms as if we were still together, I didn't move, curious to know why he was here. "Sure," I replied coolly, containing my excitement. I backed up as he walked in and shut the door.

Noah stood a few feet away from me, his hands shoved in his pockets. "I saw you at the station yesterday."

"I saw you, too. It looked pretty crazy."

"It was quite a week. Thank God the hunters finally left town."

I nodded, wondering if he had stopped by only to make small talk.

"Anyway, did your dad mention that the wolf—"

"That the wolf they killed wasn't Dakota?" I interrupted.

"Yes."

"He didn't have to. I could tell it wasn't Dakota as soon as I saw it."

"I can't tell you how happy I am that they didn't get him. I know how much he means to you. It killed me to think of you losing him."

I frowned, frustrated as I remembered my father's warning from last night. Even though Dakota wasn't dead, I had still lost him. "Thanks. But unfortunately, he can't come home now. Ever. I'm not sure what I'll do if he shows up here." I paused with a sigh, gazing at Noah. "Is this why you came by? To ask me if I knew about Dakota?"

"Well, that was part of it."

"Then what's the other part?"

"To see you. I miss you. These last few weeks have been really hard. I hate staying away from you," he admitted slowly.

"Then don't." I shook my head, sure that the somber look in his eyes meant nothing had changed. "Look, unless you came here to tell me what's really going on, I think you'd better go." I gestured to the door.

"I want to tell you," he said. "But I can't. Not yet. All I can tell you is it's not over."

I took a deep breath. "It's been weeks. How long to you expect me to wait around?"

"I wouldn't blame you if you don't wait, but I'm asking you to. I'm going to get through this, I promise."

"It's getting harder as every day goes by."

"Because of Xander?"

My eyes shifted, meeting his questioning stare. Only I didn't want to answer him. The minute he had told me he couldn't see me anymore, he'd given up his right to know anything about my dating life. I huffed with frustration. "Listen, I had a pretty rough night and I haven't had my coffee yet. So unless there's more, I think you should just leave." Tears glazed over my eyes, and I fought to hold them back.

"I'm sorry, Laken," was all he said as he lingered in the foyer.

"You seem to be saying that a lot. I don't want you to be sorry. I want you to fix whatever it is that's keeping you away."

Noah shook his head. "It's out of my hands right now. I just—I never expected to find you when I came here. I never expected that I would care this much. You have to know that."

I glared at him as I swallowed back my tears, refusing to let him see me cry. "I don't know what to think anymore. But right now, you should just go." When he made no move toward the door, I walked across the entry hall and opened it for him. Cold air stung my face as I stood beside the door-way.

"I guess I can't expect you to feel any differently right now," Noah muttered, heading toward the doorway and stopping inches away from me. "Goodbye, Laken," he said softly.

I glanced up at him, surprised to see moisture glistening in his eyes. His gaze met mine for a brief moment before he walked out the door. Without another glance his way, I shut the door and locked it as a deep sadness buried itself in my heart.

ↄ๏ↄ

There was one surefire way to get over Noah. Later that evening, I applied mascara to my eyelashes as I practiced the smile I would greet Xander with when he arrived. Several hours ago, once my sadness faded away and my heart-break over Noah turned to anger, I let go of any hope that we'd get back together. It was over, and it was about time I came to terms with that.

Forcing Noah out of my thoughts, I found myself thinking about Xander. I couldn't deny how I felt when I was with him, how the spine-tingling chills swept over me each time he looked at me or touched me. I had been holding on-to the excuse that I couldn't get involved with him because of Marlena for weeks. Now she was no longer a factor. What excuse did I have left, other than I was simply afraid that things would go too far too fast? And what about the curse? I had to admit that I was starting to believe it. If Xander really was the key to break it, I might as well give him the chance he had been asking for ever since he'd moved to town.

So I sent him a text, inviting him over tonight. I suspected that he would have turned me down after what happened last night had I not explained that my parents were going out and I was nervous to be home alone without Dakota. What he didn't know was that I planned to make tonight a night to remember.

Sliding the mascara brush back into the thin tube, I inspected my appearance in the mirror. My hair cascaded in waves over my black shirt, my diamond necklace sparkling above the neckline. Silver hoops dangled from my ears and jeans hugged my hips, revealing my slim figure. I wondered what Xander would think when he saw me.

When I left the bathroom and descended the stairs to the kitchen, I heard a knock at the front door. My heart jumped as I quickened my pace, grateful that my parents had already left. I raced around the kitchen table and through the entry hall to the front door. Before opening it, I glanced out the peephole to make sure it was Xander. Without Dakota whining eagerly at the door, I couldn't be certain. But one look outside at his dark hair and blue eyes was all I needed.

Whipping the door open, I flashed him a shy smile. "Hi."

He studied me, his expression softening. "You look nice," he said, breezing through the doorway, his long black coat rippling around his jean-clad legs.

I closed the door behind him, shutting out the darkness and cold air. Xander sauntered through the entry hall to the kitchen where he stripped off his coat and hung it on a chair. I followed him, stopping in the doorway and admiring his broad shoulders and muscular arms outlined by his gray T-shirt. His sleeve cut off the top half of his tattoo, revealing the dagger blades. "Thank you. So do you," I said. Then I wandered over to the refrigerator. "Can I get you something to drink?"

"Sure. I'll have whatever you're having."

After pulling two cans of Sprite out of the refrigerator, I

grabbed a few glasses and filled them with ice. The ice cubes clanked loudly against the glass in the awkward silence. I stacked them and carried them to the table where Xander waited, careful not to drop them as I had the afternoon I'd told him about the stranger.

I placed the glasses and Sprites on the table and sat down beside Xander. We popped open the cans, pouring soda over the ice in silence. I pretended to be more interested in my drink than him, but nothing could be farther from the truth. "How was your day?" I asked, desperate to fill the quiet.

"Fine. And yours?" he responded politely.

"Pretty boring," I admitted, wrinkling my nose and grinning. "Kind of like this conversation is right now."

Xander returned my smile. "Yeah, this is a little awkward, isn't it?"

I sipped my drink. "Yes," I answered quietly. "I'm sorry."

He tilted his head, gazing at me. "What for?"

"Last night. I don't know why I let it end so badly."

"It's okay," Xander said, but I knew it wasn't. "Any sign of Dakota today?"

I shook my head. "No, but that's a good thing. Like you said last night, Dakota can't come home now. I just hope he can take care of himself out there. Winter is coming, and that means food will be harder to find."

"I don't know why you're worried about him," Xander said. "My offer still stands. He can stay with me and my dad."

My jaw dropped open. "Really? You'd do that?"

He smiled at my surprise. "Did you think I was kidding when I offered to let him stay with us before? Of course. I mean, why not? He's housebroken, right?"

"Yes."

"And as far as I can tell, he's better behaved than any dog I've ever known. Besides, he loves me, remember?"

I couldn't help smiling as I pictured Dakota running to

the window and whining every time Xander's truck pulled into the driveway. "You have a point. What does your dad think about this?"

"I haven't mentioned it yet, but I'm sure he'll be fine with it." Xander studied me, watching my reaction. "So what do you say?"

"Um, yeah, sure. That would be great. As long as I can stop by every so often to see him."

"Hmmm, fringe benefits," Xander mused with a sly grin.

"Yes, for both of us." I flashed him a smile, nearly choking on my next sip when his eyes doubled in size.

But the moment was short-lived. He quickly composed himself and changed the subject. "You'll have to tell me what he eats and anything else you think I need to know. I won't be able to communicate with him like you can, but maybe you can teach him some signs so that I'll know when he needs to go out or when he's hungry."

"Sure. But there's isn't a whole lot to tell. He's pretty easy to take care of. You'll need to feed him more in the winter and, trust me, you'll know when he's hungry. His diet is simple. Mostly raw chicken."

Xander wrinkled his nose. "Raw chicken? What about the bones?"

"He loves them. They make great chew toys, too. But you can't cook them. They have to be raw."

"Really?"

"Yes. Cooked bones can splinter and get caught in his throat."

"Okay. I'll remember that. Is there anything else I should know?"

"No. He comes and goes as he pleases. He'll stay out all night in the summer, but not so much in the winter."

"I'll put his bed next to the fireplace. Think he'll like that?"

I shrugged. "I don't know. We don't have a fireplace. He might, but probably only on a really cold night. He doesn't like to be too hot."

Xander nodded. "So other than a bed, is there anything else I need to get for him?"

"No. In fact, you don't even have to get him a bed. Just take the one I have for him. I have to get rid of it anyway. There can't be any trace of him in the house. My dad's worried someone will find out he wasn't just an outdoor visitor." I took another sip of my drink before standing up. "It's upstairs. Let me get it before I forget."

Without another word, I rushed around the table and hurried up the stairs to my room. I walked past my bed to the nightstand where I turned on the small lamp. In the soft light, I took a deep breath as I picked up Dakota's huge bed in the corner.

"This is going well," I whispered to myself. "And now I have an excuse to go over to his house as often as I want, maybe even every day."

When I stood up, talking to myself with the dog bed in my hands, Xander appeared in the doorway, a huge grin on his face. I gasped as the bed slid out of my grip and fell to the floor.

"Do you always talk to yourself?" he asked.

"Only when I'm nervous," I told him, my eyes locking with his. "I didn't realize you were going to follow me up here."

"I thought I'd help you. He's a pretty big wolf, so I figured his bed must be huge."

I nodded. "We had to get him the biggest one we could find. Great Dane-sized."

Xander's grin faded as he scanned my room. "May I come in?" he asked.

"Sure."

He walked into my room, his eyes taking in the photographs hanging on the walls. His gaze swept across the bed, resting on my camera that perched on the desk. "Did you take all of these pictures?"

I nodded. "Yes. It's sort of a hobby of mine."

"They're good," he said appreciatively. Then he looked

back at the bed, focusing on the wolf print hanging above the headboard. "That's a nice picture, too. It's very fitting for you."

"Thanks."

"You really love wolves, don't you?"

I nodded again, suddenly feeling awkward and nervous with Xander in my bedroom. He'd never been up to my room, and I felt just as uneasy as I had the first time Noah had come up here the night he helped Dakota up the stairs. "Yes, I do. But apparently, it runs in my blood."

Forgetting about the dog bed, I walked around it on my way to the dresser. I pulled the top drawer open and reached for the shoebox filled with memories of Ivy. Turning to Xander, I held up the box.

"What's that?" he asked.

"Something I want to show you."

I approached my desk, pushing the keyboard aside and putting the shoebox in its place. I sorted through the pictures until I found my favorite—the one of Ivy in her winter jacket and hat, smiling as a gray wolf licked her cheek while the snow fell. When I turned around, my breath hitched for a moment. Xander had crept up behind me and stood inches away. I hoped he couldn't hear my heart pounding in my chest.

I backed up until my thighs hit the edge of the desk. Leaning against it, I looked up from under my lashes at him, my eyes locking with his. "Here," I said softly, handing the picture to him.

"What's this?"

"Just take a look at it."

He looked down, studying it in the dim light. "Is this her? Your real mother?"

"Yes."

"She's very pretty. Just like her daughter. You have her eyes." He paused, staring at the picture as though he was trying to memorize every detail. "And she obviously loved wolves, too. Like mother, like daughter."

"Knowing that she was my biological mother has answered some questions for me. There were so many things that didn't make sense before. I really wish I had a chance to get to know her."

Xander handed the picture back to me. "I'm sure she would have liked that, too."

I placed the picture on top of the other photographs in the shoebox and then looked back up at him. "Yeah, I think you're right, at least from what my father told me and what I read in the letter she left for me." The notion that I'd been nearly seven years old when she died crossed my thoughts, and sadness settled over me.

"What's wrong?" Xander asked, seeming to sense that my mood had soured.

"Nothing."

"You sure? Because you can tell me anything."

"I was just thinking that if I couldn't communicate with animals until she died, then she didn't die until I was almost seven years old. I wonder if my dad knows about that. Because when he told me about her, he acted like she died right after I was born."

"Then maybe you'll have to ask him. Does he know?"

"Know what?"

"About you and the animals?"

"I don't know. I didn't think so, but lately he's said some things that have made me wonder."

"Well, he did let you raise a wolf pup when you were what, thirteen?"

I smiled. "Yes, he did." I sighed, desperately wanting to change the subject. "Thanks again for offering to take Dakota in. You have the perfect place, being up on the mountain all by yourselves. He should be able to stay out of sight there."

Xander flashed a soft smile. "It's the least I can do. I feel partially responsible for this mess. If I hadn't dated Marlena in the first place, none of this would have happened."

"Or it could have happened sooner because of Noah.

Your intentions were in the right place."

"Yes, they were." Xander sighed and started backing away from me.

My heart sank with disappointment and, before I realized what I was doing, I reached out for his hand. As soon as my fingers curled around his, he glanced at me.

Stopping, he inched closer to me. "What are you doing?" he asked.

I took a deep breath to muster up my courage, my eyes glued to his. "I want to make up for last night. I'm sorry I pushed you away when you dropped me off."

Xander closed the distance between us. "Are you sure?" he whispered, his breath grazing my chin. He raised his free hand, touching the side of my face.

My breath caught and my pulse quickened with anticipation. "Yes," I whispered, mesmerized.

He leaned toward me, stopping when his lips hovered above mine. Heat and desire lurked in the depths of his eyes. "I hope you're sure about this, because there's no turning back now," he murmured before pressing his lips against mine.

His kiss started out soft and light, teasing me. My eyelids closed and I gave in to his touch. He moved his mouth against mine as an intense desire gripped my soul, sending a fire down to the pit of my stomach. Letting go of his hand, I reached up around his shoulders, pulling him closer until our bodies were flush against each other. As we molded together, his kiss deepened, sending a sense of urgency through me. Then he broke away from my lips, running his tongue along them and pitching me into a dizzy head spin.

Trembling, I waited, letting him take the lead. He pressed his mouth to mine again, this time slipping his tongue between my lips. I quivered, not sure how much more I could take. His touch sent a hot rush through my veins that I couldn't tame.

After a few minutes, he loosened his hold on me and lifted his lips from mine. Breathless, I opened my eyes, wondering if the moment was over. I didn't have to wait long to find out. Xander lifted me up and my legs circled his hips as he spun around and walked to the bed. He lowered me onto the comforter, hovering over me. Within seconds, he covered my body with his and his lips found mine again. His tongue dove into my mouth, spinning my thoughts out of control as I felt his weight crushing me, our legs tangled together.

My heart raced as I tossed my inhibitions aside. I hadn't decided how far I would let things go, but at the moment, no amount of kissing or touching seemed to be enough. Boldly, I ran my hand down his back, past his waist and down over his jeans. He deepened his kiss, pushing into me with a bruising desire.

When Xander lifted his lips from my mouth and trailed kisses down my neck, a fire erupted on my skin in their wake. Wanting to touch more of him, to feel his skin, I moved my hand up until I reached his waistband. Then I slipped it under his shirt, moving my hand up his back, and he jerked away as if burned by my touch. He sat up, his knees beside my hips and his eyes simmering with heat. Without a word, he pulled his shirttails up over his head. His chest bare, except for the shark tooth necklace and his tattoo, he tossed his shirt behind him.

Filled with a new awakening, I remembered my dream from a few weeks ago. This was like it, except real and much, much better. Xander leaned down, crushing me as he kissed me again. I closed my eyes, running my hands up and down his back. Then I slipped an arm around to the front of him, moving my hand up his abdomen to his shoulder and then back down to his waist. Before I realized what I was doing, I touched the top button of his jeans. Fire shot through me at the thought of where this was headed. I held my breath, daring myself to go further, to break past my boundaries.

But I never got the chance. Xander sucked in a deep breath and sat up. He reached for my hand, moving it away from his jeans. "Laken, whoa. Slow down. What are you doing?"

I looked up at him, hurt and disappointed. "Just what I thought you wanted me to do."

He smiled, dropping his head and shaking it. "You have no idea how much I want this. But last night you were pushing me away. And now this? I don't get it."

I lifted up to rest on my elbows. "Do you have to get it? Can't you just let yourself go in the moment? Besides, isn't this what we need to do to break the curse?"

"Well, yes. But it has to be right. This is too impulsive. I don't want you to regret anything with me. You're too important, too special." Xander slid off the bed and retrieved his shirt from the floor. He slipped it on, reaching his tanned muscular arms up to reveal the ripples across his abdomen. I watched with wide eyes, admiring him. As soon as he pulled his shirt down over his chest, I looked away, hoping he hadn't noticed me staring.

I sat upright, but remained on the bed. "So Marlena's good enough, but I'm not? Is that it?" I asked, unable to contain my jealousy.

"Laken, you couldn't be further from the truth. She meant nothing to me." He moved closer to the bed, standing above me. "What's gotten into you tonight? Last night, you were hoping Noah would come back to you. If I didn't know any better, I'd think he crushed any hope you had of getting back together with him at some point in the last twenty-four hours and now you're using me to get back at him."

I glanced to the side, avoiding his stare. He wasn't that far from the truth. When I looked back at him, the hurt shining in his eyes was unmistakable. "That's it, isn't it? You're on the rebound and you're using me?" Disappointment hung in his tone as he shook his head.

I jumped up to my feet, grabbing his wrist before he could turn away. "No, that's not it," I declared, desperate to turn this around. "Okay, yes, he came by this morning to make sure I knew that Dakota wasn't dead, and we're still not back together. In fact, I've pretty much come to the conclusion that we're never getting back together. But that's not what this is." I stared up at Xander, hoping he believed me.

"Then explain it to me," he said coolly.

"You know I'm attracted to you. I've only been fighting it since the first day of school."

He smiled coyly but then caught himself and frowned again. "You have?"

"Yes," I answered sheepishly. "But you scare me."

"I do? What are you scared of?"

"Everything," I admitted. "You're crazy. I mean, look at you. You have a tattoo and you stole a car. You're the kind of guy girls are warned about from the time they start noticing boys. You're worlds away from every other boy I've ever dated."

Xander smiled with satisfaction. "Good. I like to stand out."

"So are we okay now?"

His expression fell. "I don't know. I'm going to have to think about it. I'll let you know." He watched the disappointment sweep across my face before grinning. "I'm only kidding." He reached an arm out around my waist and pulled me against him. "Now where were we?"

As he bent to kiss me again, I heard a door shut downstairs. Then muffled voices echoed through the house. I gasped, trying to push him away, but he held me tightly. "Xander!" I whispered, my eyes wide with fear. "My parents are home early."

He shrugged with a sly smile. "So?" Then he claimed my mouth in another kiss, slipping his tongue between my lips.

For a moment, I gave in to him, responding to his kiss as desire spread through me again. But when my parents' voices grew louder, I pulled away, squirming to untangle myself from his arms. "Xander, stop! Please, not while my parents are home!"

"Why not? I like a little danger every now and then."

"Well, I don't, at least not this kind. I didn't tell them I invited you to come over while they were out. And don't forget my father carries a gun. I don't think you need to risk him finding us up here."

Xander sighed. "Okay. You win. But next time, you're in trouble." He sidestepped toward my nightstand and picked up Dakota's bed. Holding it in one hand, he gestured with the other one. "After you. I guess we should tell your parents the plan for Dakota. I'm sure your dad will be glad to know you won't ask to let him come home."

I nodded, flashing him a smile. "I just hope they buy our excuse for being up here to get his bed."

"You're way too worried about that," Xander teased. "You do realize that if I hadn't stopped when I did, you'd be scrambling to find your clothes right now, don't you?"

I rolled my eyes at him. What else did I expect? After all, this was the Xander I had come to know. Taking a deep breath as I straightened my shirt and smoothed out my messy hair, I led the way out of my bedroom.

Chapter 8

L aken, please don't keep me waiting," a voice whispered through the darkness, jolting me up from my slumber. I opened my eyes, straining to see the shadows in my room. As if in a trance, I sat up, shifted my legs to the side of the bed and touched my bare feet on the cold floor.

"Laken, come outside. It's snowing," the hushed voice continued, drawing my attention to the doorway. Wearing my pajamas, I crept into the hallway and stopped at the top of the stairs.

"Laken. Where are you, my dear? Please come. I need you." The voice was louder now, but still barely more than a whisper.

In the dark, I tiptoed down the wooden stairs. When I reached the kitchen, I circled the table visible only from the moonlight filtering in through the window. I went to the back door, unlocked it, and stepped outside into a winter wonderland. Snowflakes floated in the air, transforming the black night into a whirlwind of white.

The blanket of snow stung my feet as I walked across the

patio. Something, or someone, had a pull on me. All I wanted was to find out who kept calling my name and what they
wanted. When I reached the edge, I stopped. The flakes
landed on my shoulders and hair, but I didn't care. Instead, I
focused on the man in the long black coat standing in the
middle of our backyard. It was him, the man who wanted to
kill Xander and Caleb.

He flashed a sinister smile, holding out his hand. "Come
now, my lass. It's time."

Without hesitating, I descended the patio steps, my eyes
locked with his black stare. I knew I shouldn't go to him,
that I should turn and run as fast as I could. But my legs
kept going, taking me closer to him one step at a time.

♥ↄ♥ↄ

My eyes flew open and I bolted upright in bed, my heart
pounding. I scanned the dark shadows in my room, trying to
catch my breath. It was only a dream, and yet it seemed so
real. I shuddered, leaning back down against my pillow. The
image of the man raced through my thoughts, his coal black
eyes and evil smile haunting me.

I turned on my side, pushing thoughts of him out of my
mind. Instead, I thought of Xander, remembering how his
kisses and touch had made me tremble. I smiled at the
memory of him from just a few hours ago on my bed. But
my fantasy didn't last very long when the stranger slipped
back into my mind and fear gripped me in the darkness. I
had finally accepted my feelings for Xander and I had so
much to look forward to with him. Would the stranger take
him away from me before we had a chance to be together?

♥ↄ♥ↄ

Xander insisted on driving me to and from school the
following week, and Ethan rode with us as he'd done when

the Explorer had been stuck in the mud. Xander never left my side during the days, walking me to every class, his arm draped over my shoulders. I wasn't sure if we were a couple, but I accepted his attention without questioning it. He kissed me whenever he got the chance, not caring where we were or who might be watching. At first, I worried that Marlena would see us. But she looked smug, happy that she'd hurt me by getting Dakota killed, and left both of us alone.

I didn't tell a single soul that Dakota wasn't dead. Not even Brooke or Ethan could know. I forced myself to act as though I was still in mourning, reminding myself that Dakota's life depended on my convincing performance.

Friday afternoon, when Xander and I entered my house after saying goodbye to Ethan, we heard a faint scratching at the back door. Leaving Xander in the entry hall, I raced into the kitchen still bundled up in my parka and gloves. I threw my book bag on the table and rushed to the door. Flinging it open, I felt a huge smile break out across my face. Joy swept through my heart when Dakota bounded through the doorway, nearly knocking me over. He jumped up, placing his front paws against my shoulders, and slopped wet kisses on my neck. "Dakota!" I laughed. "Stop. Yuck!"

With a push, he lowered his body to the ground. I dropped to my knees, burying my face in his fur as Xander's footsteps trailed in behind me. "Hey, big guy. I missed you!" I said, pulling my gloves off and running my fingers along his back and ribcage.

He felt a little bony, and I attributed his weight loss to the energy he must have spent catching meals on his own and keeping warm at night. "And you're too skinny. Are you hungry?"

He met my gaze, his head moving with a swift nod.

Holding my gloves, I stood up and turned to Xander. I unzipped my coat, pulled it off and folded it over the back of a chair before tossing my gloves on the table. "I'm not sure if we have anything for him," I said, crossing the kitchen and opening the refrigerator.

"Hey, Dakota," I heard Xander say as I scanned the shelves.

I frowned, not finding any chicken or other raw meat for Dakota. Frustrated, I closed the door and turned to see Xander on his knees, his black coat matching Dakota's fur. He smiled and stroked Dakota between the ears as though they had been friends forever.

"I need to go to the store and get him something to eat. We don't have anything," I explained.

Xander glanced up, his blue eyes meeting mine. "No problem. I got it covered. I stocked up on chicken for him this week. And we should probably get him over to my place before your parents get home."

I nodded, shifting my gaze from Xander to Dakota. Dakota looked at me, his amber eyes curious. With a sigh, I approached them and knelt down. "You can't stay here anymore, Dakota. Dad's worried that the people in town will be watching us. If they find out you're still alive, they'll come after you," I told him as I rubbed his cheek. "You have to live at Xander's house from now on. You'll love it there, I promise. It's way up in the mountains. You'll be safe there." I took a deep breath, glancing at Xander after seeing the understanding in Dakota's eyes.

"Maybe you should tell him about us," Xander suggested. "I don't want him to bite my head off when I kiss you."

I smiled shyly. "What about us?" I asked. "What is this? I mean, I'm not sure what I should tell him."

"Just tell him we're together now. I have no interest in anyone else. I never did. You should know that by now."

"But you can have any girl you want. Why me?"

I hesitated, worried that since he'd finally gotten what he wanted, I wouldn't be as exciting as he expected. Putting the curses aside, I found it hard to believe a hot guy from California like him would stay interested in a small-town girl like me.

Xander smiled coyly. "You aren't seriously doubting how I feel about you, are you?"

I shrugged. "Maybe. It's just weird now. I don't want you to be with me just because of these old curses that can't be proven."

Xander raised his eyebrows. "Every one of your female ancestors that you know about died young. Every woman who has married my male ancestors died young. What more proof do we need?"

"Okay, so even if they are real, you don't have to be with me. This isn't out of pity or fear, is it?"

He smiled, shaking his head. "I'm crazy about you, end of story. But I'm also going to admit that the idea of ending up like my dad kills me. He puts up a good front, but it's not just loneliness he deals with every day. It's guilt."

"Guilt?"

Nodding, Xander continued. "He feels responsible for my mom's death. He knew about the curse and yet he married her anyway. You're my chance at a better life. And I have to say, I couldn't be happier about that." He smiled, a twinkle in his eyes. "I'd kiss you right now if I knew how Dakota would react."

"He won't care. But he'll probably kill you if you break my heart. So consider that a warning."

Xander grinned. "Are you saying you like me enough that I could break your heart?"

I whipped my eyes away from him, not sure what to say. The answer was undeniably yes, but I wasn't ready to let him know that. I returned my attention to Dakota who watched us. "There's something else you should know," I told him. Taking a deep breath, I let my thoughts take over. *'Xander and I are together now. That's a good thing because it means I'll be able to visit you at his house a lot.'*

Xander watched me curiously. "What are you telling him?"

"That if you hurt me, he has my permission to kill you," I teased.

"Then I have nothing to worry about." Xander locked his eyes with mine and leaned toward me. "So back to my original question. Is it safe for me to kiss you in front of him?"

"I'm not sure. You'll just have to try it and see what happens."

"Hmmm," Xander mused. "It's a good thing he can't read my thoughts right now." He snaked his arm around my shoulder and drew me close to him. Then he gently pressed his lips to mine.

His lingering kiss was light, and after a few seconds, Xander pulled away from me. "Why don't we take Dakota over to my place? It's a little awkward kissing you here on the kitchen floor. I think my bed might be a little more comfortable."

My heart skipped a beat at his suggestion as I remembered last Saturday night. A smile curled upon my lips as we rose to our feet. "Let's go then." I looked down at Dakota who sat patiently, watching and waiting. "Ready, big boy? Xander has plenty of chicken with your name on it."

Dakota swiped his tongue across his lips before jumping to his feet and trotting out of the kitchen, his nails clicking on the floor from where he paced in the entry hall.

"I like your enthusiasm," Xander said, smiling.

I felt a hot blush race across my cheeks. "I was just thinking that it might be a little embarrassing if my mom walked in while we were kissing on the kitchen floor," I replied, trying to dismiss the thought of what we might do in his bedroom once we got over to his house. "Besides, you're right about Dakota. I don't want my parents to see him. Out of sight, out of mind, right?" I smiled before grabbing my coat and gloves from the table. After slipping into my parka, I followed Xander to the front door.

"How is Dakota at riding in cars?" he asked, opening the door. Dakota shot outside, racing across the lawn to the truck.

"I don't know. He hasn't ridden in a car since my uncle brought him up here when he was about three months old,"

I told him as I shut the door behind us and locked it.

"Great," Xander muttered. "This ought to be fun."

Slipping my gloves on, I looked out across the front lawn at Dakota who stood beside the truck in the driveway, staring up at the door as he waited patiently. "Don't worry. I'll get him in. Is the backseat big enough for him?" I asked.

"Should be."

"Good. I'll take care of this."

I marched ahead of Xander toward the truck and had no problem getting Dakota into it. He eagerly jumped into the backseat as if he'd done it hundreds of times. Then he sprawled out on the seat and didn't make a sound on the way to Xander's house. It helped that he knew where he was going and why.

The sun had dropped below the mountains when we pulled up to Xander's house. Although the sky still glowed with the purple hint of twilight, the outside lights shone brightly.

The three of us hopped out of the truck and headed toward the front porch. When Xander and I reached the door, we noticed that Dakota had stopped in front of the steps. He stood still, his ears alert while he scanned his new surroundings. "Dakota!" I called as Xander unlocked the door and held it open, waiting for us. "Come on, boy!"

Without another look at the woods, Dakota bounded up the steps and into the house. I followed him into the foyer as Xander locked the door. "Can I take your coat?" he asked, approaching behind me.

"Of course." I stuffed my gloves into the pockets before shedding my parka and handing it to him. "Is your dad home?" I asked, observing the dark room and empty fireplace as Dakota trotted through the house, inspecting room after room. He quickly found his bed near the fireplace and, after giving it a quick whiff, he continued wandering around.

"Doesn't look like it, otherwise the lights would be on and he'd have a fire going." Xander hung our coats in the hall closet and walked up behind me. "He probably just ran out to get some groceries. He likes to do that on Friday evening." Xander closed the distance between us and slid his arm around my waist, twirling me around to face him. "Now where were we before we left your kitchen?" he asked before kissing me.

I pulled back, worried that his dad could come around the corner if he actually was home. "Wait. Don't you think you should check in with your dad first? You could be wrong. He could be downstairs, and I don't want him to come up here and find us making out."

"Why not?" Xander asked with a chuckle. "He doesn't care. I have girls over all the time." When I raised my eyebrows, he added, "I mean, I used to. Back when we were in California."

I scowled, wondering how many times Marlena had been over here. But I pushed that thought out of my head as quickly as it had appeared. "Seriously. Don't you want to just check in with him? Make sure he's okay?"

Xander sighed, placing his hands on my shoulders and leaning his forehead against mine. "You're right. Why don't you get some chicken out for Dakota while I call him? But after I find him, I'm building a fire and I want you to relax."

I smiled. "That sounds great." Then I broke away from him and headed toward the kitchen, enjoying the sound of Dakota's nails tapping on the floor when he followed me through the doorway.

After turning on the lights, I found a whole chicken in the refrigerator right away. Then I searched the cabinets until I found a plastic bowl. After rolling up my sleeves, I unwrapped the chicken while Dakota danced beside me, whining softly and drooling. "I know you're hungry. I'm going as fast as I can," I told him before putting the bowl of chicken on the floor. As I kneeled beside him, he sank his teeth into the meat, his tail wagging.

"That should keep you busy for a while," I said, standing up. After washing my hands, I found another bowl and filled it with water. I placed it on the floor beside the chicken and, when I rose to my feet, Xander appeared in the doorway.

He leaned against the corner, folding his arms across the black shirt he wore with blue jeans. "I started a fire," he announced. "Care to join me in the living room?"

As tempted as I was to say yes, I hesitated. "Did you get a hold of your dad?"

"Yes. He's fine. He's out shopping just like I thought."

"And what about dinner? You know, it's customary to feed your guests when they're visiting at dinner time."

Xander glanced at his watch and shrugged. "It's still early and I'm not hungry yet. Do you normally eat this early?"

"I guess not."

"Come on, then." Xander nodded his head in the direction of the living room. "Let's go work up an appetite."

I couldn't resist smiling as I walked over to him. "Not so fast," I said, very aware of the fact that we were alone. If last Saturday night was any indication, there was no telling how far things would go. It was exciting, but also a little scary. "I have a better idea. I want to see your dad's workshop. I'm really curious about his jewelry. Do you mind?"

"Seriously?" Xander asked as if surprised by my request.

"Yes. I was fascinated before he told me he can make diamonds, but now it's really amazing. Please."

Xander huffed, seeming disappointed. "Okay. I'll give you a quick tour. But we have to be fast. He doesn't like anyone going down there, and even though I think he'd be okay with you, I'd rather not take any chances."

I shrugged. "That's fine. A quick tour is better than nothing."

Xander smiled. "Follow me." He turned, leading me to the foyer. We continued down a dark hallway extending in the opposite direction of the living room. He flipped a light on, but even then, the hallway supported by wood beams crossing overhead was dim.

At the end, he opened a door, turned on another light and

led me down a narrow stairway. I held the railing, taking the steps slowly as I squinted into the darkness.

"This basement was actually built to be a wine cellar, so it's pretty cold down here."

"Then why doesn't your dad use a warm room upstairs where he can enjoy the beautiful views while he works?"

"He won't work where there are windows. He likes his privacy."

"I guess I can understand that," I mused.

At the bottom of the stairs, we entered an unfinished room. Xander turned on the lights that were nothing more than bulbs wired into the ceiling. Cement walls surrounded the cellar, except for one side where an empty wine rack covered it.

"Maybe. Until now, I thought he was crazy." Xander glanced at me, catching my eye. "So this is it," he said, sweeping his hand out. "I'll show you around." He led me to the center of the room where a long workbench was centered under the lights. Lamps had been positioned on both sides of it. Tools including small knives, wrenches, pliers and other items I couldn't name cluttered the table. A microscope, or at least something that looked like a microscope, sat in the middle.

I walked along the bench, studying the tools. "So this is where he works? This is really cool. What's he working on now? I don't see any jewelry."

Xander pointed to a gray safe in the corner of the room. "He locks everything up when he finishes working for the day."

"So you guys have a driveway gate, an alarm system, and he still locks everything in a safe?" I asked with a teasing grin. "I suppose that might make sense in Southern California, but you do realize this is northern New Hampshire? Your house is more likely to get raided by hungry bears than burglars."

Xander stood on the other side of the table, his eyebrows raised. "Well, someone found us here."

My smile faded quickly. "Yeah, but I don't think he wants to steal what you have down here. Otherwise, he probably would have done it by now." I scanned the tools again, running my finger over a small knife. "Do you know how to use all of these?"

Xander nodded as he circled the table, stopping beside me. "Yeah. I started learning when I was about ten."

"What kind of jewelry do you like to make?"

"Necklaces or bracelets. Anything except earrings. Earrings are really hard because they have to be identical."

His eyes locked with mine, and he lifted his hand to touch my necklace pendant. "Someday, I'll make something for you." He raised his other hand and ran his fingers along the chain to my neck, grazing my skin as he did. When he reached my shoulders, he stopped, resting his hands under my hair. "I already have an idea of something I'd like to make for you."

"You do?" I asked, my heart racing from his touch. "What is it?"

"I can't tell you," he whispered. "It's a surprise." He slid one hand behind my neck and trailed the other one along my jaw. As he lifted my chin, he leaned toward me, stopping when his lips were a breath away.

My eyelids started to fall when his phone buzzed, breaking the mood. I looked up at him, noticing the frustration in his eyes.

"Damn it," he swore under his breath, reaching into his back pocket for his phone. He swiped the screen, turning away from me with it in his hands.

I watched as his back stiffened. "Everything okay?" I asked.

Xander spun around to face me, an annoyed look in his eyes. "Yeah. Dad can't remember if we need milk and eggs. I need to run upstairs and check the refrigerator. I'll be right back, okay?"

Before I had a chance to respond, he darted around me and up the stairs. I heard his footsteps while he walked down the hallway, but they quickly disappeared. An eerie silence settled over the cellar as I stood beside the table, studying the tools again. I imagined Caleb at the workbench every day, crafting beautiful necklaces, earrings and bracelets that sparkled in the sunlight. It seemed like something from another time when people used their hands to make something beautiful.

After several minutes passed and Xander didn't return, I headed upstairs to find him. At the top, I turned off the light and shut the door before entering the dimly lit hallway. I jumped when I nearly ran into him, almost knocking a glass out of his hand. "Oh!" I gasped. "I was just coming to look for you. I didn't know you'd be gone so long."

"Sorry," he said sheepishly, steadying his hand to keep the dark liquid from spilling over the edge of the glass. "I started a fire and then got you a Diet Coke." He handed it to me.

"Thank you. Did you answer your dad?" I asked before sipping the soda.

"Answer my dad?" Xander repeated, confused.

"Yes," I said slowly. "About the milk and eggs."

Recognition washed over Xander's face. "Oh yeah, that. We're out of both, so it's a good thing he asked. You'd think the guy would have learned how to make a grocery list by now."

"We keep one going all the time," I said before taking another sip of the Diet Coke.

"I've told him that's what normal people do, but he still forgets." He glanced at the drink in my hands for a moment before turning beside me. Wrapping his arm around my shoulders, he led me back to the living room. "You know, as fun as it is to talk to you in the hallway, I think we'd both be a lot more comfortable on the couch. The fire's really going good now."

As we turned the corner, the orange flames dancing in the stone fireplace caught my eye. A smoky scent filled the room and loud pops crackled. Dakota was sprawled out on his bed, sleeping off the big meal he'd just finished.

Xander led me to the couch and I sank onto it with my back against the armrest before taking another gulp of the soda. "Thanks for the drink. How did you know I was in the mood for a Diet Coke?"

"I just had a feeling," he said with a smile, sitting down a few feet away from me.

He watched me, his steady stare unnerving me, and I couldn't help but smile.

"What are you looking at?" I asked self-consciously. "Is my hair all frizzy with static or something?" I reached up with my free hand to smooth it down.

"No," he laughed. "I'm just enjoying this moment with you. I waited a long time to get you over here for fun, not to work on our History project."

"I thought we came over here to get Dakota settled in." I raised the glass to my lips, finishing the soda. Then I placed it on the coffee table.

"Yes, but I'd like to think you're here for me more than him." Xander slid over to me until his leg rubbed up against mine.

I grinned at him. "Dakota's been in my life for five years, and I've only known you for a few months. So you can't make that comparison. It's not a competition."

"Good. I don't need any more competition," Xander said, reaching for my hand.

As I felt his touch, a sudden dizziness washed over me. I lifted my free hand to my forehead, rubbing my temples above my eyebrows. "Whoa," I said, confused by the numb feeling taking over me.

"Laken," Xander said, leaning closer to me. "Are you okay?"

"I—I don't know." I took a deep breath as the room spun around me. "Everything is moving. I think I need to lay down."

"Were you feeling sick today?" Xander asked, his eyes worried as he stood and helped me lift my legs up.

"No," I whispered, shifting down along the couch until I leaned my head on the armrest. "I felt fine all day." I paused, sucking in a deep breath. "I don't know what's happening. The room is spinning." I glanced beyond him at the fire, the flames mesmerizing me. They swayed in the fireplace at first, but then became blurry like everything else around me.

Xander reached for the plaid blanket on the opposite end of the couch and opened it up. He draped it over my legs, pulling the edge up to my chest. "Here you go."

Sleepy, I shifted my gaze to him, the fire reflecting in the empty glass on the coffee table catching my attention. My eyes whipped open with fear and I looked at him, alarmed. His handsome face and black hair blurred above me. "What did you give me?"

"Shh," he said, leaning over me to kiss my forehead. "You're going to be fine. Get some sleep."

I tried to glare at him, wanting to demand that he tell me what he put in my drink, but I couldn't hold my eyes open. With one last sigh, my eyelids fell and I surrendered to a deep sleep.

Chapter 9

S unlight was bursting in through the windows when I
woke up the next morning. My eyes opened, and I
recognized the gray walls and blue plaid comforter of
Xander's bedroom. I sat up, trying to remember what had
happened the night before. Looking down, I narrowed my
eyes when I saw that I wore an unfamiliar black button-
down shirt. My purple sweater and blue jeans were folded
neatly on the dresser, and my legs were bare under the covers. At least my bra and underwear were still where I'd left
them—on my body.

I leaned against the headboard as Dakota ambled over to
the bed, nudging my thigh. With a sigh, I stroked the fur
between his ears, bits and pieces of the night before coming
back to me. I remembered bringing Dakota to Xander's
house, feeding him, and then checking out Caleb's workshop in the wine cellar. But after that, my memory was hazy. I vaguely recalled drinking a Diet Coke and crashing on
the couch. After that, how I ended up in Xander's room
wearing only his shirt over my underwear was a mystery.
The idea that something intimate had happened between us

darted through my thoughts, but I dismissed it. Xander might be arrogant and infuriating at times, but I refused to believe he would drug me to have his way with me.

"What happened last night?" I whispered, looking down at Dakota and wishing he could answer me. "Xander had his mind on one thing up until he gave me that drink." I shook my head, going over the evening's events and his behavior in my mind. But nothing made sense. *There has to be a good reason he resorted to drugging me,* I thought. I shuddered at the frightening possibilities that went through my head, all of which reeked of the stranger's threats.

My nerves on edge, I noticed a folded piece of paper on the nightstand and reached for it. My name was scrawled across the blank side. I whipped it open as a feeling of dread washed over me.

Laken, I'm sorry about last night. My father's in trouble. The text I received wasn't from him. He's been taken. I had to go, to try to get him back, and I couldn't let you come. I needed to keep you safe.

I lifted my eyes from the letter with a heavy sigh. Of course, I would have wanted to go with him. Fear sinking its claws into me, I dropped my gaze back to the note. He explained that he'd contacted Brooke and Ethan and asked them to cover for me being out all night. He had also arranged for Ethan to pick me up this morning and listed the house alarm and driveway gate codes so that I could leave. *I'll see you soon,* was all he wrote at the end.

I read it several times, wishing he'd told me where his father was. But perhaps he hadn't known that when he'd written it. Frustrated, I crumpled up the note and left it on the bed before standing up. Rushing over to the dresser, I pulled Xander's shirt off and tossed it onto the bed. Then I got dressed before looking for my shoes and socks.

I found them on the carpet in the corner next to the dresser. After zipping up my boots, I hurried out of the room with Dakota in tow. We raced down the stairs through the empty house, oblivious to the sunlight streaming in through the huge windows. A dark cloud hovered above me that would only go away as soon as Xander and his father were safe once and for all. In the living room, the fire from last night had burned out, leaving ashes and soot in the fireplace.

It seemed strange to wander through Xander's house alone. I half expected Xander or his father to come bounding around a corner at any moment, but the house remained deathly quiet. I could have heard a pin drop in the silence. At least Dakota was here, trotting from room to room as if looking for any sign of life.

Not sure what to do, I retrieved my jacket from the coat closet. As I stood in the entry hall, Dakota pacing at my feet, I pulled my phone out of my pocket. After dialing Ethan's cell phone, I held my breath until he picked up on the second ring.

"Hi, Laken. I was wondering when you'd call."

"Ethan, hi." I paused, wondering how much Xander had told him.

"How was your night? I have to admit, I'm a little surprised. First Noah, now Xander? You're going to get quite the reputation," he teased, laughing on the other end.

One thing was certain. He would never joke around if he knew Xander and his father were in trouble. "Ha, ha," I muttered, acting as though his teasing was the only thing on my mind. "Can you give me a ride home?"

"Sure. I'll leave in a few minutes. What's the address?"

I gave him the street name and then explained, "I'm not sure what the house number is, but it's pretty much the only house up here."

"I'll find it. Don't worry."

"Wait. Don't hang up. You're going to need the gate code. Damn it," I swore, realizing I'd left the note with the codes upstairs on Xander's bed. "Hang on, I have to go get it." Holding the phone up to my ear, I hurried back up the stairs to his bedroom. The exertion took its toll on me as I still felt groggy. But I pushed myself, running into the room and to the bed. As soon as I grabbed the crumpled note, I opened it. "Here it is. The gate code is eight one three."

"Eight one three. Got it. I'll be there in about fifteen minutes, and then you can fill me in on all the tawdry details of your night."

"Nice try," I grumbled. *There's nothing to tell.* "Call me if you get lost or you're going to be late. Otherwise, I'll be waiting outside."

After hanging up, I sat on the bed and checked my messages. But there was nothing new. Not a single text or voice mail. Without hesitating, I dialed Xander's cell phone, my heart sinking when the call went directly to voice mail. Something was very, very wrong. He never should have ventured out to find his father on his own. Unfortunately, it was too late to convince him of that.

After the beep, I left him a message even though I held little hope that he'd get it any time soon. "Xander. It's me, Laken. I got your note this morning and I'm really worried. Call me as soon as you get this." I hung up before mentioning last night. As much as I felt he owed me an apology for slipping something into my drink, it seemed small and insignificant at the moment. And what good would it do to stay mad at him if I never saw him again?

Before getting up, I sent him a text. *What's going on? Call me ASAP*, was all it said. Hopefully, he would get one of my messages soon and let me know he was okay. Until I heard from him, I would be a nervous wreck. I tried to convince myself that Xander was tough enough to take care of himself in any situation, but my efforts were wasted. I wouldn't relax until I heard his voice or saw him.

I stared at my phone as the screen went dark, lifting my eyes when Dakota appeared in the doorway. He looked at me, his expression concerned. "I know, big boy. I'm worried, too," I said with a nervous sigh.

After a minute, I stood and trudged back downstairs. A dull pain was beginning to settle into my forehead above my eyebrows. My adrenaline was fading fast, and I felt the lingering effects of whatever Xander had given me. As I paced across the entry hall, waiting for Ethan to arrive, I yawned, feeling tired and run down.

A few minutes later, I slipped into my parka and typed the code into the alarm keypad on the wall. The red *Armed* reading blinked to a green *Open*. When I stepped out the front door with Dakota, I realized that I didn't have a key to lock up with. As much as I hated it, I had no choice but to leave the house unlocked and the alarm unarmed.

I walked across the porch, shivering, as I zipped up my jacket. Beyond the house and driveway, trees stretched up to the blue sky with spider like-limbs. Cold air nipped at my cheeks and the porch was freezing when I sat down to wait. Dakota stayed with me, refusing to leave my side. Grateful for his company, I reached my arm around him and leaned my head against his neck. "Okay, Dakota, it's up to you. I need you to find Xander and his dad." I lifted away from him, staring into his sober eyes. "Can you do that? I have to go home now so Mom and Dad won't worry. But I'll come back as soon as I can."

Dakota gave me a swift nod, and I knew he understood. I sighed, trying to keep my imagination from running away with thoughts of what might have happened to Xander and his father, when a car hummed in the distance. Ethan.

I rose to my feet as Dakota leaped off the front porch and took off around the side of the house. He disappeared into the woods, heading out on his mission.

When Ethan pulled up to the garage doors, I rushed over to the passenger side and jumped into the warm car, tossing him a grateful smile as I pulled the door shut. "Hi. Thanks again for the ride."

He smiled warmly. "You know you can count on me," he said, backing the car around and heading down the driveway. "Maybe the next time I come up here, Xander can give me a tour. That's a pretty big house for just him and his dad."

"Yeah," I mused, wondering if Xander and his father

would live to come back to it. Scolding myself for my morbid thoughts, I threw on a smile for Ethan's sake. "And it's gorgeous inside, too."

"I bet. What does his dad do? Are they independently wealthy or something?"

"Something like that," I muttered, watching the barren trees out the window.

When we reached the gate, Ethan slowed to a stop. He rolled down his window and punched in the code. After the gate opened, he eased the car between the pillars on each side. "Maybe he was in the movie business. After all, they are from LA."

I shrugged, not sure what to say. I knew a lot more about Xander and his father than anyone else, but I couldn't trust my voice to hold up if I talked about them. Just the thought of them and the fear that I might never see them again brought tears to my eyes. And I couldn't let Ethan know how scared I was. I had to be strong, at least for the few minutes it took to get home.

"So what were you doing at his house all night?" Ethan asked, changing the subject.

I glanced at him, meeting his curious brown eyes for a brief moment. "What did Xander tell you?"

"That you're having trouble adjusting to being home without Dakota."

I nodded with a weak smile. He wasn't that far from the truth. "Do my parents know where I was last night?"

Ethan tossed me a confused look. "I thought you told them you were staying at Brooke's."

"Did I? Oh, that's right, I did." I tried to hide my surprise as I dug my phone out of my pocket. I swiped the screen and checked my outgoing text messages, something I hadn't thought to do earlier. Sure enough, the last one sent before my text to Xander this morning was a note to my mom telling her I'd be staying at Brooke's. It had been sent at seven o'clock last night, nearly an hour after I remembered touring Caleb's workshop in the cellar.

Leaving my phone in my lap, I stared out the window as Ethan reached the road and turned in the direction of town.

"You still haven't answered my question," Ethan said.

"What question is that?" I asked, even more annoyed with Xander now that I knew he'd lied to my parents pretending to be me.

"About last night? It's me, remember? Your best friend. You can tell me anything, okay?"

I shook my head stubbornly. "There's nothing to tell. Nothing happened."

"You don't seem very happy about that."

"It's a long story."

"But everything's okay between you and Xander, right? I mean, he's free from Marlena now and I know you've liked him for a long time, even when you were seeing Noah. Don't deny it."

"Okay. You got me there. But I'm not really sure what's going on right now. He was gone this morning when I woke up."

"Seriously?" Ethan glanced at me, his eyebrows raised. "You just spent the night at his house. I wouldn't worry about it. I'm pretty sure he likes you, a lot. He told me he had an appointment this morning or he would have taken you home himself. Must have been a pretty early appointment."

"Well, I don't know what to think and I don't feel like talking about it, okay?"

Ethan sighed. "Sure. But I'm here whenever you change your mind."

I shot him a grateful smile. "Thanks. What did you and Brooke do last night?"

For the rest of the ride, Ethan moaned about the chick flick he and Brooke had watched the night before. But a smile lingered on his face, as if he'd secretly enjoyed his evening. As he talked, jealousy shot through me. They didn't know how good they had it. Their lives were blissfully normal, something I'd give anything for. He had no idea that Xander and his father were missing right now, and that I felt responsible for the danger they were in. And I wasn't about to tell him.

When he pulled into my driveway, I thanked him before stepping out of the car. As I shut the door, I gazed at the house, longing for the comfort being home usually gave me.

I waved to Ethan, trying to smile as though I didn't have a care in the world. After his car disappeared in the distance, I headed up the sidewalk on my way to the front door, trying to think about taking a hot shower. As good as one would feel, nothing could shake my fear. Xander and his father were in trouble because of me and there wasn't a single thing I could do about it right now.

e⌒ɔe⌒ɔ

After a hot shower and a quick lunch, I spent the rest of the day pacing in my bedroom. I checked my phone every few minutes even though it remained silent. A few times, I sat down at my desk in an attempt to get a little homework done, but to no avail. At four o'clock, I pulled my hair into a ponytail and slipped into a pair of hiking boots. I couldn't handle the suspense any longer. If Dakota found any trace of Xander or Caleb, he would wait for me at Xander's house. He'd never try to track me down at home. He knew better than to come this close to town.

With my phone in my pocket, I rushed out of my bedroom and down the stairs. Then I ran through the empty kitchen and into the entry hall. When I opened the coat closet, I heard my father's voice behind me.

"Going somewhere?" he asked calmly.

I whipped around, my parka still hanging in the closet as I met his brown eyes. "Hi, Dad," I said with a faint smile. "Yes, I was going over to Xander's."

Dressed in a plaid flannel shirt that hung untucked over his jeans, he leaned against the family room doorframe.

"You've been gone a lot lately. It would be nice if you stayed home tonight."

I sighed, hoping he wouldn't insist on that. "Sorry. It's just not the same around here without Dakota. Even before when he stayed out all night, I always knew he'd come home at some point."

"I know what you mean. Your mom and I were talking about him last night. It's going to take some getting used to. We miss him, too."

I nodded, not quite sure what to say.

My father continued. "Unfortunately, I have to stick to my decision. I wish he could come home, but we can't afford to risk the mayor finding out he's still alive and living close to town."

"I know, Dad. You don't have to explain."

He smiled softly. "How did last night go? Did he settle in at Xander's okay?"

"Yes. I think he'll like it over there. He took to Xander right away the first time they met."

"I remember. I guess you'll be spending a lot of time over there now."

I shrugged. "I don't know. We'll see how it goes." I turned back to the closet and reached for my jacket. After pulling it off the hanger, I put it on and then grabbed my hat and gloves. "I want to get going before it gets dark. I'll be home later, okay?"

"Should we save you some dinner?"

I shook my head. I still felt full from lunch and, as long as Xander and Caleb were unaccounted for, food was the farthest thing from my mind. "No, that's okay. I'll probably grab something at Xander's." I shut the closet and approached the front door, but stopped and turned back to my father. "Where's Mom?"

"You know your mother. She's working on next week's lesson plans."

"Tell her I said goodbye, okay?"

"Sure. Be home by midnight. Got it, Laken?"

I nodded. "Yes. Bye, Dad," I said before slipping outside into the cold air.

I couldn't help feeling like I was going to a funeral as I hurried down the sidewalk to the Explorer. My heart accelerating, I jumped into the SUV and backed out of the driveway.

Ten minutes later, I pulled up to Xander's house and shut off the engine. I had held on to a sliver of hope that Xander's truck would be in the driveway when I arrived even though I hadn't heard from him, but as I expected, the driveway was empty.

I stepped out of the Explorer, taking a deep breath of the cold mountain air. Silence greeted me and the descending sun cast hues of pink and purple across the sky. I scanned the woods, the trees reaching up to the sky, their branches still and lifeless.

Alone in the driveway, I shoved my hands into my coat pockets looking for my phone. "Damn it!" I swore under my breath, realizing I had left it in the truck.

I rushed to the Explorer, pulled the door open, and leaned across the seat to get it out of the cup holder. As I straightened up, I checked again for any missed calls or new text messages. But nothing had been received in the few moments I'd been standing in the driveway.

With a disappointed sigh, I shoved it into my pocket and shut the door. When I turned, Dakota stood in front of me. "Dakota!" I knelt beside him on the pavement and stroked his fur. "I hope you know something because I haven't heard a word from Xander."

Dakota stared at me before swiftly nodding his head. Then he whipped around and trotted to the edge of the driveway. He stopped, turning to look at me as if beckoning me to follow. I hurried toward him. "What is it? Do you know where they are?" I knew he couldn't answer me in words, but I hoped he would show me a sign.

With another nod of his head, he took off into the woods. I ran after him as fast as I could, dodging the trees in my way. He darted around bushes and leaped over logs and, like the night we had set out to find Ryder, I struggled to keep up. At least I still had a little daylight this time, although it was fading fast. Within an hour, the woods would be pitch black.

"Dakota!" I called, my breathing labored. "Slow down! Please!" I shook my head, running around the trees after him. The ground sloped downward, and I fought to keep my balance, but it was no use. As I sped up, I tipped forward. Knowing that I was about to fall, I reached my arms out, bracing for the impact. I slammed into the ground, rolling once before coming to a stop in front of a huge tree. My nerves rattled, I sat up, brushing the leaves and dirt off my jacket.

Frustrated, I scrambled to my knees as Dakota appeared in front of me, tilting his head with concern. "I'm all right," I muttered. "But slow down. I only have two legs, and I can't keep up with you."

I was about to stand up when a rustling noise came from the side. I turned to see a female moose ambling toward me, her big brown eyes gazing at me. When she stopped, she lowered her head, sniffing my hat as though asking if I was okay. I looked up as her muzzle grazed the tip of my nose, her breath whispering across my face.

"Hello," I said softly, rising to my feet. I reached up to stroke her neck, smiling when she leaned in against my touch. "I could use a little help here. Would you mind giving me a ride? I can't keep up with him." I nodded at Dakota who stood a few feet downhill from us.

The moose shot me a curious look before dropping to the ground. She lay still, her belly resting on a bed of leaves, watching me while she waited. I glanced at her eyes, hoping she knew that I was about to climb onto her back. I had never tried to ride a moose before, but I was desperate to keep up with Dakota.

Slowly, I lifted my right leg up and over her back just behind her shoulders. I lowered my weight onto her and held my breath, not sure what to expect. As I leaned my hands against her neck, she rose to her feet, her movements abrupt. I struggled to stay in position until she stood on all four feet with her back level, only then scanning the ground and realizing how high up I was. I had never even ridden a horse, much less a moose. But I didn't have time to worry about this. All I needed to do was tell her to keep up with Dakota and hang on for dear life.

"Thank you," I whispered, petting her fur. "Now follow the wolf. I don't know where he's taking me, but I know we need to get there fast."

Dakota whirled around, shooting off through the woods, and the moose launched forward, loping after him. I hugged my legs tightly around her chest as her abrupt stride nearly knocked me off balance. Grabbing at her shoulders, I discovered that there was nothing to hold on to. Even when I leaned my hands against her neck, I felt loose and wobbly. Finally, I bent down and wrapped my arms around her neck, not only feeling more secure but also avoiding the tree branches.

The moose kept up with Dakota remarkably well. She traveled down the mountain and up another hill effortlessly, as if I didn't add an extra burden to the journey. Occasionally, Dakota slowed and circled back, his movements silent compared to the moose's footsteps rustling through the leaves. I looked ahead between her big ears as the trees passed by, wincing when my legs brushed against them. But any bruises I ended up with would be worth it if I found Xander and Caleb.

We continued through the forest for what seemed like hours. I had no idea if we were near any roads or what direction we were going. The sunlight was fading fast, and the sky peeking in between the branches overhead was dark purple. When we reached a clearing, Dakota stopped at the edge and the moose pulled up behind him.

I lifted my shoulders to sit straight and tall, grateful for the bird's eye view of the opening beyond the trees. A hillside dropped below them, giving way to a small meadow of tall grass surrounding a weathered log cabin. The windows had been boarded up, and the property appeared abandoned except for a Jeep Wrangler parked out front in the gravel driveway.

Stroking the moose's neck, I whispered, "Thank you. I'll get off here." After she dropped to the ground, I hoisted my right leg over her body and slid to my feet beside her.

I remained by her side, staring at the cabin as she stood up. "Please stay here," I requested quietly. "I may need a ride home." Then I crept over to Dakota and knelt beside him to wait behind the trees, hidden from sight. The cabin was dark, except for the light shining through the cracks between the boards covering one of the windows.

Panic slid over me and I had no idea what to do next. I could only assume that Xander and his father were here, but I wasn't about to knock on the door.

Trying to come up with a plan, I was distracted when I heard the crunch of tires rolling along the driveway. A Lincoln police cruiser emerged from the woods and pulled up beside the Jeep. I felt my heart almost stop, my body numb, when Noah stepped out of the car, his hands buried in the pockets of his fleece-lined jean jacket. "Noah? What's he doing here?" I muttered, confused and scared.

Noah walked toward the cabin's rotting front porch, his nervous eyes scanning the woods. When he reached the door, it opened and the stranger with the black ponytail stepped out. They talked for a minute, but I couldn't hear what they said before they disappeared inside.

Utter shock struck me like a knife in my heart. Mixed emotions of anger and disappointment tumbled inside me, and questions raced through my mind. How did Noah know that man? Was he involved with the stranger threatening Xander, Caleb, and even me? And what were they doing here? What, or who, were they hiding?

I wanted answers. I had trusted Noah, and if he had anything to do with Xander and Caleb's disappearance, I would never forgive him. I was crushed and felt betrayed. *Don't jump to any conclusions,* I told myself. *You have no idea what he's doing here.*

I shook my head, annoyed with my inner self for wanting to give Noah the benefit of the doubt. One thing was certain. He wasn't here for anything good.

I suddenly knew what I needed to do. I glanced at Dakota, sharing my plans with him through my thoughts. Then I stood and faced the moose for a moment, telling her I no longer needed her help and dismissing her. She turned, lumbering through the trees until the shadows of the forest swallowed her up.

With a deep breath, I looked back at the cabin. Seeing no sign of Noah or the man, I ran down the steep hillside as quickly as I could without falling. Then I raced over to the police cruiser and ducked beside it, in case one of them came outside. Praying silently, I tried the back door handle, not sure whether to be relieved or worried when it opened right away. *Here goes nothing,* I thought, slipping into the back seat before quietly shutting the door.

As a veil of black fell over the mountains, I crouched behind the passenger seat and waited for Noah to return.

Chapter 10

I didn't have to wait very long. A few minutes later, the door to the driver's seat opened and Noah slid into the car. I held my breath, hoping he wouldn't look into the back and see me. I planned to wait until we were far away from the cabin and the man to let Noah know he wasn't alone and demand he explain what was going on. After starting the engine, he backed the car around and headed down the driveway, the tires crunching on the gravel.

Dark shadows rolled across the back seat as the car bumped over ruts in the driveway. I took shallow breaths, my mind filling with doubts. I wondered how Noah would react when he realized I had stowed away in his police car and I hoped he wouldn't hurt me. I suddenly didn't know which side he was on. As badly as I wanted to trust him, he was obviously hiding something. But unlike the man with the black eyes, Noah didn't frighten me, at least not yet.

The car lurched to a stop before turning onto the smooth pavement. Then we picked up speed, cruising along a winding mountain road. I wedged myself between the seats to keep from pitching back and forth and side to side. I fought hard to stay still, worried that one false move would catch Noah's attention. If I surprised him while he was driving along a treacherous road, one accidental jerk of the steering wheel could catapult the car down a ravine or wrap it around a tree. I had no choice but to wait until the car came to a complete stop to reveal myself.

My chance came a few minutes later when Noah slowed down and pulled onto the shoulder of the road. I felt a slight bump as the passenger side dropped off the pavement. Raising my eyebrows, I wondered why he was stopping on a desolate mountain road. But then again, why had he shown up at the cabin and spoken to the stranger as if they knew each other?

I heard Noah shift the car into park, but he left the motor running as he reached up to turn on the overhead light. At that moment, I took a deep breath and lifted up onto the back seat. "Hello, Noah," I said calmly.

"Jesus!" Noah gasped, meeting my gaze in the rearview mirror. His jaw dropped open, his face growing pale. He whirled around in his seat to face me, his brown eyes startled and confused. "What are you doing back there? You just scared the hell out of me!"

"What were you doing at the cabin with that man?" I asked.

His gaze slid away from mine. "It's a long story," he replied slowly.

"Really? That's your answer? Have you known him all along?"

Noah nodded as he raised his eyes to me. "Yes. But it's not what you think."

"How do you know what I'm thinking right now?" I fumed.

He was hiding something, and I wished he would stop beating around the bush and come out with it.

"How did you get here anyway?" he asked.

"You're changing the subject," I said, taking a deep breath in frustration. "I was at the cabin."

"Did he know you were there? He didn't drag you up there, did he? Because if he hurts you, I'm done with this."

"Who? That guy? No. Dakota led me there through the woods. And a moose gave me a ride."

"You rode a moose?" he asked with a chuckle.

"Yes. It's one of the perks of being able to talk to wild animals, although it was the first time I've ever ridden a moose. Desperate times call for desperate measures." I paused, feeling awkward talking to him from the back seat like a child. "Mind if I sit up front?"

Noah shook his head, stepped out, and opened the back door. I scrambled out of the car and we returned to the front seats. As I shut the door, I turned to him. "Are you going to tell me what's going on, or am I going to have to turn this over to my dad? I'm sure he'd be interested to know that you're not who you seem to be."

"I guess I deserve that." Noah looked straight ahead, dropping his chin as he spoke. "That man is my uncle," he admitted.

"What?" I gasped. "You've known him this whole time? Even when he helped with the drunk kids on our first date?"

"He was like the father I never had. But just because I'm related to him, and he helped my mother raise me, doesn't mean I like him. I'm not happy about any of this, but he has something I want. He's using it to control me."

"What does he have?"

"It's actually not a thing. It's someone I care about." Noah looked back at me with desperation in his eyes. "I'm sure you're thinking that I'm a horrible person right now, but I never intended for any of this to happen. My uncle is a ruthless, dangerous man. He knows what he wants, and he'll stop at nothing to get it. I've been trying to figure out how to get everyone out of this mess safely, but it's not something I can fix overnight."

"Who is it?"

Noah took a deep breath before answering. "My ex-girlfriend. Before I took the job here, we were dating. But I broke it off when I found out I would be moving. It wasn't fair to ask her to wait for me. I didn't know how long I'd be here."

"Why did you move here? Did that have something to do with your uncle? And me?"

He nodded slowly. "Yes. He wanted to make sure you were the one Xander and Caleb were looking for."

"So you know about them, too?" I shook my head, my mind spinning. "Can we back up a moment? Where is your friend now? Is she in the cabin back there?"

Noah shook his head. "No. My uncle won't tell me what he's done with her."

"I'm sorry if he took her because obviously I don't want anyone to get hurt, either. But all that time we spent together, it was really just a ruse? You used me to find Xander and his father?" Bitterness crept into my voice, and I held my tears at bay. I would not break down, no matter how badly his betrayal crushed me. Staring out the windshield into the black night as if in a trance, I asked, "Did you go out with me just to get information for your uncle?"

"He wanted me to get to know you, yes. But I know what you're thinking and you need to know everything I said and did was real." He leaned across the console, his expression hopeful.

I slid back until I bumped against the door. "I want to believe you, I do. But I don't know how I can trust you now. You've been lying to me for months."

"Laken—"

When he reached out to touch my arm, I flinched. Fear snapped me out of my trance and I wondered if he was lying. Not waiting to find out, I turned and flung the door open. Without another word, I jumped out of the car and started running down the road. Footsteps followed me, but I kept going, pushing myself as fast as I could go until Noah caught up to me. He grabbed me from behind, jerking me to a stop. Then he whipped me around to face him. "Laken," he said, his teeth clenched. "I'm not going to hurt you. You have to trust me."

I struggled against him, but his hold on me didn't budge. Looking up at him through the tears I could no longer hold back, I shook my head. "You've got some nerve asking me to trust you. You should have told me about your uncle weeks ago, at least when he showed up behind my house. You aren't the person I thought you were. Now let me go."

"Are you going to run if I do?"

"I—I don't know." I wasn't sure what scared me more, Noah or being stranded out here alone after dark.

"That's not good enough. You need to stay with me. The wolves are still out here."

A vision of them chasing me the night I ran off the road flashed through my mind, but the thought of them didn't scare me as much as Noah did at this moment.

I shook my head in contempt. "They're his, aren't they? He brought them here, and you knew about them, didn't you?"

Noah's shameful eyes shifted away from my stare. "Yes."

"Why would he do that? And how?"

"My uncle is a resourceful man. He bought them from a breeder out west. I think he released them here to scare you. For fun."

I shuddered, remembering his uncle's black eyes and wicked smile. "What does he hope to gain from that?"

"I don't know. Entertainment, I guess. He's sick and twisted. Something tells me he has another use for them, but I'm not sure what it is."

"So they're still out here? Running loose?" I was thankful that they hadn't found me and Dakota earlier this evening. Realizing they could be anywhere, I scanned the woods along the road, but saw nothing except pitch black.

"As far as I know. Now, will you please get back in the car so that I can take you home?"

"I guess I don't have a choice," I relented with a huff.

"But if you try anything, I'm turning all of this over to my dad."

He let go of me, and we headed back to the car. When he tried to come closer again, I shrugged him away. I might be stuck letting him give me a ride home, but I wasn't about to enjoy it.

As soon as we were back in the car, Noah eased it onto the road. "Where do your parents think you are right now?"

"At Xander's house, which is where I need you to take me. Do you know where he lives?"

"Yes."

"What else do you know? Do you know where Xander and his father are right now?"

"Caleb's at the cabin," Noah admitted, his voice quiet.

I swallowed the sudden panic threatening to choke me. "What about Xander?"

A strained silence filled the car, and I forced myself to stay calm. "Well?" I asked, my teeth clenched and fury simmering in my veins.

"No sign of him."

"Whew," I said, letting my breath out. "How is Caleb? Is he okay?"

"He's alive, for now," Noah replied grimly.

"What! Noah, how can you leave him there? Arrest your uncle. You're the law, remember?" I cried, shocked by his casual reference to Xander's father.

"Believe me, I'd like nothing more than to put my uncle behind bars. But if I do that, I may not find Jenna until after it's too late."

The notion that another life was at stake in this mess pitched my thoughts into a whirlwind. "Did you see Xander's father?"

"Just for a moment."

"How did he look?"

"He has a few bruises, but other than that, he's okay."

"Bruises?" Sympathy took up residence in my heart as I imagined Caleb imprisoned in a dark room. Was he cold and hungry? I was too scared to ask what the conditions were like inside the rotting cabin.

"Have you heard from Xander today?" Noah asked.

"No. He disappeared last night, sometime after I…" My voice trailed off and I frowned at the memory of feeling drugged from whatever Xander had slipped into my drink. Even though I knew he had done it to make sure I would stay safe, I couldn't help feeling a little angry with him.

"After you what?"

"After I fell asleep," I said, scolding myself for letting last night get to me when lives were on the line. "He left a note saying that his dad was gone and I haven't heard from him since. I thought that maybe he was in trouble, too."

"If my uncle has him, he's holding him somewhere else. Because he wasn't at the cabin with his father."

"Do you know what your uncle wants to do to them?" I glanced at Noah, watching a dark shadow slide over his expression.

"Yes, I do."

"What are you going to do about it? You can't just let him murder two innocent people."

"If I save either one of them, he'll kill Jenna. I'm trapped. I don't know what to do."

I stared at him, surprised at the defeat in his voice. "You have to save all of them."

"And how do you propose I do that? I only know where Caleb is. For all I know, Jenna's tied to a tree in the middle of nowhere. Looking for her would be like looking for a needle in a haystack."

"But you're sure your uncle has her and she's still alive?"

"Yes. He calls me when he checks on her to let me hear her voice. He wants me to know she's alive so that I won't interfere with his plans."

"Oh." I could only imagine how torn Noah felt right now caught in the middle. Saving one life would sacrifice another. It was a choice no one ever wanted to have to make.

As hard as I wanted to stay mad at him, a part of me felt sorry for him. But not all of me. I was still hurt that he had used me, and I wondered if any part of our relationship had been real. Silence filled the car, and I pulled my phone out of my pocket, checking it for new messages. As I suspected, there were none.

Noah glanced at me out of the corner of his eye. "Anything?"

I shook my head. "No." I dropped the phone in my lap, my heart sinking as the screen turned dark. We drove for a few more minutes without talking before Noah turned onto another road. A few miles later, he turned into Xander's driveway.

"Stop here," I instructed when we reached the gate. "I'll take care of this." After unfastening my seatbelt, I jumped out of the car and rushed around the front through the headlight beams.

Reaching the control box, I blocked Noah's view and punched in the code. As the gate lurched forward, I ran back to the passenger side, hopping in before Noah pulled away. Then we continued up the winding driveway. "Have you been to their house before?" I asked.

"Not really."

"What does that mean?" I muttered, frustrated with him.

I still wasn't sure how much he knew about Xander and his father. But my thoughts of Noah disappeared when I saw the log house looming ahead, lit up like a beacon in the night. Xander's pick-up was parked in front of the garage, the porch lights reflecting off the shiny black paint.

My heart fluttered with relief. "He's here!" I murmured.

I didn't even wait for the car to stop before opening my door. "Laken, slow down," Noah said as he jerked it to a halt.

"I can't," I said under my breath.

I leaped out of the car, not bothering to shut the door before I ran across the driveway and up the steps to the front porch. I was about to knock on the door when it flung open and Xander stepped out wearing a black T-shirt and jeans. His dark hair was messy and his eyes tired, but his expression softened when he saw me.

"Xander!" I said before rushing into his arms and leaning my head against his shoulder.

"Where have you been?" he asked, rubbing my back. "I was worried sick when I got home and found your truck, but no sign of you."

I drew in a sharp breath, remembering the last time I had seen him right before falling into a drug-induced sleep. Placing my palms on his shoulders, I pushed him away. "You were? Was that before or after you slipped something into my drink?"

"What?" came Noah's voice behind me. "He drugged you?"

Before Xander could say a word, I whirled around to glare at Noah. "You have no room to talk since you lied to me and used me."

"He did what?" Xander asked, his eyes shooting sparks at Noah.

I turned back to Xander. "Let it go. I'm handling this."

"What's he doing here, anyway?" Xander asked suspiciously.

"He knows where your father is."

"Good. Then that makes two of us."

"Three of us," I corrected. "Where were you? I called you. I left you several voice mails and sent you a dozen texts. Why didn't you call me back?"

Xander raised his eyebrows. "I couldn't. My service went out. You know as well as anyone that you can't always catch a signal in these mountains. And I just got home a minute ago."

"Oh," I said, my frustration deflated. He had a good point. "I didn't think of that. Can we go inside now? It's a little cold out here and you don't even have a jacket on."

"Yes, of course." Xander moved out of the doorway to let me into the house, but he blocked it again when Noah walked up the porch steps. "Where do you think you're going?"

"Xander, he knows the guy who's after you and your dad," I explained. "I think we need his help." I hated to admit it, but if Noah had told me the truth on the way back to Xander's, then he would be an ally. Xander and Noah each wanted to save someone they cared about, and they had a better chance at succeeding if they banded together instead of fighting one another.

"How do we know we can trust you?" Xander asked him, narrowing his eyes.

"You don't. You're just going to have to take a chance on that," Noah replied, his voice calm.

"I don't take those kinds of chances," Xander told him coldly.

I turned in the entry hall, watching their confrontation. "You both need to trust each other. If I'm still in this after all that has happened, then I think you need to put your differences aside until everyone is safe. After that, you can go your separate ways. But for now, Xander, please let him in so we can talk."

With a huff, Xander stepped aside, letting Noah through the doorway as I pulled off my jacket, hat and gloves. After shutting the door, Xander draped an arm around my shoulders while Noah scanned the house, letting out a low whistle.

"Nice place you and your dad have here," he commented.

Xander shrugged. "It's just a place," he said as Noah wandered past us into the family room. "Come on in. Make yourself at home," he offered sarcastically, earning him a sharp poke in the ribs from my elbow.

"Be nice," I warned in a low voice.

My eyes met his for a moment before I slid out from under his arm and followed Noah through the house. The glow of the only lamp in the family room reflected in the window behind it. Other than that, the room was cold and dark. No fire crackled in the hearth tonight, sending a chill through the house that used to seem so inviting and friendly. Caleb's absence hung in the air, turning the mood solemn.

I approached the couch, dropping my jacket, hat, and gloves onto the armrest. Then I turned to face Xander who lurked behind me. "It might be time for me to ask my dad for help," I said.

"No way," Xander and Noah protested in unison. They glanced at each other before Xander continued. "It's too dangerous. I think that would only make things worse for my dad and, at the same time, put your dad at risk. Noah, why haven't you arrested this monster? You're the deputy in this town, aren't you?"

Noah stood by the coffee table, his gaze directed at us. "Your father isn't the only one in danger. A friend of mine disappeared a few weeks ago and he has her. If I don't do what he asks, he'll kill her. And I don't know where she is, so there's nothing I can do right now."

"Oh," Xander said with a thoughtful sigh. "That puts a wrinkle in my plans to take him out. Who is she?"

"Just someone I care about who doesn't deserve to pay for my uncle's greed." Noah's brown eyes settled on me as he spoke.

"That guy is your uncle?" Xander asked, shaking his head.

"Yes," Noah confirmed. "Good old Uncle Efren. I've known him my whole life. You don't want to cross him. He's greedy, and he's smart."

"So the whole time you've been here, working as the deputy in town, you knew he was planning to kill us?" Xander huffed, a look of disbelief in his eyes.

"It's a long story," Noah said before repeating what he'd told me on the way back. When he stopped, his eyes shifted as if he was worried about how Xander would react.

"Great," Xander muttered. "Well, since you're in this, you can help me get my father back and then I'll help you find your friend. And Laken—" He glanced at me, his eyes locking with mine. "—you should go home."

"What? I'm not going home now!" I objected. "Not while you two are out there risking your lives. And what about Dakota? If you need him, then you need me."

"Sorry, Laken. There's no way you're coming with us," Xander said firmly.

"I haven't agreed to this," Noah stated, earning him an icy glare from Xander.

"You don't have a choice. We'll have a better chance getting my father and your girlfriend—"

"She's not my girlfriend," Noah interrupted.

"Whatever," Xander said, rolling his eyes. "All I'm trying to say is that we'll have a better chance if we're not worried about keeping Laken safe."

I raised my eyebrows. "But I get to worry about both of you?" My question earned me shocked looks from both of them and, in that moment of silence, a faint scratching sounded at the front door. "Dakota!" I ran into the entry hall and opened the door.

Dakota charged into the house, heading straight for Xander. But he stopped as soon as he spotted Noah, a deep growl rumbling in his throat.

I shut the door before hurrying to Dakota's side and touching the top of his head between his ears. "That's enough, Dakota. He's here to help us, I think." I looked at Noah, still not sure if we could trust him. Even though I wanted to, I wouldn't let myself.

"He's got good taste," Xander murmured in a sarcastic tone.

I shot him an unamused look. This wasn't the time or the place to hold a popularity contest judged by a wolf.

"Well, good. Laken, Dakota has perfect timing. He can help us, too," Xander said. "And with him covering our backs, you'll have nothing to worry about."

"I wish I could be as confident as you are," I said.

Xander ignored me. "Come on. I'll walk you out. Noah, wait here. I'm not done with you." Turning back to me, he asked, "Can you have Dakota stay here to keep him from going anywhere?"

"Maybe." Before picking up my coat from the couch, I gazed at Noah. "Do you agree that I should go home?" He was my only chance to stay and help.

"If you don't go home tonight, your father will have the whole town out looking for you. So yes, I do," Noah replied calmly.

"I guess I'm out-voted."

"If your dad figures out what's going on, it will only put him in danger," Xander reminded me, reaching over and squeezing my hand.

As my eyes met his, I noticed Noah's subtle wince out of the corner of my eye. Ignoring his reaction, I pulled my hand away from Xander's. Then I reached for my jacket and put it on. My hat and gloves in my hands, I said, "I guess I'll be going, then."

Before heading for the front door, I stooped beside Dakota and wrapped my arms around his neck. "Please keep them safe," I whispered into his fur. "And you stay safe, too. I almost lost you once, and I'm not going through that again."

Standing, I swept my gaze across the room from Xander to Noah before walking toward the front door. A shudder rippled through me as I wondered if this was the last time I would see any of them.

When I reached for the door handle, footsteps sounded behind me. Xander rushed up to my side, putting his hand over mine. "I'll walk you to your car."

Without bothering to put a jacket on over his T-shirt, Xander stepped outside with me. He took my hand as we walked down the steps of the brightly lit front porch, his touch warm, his grip firm, yet gentle.

"He knows about my abilities with animals, so you don't have to act weird when you want me to tell Dakota something."

We stopped beside the driver's door, and Xander looked

at me. "Really? How did that happen?"

"There was a situation with a moose last month."

"A moose?"

I nodded, remembering that cold afternoon at the Owens' property. "A moose got tangled up in barbed wire on a farm at the edge of town. My dad sent Noah up there to shoot it, but he couldn't do it. So he called me."

"Why would he call you?"

"I wondered the same thing, but I do have a wolf. I guess he thought I had a way with animals." *Or he already knew,* I thought. *Let's face it. Xander was right. You are naïve. It all makes sense now. Noah never would have asked you to help with the moose if he hadn't known.* I felt as though the voice in my head was scolding me. Maybe I was naïve, but that didn't mean I could forgive Noah for lying to me. I may not have seen through him, but he should carry the blame for not being truthful and I should stop beating myself up for not second-guessing him sooner.

"That's not hard to see," Xander said.

"I guess not. I tried to cut the wires by myself, but I wasn't strong enough. So Noah had to do it while I kept the moose calm."

"He must have been amazed by that."

"Pretty much." I paused, looking up at Xander, the bright lights along the front of the house blurring behind him. "Aren't you getting cold?"

Xander rubbed his arms. "A little. With everything going on, I think my blood is running hot right now. But I should let you get home."

"What? No escort service? You're going to let me drive home alone?"

Xander sighed, his eyebrows furrowed with concern. "It seems so. Against my better judgement, I might add. But I think you'll be fine. That guy wants me, not you. The farther away from here you get, the safer you'll be."

I nodded and turned, but before I could open the door to the Explorer, Xander reached around my waist, pulling me against him. "Not so fast," he murmured, gazing into my eyes. "You're not mad about last night, are you?"

I slid my arms up around his shoulders. "I know I should be, but right now, I'm just glad you're safe. And I'm worried about your dad."

"Me, too," Xander said. Then he leaned toward me, softly kissing my lips. I closed my eyes, savoring the only peaceful moment we had as danger closed in around us. He deepened the kiss, pulling me closer to him. When I touched his neck, he shuddered.

Lifting away, Xander looked at me, heat simmering in his blue eyes. "You're very distracting," he whispered.

"I'm sorry."

He chuckled, his worried eyes flashing with amusement for a brief moment. "So, am I forgiven?"

"As long as it never happens again."

"I will always do whatever I must to protect you."

"I can take care of myself," I insisted, still caught up in the memory of his kiss.

"You'd better go. Where's your phone?" he asked, releasing his hold on me.

I unzipped my pocket and pulled it out. "Right here. See?" Then I opened the door and slid into the driver's seat, dropping my phone into the cup holder.

Xander leaned into the truck as I turned on the engine and flipped on the lights. "Call me as soon as you get home. And I don't mean when you pull into the driveway. I want to hear your voice once you're inside with the doors locked. I presume your parents are home tonight?"

"They are. At least they were when I left, and they didn't tell me they had any plans for tonight."

"Good. So I should hear from you in about a half hour?"

I nodded.

"Okay. I'll be watching the time while I try not to kill Noah."

"Hey," I scolded. "You guys are going to have to try to get along, at least until everyone is safe."

Xander frowned. "Don't worry. I won't harm a hair on his head unless I have to."

"Good."

"Besides, if it comes to that, I think Dakota will do the dirty work for me."

It was my turn to frown. I had a feeling he was right about that.

"Okay, you need to get out of here. Drive carefully."

"I will." I smiled at him one last time before he shut the door and backed away from the truck.

After fastening my seatbelt, I turned the Explorer around in the driveway and pulled away from the house. I guided the SUV through the darkness, stopping at the gate to enter the code before continuing down the mountain, my thoughts more focused on leaving Xander, Noah and Dakota to save Caleb and Noah's friend than on the road.

Fifteen minutes later, I pulled into my driveway. I shut off the engine and lights and, in the darkness, ran up the sidewalk to the house. After unlocking the door, I hurried inside and twisted the deadbolt back into place.

Making my way into the dark kitchen, I heard my parents' bedroom door open down the hallway.

"Laken, is that you?" my father asked in a tired voice.

"Yes, Dad," I answered, hoping he wouldn't come around the corner to ask me about my night.

"Okay. Are you headed up to bed?"

"Yes. It's been a long night."

"Goodnight, then. We'll see you in the morning."

Whew! I thought. "Goodnight, Dad." As I heard the bedroom door shut, I turned on the kitchen light. After slipping out of my parka, I hung it on the back of a chair and tossed my hat and gloves on the table, feeling exhausted. I paused, remembering my promise to call Xander when I got home only to realize that my phone was still in the Explorer. "Man!" I whispered. "Why do I keep doing that?"

Grabbing my keys, I left my parka, hat and gloves where they were and returned to the entry hall. I crept outside into the darkness and ran down the sidewalk to my truck, the cold seeping in through my shirt. Approaching the Explorer, I clicked the remote and the parking lights flashed. Then I opened the door and grabbed my phone from the cup holder.

I had just started to head back to the house when Noah's uncle stepped into my way. Bone-chilling fear rattled me as my eyes locked with his sinister stare.

"Laken," he said with an evil smile. "It's time for you to come with me."

An icy blast of panic shot through me. I looked around him, searching for an escape route. But it was hopeless. I was trapped between him and the Explorer, and I had no doubt that he'd catch me if I tried to run. My nerves on edge and my heart nearly jumping out of my chest, I forced myself to remain calm. "But you don't want me. You told me that."

"That's right. I want your boyfriend. But he had twenty-four hours to show up, and yet he's nowhere to be found. So it's time for plan B. If he won't come for his father, perhaps he'll come for you." Efren grabbed my arm and, as I opened my mouth to scream, he darted behind me, covering my mouth with his free hand. "You really don't want to do that," he whispered in my ear. "Let your parents sleep. I don't want to have to hurt them."

Tears burst from my eyes. I couldn't believe this was happening. How could I have been so stupid to leave my phone in the truck? Dakota wasn't even around to protect me. Left with no choice but to obey Noah's uncle, I held still as his hand dropped from my mouth to my ribs, anchoring my body against him.

"There, now. It's much easier to cooperate, isn't it?" he asked. One of his arms released me and a strange pop sounded, like that of a cap coming off a container. Then a needle pierced my upper arm through my sleeve and something cold was pumped into me. As the liquid circulated through my veins, the dim light from the single bulb outside the house blurred. I fought to stay awake, but I lost that battle, watching the shadows whip around me for a split second before my world went black.

Chapter 11

A dull ache worked its way through my head, spreading from my eyebrows to my hairline when I woke up. My eyes still closed, I felt a hard surface beneath me. I tried to move, but my hands were secured behind my back, and a rope cut into my wrists when I shifted, hoping to release the pressure. But the knot only seemed to tighten, making it worse. I stretched out my legs, realizing that my ankles had also been tied together above the tops of my hiking boots.

With a deep breath, I opened my eyes to see an empty room. The walls and floors consisted of weathered wooden planks, including those that boarded up the single window. Very little light slipped in between boards, shrouding the room in darkness. I shivered in the cold, wishing I had my parka or a blanket to put over my jeans and turtleneck.

The memory of Noah's uncle grabbing me was hazy, but I could practically feel the cool injection he had pumped into my veins. Everything else that had happened since my world had gone dark was a mystery. I didn't know where I was, and I didn't know what time it was. My stomach growled, but I had a feeling I wouldn't be eating any time soon.

I lifted my shoulders from the wood floor, inching up until I leaned against the wall. I stared at the shadows in the room, scanning the perimeter until I noticed a door made of the same weathered planks. But getting up to leave through it seemed impossible from where I huddled on the floor. My head ached, and I longed to reach up and rub it. I wiggled my wrists again, wishing I could squeeze a hand through the ropes, but to no avail. They had been tied so tight, it was more likely that I'd end up with rope burns than get them to loosen.

"Hello?" I whispered, my voice hoarse and raspy. I cleared my throat, raising my voice. "Is anybody out there? Please answer me if you're there."

Silence loomed in the room and beyond. Sighing in defeat, I leaned my head back as my eyelids fell. Listening carefully, I hoped I would hear any sign of life, even that of my abductor, but I heard nothing.

Shivering and hungry, I remained on the cold floor for what seemed like forever. I tried to fall asleep, but the pain throbbing in my head kept me awake.

Sometime later, whether it had been hours or days, I couldn't tell, the door handle rattled. My eyes flew open and I stared at the knob, holding my breath with the hope that Xander or Noah was coming to my rescue. But it escaped from my lips in disappointment and fear when the door opened to reveal the man in black.

Efren stepped into the room, the light behind him nearly blinding me. He held something in his hands as he walked across the floor to where I sat, his footsteps echoing in the empty room. He knelt beside me, a frown etched onto his face. "You're awake. Good. Someone wants to hear your voice." He turned on the phone in his hand and, as I watched him, I recognized it as mine.

He dialed a number and turned on the speaker before holding it up in front of me. I glanced at him and then down at the phone, nervous as I read Xander's name. The other end rang twice before Xander picked it up. "Laken? It's about time. I've been calling you all morning. Why didn't you call me last night? I got your text, but I really wanted to hear your voice."

I wasn't sure if Efren intended for me to speak right away, so I remained quiet, waiting for his cue. But he spoke first. "Hello, Xander."

"Who is this? Where's Laken?" Xander demanded, his voice tense and worried.

"You know very well who this is. And Laken's right here. Would you like to speak to her?"

"Yes, of course."

Efren nodded, prompting me to speak. "Xander, it's me."

"Laken," Xander breathed with a mixture of relief and alarm. "Are you okay? Where are you?"

"I'm—scared. I don't know where I am."

"That's enough," Efren said, turning off the speaker and holding the phone up to his ear. He stood, pacing the length of the room. "Okay, California boy. You heard her, so you know she's alive. Now if you want her to stay alive, you're going to do exactly as I say. Meet me at the bridge on Old Oak Road off of Route Three in one hour. And come alone. Once I have you, I'll let her go. Don't be late." He hung up the call before Xander could have possibly answered him.

Efren walked toward me, kneeling in front of me again. "As long as he does what I ask, you'll be home by sunset."

"And what if he doesn't?" I held my breath for a moment, not sure I wanted him to answer me.

"Let's not worry about that right now. He'll come, I'm sure of it." He smiled with satisfaction. "By the way, you haven't thanked me."

"For what?" I asked with a huff.

"I heard your wolf survived the hunt thanks to one of the wolves I brought up here." His eyes showed no sign of sorrow or remorse for the wolf that had been killed instead of Dakota.

In spite of his cold stare, I replied, "I'm sorry. I had no idea they would get one of your wolves."

He shrugged indifferently. "She was just a means to an end. And I still have the rest of the pack." He stood up, my phone in his hands. "Well, I'd better be going. I don't want to be late to meet your boyfriend." A broad smile broke out across his face. "Don't go anywhere, my dear," he said before heading toward the door.

"Wait!" I cried out, not wanting to be left in the cold room again. I shivered, my head throbbing with pain and my empty stomach growling. He stopped and turned, his icy stare daring me to tell him what I wanted. "I know you have to leave right now, but I don't suppose you could loosen these ropes and get me a blanket?"

"Sure. And why don't I get you some tea and cookies while I'm at it?" He laughed. "You're kidding, right? After growing up around here, I'm sure you can tough it out. This will all be over soon. You'll survive. You have no idea how many nights I went to bed cold and hungry as a boy. You can handle a few more hours." Without another word, he stalked out the door, shutting it behind him and pitching the room back into darkness.

The sound of his footsteps faded within seconds, and silence returned. Tears welled up in my eyes and I trembled, not only from the cold, but also from fear. If Xander showed up at the bridge like Efren had instructed, what would happen to him? But if he didn't, what would happen to me? I shuddered at the memory of Efren's stare. He clearly had no conscience and, as Noah had explained, would stop at nothing to get what he wanted.

The seconds ticked by slowly. Noah's uncle still had my phone, and I wondered if he was using it to send messages to my father. Surely if my parents woke up to find me gone on a Sunday morning, they would want to know where I was. If Efren was smart, he'd make sure they thought I was safe.

The darkness and silence surrounded me. All I could do

was rest my forehead on my bent knees and cower in the shadows. I cried for a while, but my tears eventually dried up. I told myself that Xander and Noah would get all of us out of this mess safely, but I wasn't convinced. Something very bad was bound to happen soon, and there wasn't a single thing I could do about it.

In spite of my headache, my eyes closed and I prayed that I would fall asleep as I waited.

ᕙᕗ

The rattling door handle woke me from my light sleep. My eyes flew open and my heart fluttered anxiously, conflicting emotions of fear and relief taking a hold of me. The hope that I might be let go was overshadowed by the guilt I felt knowing that I would only be released if Xander surrendered. I lifted my gaze, staring at the door and expecting to see Efren any moment now.

To my surprise, Noah rushed into the room. "Laken!" He ran over and knelt beside me, worry lurking in his tired brown eyes.

As I looked at him, too exhausted to talk, he ran his fingers along my cheek. "Are you okay?"

I nodded slowly. "I'm cold. So cold," was all I whispered, shivering.

Noah pulled off his fleece-lined jean jacket and slipped it between my back and the wall. After wrapping it around my shoulders, he rubbed my arms. "He couldn't even give you a blanket?" he muttered with a frown.

"Did you know he was going to take me?" I asked, still not sure if I could trust Noah.

"No, I didn't. But he knows that if he told me his plans, I would have tried to stop him." Noah paused, studying me with concern in his eyes. "You look freezing. Your lips are practically blue." He tucked a loose strand of hair behind my ear. "How do you feel?"

"How do you think I feel?" I knew he didn't like seeing me in this condition, but I couldn't help holding him partially responsible. "I have a horrible headache. I'm miserable and hungry. I didn't even eat dinner last night."

"I'm sorry, Laken. There's no excuse for this."

A sudden commotion at the door caused both of us to turn our attention to it. Xander shuffled into the room, his arms tied behind his back. Noah's uncle pushed him, and he fell to the floor with a heavy thud. His hair flopped across his forehead, a black and blue bruise circled one of his eyes, and his black shirt was ripped open across his shoulder, exposing a bloody scrape.

"Sure there is, Noah," Efren said, towering above the three of us. "And she served her purpose. I got him. It's time to end our pitiful existence and start living the good life. We're almost there."

"We?" I repeated, looking at Noah for answers.

"Get up, Noah!" Efren grabbed Noah's upper arm, jerking him to his feet. "You don't need to be on the ground with them. You're with me. We're a team, remember?"

"Laken wasn't part of the deal," Noah stated.

I stared at him incredulously, tears forming in my eyes. Did Noah really want this? Could he blindly look the other way while his uncle murdered innocent people?

"What was the deal, Noah?" I asked.

He gazed at me, shame and guilt crossing over his face. "I'm sorry," he mouthed.

I swallowed the lump forming in my throat as I choked back sobs.

Xander groaned from where he lay in a crumpled heap on the floor. "Laken," he murmured. "Is that you? He told me—he would—let you go if I cooperated."

"I know," I whispered.

"Okay, enough sentiment," Efren interjected. "Noah, get the girl. I want you to personally deliver her to her parents." He gazed at me, studying me with his black eyes. "You might want to clean her up and feed her something first. She looks like she could use it and we don't want her going home looking like she just got beat up."

I glared at Noah as he approached and bent down to help me to my feet. My ankles were still bound together, but he managed to lift me up so that I could lean against the wall. "Ow," I said, wincing as the ropes seemed to cut into my wrists and ankles.

"Here, I'll get those." He knelt down at my boots and un-tied the rope.

I felt instant relief when it unraveled around my ankles. I picked up my feet, flexing them up and down to stimulate my circulation, as Noah stood up, the rope in his hands. "You didn't answer me. What was the deal?" I demanded.

He shook his head, his eyes begging for forgiveness. "I promise it never involved kidnapping you." He tossed the rope across the room to his uncle. "Here. Take that. I'm not doing your dirty work for you."

Efren caught the rope with a swift movement. "We agreed we would do whatever it took," he replied, shaking his head. "I warned you not to fall in love with her. It's weakened you, and now you can't see what we need to do."

I gasped, flashing my eyes at Noah. "What?" I asked, feeling my heart drop into my stomach. "Is that true?"

Noah met my gaze but didn't answer me. "Come on. Let's go." He wrapped an arm around my shoulders and started leading me toward the door.

"You both have no idea what you're doing," Xander muttered from the floor.

He rolled onto his side and slowly sat up. Wincing in pain, he glared at his captor, defiance in his eyes.

Efren smiled wickedly, seeming amused by Xander. "Think what you want, but I know exactly what I'm doing. Why do you care, anyway? Soon you and your father will be dead, so you don't need to concern yourself with this."

I stopped, wanting to hear anything that might explain Efren's motives. Noah tried to keep me moving, but I stood firm.

"Once my father and I die, so does the magic to make diamonds. There's no one left after me. You need me," Xander said, his voice low and husky.

"You couldn't be more wrong. Maybe I'll give you a few minutes with your father before I set fire to this place. You might ask him who Violet Lawson was."

I sucked in a sharp breath, my jaw dropping as I snapped my gaze back to Noah, suddenly knowing why Caleb had seemed familiar the day I met him. Noah had his eyes. In that one moment, it all made sense.

"What are you talking about?" Xander asked, not making the connection. "Who cares about some girl he knew a long time ago?"

"Your father met a woman shortly after your mother died. He wined and dined her, and well, I don't think I need to tell you where the evening led. Nine months later, she gave birth to a baby boy."

"That's impossible," Xander said. "My father never would have abandoned a child of his. If he had another son after me, I'd know about it."

"Not if he didn't know."

"Xander," I whispered. "It's Noah."

"What?" Xander shook his head in disbelief. "Wait a minute, that's impossible. He's not—he couldn't possibly be—" Xander stuttered, barely able to get the words out.

Silence settled over the room, and Xander's expression fell as the realization of who Noah was seemed to sink in.

Turning to Noah, I choked out, "Why didn't you tell me?"

He shook his head. "How could I? If I'd said a single word about any of this, you would have been in danger. I couldn't take that risk."

"Hey!" his uncle said, shooting a warning look at Noah. "That's enough. Now get her out of here before her father sends out a search party. I don't need the sheriff running around looking for his daughter."

"What about her phone?" Noah asked.

"Oh yeah." The man reached into the side pocket of his coat. "Here." He tossed it to Noah. "Give it to her when you drop her off." Then he looked at me, a warning look in his eyes. "Wait a minute." He approached me, stopping inches away as he lifted his hand to my face. Tilting my chin up, he locked his dark eyes with mine. "One word out of you about any of this and I'll feed Noah's friend to the wolves. Got that? You don't want her blood on your conscience, do you?"

"No," I whispered, afraid to move.

"Good. Then we have an understanding." He pulled his hand away from me and smiled. "Thank you, Laken. You've been most helpful and we appreciate that. I'm sure Noah will buy you anything you want once we cash in on the diamonds."

"I don't want his gifts," I told him. "I want you to let my friends go."

Efren laughed, sending shivers up my spine. "After all this? Not a chance. Forget about them. They're as good as dead."

I glanced at Xander, meeting his blue eyes. Fear struck me as tears spilled down my cheeks. I couldn't believe this was happening. How could I leave him here like this, bruised and beaten? He had always been so strong, so confident. It ripped at my soul to see him on the floor, at the mercy of this monster who couldn't wait to steal his last breath.

"Come on, Laken." Noah turned me around and led me through the doorway. "There's nothing we can do. It's over."

I refused to believe this was over, but I had no choice other than to let Noah lead me out of the room. We walked through another empty space, our footsteps echoing on the wooden planks. The only difference between this space and the room I had been locked up in was that it was a little bigger and a small kitchen sat off to the side. The walls were lined with the same wooden boards and every window had been covered up with plywood. Two more doors were located at the back, and I wondered if Caleb was being held against his will behind one of them.

Noah walked me through the front of the cabin, but I stopped and spun around as the door to the room we had left slammed shut. I listened carefully, hearing a thud and then a painful moan. "Are you going to let him get away with this?" I asked, squirming out from under Noah's arm and ignoring his jacket when it fell off my shoulders to the floor. Then I rushed back to the door as fast as I could, my hands still tied behind my back. "Noah! You have to help him!" I begged.

Noah ran up behind me and wrapped his arms around my chest, pulling me away from the door as I struggled against him. "Laken, I can't do anything. It's them or Jenna."

"You have a gun. Where is it? Put a bullet in him and everyone is saved."

Whipping me around to face him, Noah shook his head. "No, Laken. You don't get it! I don't know where Jenna is. If I kill him, I may never find her. All he told me is that if she's not found in time, she'll die. He wasn't kidding about feeding her to the wolves. I hate this, you have to believe me. But there's nothing I can do!"

Taking a deep breath, I tried to calm down. I stopped struggling against him, and his arms loosened as he felt me relax. "Can you at least untie my wrists?" I asked.

"Only if you promise not to do something stupid."

"Maybe you should clarify what you mean by that."

"Do you promise to come with me and not look back?"

I sighed with frustration. "He has innocent people here," I said quietly.

"I know, but that's not an excuse to do something reckless. You're not going back in after Xander. You're no match for my uncle. Do you promise?" he repeated.

"Fine," I huffed. "I promise I won't barge in there and try to save him."

"Can I trust you to live up to your word?"

I narrowed my eyes at him in disbelief. "You have no room to talk about trust."

Guilt washed over his face as he took a deep breath. "I guess I deserve that. Now turn around so that I can untie you."

I did as he asked and stood patiently while he untied the knot. After a few minutes, the rope slackened and dropped away from my wrists. Feeling instant relief, I pulled my arms in front of me, rubbing them. "Thank you," I whispered, watching the door to the room that his uncle and Xander still occupied.

"Laken," Noah started, noticing my gaze. "You're coming with me, right?"

"Yes," I said, shifting my attention back to him.

As Noah bent down to retrieve his jacket off the dusty floor, my mind raced. Didn't his uncle realize I would tell my father that Xander and Caleb had been kidnapped and their lives were on the line? Efren might be controlling Noah with the girl he held hostage, but I had no allegiance to her. In fact, I couldn't even be sure that she existed. What if Noah had made the whole thing up to get me to trust him? What if there was no missing girl and this was simply a cover story to let his uncle kill Xander and Caleb? What if he was just as greedy and ruthless as his uncle?

I wished I knew what to believe about Noah. I wanted to trust him, but I couldn't. Not when he'd kept so many secrets from me. But any decision I needed to make about him could wait.

Xander and Caleb were my top priority right now. If I didn't figure out a way to save them before Noah took me home, they would be dead before help could arrive. There was no way this man would risk me telling my father. He would kill them before I ever reached my house.

Noah straightened up with his jacket in his free hand. He dropped the rope to the floor and dusted off the dirty sleeves. "Here," he said, offering it to me. "Wear this. I don't want you to be cold."

"How kind of you," I muttered, taking the jacket from him even though being cold was the farthest thing from my mind. I slipped my arms into it and zipped it up halfway. "Can I have my phone now?"

"When we get to your house."

"Fine," I scoffed, brushing past him to what I believed was the front door. I heard his footsteps behind me as I yanked the door open. It creaked and groaned, wobbling on its hinges. When I stepped outside onto the porch, sunlight peeked through the bare trees surrounding the cabin, but the air was bitter cold. The Jeep I remembered from last night sat beside the police car. "I'm sure you're not on duty."

"My car's in the shop. Your dad said I could use the cruiser, but only until my car is ready."

"What difference does it make? Looks like by tomorrow, you'll be able to buy a new one." I paused, frowning. "I wonder what my father would say if he knew you were using it to commit a crime." Without waiting for him to respond, I headed down the steps to the gravel, my shoes crunching on the stones.

Rushing up behind me, Noah grabbed my arm and jerked me to a stop. Then he spun me around to face him. "I told you I don't have a choice. I will find Jenna. I won't let him hurt her just like I won't let him hurt you."

As he spoke, a shadow darted through the trees in the distance behind him. I stared at the woods, my heart fluttering when Dakota charged into the grass and across the driveway, stopping behind Noah. He emitted a loud growl, his lip curling up to reveal his fangs.

Noah slowly turned, his eyes locked on Dakota who glared at him, the hair on his back standing straight up. Dakota moved toward Noah, forcing him to back up until he bumped into the police car. Then Dakota halted a foot away from him, trapping him.

"Laken," Noah said nervously. "Can you please call him off?"

"Why? So you can take me home while my friends are

murdered? Not a chance." I shot him an icy stare, recognizing the uneasiness in his eyes.

"Laken, don't do this. You promised."

"I only promised that I wouldn't barge into that room and take on your uncle. I kept that promise." I glanced at Dakota. "Nice work. You always knew about him, didn't you? I should have trusted your judgement." I raised my eyes, catching Noah's warning look as I started backing away.

"Laken," Noah begged. "Please, don't do anything crazy. I don't want to lose you."

I stopped, staring at him, my jaw dropping open. "To lose me would imply that you have me. You lost me weeks ago when you left."

"I'm sorry about that. But I still don't want you to get hurt. My uncle has no intention of hurting you, but he won't think twice if you get in his way."

I threw my hands up in the air and shook my head, tears brewing in my eyes. "I have to try. Surely you can understand that." Then I returned my attention to Dakota. "Keep him there as long as you can."

With a subtle nod, Dakota kept his eyes focused on Noah. When Noah started to move, Dakota growled. Clearly realizing he was trapped, Noah froze again, his back still pressed against the car.

Without another word, I whipped around and ran across the driveway. After scaling up the hill, I escaped into the woods, confident that Noah wouldn't come after me.

Chapter 12

The branches overhead cast shadows on the ground as I ran quietly through the woods surrounding the cabin. I darted from tree to tree, cringing when the leaves crunched under my shoes.

After reaching the other side of the cabin, I crouched behind a thick tree trunk and watched the scene unfolding in the driveway. Dakota slowly backed away from Noah, never taking his eyes off of him. His growl faded, his lip unfolding over his fangs. As if he had accomplished his mission, he spun around and charged across the driveway in the same direction I had gone. *Good boy,* I thought. Hopefully, Noah would think I was still on that side since that's where Dakota headed.

My attention was quickly drawn back to the cabin when the front door swung open and Noah's uncle stepped outside, his long coat swaying against his legs. From where I watched in the distance, I could see the anger flashing over his expression. He slammed the door and stormed down the porch steps. Noah lingered by the car, watching the woods, probably looking for me, when his uncle approached him.

"Where's the girl?" Efren demanded.

"I don't know. She got away," Noah answered, his voice distracted as he stepped away from the car, still focused on the woods.

"How the hell did that happen?"

Noah turned to him, his eyes defiant. "The wolf, that's how it happened."

Efren shook his head in disgust. "I don't believe it. I give you one simple thing to do, and you can't even get her home? You incapable idiot!" He swung his fist at Noah's jaw, the force knocking Noah to the ground.

My breath caught as Noah fell. No matter how upset I was with him for the secrets he'd kept from me, I didn't want to watch him suffer.

I flinched when his uncle kicked him in the stomach. "Get up, you fool. You're going to need a stronger backbone if you want to stay with me."

Noah groaned as he lifted his shoulders. Rising to his feet, he stared at his uncle through narrowed eyes. He raised his hand, wiping at the blood streaming down his chin from a cut on his lip. "Remind me when I said I *wanted* to do this."

"I refuse to believe you'd rather work a dead-end police job that will never get you anything more than a tiny apartment and a beat-up old car than be rich."

"I told you before, and I'll tell you again, it's not worth killing people."

"It's your birthright. Are you going to let Xander win? Once he's gone, you can have anything you want. Now, shall we get started? The sooner we do this, the sooner we can get out of this town."

It seemed that Noah couldn't hold back any longer. He curled his hand into a fist and struck at his uncle. But he wasn't fast enough. In a flash, Efren caught his wrist in mid-air. He spun Noah around, locking him to his chest with one arm, the crook of his elbow cutting across Noah's neck. "Don't cross me, boy," he gritted out. "I'm older, and

I'm stronger. You don't stand a chance. The more you defy me, the longer I'll wait to tell you where Jenna is."

At the mention of Jenna, Noah relaxed, yielding to his uncle's threat. "Fine. Let me go. As long as we're fighting, I can't get out there to find Laken." As soon as his uncle released him, Noah jumped away and rubbed his throat. "Before I look for her, let's get one thing clear," he said.

Efren narrowed his eyes. "You're wasting time, but go on if you must."

"I won't make any diamonds for you until you let Jenna go and I know she's safe from you forever."

"We already agreed to that. Why are you bringing it up for the hundredth time?"

"Because I don't trust you."

"Noah," Efren said, letting out a huff. "You should know me better than that. Now stop standing around and find Laken. Then bring her to me. I have half a mind to let her burn with Caleb and his son."

As his uncle turned, Noah grabbed his arm, pulling him around to face him. "You wouldn't dare touch her."

Efren shook his head, chuckling. "Get over her, Noah. She's not coming back to you now that she knows you lied to her. And that's really a shame. Because as soon as Xander dies, unless she chooses you, she'll die young just like her mother."

I gasped. How did he know that?

"We don't know that for sure," Noah snapped.

"It's what the book says. And it's been proven every generation before her as far as I could tell when I researched Ivy's ancestors. But I am sorry she picked Xander. After all that time you wasted getting to know her," he sneered.

"She didn't have a choice. I left her, remember? You took Jenna and told me I was getting too close to Laken. You forced me to leave her."

"I protected you. There's nothing but trouble with that one."

Noah let go of his arm. "We'll see about that," he muttered before jogging across the driveway in the direction Dakota and I had gone.

I watched Noah run up the hill and into the woods. It would only be a few minutes before he found me, so I had to hurry up and figure out what to do next.

Efren's gaze followed Noah's retreating figure until he disappeared between the trees. Then the older man turned and walked around the police car. When he reached the Jeep, he opened the back door, lugging out two red gasoline containers. He placed them on the ground for a moment to shut the door. As soon as it was secured, he lifted the containers and carried them toward the cabin, his strides long and determined.

My breath caught deep in my lungs as panic raced through me. Time was running out, fast. In minutes, the cabin would be set on fire, and Xander and Caleb would be left to burn to death. I was their only chance. Frantic, I watched Noah's uncle carry the gasoline containers up the porch steps.

Think! Think fast! Desperate to do something, I scanned the forest, looking for anything I could use as a weapon. I quickly spotted a black shape jutting out from under the fallen leaves. Jumping up, I rushed over to it and brushed the leaves aside, uncovering a football-sized rock. I pried it out of the earth and lifted it with both hands.

Standing up, I shifted my attention back to the cabin. Without a second of hesitation, I hurried out of the woods and down the hill. As if in a trance, I marched across the gravel driveway, heading straight for the front porch. After skimming up the steps, I stopped at the door that had been left open and peeked inside.

Efren was nowhere to be seen, but I smelled the toxic odor of gasoline. It burned my nose, and I trembled, wondering what in the world I was doing. Did I really think I could take him down with a rock? *I can do this. The only thing I know for sure is that if I don't try, Xander and Caleb will die.*

With a deep breath, I waited and listened. Noah's uncle came out of a room and entered another one. When he disappeared, I slipped into the cabin by nudging the door open with my foot. I crept across the room, stepping lightly on the creaky floorboards. Reaching the doorway he had just walked through, I braced my back against the wall next to it, waiting for him to emerge. I heard liquid splashing against the floor and walls, and an image of him tossing gasoline everywhere flashed through my thoughts.

Then suddenly, I heard a soft groan. Caleb! He was here, and he was alive!

The splashing sounds stopped and footsteps approached the door on the other side. Holding my breath, I raised the rock up over my head, preparing to slam it against Efren's head as hard as I could. When he stormed out of the room, I waited until he cleared the doorway before rushing up behind him. As I started to bring the rock down on him, it shifted in my hands. I struggled to get a firm grip on it, but it was too late. I had lost my chance.

Noah's uncle dropped the gasoline container to the floor and spun around, knocking the rock out of my hands. It fell to the floor with a loud thud. My heart sank as I looked up, not sure what to do now after my epic failure. Efren's black eyes met mine for a quick moment, and then he smiled, chuckling with an evil satisfaction.

On instinct, I bolted toward the front door. My only chance to save myself was to run. But he chased me, grabbing my hair when he got close. "Ow!" I screamed, my scalp stinging. I skidded to a halt, backing up to relieve the pressure.

He released my hair and reached for me, one arm wrapping tightly around my neck, choking me. His other arm circled my abdomen, squeezing the breath out of me. "You didn't really think you could knock me out, did you? You bitch. You should have left with Noah while you had the chance."

I struggled against him, but it only earned me a tighter

chokehold around my throat. "Let me go," I muttered. "I'll leave now, I promise."

He laughed. "What kind of fool do you think I am? You had your chance." He dragged me across the room to the other door. Kicking it open, he lugged me into the room and threw me against a wall. I slammed into the wooden boards, the impact knocking the wind out of me. Weak from fear and exhaustion, I crumpled to the floor.

Xander lay in a heap a few feet away, his hands guarding his stomach as if he'd been hit since I had left. "Laken?" he whispered, his blue eyes meeting mine. "What are you doing here? I thought he let you go. You should be halfway home by now."

Tears brimmed in my eyes as I shook my head. "I couldn't leave you. I tried—"

"That's enough!" Noah's uncle shouted. "I didn't want to do this, but you've given me no choice." He stormed out of the room, returning seconds later with one of the red containers.

I sat up, watching with wide eyes as he poured gasoline around the edge of the room. "Why?" I demanded, staring at him.

He stopped and turned, tilting his head to the side as he shot me a curious look. "Excuse me?" he asked, his voice calmer than just a moment ago.

"Why are you doing this? What did they ever do to you?"

Efren sighed as if remembering something painful. "My father was the grounds keeper for Caleb's father. We had nothing, and they had everything. Every day, I watched Caleb roll into school with his expensive clothes and fancy cars. He had everything that money could buy, including any girl he wanted. It didn't make sense. His father practically never left the house. I didn't know how anyone could have so much money if they weren't a doctor or a lawyer or at least went to work somewhere. So I started snooping around. My father didn't care, though. He was happy with the little pay he received as long as he could buy booze."

I listened carefully, not once feeling the urge to feel sorry for him. No matter what was driving him to kill Xander and his father, I couldn't see him as anything other than a monster driven by greed and jealousy.

Xander stirred on the floor, taking a deep breath as he sat up. "How did you find out where the money came from?" he asked.

Efren pulled a worn leather-bound book out of his inside coat pocket. "I found this."

"What is that?" I asked.

"A journal from some guy who lived thousands of years ago." He ran his fingers along the ratty edges. "I must have read this a hundred times. At first, I thought it was just some crazy story written by a crazy old man. But then I found a key to Caleb's father's house. He wasn't nearly as concerned about home security as Caleb is. I couldn't believe what I found in the basement. Coal and tools for making jewelry. That's when I realized every word written in this journal is true."

"So you've been planning this for a long time?" I asked.

"Pretty much. The biggest chance in the entire plan was getting a son out of Caleb. But for once in my life, fate was kind to me."

"Twice," Xander groaned.

"What's that?"

"I said twice. My father never would have gotten another woman pregnant if my mother hadn't been killed by a drunk driver."

"That's very true. But according to this—" He waved the book in the air. "—it was bound to happen sooner or later. Well, enough of the reminiscing. It's been fun, but I have to get on with my work." He shoved the journal back into his pocket and leaned down to grab the container.

As Efren resumed soaking the room with gasoline, Xander rose to his feet. He wobbled for a moment before balancing, his hands still tied behind his back.

Then Xander ran at him, slamming his shoulder into Efren's back. "No, you don't!" But he was no match for the older man without being able to use his hands. Noah's uncle dropped the gasoline can, the liquid in it sloshing from side to side. He swung a fist at Xander, slamming his jaw and pitching him back onto the floor with a thud.

I winced, looking away. I couldn't bear to watch anyone else get hurt. I just wanted this nightmare to end.

Efren shook his head with a smug grin and reached for the gasoline container. After dousing the last corner, he stopped in the doorway. Digging into his pocket, he pulled out a tiny matchbox. "Laken, I sure hope Xander is worth dying for."

Crippled with fear, I couldn't believe this was happening. I wasn't ready to die, let alone burn to death at the hands of a mad man. My eyes squeezed shut, I felt the sting of tears under my lids. My arms and legs shook as panic wormed its way into every part of me. There was nothing I could do but hope that my suffering would end quickly.

I waited to feel the heat of the flames, but instead, I heard a door slam and a struggle. I opened my eyes to see Noah holding a rope around his uncle's neck and Efren gasping for air.

"Laken," Noah said between clenched teeth. "Run while you can!" He bit down on his lip, tightening the rope.

I jumped up, racing over to Xander. "Come on!" I helped him scramble to his feet. Holding his upper arm, I pulled him toward the door.

"No!" Noah's uncle cried hoarsely. "Don't let him escape!"

"It's too late," Noah hissed into his ear. "I won't let you hurt Laken. If that means Xander gets away too, then so be it."

As we ran past them, Xander tripped and fell to the floor, breaking away from me. I stopped and spun around to see that Noah's uncle had stuck his leg out. Xander moaned, lifting his shoulders off the floor. He gazed at me, pain raging deep within his blue eyes. "Get out of here, Laken. Leave me."

My vision blurred from the tears in my eyes. I glanced from him to Noah who continued struggling to restrain his uncle. Hesitating, I watched his uncle drop his shoulders, pulling Noah up over him and flipping him onto his back. The rope fell to the floor as Noah leaped to his feet and faced his uncle, staring at him. But his gaze quickly drifted to me. "What are you waiting for?" In his moment of distraction, his uncle whipped around and grabbed him from behind.

"Don't let her ruin our plans," Efren warned. He kept a strong hold on Noah with one arm while he reached down to grab the rope with the other. "Are you forgetting whose side you're on?"

"No," Noah stated. "I know exactly whose side I'm on. Jenna's, and now Laken's."

"I'll give you Jenna as soon as we're done with this," his uncle said as he jerked Noah's arms behind him and tied the rope around his wrists. "And Laken, well, I tried to let her go. You know I never planned to hurt her. But now, she's left me no choice." He pushed Noah toward me.

I started to run through the cabin, but he whipped past Noah and grabbed my upper arm, jerking me to a stop. He spun me around and, with one hand still holding the rope securing Noah's wrists, he pulled me back into the gasoline-soaked room. Then he shoved me, hard. I fell to the floor as the door slammed shut and the lock clicked.

"No!" I heard Noah cry, his voice muffled from the other side of the door. "You promised!"

"And you crossed me!" his uncle yelled. Their footsteps shuffled across the cabin and it sounded like the front door opened. Then silence fell over the cabin.

"Xander!" I rushed to him, kneeling as he slowly sat up. Tears rolled down my face and I lifted a hand to run my fingers along the side of his face, the dark stubble on his cheek prickling me.

"Ow," he moaned, trying to smile.

I shook my head slowly. "I'm sorry," was all I could think of to say.

"You have nothing to be sorry about." He started to smile again, but ended up cringing from pain.

"This is all my fault. I'm the reason he found you and your dad."

"You've got it all wrong. He did me a huge favor," Xander managed to say in a strained voice.

"How's that?"

"He led me to you." Xander gazed at me and, in spite of being trapped in a gasoline-soaked room that would be set on fire in the next few minutes, butterflies danced in my stomach. "Listen, I'm not sure if we're going to get out of here, so I have to tell you something." He paused with a long sigh before continuing. "You turned my world upside down. I know we had our differences and that I annoyed the hell out of you at times, but I'm in love with you."

My breath hitched and my jaw dropped. "What? How? When?" I stuttered in shock before composing myself. "But, we hardly know each other. We're not even dating."

"We're not?"

"Well, I...I don't know. I can't think about this right now. We have to try to get out of here!" I cried.

"Not until you know how I feel. If this is the end, I'm not about to go down keeping this all bottled up inside."

"You should have told me sooner," I said, shuddering from mixed emotions of fear and love, excitement and desperation. Never had I felt so alive before, and yet we were about to die.

"I wanted to, oh man, you have no idea how much I wanted to. You had me tied in knots ever since the first day of school."

"You had a funny way of showing it."

"Have you ever heard the saying, 'If you love something, set it free. If it comes back to you, it's yours. If it doesn't, it was never meant to be.'? Well, that's what I had to do. You chose Noah in the beginning, and I had to let that run its course."

"I guess I didn't give you much of a choice, did I?"

He smiled. "No, and you drove me out of my mind. Even with Marlena to distract me, you were all I could think about."

"Oh," was all I could muster. I wanted to tell him how I felt, that I thought I was in love with him, too, but I couldn't find the right words. "Let me try to untie these ropes." I leaned to the side, planning to move around him when he caught me with a kiss. I placed my hands on each side of his face. He tasted like sweat and blood, but I didn't care. His lips moved against mine, his kiss filled with passion, desire, and sorrow, as if it would be our last one.

"You haven't told me how you feel," he whispered when I broke away from him. "Am I just a rebound to you?"

I shook my head. "No," I said in a hushed voice. "You never were. But there will be time to talk about this later." Before he could say another word, I shuffled around to his back and reached for the ropes around his wrists. They had been secured tightly, and I worked frantically to untie the knot. "I think I heard your dad a few minutes ago. He's in the next room," I said as I pulled on the middle rope. The knot finally loosened and I threaded the rope through an opening. When it fell, Xander pulled his hands apart, bringing his arms in front of him and rubbing his chafed wrists.

He shifted around to face me. "We're getting out of here!" he declared before plucking a quick kiss on my lips. Then he stood and extended his hand down to me, pulling me to my feet. "When Noah's uncle comes back, I'll go after him and you run."

I nodded. "I'll see if I can find your dad."

"Only if there's time. If this place becomes an inferno, I want you to get out, run as fast as you can and not look back. Where's your phone?"

I patted the fleece-lined jean jacket, my heart sinking when I felt the empty pockets. "Noah has it."

"Well, if you can get it back from him and you have service, call your dad. Tell him to send a fire truck."

I nodded and hope swelled inside me. Maybe we had a chance to get out of here after all. But my optimism disappeared the moment the door rattled. Xander and I snapped our attention to it, watching as it opened and Noah's uncle returned. In a flash, Xander whipped his hands behind his back.

"I'm so sorry to keep you two waiting. Now where were we?" Efren flashed an evil smile, holding the matchbox out in front of him. "I hope you two said your goodbyes because it's the last chance you'll have." Without another word, he struck a match and the flame hissed. He glanced at us for a moment before dropping it. Then he disappeared again.

Fire erupted around the perimeter of the room, and flames shot up, licking the walls. Heat seared my face and smoke filled my lungs. Within seconds, the fire surrounded the room and a heavy realization hit me. We were trapped.

Chapter 13

"Laken, run!" Xander yelled from beside me. "I'm going to find my dad!"

"How? We're surrounded!" The flames were growing bigger as we stood in the center of the room. The scorching heat made me so hot, I was afraid I would pass out. Sweat began oozing from my pores, coating my arms and chest under my clothes.

He grabbed my arm, turning me around to face him. Even through the smoky haze, his blue eyes were as clear as the sky. "Just run through it. It's the only way!"

I nodded before shifting my attention to the narrow gap between the flames in the doorway. Mustering up my courage, I bolted across the room and shimmied through them, praying I wouldn't catch on fire. My breath sputtered as my lungs burned from the thick smoke. Air. I needed air.

Without looking back, I ran through the front of the cabin, dodging the flames as best as I could. I had almost reached the door when Noah's uncle stepped into my path, a gasoline container in his hand. "Not so fast," he sneered. He walked through the doorway, forcing me to back up. I glanced over my shoulder, stopping when I got too close to the fire. My back burned, the heat unyielding, but I focused on Noah's uncle instead of the flames about to devour me.

"Please," I begged, my voice a whisper. My only chance to escape hinged on his sense of compassion, if he had any.

"Nice try. Don't you want to go down with your boyfriend? You two will have an eternity together in death. Besides, unless you break the curse, you'll die soon anyway. Why not get it over with?"

I swallowed back tears, fighting to keep my resolve. I would stay strong until I took my last breath.

Before I could respond, Xander launched at him from the side. He toppled Noah's uncle, and the two of them flew toward a line of fire. I heard them struggling, the vision of them tumbling to the floor hidden by the thick smoke. My gaze swept around, locking on the gasoline container sitting in the doorway as flames swirled inches away from it.

Without a second to spare, I raced across the room, grabbed the container, and ran out the front door as it bumped against my leg. I felt it sway unevenly, the liquid inside rocking back and forth. Dashing across the front porch and down the steps, I sucked in a deep breath of fresh air. The sky had darkened, gray clouds skimmed the treetops, and the sun had dropped behind the mountain. I couldn't believe how late it was, but I chided myself for thinking about the time. Day or night, what did it matter when we were fighting for our lives?

As soon as I reached the driveway, I dropped the container and turned to look at the cabin. Flames skated across the open doorway and smoke drifted up to the sky. A feeling of dread consuming me, I was afraid to hope that Xander would win his battle with Noah's uncle. Efren was big and strong, and Xander was weak from being beat up. Desperate to know what was happening, I resisted the urge to run back into the inferno, sure that there was nothing I could do.

A low moan coming from the other side of the police

cruiser broke my thoughts away from the fire. I ran around the car to find Noah lying on the gravel, blood trickling from a cut on his jaw. I rushed over and knelt beside him. He looked bruised and beaten, but his wounds appeared superficial.

"Noah," I said, touching his shoulder.

He stirred slightly.

"My phone. Where's my phone?" I asked, a sense of urgency in my voice. But his eyes remained closed. Knowing that I couldn't wait for him to wake up, I slid my hands under his back and heaved him onto his side. Trembling, I found my phone in his back jeans pocket.

After easing him to the ground, I swiped my phone and it lit up immediately. Forgetting about Noah, I rose to my feet and watched as a notification appeared on the screen. Low battery. *No!* I thought as fresh tears formed in my eyes. I touched the OK icon, and the message disappeared. Then I frowned at the empty right-hand corner where the bars were missing. What difference did having a low battery make if I couldn't get a signal?

I walked around the police car, my gaze not leaving my phone as I paced back and forth, praying that I would find a signal. No one emerged from the cabin, making each second feel like an eternity. Flames danced in the doorway and the cloud of smoke above the roof had doubled in size. Panic lodged in my throat, I prayed that Xander and his father would get out alive. But as each moment passed, my hope faded.

When nothing happened on my phone, I hurried down the driveway. Finally, three bars lit up the corner of the screen. I stopped, my hands shaking as I dialed my father's cell phone. I pictured him in the family room, his eyes glued to the Patriots game on TV. He had no idea what was happening out here, and he was about to get a rude awakening.

The other end rang once before my father answered. "Laken. We were wondering when you might be home. I assume you have homework to finish for next week."

"Dad!" A lump formed in my throat and tears burst from my eyes. "Dad, I need your help!"

"Laken?" Alarm rang out in my father's voice. "Where are you? What's going on?"

"I'm at the abandoned cabin on Old Oak Road. It's been set on fire. We need an emergency crew out here now!"

"What? How? Why are you there?"

"It's a long story and there's no time to explain. You have to hurry! Xander and his dad are trapped inside. Please!" I cried urgently.

"How did this happen?"

"Dad! Please just get here and we'll explain later. Noah's here, too."

"He is? Put him on."

"I can't. He's unconscious. You better send an ambulance, too." I paused, noting silence on the other end. "Dad?" When he didn't respond, I pulled the phone away from my ear and swiped my finger over the screen, but it wouldn't light up. The battery had died. "Damn!" I swore. At least I'd had enough time to tell my father where we were and what was happening.

I shoved my phone into the back pocket of my jeans and ran toward the cabin, my shoes kicking up stones behind me. Skidding to a stop in front of the porch, I stared up at the blazing flames in the doorway. The heat blasted me in the face, but I ignored it. I couldn't stop worrying about Xander and his father. Without another thought, I raced up the steps and peered into the cabin, unable to see anything except the fire burning everything in its path. "Xander!" I called, although I doubted he would hear me over the hissing fire.

I started to walk into the cabin, but arms grabbed me from behind, dragging me backward. "Laken!" Noah gushed into my ear. "What are you doing? You're not going back in there!"

I struggled against his solid frame. "Let—me—go!" I cried.

But I was no match for his strength. His arms locked around me in a death grip, not budging.

Noah pulled me down the steps and across the driveway until I no longer felt the scorching heat. "Stay here," he ordered.

"But Xander and his dad are still in there," I protested, my voice frantic. The longer they stayed in the burning cabin, the more likely it was that they wouldn't get out alive.

Noah turned me in his arms, keeping a strong hold on me. "What happened?"

"Xander wanted to find his dad, but your uncle came back and they got into a fight. That's when I ran." I looked up at him through tear-filled eyes. "We have to do something! We can't let them die in there!"

"I'll go, but you stay here. It's too dangerous. Can I trust you this time?"

I nodded. "Yes! Just go! Hurry!"

Without another word, Noah released me. He raced across the gravel and up the front steps. After he disappeared into the burning cabin, I ran toward it until the heat blasted me in the face. Stopping, I gasped when two figures appeared in the doorway.

"Get out of here, Noah! You're no good to me dead!" Efren yelled, shoving Noah out the front door.

Noah stumbled before regaining his balance. A glistening sheen of sweat plastered across his forehead, he backed away from the doorway. He glanced at me, his eyes helpless, before turning his attention back to the burning cabin.

Suddenly, Xander emerged beyond the flames, running toward the doorway. My breath caught as I realized he was alive, but my moment of happiness was crushed when Noah's uncle grabbed him and shoved him back into the cabin. "You're not going anywhere!"

"Noah, do something!" I begged, wondering how much longer Xander could survive the smoke and fire.

Noah didn't have a chance to act. Dakota bolted past me, charging up the steps and launching at Efren. "Dakota, no!"

I screamed. Instinctively, I raced up the steps and watched in shock as Dakota leaped at Efren. Growling fiercely, Dakota bit into his neck, breaking it with a sharp snap as they fell to the floor.

Noah's face paled to a ghastly white. "No!" he yelled, running into the flames and dropping beside his uncle. "No! You can't die!" He shook his uncle, trying to revive him, but it was no use. He was dead.

Xander hauled himself to his feet, running through the doorway and directly into my arms. He gasped for air as he held me tight. I lifted my hand to his sweaty cheek, tears of joy and relief running down my face. Without a word, I kissed him, not caring about the dried blood, sweat and soot covering him.

When I pulled back, sweat ran down my face and along my arms, back and abdomen under my clothes. Dakota rushed through the cabin doorway, his tongue hanging from his mouth as he panted in the heat.

"Come on," I whispered to Xander. "We have to move. We're too close." With his arm draped over my shoulders and mine circling his waist, we hobbled down the stairs together. We managed to cross the driveway, the cold air offering relief from the intense heat. Dakota followed, stopping beside Xander as we watched the flames engulfing the cabin.

Xander took several deep breaths and then coughed a few times. I looked up at him, instantly thinking about his father. "Did you find him?" I asked quietly.

Xander nodded as a tear rolled down his cheek. "He's gone," he choked out. "It was too late." His chest heaved with a sob and he shuddered.

"Xander, I'm so sorry," I whispered. I hugged him, standing tall as he leaned into me. "My dad should be on the way with the fire department. They'll find him." My voice dropped off when I thought about what they would find. Caleb's burned, lifeless body.

After a few moments, Xander broke away from me. "I

need a minute alone," he whispered before heading toward the woods. Dakota raced after him, and their shadows disappeared into the forest. With a sad sigh, I turned as Noah emerged from the burning cabin, a distraught expression on his face.

His gaze focused on the ground, he descended the porch steps. Then he looked up, his eyes meeting mine when he walked across the driveway.

"It's over," I said as he stopped in front of me.

Shaking his head, he stared at me. "No, it's not even close to being over."

"What do you mean? Your uncle—he's dead. I saw it."

Noah gazed at me, his eyes glistening with tears. "I don't know where Jenna is. All I cared about was finding her. I tried so hard to go along with everything my uncle wanted just to get her back, and now it's hopeless."

"There has to be a way. We'll find her." I started to reach for his hand when Xander lunged at him from the side, pushing him to the ground.

"How could you do this?" Xander hissed as he landed on top of Noah. He slammed a fist into Noah's jaw, and the two of them rolled across the gravel, their arms flying at each other.

I ran after them, but kept a safe distance as they wrestled on the ground. "Stop it, you two! Please! Enough is enough!"

When they finally stopped, Xander emerged on top and pushed Noah's shoulders into the gravel. "I ought to send you to the grave with your uncle!" He lifted a hand, curling it into another fist.

I rushed over and touched Xander's back. "Hasn't there been enough bloodshed today? Xander, please, he was trying to protect his friend. Wouldn't you do the same thing if I had been taken?"

Xander sucked in a deep breath, relaxing slightly, his fist still clenched. His anger broke for a moment and I knelt beside him, staring into his eyes.

"Nothing you do now will bring your father back," I said softly. "And my dad will be here any minute. I don't think he's going to like it if you take your frustrations out on Noah. The last thing you need right now is to be hauled off to jail." He glared at me, the anger in his blue eyes crumbling to grief. "Please, for me."

"Fine," Xander gritted out. He pushed himself off to the side and dropped onto the gravel, exhausted.

Noah sat up, his chest heaving with deep breaths and his eyes worried. "Look, I'm really sorry about your dad," he said, watching Xander.

"Why should I believe you're sorry about any of this?" Xander muttered, staring blankly ahead.

"Because he was my father, too. Only I never had a chance to get to know him. My uncle made sure of that."

Xander glanced skeptically at Noah, narrowing his eyes. "You had plenty of time to come clean with all of this since you got here."

"I know it seems like that, but a lot of this was new to me. I was trying to figure things out when—" Noah paused, glancing at me. "—when I got to know Laken. I didn't want her involved in this. But then he took Jenna, and I had no choice but to do whatever he asked."

"Likely excuse," Xander said with a huff.

I frowned, the grief in Xander's voice pulling at my heart. But my attention was diverted away from him when sirens blared in the distance. We turned our attention to the driveway as red and blue lights flashed between the trees.

My father's police car led the entourage of two fire trucks and an ambulance racing up the driveway. They skidded to a stop beside Noah's police cruiser, the doors opening as I rose to my feet. My father shut off his car, the lights on top of it immediately becoming dark. He jumped out and ran around it to us, worry lurking deep in his eyes. "Laken!" he gushed, sweeping me into his arms, his green coat stiff.

When he broke away from me, he studied Xander and

Noah who still sat utterly exhausted on the gravel. He took a deep breath, taking note of their bruised, bloody and soot-covered faces. "I'm going to need to know what happened here," he said as he approached them and extended his hand to Noah. Noah reached up to grab it, letting my father haul him to his feet.

Then my father moved over to Xander, helping him up as four men in black fire-proof suits and hats with face masks dragged two thick hoses from the trucks to the cabin. The four of us backed out of their way and my father looked at Noah. "Is anyone inside?"

I glanced nervously at them, wondering how Noah would answer that. Xander looked especially distraught when Noah said, "Yes, sir. Two men, but they didn't make it."

"Oh, geez," my father gasped, wiping his hand across his forehead. "Who are they?"

"Caleb Payne," Noah answered soberly. "And another man. Both deceased."

My father glanced at Xander, sympathy and sadness brimming in his eyes. "I'm sorry, son."

Xander merely nodded. He seemed to be on the verge of breaking down, but he held on to his silent composure.

"Noah, stay with Xander and Laken. I need to help the crew." Without another word, my father approached one of the firemen holding the hose as water shot out of it. Pressure sent the white spray up into the air where it arched before raining down on the burning cabin.

The three of us moved toward the police car to get out of the crew's way as they struggled to hold the heavy hoses steady, dousing the flames. Xander stayed by my side, and I couldn't help feeling as though he was trying to keep Noah away from me.

As we lingered by the car, an EMT jumped out of the ambulance. "Noah, hey," the young auburn-haired man said, his expression worried. "I heard you guys need an ambulance."

"We're fine. Thanks, Billy."

"Anyone inside?" Billy asked.

"No one you'll need to treat," Noah explained. "But you're going to need some body bags."

The EMT shook his head and slapped Noah's shoulder. "Oh, shit! You mean there are people in there?" He paused, his jaw dropping before he continued. "Well, I'm going to see if the sheriff needs my help. I'm glad you're okay."

After Billy walked away, Xander glared at Noah. "I want to go home," he said. "You don't need me to stay now that the fire department is here. And I don't want to watch them drag my father out of there."

I reached over to Xander, placing my hand on his forearm and offering him a sympathetic smile. "I'm coming with you. You shouldn't be alone." His eyes met mine, his expression grateful.

"Okay," Noah said. "Let me tell the sheriff we're leaving, and I'll take you two home."

As Noah walked away, Xander and I stood in silence. I didn't know what to say and, even if I did, my attempt to speak would probably turn into gut-wrenching sobs.

Noah returned a few minutes later and gave us a nod. Without a word, Xander and I climbed into the backseat of Noah's police car.

We arrived at Xander's house about fifteen minutes later. After slipping out of the car, I followed Xander until Noah approached, causing Xander to stop dead in his tracks, his posture stiff and tense. "Where do you think you're going?" he demanded.

"I want to talk to both of you. I need your help," Noah said.

"What makes you think either one of us is going to help you after all the grief you caused us?" Xander hissed in an angry whisper.

I reached up to touch his upper arm. "Please hear him out," I said softly before turning back to Noah. "This is about your friend, isn't it?"

Noah nodded, taking a deep breath. "Yes. She's in trouble. She could die if we don't find her. Haven't we all seen enough death today?" Before he finished, leaves rustled in the woods behind him and Dakota emerged from the shadows. He trotted over to us, halting beside Xander and facing Noah.

I gazed up at Xander and shivered, not from the cold since I still wore Noah's jacket, but from the thought of another innocent victim struggling to survive. From all that Noah had told me, she'd simply been caught in the crossfire of his uncle's scheme. She was nothing more than a pawn just as Ryder had been. "Xander, we can't turn our backs on her. At least I can't, so if you don't want to be a part of this, I'll go with Noah from here."

"Fine." Xander approached Noah, stopping inches away from him and glaring at him. "But if you're lying about this or Laken gets hurt, I'll kill you. And I mean that." Without waiting for Noah's response, Xander marched away from him. He walked up the front steps, and Dakota followed him, leaving me alone with Noah.

I stared at Noah as he hung his head. With a sigh, I walked up to him and stopped about a foot away. The front door to the house opened and the lights turned on, but I kept my attention focused on Noah. "You're going to have to give him some time. He just lost his dad," I said softly.

Noah lifted his eyes to me, nodding slowly. "He's my brother and, aside from my mom, the only family I have."

"And now you're the only family he has. Imagine if you had just lost your mom."

"I know."

I offered him a weak smile. "Well, let's get inside. It's getting really cold, and we're not going to accomplish anything out here in the driveway." I led the way up the front steps and into the house. Noah trailed behind, shutting the door as soon as he stepped into the entry hall.

I headed into the family room, pulling my arms out of Noah's jacket and folding it over the back of the couch. The sound of glasses clanking in the kitchen lured me around the corner to where I stopped in the doorway. Xander stood at the island, the pendant lights suspended from the ceiling reflecting against the bottle of whiskey in his hand. With teary, bloodshot eyes, he poured the liquor into a cocktail glass. When it was half-full, he lifted it to his lips, swallowing a huge gulp as if he'd done it hundreds of times.

I suddenly realized there was still a lot I didn't know about him. I tilted my head, trying to calculate the age difference between him and Noah. "I presume you're not eighteen," I said.

He raised his eyebrows. "Good guess," was all he said before downing another gulp of whiskey.

"And high school? Really?"

He shrugged. "I needed to get to know you."

"Well, I guess it worked." I paused, not quite sure how to bring up Noah. "Noah's waiting for us," I finally said.

"So? Why should I care?" he asked, glaring at me.

"Because he's your brother, whether you like it or not."

"Fine. I don't like it." His cold stare sent shivers down my spine, but I ignored them as I walked around the island to him.

"He kept secrets from us, yes. I'm not going to try to defend him about that. He made his mistakes, and he's sorry. But you weren't up front with me, either. My point is, what's done is done. If anyone should be upset with anyone here, it's me. And if I can look past all of this, then so can you. He needs us right now."

"Like hell! My father is dead! Where was he when his uncle locked my dad in that cabin? He can't bring him back!" Xander shuddered as sobs wrenched through him. "Damn it!" In a swift movement, he threw his glass across the kitchen. It slammed against the wall beyond the table, shattering into pieces that crashed to the floor. "He's gone! And there isn't a damn thing any one of us can do to bring him back!"

I threw myself against him, wrapping my arms around

his trembling shoulders. "I'm sorry," I whispered, tears running down my face as I rubbed his back, trying to reassure him in his moment of grief. "You're going to get through this, I promise. I'm here for you. Just tell me what you want me to do, and I'll do it. I'm not going anywhere."

"He was my only family. I have no one else. And now, I just want revenge. I want to kill someone!"

"The man responsible for your dad is dead. Don't take this out on Noah. He's no more at fault than either one of us."

"I wish I could believe that." He backed away from me, and I heard Dakota's nails clicking on the kitchen floor.

I spun around to see Dakota heading straight for Xander. "Dakota! Out of here until we clean up the glass." He glanced at Xander and then at me before turning and trotting out of the kitchen.

Xander sighed, seeming calmer, and dropped his gaze to the broken glass littering the floor. "Sorry about that," he said quietly. "I guess I forgot about Dakota."

"It's okay. You had bigger things on your mind. But if he steps on even the tiniest piece of glass and cuts his paw, he'll get blood everywhere. I didn't think you'd want that."

"You're right. I guess I'll have to get used to living with a wolf."

I offered him a grateful smile. "I'll help you."

"Good. Because I want you here as much as possible." He smiled weakly before walking across the kitchen to a narrow door, opening it and pulling out a broom when Noah appeared from around the corner. The broom in his hand, Xander stopped as soon as he noticed Noah. "Look what the wolf dragged in," he muttered.

I frowned, realizing it could be a very long time before Xander accepted Noah.

"Everything okay in here?" Noah asked hesitantly, glancing at the broken glass.

"Are you kidding?" Xander shot back. "You're not seriously asking that. Everything is *not* okay." He stormed across the kitchen, glaring at Noah. Just when I thought Xander was about to strike at Noah again, he lowered the broom to the floor and began sweeping the broken glass into a pile.

Silence, other than the sound of glass clattering against glass, loomed in the kitchen. Finally, I glanced at Noah and offered him a faint smile when our eyes met. "We'll be right out. I know you're anxious to find your friend."

"Thanks," he said before casting his gaze across the room to settle on Xander. "But first, Xander, I have something for you. It belonged to your family for generations until my uncle stole it from your grandfather." Noah held up the leather-bound book his uncle had flashed in front of us before setting the cabin on fire. "Call it what you like, but I hope you'll accept this as a peace offering. We are brothers, and I never meant you or our father any harm." Noah walked across the kitchen, placing it on the island. "I managed to get it out of his coat before he knocked me out. It belongs to you."

Xander stopped sweeping long enough to glance at it. He nodded, but didn't say a word.

"Anyway," Noah said awkwardly. "I'll leave you two alone to finish up in here. I'll be in the living room when you're ready." He turned, heading toward the doorway and disappearing around the corner.

I glanced at the book, hoping that Xander would start to come around. I was sure that it meant something to him. If he couldn't get his father back, perhaps he would at least find comfort in the book that explained the secrets of his legacy.

Looking up from the book, I met Xander's sad blue eyes as he swept the shattered glass into a pile. "I know it's hard for you to think of anything else at a time like this, but Noah needs our help right now."

He nodded, tears glistening in his moist eyes as he leaned the broom against the wall. When he walked across the kitchen, I met him halfway, wrapping my arms around him again. He smelled like smoke, but so did I, and I didn't care. All I could think about was the loss of his father. The tears I had been holding back streamed down my face, soaking his shirt as I leaned my cheek against his shoulder. "Will you help?" I choked out.

After several moments of silence, he shuddered with a deep breath. Then he whispered, "I'll try. No one else needs to die in this mess."

Stepping away from him, I looked up to meet his gaze. "Thank you. I'll be in the living room. Join us when you're ready." Then I walked out of the kitchen, exhausted, but ready to take on the next crisis. I dreaded another rescue mission, but I prayed that we would find Noah's friend before it was too late.

Chapter 14

Noah was pacing in front of the fireplace when I wandered into the family room. The house felt cold without Caleb's warm smile and a bright crackling fire. Silence filled the air instead, sorrow and dread setting the mood. The windows were dark, a single lamp on the end table lighting up the corner while shadows lurked on the other side of the room.

I sank onto the couch with a big sigh as Dakota trotted over and sat beside me, resting his big black head on my knees. I ruffled my fingers through his fur, watching Noah.

"Do you have any idea where she is?" I asked softly.

He stopped, crossed his arms over his chest and shook his head. "No. I suspect my uncle is, or was, hiding her in the woods. There's no telling what he did with her. For all I know, he could have left her hanging from a cliff somewhere. That would be just like him."

I pictured a girl not much older than I was tied helplessly to a tree in the unforgiving mountain air, and shuddered for a moment. Then my thoughts were interrupted when I heard footsteps behind me. Dakota raised his head to look up over my shoulder, but I didn't need to see Xander to know that he had joined us.

"So we have no idea where to even begin. This ought to be fun," he commented.

I turned my head to look up at him, trying to ignore the amber drink in his hand. "Even if we don't, we have to try," I whispered, frustrated by his negativity. *Go easy on the poor guy,* a sympathetic voice rolled out in my head. *He just lost his father. He has a right to be negative. His whole world changed today. No matter how he handles this, he deserves some credit if he helps Noah, regardless of his attitude.* When my inner self finished lecturing, I tossed another glance over my shoulder, catching Xander's gaze for a moment. A weak smile slid across my face as a peace offering.

"Sorry, but I'm not sure I believe it," Xander said before directing his attention at Noah. "How do I know you don't want to send me out on a wild goose chase? Maybe you're hoping I'll fall off a cliff or freeze to death. Then you get the diamonds and Laken."

Noah glared at him before moving his gaze to me. "I never cared about the diamonds. From what I've seen, being rich doesn't always make people happy." He reached into his back pocket and pulled out a newspaper clipping. Unfolding it, he walked across the room and handed it to me.

I took it from him, noticing that the top margin read *Pittsburgh Post Gazette* on the left and October fourteenth of this year on the right. The next thing that caught my attention was a black and white photograph of a pretty girl with long brown hair, brown eyes, and a dazzling smile. The caption below her picture stated, *Senior class photograph of Jenna Kierosky, last seen October 12.* I quickly read the article, learning that she had last been seen at the restaurant where she worked as a waitress. She had closed up and left around midnight after declining another employee's offer to walk her out. Only she never made it to her car or home. When her parents reported her missing the next day, her car was found at the restaurant, but there was no sign of her.

Everything I read validated Noah's story, even down to the dates. The week she disappeared corresponded to when Noah had first seemed withdrawn. I turned, holding the newspaper up to Xander. "Here. Read this. Everything he told us is true."

Xander snatched it out of my hand, barely managing to keep it in one piece. I turned back to face Noah who now sat on the large chair near the fireplace, watching Xander. I heard Xander take a big swallow, and I hoped it would be the last. Getting drunk wouldn't help us find Noah's friend.

After a few moments, Xander took a deep breath. "So, you're telling the truth. That's great, but I still don't understand how you think the three of us can find her."

"Four of us," Noah stated, nodding his head at Dakota.

"I stand corrected. But there's only so much ground we can cover in one night," Xander said.

"We?" I asked. "We're not going out there tonight. Dakota will go alone. He'll be able to go much farther if he doesn't have to wait for us. If she's out there, he'll find her."

"Laken," Noah started to protest.

I shook my head. "I know what you're thinking, but it's not worth the risk. We have to let Dakota do this on his own."

"She could freeze. I'm really worried that my uncle left her exposed to the elements," Noah said before pulling his phone out of his pocket. He swiped the screen and began typing something as he stared at it. Then he frowned. "Damn! You've got to be kidding!"

"What?" Xander and I asked simultaneously.

"There's a snowstorm moving in tonight. When the hell did that happen?" Noah jumped to his feet and crossed the room to show me and Xander the radar map on his phone. A huge section of blue indicating snow loomed just to the west of town.

"Welcome to New Hampshire, boys," I said, not surprised. I was used to the changing weather patterns. My motto regarding the weather was to expect the unexpected.

Xander sucked in a deep breath. "We're definitely not going out in that. You're on your own."

"Let me see that." I snatched the phone out of Noah's hand and pulled up the forecast details. "Accumulations could reach six inches with more in the higher elevations," I read.

"Great," Noah groaned. "I don't know how I'm going to sit around here all night. I feel like I need to be out there looking for her."

"Well, you can't," I told him. "You won't help her by getting lost in a blizzard."

"She's right," Xander chimed in, seeming genuinely concerned for the first time. "I agree with Laken. We'll send Dakota out tonight. He can do this. You're just going to have to trust him."

"But, Laken, you went with him to find Ryder. What if you hadn't taken a chance that night?"

"I took a calculated risk. Ryder's backyard is just down the street from mine, and I knew he couldn't have gone too far. This is completely different. She could be anywhere in hundreds of square miles."

Noah shook his head. "I still think I should go with Dakota. I don't think I can wait here."

"Then go. We're not going to hold you back," Xander scoffed, earning him a disappointed glance from me.

Then I turned back to face Noah. "Please, just trust Dakota," I begged. "He can do so much more if he doesn't have to wait for you to catch up every few minutes."

"Fine," he relented. "But what's up with this weather? Does it always snow around here in November?"

"Actually, no. Early snowstorms are rare, although they do happen from time to time," I replied. "The good news is that it's early in the season and any snow we get should melt in a day or two. We usually don't get snow that lasts all winter until December." I handed the phone back to him before standing up and looking at Dakota. "Ready, boy?"

Dakota jumped up to his feet, shook his head and backed up between the sofa and coffee table, his tail wagging. Then he spun on his heels, running into the entry hall as I hung back with Xander and Noah. "Stay here. I'll be right back. And be nice." They glanced at each other like young boys who had just been scolded for fighting. I frowned. Convincing them to get along might be harder than I expected, but I would have to worry about that later. "I mean it. We have to work together." I started to walk away, but stopped when I reached the end of the couch and turned back to them. "Xander, can I borrow a coat? I didn't have one last night when—" I started to say when I was kidnapped, but I couldn't bring myself to say it out loud.

"Of course," he replied. "Take any one you want." A calculating look crossed over his blue eyes. "On second thought, why don't I come with you?" He approached me, stopping inches away.

With a deep breath, I gazed up at him. "No. I need to do this alone. Please." Even though he knew my secret, I still felt self-conscious talking to Dakota in front of him.

"I'm not sure I'm comfortable with you going outside alone."

I shook my head. "Why? There's nothing to worry about now. He's dead, remember?" I shot Xander one last imploring look before whipping around and rushing into the entry hall. Dakota paced as he waited, his nails tapping against the hardwood floor.

After grabbing a black jacket from the coat closet, I slipped into it. The sleeves extended a few inches below my wrists and the sides hung loosely around me, but it would do. With Dakota by my side, I escaped out the front door into the cold night. The clouds hung low, their rosy glow a sure sign that snow was on the way. On any other night, I would have welcomed the first snowstorm of the season, but tonight, the only thing that mattered was finding Noah's friend before we had another casualty on our hands.

Dakota ran ahead of me as I closed the door, bounding down the porch steps. I hurried after him, leaving the bright lights behind when I passed between Xander's truck and the garage. After we crossed the driveway, I stopped at the edge of the woods while Dakota ducked between two trees, disappearing into the shadows.

"Dakota!" I called. "Come back!" I waited for a moment, listening for him. As expected, he returned within seconds, his eyes locked on me. He halted and I kneeled down beside him. "You know what you need to do, don't you?"

He nodded swiftly, waiting for my cue to turn him loose.

"Good. I know I can trust you. But come back tomorrow even if you don't find her. You'll need to eat and get some rest."

Dakota huffed, as if annoyed. His attitude reminded me of Xander who also didn't seem to like it when I worried about him. I couldn't help wondering if the two of them were somehow related. Or was I just too overprotective?

"Okay. Go. Just be careful." I wasn't sure that he heard my last few words because he whirled around and took off before I finished. In seconds, his dark shadow vanished between the trees, leaving me alone.

Silence fell over the mountain as I stood at the edge of the driveway. As much as I wanted to run back into the house, I refused to give in. Dakota could use some help.

Hugging the coat around me, I trudged deeper into the forest. With every step I took, the dried up leaves crunched under my feet and my breath billowed out in front of me in a hazy glow.

A fluttering motion in a nearby tree caught my attention. I froze, my eyes meeting a pair of yellow ones belonging to an owl perched on a branch. Silently, I explained that a girl was lost in the mountains and Dakota had just set out to look for her. Then I asked the owl to keep an eye out for her. *'If you find her, please get the wolf's attention and lead him to her.'* As soon as I finished, the owl launched itself into the air, its wings outstretched, and flew off into the night.

I would have liked to have found more animals to help, but I was getting cold. Dakota and the owl would have to do for now. As I walked back to the house, snowflakes began to drift down from the sky, stopping me in my tracks and mesmerizing me. But when I heard the front door shut, my attention shifted to Noah who stood on the porch.

"Laken!" he yelled softly.

"I'm right here," I announced, approaching the house and hurrying up the steps. "What is it?"

He held up his phone. "Your dad called. He's worried about you and he wants you to come home."

I nodded, surprised that my father hadn't tracked me down sooner. "Is he still on the line?"

"No. But I'll call him back." Noah swiped the screen, touched it a few times and then handed the phone to me.

Taking it, I asked, "Can you wait for me inside?"

"Sure." Noah opened the door and slipped into the house, shutting the door behind him.

I listened to the ringing on the other end as I leaned against one of the porch posts.

"Hello? Noah? Laken?" my father answered, his voice heavy with worry.

"Dad, it's me. Noah said you called."

"Yes, I did. I've been trying to reach you for the last hour. Your phone must be dead because it keeps going directly to voice mail."

"It is," I admitted, feeling a little guilty that I hadn't tried to call him since arriving at Xander's house. "The battery died earlier and my charger's at home."

"Which is where you need to be."

"Dad, I'm really worried about Xander. His father was the only family he had." *Although now he has Noah,* I thought, wondering once again how long it would take them to get used to being brothers.

"How is he? Are you still with him?"

"Yes. Noah and I are at his house. He's taking it pretty hard. I can't leave him. He shouldn't be alone."

My father let out a loud sigh. I could tell he wasn't happy with my determination to stay with Xander, but I also knew he would eventually give in. "Okay. But it is a school night—"

"Dad, school, really? After what we went through today?"

"Yeah, you're probably not going to make it to school tomorrow. Okay, you can stay under two conditions. One, Noah stays up there with you two, and two, the three of you meet me at the station in the morning. I need Xander to ID his father. And I need statements from all of you."

My heart sank at the thought of Xander being forced to examine the charred remains of his father. "Dad, I don't understand. Why does Xander have to see his dad, or what's left of him?"

"I never met the guy and there's no ID on him. We already looked. In order for the coroner to make up a death certificate, we need a positive ID."

"I met him. Can I do it?"

"It's always better to get it from a close relative. Sorry, Laken. I know this is going to be hard on Xander, but he's going to have to get through it."

"Fine," I gritted out, gulping back the lump in my throat. "But I can't make any promises."

"If he doesn't come to the station, then we'll have to drag him down here. But I don't want to do that. So please tell him that he can either do it the easy way or the hard way."

I sighed, staring out at the driveway. The snow was falling harder now, and a white dusting covered the pavement. "Got it," I muttered. "We'll see you tomorrow."

I hung up the phone without waiting for him to answer. As I watched the snow, my thoughts returned to Noah's friend who could be anywhere in the mountains. I shivered, hoping she was warm where ever she was.

Shaking my head, I turned around to the door and re-treated into the house. After returning the jacket to the clos-et, I headed into the family room. Noah once again paced in front of the fireplace, practically wearing a path into the floor. Xander sat on the couch, a glass of amber liquid in his hand and the half-empty bottle of whiskey on the coffee ta-ble.

"I did what I could," I said quietly. "Now we wait." I scanned Xander's glass and bottle, my heart brimming with sorrow as I imagined what he must be going through to know his father was never coming back. "My dad expects all of us down at the station tomorrow morning. He needs our statements about what happened for his report." I delib-erately left out the part about Xander identifying his father.

They both nodded.

"Noah, thank you for letting me borrow your phone." I crossed the room and handed it to him. "Now if you'll ex-cuse me," I continued. "I'm exhausted and dirty. Xander, do you mind if I take a shower? My hair smells like smoke. And can I borrow a shirt to sleep in?"

Xander jumped to his feet. "Of course. You don't need to ask. In fact, I think I'll join you."

I raised my eyebrows, confused. "Excuse me?"

The glass and bottle forgotten on the coffee table, he ap-proached me, stopping inches away. "I didn't mean in the same shower. We have several bathrooms. I'll show you to the guest room."

"Thanks," I said, relieved. Then I shifted my attention to Noah. "Goodnight, Noah." Without another word, I headed up the stairs, my feet heavy from the long day.

"Goodnight, Laken," Noah said. "Xander, mind if I take the couch? I want to stay near the door in case Dakota comes back during the night."

"Suit yourself," I heard Xander say before his footsteps sounded behind me.

Once upstairs, Xander escorted me to the guest bedroom at the end of the hallway. A queen-sized bed with a burgundy comforter and piles of decorative pillows looked as if no one had ever slept in it. Attached to the room was a private bathroom with beige walls and wine-colored towels hanging from a rod across from the sink.

"I'll leave a shirt on the bed for you while you're in the shower, but the bathroom should have everything you need. Shampoo, conditioner, soap, razor, toothbrush, toothpaste. All still in the original packages. We keep the guest bathroom stocked for guests." Xander paused as sadness swept over his expression. "Actually, that was always my dad's doing. Now it'll be up to me, so it'll probably fall by the wayside."

Tears stung my eyes as I realized how many reminders of his father Xander would have to face in the coming days. I walked over to where he stood in the doorway, gently touching his hand. "It's perfect. Your father was a very thoughtful man. Thank you."

Without a word, Xander nodded before turning to leave. Then I shut the door behind him and, in the heavy silence, escaped into the bathroom for a hot shower.

こうこう

Twenty minutes later, I emerged from the bathroom wrapped in a towel, my wet hair dripping on my bare shoulders. I approached the bed to find a white button-down shirt folded neatly on the comforter. Too bad I didn't have any clean underwear, but I wasn't about to ask Xander if one of the dresser drawers was stocked with panties for overnight guests. I would just have to make do.

As I bent down to pick up the shirt, the bedroom door opened and I snapped up to see Xander standing in the doorway. His damp hair fell unevenly across his forehead. The dirt and soot had been washed off his face, the faint bruise below one eye all that was left from the fight for his life. He wore gray sweat pants with a dark green shirt hanging open, and I couldn't help noticing his tanned muscular chest exposed in the middle. I scolded myself for admiring him when the only thing I should be thinking about was the loss of his father. The despair lurking in Xander's eyes pulled at my heart, and I felt the threat of tears starting to fill my eyes.

"Xander!" I gasped. "Could I get a little privacy?" I folded my arms over my breasts, holding the top of the towel in place.

He stepped into the room, leaving the door wide open. "What if I say no?"

I took a deep breath, my eyes locked with his. "You wouldn't do that," I whispered.

He closed the distance between us, only stopping when he was close enough to bend down and kiss my neck. Mind-numbing shivers raced through me and I was suddenly very aware that I wore nothing under the towel. I sucked in a deep breath, holding it and wondering what to do.

"Xander, I'm really sorry about your dad," I said quietly, trying not to be distracted by his kisses.

He lifted his head, his eyes full of pain and grief. "I don't want to talk about it."

"You can't run away from it."

"Sure I can. And I know exactly how." He leaned down, trailing his lips along my neck again. "Mmmm," he murmured sleepily in between kisses. "You smell really good."

Not sure what to say, I leaned toward him. "So do you," I said awkwardly. When I raised my head away from him, I saw him staring at me. "What?"

"Do you really need to ask?"

I swallowed nervously, trying to guess what he meant. Only one thing came to mind between my half-nakedness and the bed beside us. "Xander, no," I protested. "We can't. Not now, not like this. You're grieving, and you've been drinking."

"I can handle my alcohol. I'm not the teenager you thought I was. I assure you I am not drunk right now."

I backed up a step, my heart racing. "Look, it's not that I don't want to, but…"

Xander stepped toward me, snaking his arm around my waist and jerking me up against him. "But what?"

"But—I—" I started to explain that I had never done this before, that I was a virgin, but he didn't give me the chance.

He lowered his mouth to mine, claiming my lips in a kiss that sent fire shooting through me. At first, he was urgent and impatient, and he tasted sour from the whiskey. But after a moment, he softened his kiss, gently flicking my tongue with his. My senses whirled out of control, and I moved my arms up around his shoulders, pulling him closer to me. He flinched when I touched his left one, a sign that he was still sore from his fight with Noah's uncle. "Sorry," I muttered into his kiss, sliding my hand down his back.

That was the last word I said before I lost myself in his kiss. I forgot that all I wore was a towel because I wanted this. I wanted him now more than ever before. We had almost been killed today, and I wasn't ready to die. If the curse on my bloodline was real and giving in to Xander was the only way to break it, then maybe it was time to let go of my inhibitions.

I slid a hand up his neck and sifted my fingers through his hair, responding to his kiss with a renewed sense of urgency. He felt warm and strong, his chest hard and solid. Then I pulled my hand over his shoulder and moved it down his chest. As I touched his smooth skin, he shuddered, pulling me closer.

"Laken," he murmured, breaking his mouth away from mine. "Do you have any idea what you're doing to me?"

I gazed up at him, slipping my fingers under his waistband and daring myself to keep going. But I couldn't. This was all wrong. I hadn't thought this through, and I knew I would regret it in the morning. My first time had to be special, not overshadowed by the tragic death of his father.

"I'm sorry," I said, whipping my arms away from him and hanging them by my side. "I can't do this."

"Yes, you can," he insisted.

I shook my head and looked away. "It's not the right time. Please," I begged, before shifting my gaze back to him and meeting his smoldering eyes. "Noah is downstairs. We can't, not with him in the house."

Xander laughed. "Is that all? No problem. He's history. I'll get rid of him right now, brother or not."

"It's not just him, it's everything. This whole day. You almost died, and I know it's killing you that your dad is gone. I don't want our first time to be an escape from all these horrible things. It should be about us."

A faint smile formed on Xander's face. "Are you saying you've thought about our first time?"

"Maybe," I shot out, hoping he couldn't tell how nervous I was.

The truth was, yes, I had thought about it. But I figured it was months away, if not longer. If my mother had died in her twenties, then I still had several years before I needed to break the curse.

"That's a yes," Xander said confidently, pulling me against him again. "I can shut the door, you know. I think he's finishing off the bottle of whiskey I started, so we should be safe."

I scoffed, not surprised that Xander wasn't giving up. "That's just one little thing. There is so much else to consider here."

"This isn't business, Laken. This is about us. Forget about everything that happened today. Just focus on how you feel about me. What do you want right here, right now?" He stared down at me as he held me against him with one arm. Then he ducked down, reaching his other hand behind me to touch the back of my thigh. I sucked in a sharp breath as he ran it up my leg until he reached the curve of my butt.

I gasped when his hand moved higher, rubbing me under the towel. "Xander, what are you—"

He cut me off with another kiss, and my eyes fell shut as

I gave in to my desire. I parted my lips, meeting his tongue in a moment that sent my world spinning all around me. Or was it his hand massaging me in a place no boy had ever touched? *Boy?* Xander was clearly no boy. That thought sent a wave of fear rushing over me. I wasn't ready for this.

To my relief, he pulled his hand out from under my towel. Then he grabbed my waist with both hands and twirled me around toward the bed. Setting me down, he pushed me onto my back. Our kiss continued, the intensity building as he ravaged my mouth, touching, tasting, exploring. He pushed his legs between mine, sending a fiery heat through my veins as he lowered his weight on top of me.

Lifting his lips from mine, he hovered above me so close that I felt his breath against my mouth. I opened my eyes to see a storm brewing in his. His breath, hot and heavy, whisked across my mouth. As I stared at him, my heart pounding with anticipation, he slid down, trailing kisses along my neck and then even lower. He touched my knee, running his hand up the inside of my thigh. My breath hitched, and I clutched his neck, threading my fingers through his hair. His hand, warm, soft and strong, continued up my thigh until—

He slowly skimmed his fingers around to the top of my leg until he reached my hip. Then he folded the bottom of the towel up. A draft of cool air whispered across my stomach. I trembled, barely catching my breath as he caressed my abdomen.

"Xander," I murmured, my senses on fire from his touch.

Without a word, he repositioned the towel to cover the top of my legs again. Then he moved up, his mouth lingering over mine as he watched me. "Are you afraid?" he asked.

"No," I answered a little too quickly before changing my mind. "I mean, yes."

"Don't be," he whispered. He leaned down, and I closed my eyes, waiting for his kiss. Instead of pressing his lips to mine, his tongue tickled my bottom lip. I sucked in a quick breath as he licked my lips, first the bottom one and then the top one. When he stopped, I opened my eyes halfway to see him staring at me again. "I want to touch you where no one has ever touched you before. I want to make you feel more alive than you've ever felt."

"You already have," I muttered as he bent down, trailing kisses along my neck.

His hand slid across the top of the towel over my breasts, stopping at the center and flipping the corner out from where it had been tucked under the edge. The towel loosened, and I shook with desire—and fear.

Xander shifted up to kiss my mouth again, and I trembled. I couldn't believe this was happening. Would it hurt? How would I feel in the morning? What if Dakota came home early and Noah came upstairs to tell us only to find us in bed together?

I couldn't do this! Not tonight! Panic shot through me, and I pushed Xander away as hard as I could. He lifted his lips away from mine, and somehow I managed to roll him off of me. "Xander. I'm sorry. I can't do this tonight. It's just not right. I'm sorry. I'm so sorry," I said, staring up at the ceiling because I didn't want to see his reaction.

When a hush fell over the room, I turned to my side and propped myself up on one elbow. "Xander?" My mouth dropped open as I looked at him. He must have had more to drink than he thought because he had just passed out.

"Thank you," I mouthed. Under any other circumstances, I would have been upset, but tonight, I only felt relief.

With a sigh, I sat up and tugged the towel down over my butt as if he could see me. Then I reached for the white shirt at the foot of the bed and slid it over my head. After hanging the towel in the bathroom, I turned off the lights and went back to the bed. I left Xander where he was and slipped under the covers on the other side, hoping to get some much needed sleep.

Chapter 15

"L aken. Wake up," Xander said, jostling my shoulder until I opened my eyes. "Noah's gone."

"What?" I asked, squinting and rubbing my aching forehead as I sat up. I vividly remembered the night before and felt a blush race across my cheeks. Trying to distract myself, I scanned the room lit only by the sunlight streaming in through the window.

I yawned, glancing outside to see snow-covered tree branches stretching up to the blue sky. Then I returned my gaze to Xander who stood beside the bed in blue jeans and a gray shirt, his alert expression showing no trace of his drinking the night before.

"His car is still here, but he's gone. It looks like Dakota came home and they went back out together."

I shook my head, frustrated. "Why wouldn't he wake us up? He never should have gone out there on his own. What was he thinking?"

"I'm not sure. Their footprints look fresh, so I don't think they've been gone too long. They must have left after it stopped snowing. We should be able to follow their tracks, but we need to leave as soon as we can. How'd you sleep?"

"Awful," I admitted without explaining that I had tossed and turned for most of the night as my thoughts flip-flopped from visions of the burning cabin to my memory of kissing Xander while I was practically naked. Not to mention the tears that welled up in my eyes every time Caleb flashed through my mind, but now wasn't the time to bring that up, either. "What time is it?"

"Eight o'clock. Think you can be ready to go in five minutes?"

"Yes. But we have another problem."

"What's that?"

"My father. He's expecting us at the station this morning, remember?" I searched Xander's blank face for a sign of recognition, but he stared at me, not seeming to remember what I'd told him last night. I frowned, wondering if he also didn't remember kissing me.

"Damn. I'm going to guess that if we head out after Noah, your dad's going to wonder where we are."

I nodded in agreement. "So what do we do?"

Xander sighed, his eyes shifting. When his gaze settled back on me, he sat down on the bed. "I think we need to tell your dad what's going on. I mean, now his deputy has disappeared. Maybe he can help."

"You really think we should tell him?" I asked skeptically.

"Yes, I do. So get up and get dressed. I'll make some coffee. Meet me downstairs in five." He patted my thigh still buried under the covers before standing and heading for the door.

I watched his back with a bit of disappointment. Shouldn't one of us say something about last night? Then again, he wouldn't say anything if he didn't remember it.

Sitting up, I twisted my legs around, dangling them out from under the comforter as Xander stopped and turned. He eyed my feet and calves before raising his eyes to meet mine. Then he shot me a teasing grin. "And Laken, when this is all over, we'll have to pick up where we left off last night."

The hot blush returned to my face as I remembered his hands all over me. My heart fluttered with mixed emotions when he shut the door, leaving me alone.

Shaking my head, I pushed thoughts of last night out of my mind. We had far more important things to deal with today, and I didn't need reminders of his kiss and his touch distracting me. But at least he remembered, and that made my heart glow. I wanted every kiss, every touch to matter to him, even in times of mourning.

I took a deep breath, ready to face the day. Without another thought about last night, I walked across the room to gather my clothes from the top of the dresser.

Fifteen minutes later, my hair was brushed, my teeth were clean, and I was dressed. Wearing my black shirt and jeans still smudged with ashes and soot from yesterday, I wandered downstairs to meet Xander in the kitchen. The nutty aroma of coffee creamer lofted through the house, and bright light filled every room from the sun's reflection off the snow covering the mountains beyond the windows. I almost needed sunglasses just to walk through the house.

"That smells good," I commented as I entered the kitchen.

Xander didn't say a word. Instead, he sniffed and turned away the moment I noticed moisture in his eyes. Sympathy settling over me, I realized that every day would be a struggle for him for a while. Approaching him from behind, I touched his shoulder. "Hey," I said softly. "Are you okay?"

Xander sucked in a deep breath, shuddering as he exhaled. "I'm sorry," he said as he turned, wiping the tears from his cheeks. "My dad was always an early riser. By the time I usually get up, he already has the coffee going. It was really weird to start it myself this morning." His voice cracked as if he would break down in tears again, but he swallowed them back.

"You don't have to be sorry. You're going to have moments like this for a long time. I'm here for you, okay? I want to help in any way I can."

He nodded and just when I thought he would pull me into his arms, he backed up a step, wrinkling his nose. "Ew. Your clothes reek!"

"Gee, thanks," I said sarcastically. "There isn't much I can do about that."

"Maybe you should keep some clothes over here. You know, just in case."

"In case what? That we're trapped in a burning cabin again?"

Xander shrugged. "I don't know. What if you come over to visit Dakota and get snowed in?"

"I'm pretty good at keeping an eye on the weather. You have to be when you live around here."

He frowned. "Well, you're no fun." A smile returned to his face as he sighed. "I probably could have washed those for you last night had I thought of it."

"I think you were too busy passing out from the whiskey or whatever it was you were drinking."

He narrowed his eyes thoughtfully. "Yeah. About that. You should know that the next time I kiss you when all you're wearing is a towel, I'm not going to pass out. I can't believe I let that happen!"

I smiled, my pulse quickening when our eyes met. "Is that a promise?" As soon as I spoke, I bit my tongue. I didn't need to ask for something I wasn't sure I was ready for.

"If you want it to be," he replied. Then he looked away from me and reached for his phone on the granite counter. "Here. Call your dad. We're wasting time. I'll pour you a cup of coffee."

I nodded as I took the phone from him, thankful for the distraction. After dialing my father's number, I held it up to my ear and walked over to the windows, staring out at the winter scene. Nearly a foot of snow blanketed the land, hiding the leaves and fallen branches on the ground. All that could be seen were waves of sparkling white under the blue sky.

"Hello?" my father answered, breaking me out of my trance.

"Hi, Dad, it's me. I'm using Xander's phone."

"Oh, that explains the odd number. He must still have his California number. Everything okay? You three are still meeting me at the station this morning, aren't you?"

"That's kind of why I'm calling. There's a little problem."

"Laken, I don't think I can handle any more problems after yesterday."

"Noah's gone," I blurted out, offering no explanation.

"Gone? What do you mean?"

"I mean we woke up and he's not here." I turned around to see Xander pushing a mug of coffee across the island. He held up a bottle of hazelnut creamer with his eyebrows raised. When I nodded, he put it next to my cup. "He couldn't have gone very far because he left on foot. His car's still here."

"On foot? What's this all about? You're scaring me now."

"It's kind of a long story, but to make it short, the guy who set the cabin on fire yesterday kidnapped a friend of Noah's. Noah doesn't know where she is, but he thinks she's somewhere in the mountains. He's worried that she doesn't have any protection from the cold."

"So he's traipsing through a foot of snow in the back country? Is he nuts?"

"Not completely. We think he's with Dakota. We're going to head out in a few minutes and follow their tracks." I reached for the creamer and poured a dash into my coffee, wondering what my father must be thinking.

"I have a better idea. None of you will get very far on foot, especially in snow this deep. Red McArver has been dying to fire up his sleds since they started talking about an early snowstorm. He's got three of them, and I happen to know that they're gassed up and ready to go."

I sipped my coffee, knowing that by sleds, my father was talking about snowmobiles. They were a popular mode of transportation in the winter around here. "Dad, that's great. Do you think he can bring them up here?"

"I'll call and ask him. He owes me a favor."

"Okay. It might be the only chance we have to catch up with them." I paused when another thought crept into my mind, spoiling my hope that the snowmobiles would help us today. "Wait a minute. I don't know if that's such a good idea. What about Dakota?"

Silence hung on the other end for a moment before my father took a deep breath. "Hmmm, that does present a problem. But we're talking about Red McArver who spends more time on the mountain than with people. If there's any-one I think we can trust when it comes to Dakota, it's him. He's never been a fan of the mayor, and the last thing I would expect him to do is tell a soul. But ultimately, it's your decision."

I hesitated, an image of the girl in the newspaper photo-graph shivering out in the cold all night flashing through my thoughts. From the little I knew about Red, his property was secluded far away from town. He rarely ventured down from the mountains, seeming to prefer his privacy. My fa-ther would be taking a big risk if he let someone know that Dakota had survived. If the mayor found out, not only would another bounty be put on Dakota, but my father would also lose his job.

It didn't take me long to make up my mind. If my father trusted Red, then I could, too. "Okay. I don't want to see anyone else get hurt, so if you think we can trust him, then I'm in."

"I do. Now I'd better hurry because he might already be out on the trails. I'll see if he can haul them up to Xander's place."

"You know where it is, right?" I set my coffee down on

the counter, meeting Xander's curious stare from across the island. I smiled, nodding at him.

"Yes. Give me a half hour or so."

"Thanks, Dad."

"Don't thank me yet. It sounds like you know a lot more than you're telling me. You and Noah have some explaining to do once this is all over." He hung up before I had a chance to protest. The problem was, he was right. We owed him an explanation, and he wouldn't give up until we told him the whole story. As long as I could avoid explaining my ability to communicate with animals, Caleb's gift for making jewelry, and the curses that sounded more like a fairy tale than something real, I would tell him anything he wanted to know.

I placed the phone on the countertop and took another sip of coffee, trying to ignore Xander's curious expression.

"You're killing me over there," he said. "What's happening? Your dad's coming here? We're going to lose time if we wait for him."

I shook my head with a sly grin. "No, that's where you're wrong. What he's bringing with him will get us to Noah and Dakota much faster than if we leave now on foot. It'll be worth the wait, trust me."

"He's not bringing snowshoes, is he?" Xander groaned.

"Nope. Snowmobiles."

Xander's jaw gaped open. "You're kidding. Snowmobiles?"

"That's what I said. Ever ride one before?"

"No. I've ridden just about everything else, though. Jet skis, four wheelers, skateboards, surfboards, snowboards." He paused, sipping his coffee and quirking his eyebrows in thought. "Wait a minute. Are they yours?"

I nearly choked. "With what my parents make as a cop and a school teacher? Are you kidding? No. My dad knows just about everyone in town. One of his friends has three. So he's going to ask him to bring them up here. Speaking of which, you'll need to open the gate soon."

"Yeah, sure. No problem." His face lit up. "Wow. Snowmobiles." Then suddenly, his smile collapsed.

"What's wrong?" I asked.

"My dad would have loved to ride a snowmobile."

"Really?" I asked. "He never seemed to be into anything other than his work."

"You didn't know him fifteen years ago. He used to surf and ski all the time. It's only been in the last few years that he became more obsessed with his work." Xander's eyes clouded over with tears, and my heart ached from the pain I saw in them.

I was trying to think of the best way to comfort him when he took one last gulp of coffee and set the mug down. "Well, I'd better go open the gate. Wait here. I'll be back in a few minutes."

I nodded as he left the kitchen. I heard the closet door open and shut, and then the front door followed suit. Silence filled the house, and I tapped my fingers against the granite. There was nothing like the quiet that lingered after a snowstorm, but today, instead of being at peace, I felt anxious and worried.

I quickly finished my coffee. As soon as I set the empty mug down, I hurried out of the kitchen, ignoring my grumbling stomach. I couldn't wait another moment for Xander even though he'd only been gone a few minutes. I laced up my hiking boots and found a winter jacket in the closet. Black, heavy and a little too big with the sleeves reaching to my knuckles, it would have to do. Then I found a pair of ski gloves on the closet shelf, slid them on, and rushed outside.

Over a foot of powder blanketed the driveway, Xander's truck, and Noah's police car. Random snowflakes caught the sunlight, sparkling like diamonds. With hardly a glance at the wintry landscape, I shuffled down the front steps as best as I could in the deep snow that spilled into my boots. I ignored the cold around my ankles and stopped where two sets of footprints led in separate directions. One went down the driveway, the other trailed to the side.

I followed the tracks leading to the woods until the trail cut through the trees beside a set of paw prints. Dakota. I stopped, staring into the woods and wondering how far they'd gone, when a dark spot on the snow caught my eye.

I stooped down, narrowing my eyes as I realized it wasn't one dark spot, but a line of spots following the paw prints. "What is that?" I whispered, furrowing my eyebrows.

The drops were red, the color of dried blood. I scanned the blood as far as I could see, my nerves frazzled once again. Dakota might be hurt, but I knew that wouldn't stop him from helping someone in trouble.

I stood up, trying to keep my composure. When would this nightmare end? I couldn't handle any more blood. Even though it was only a few drops, I couldn't shake the feeling that something was very wrong.

"Why didn't you wait for me inside?" Xander asked suddenly from behind me.

I spun around to face him, surprised since I hadn't heard his quiet footsteps in the snow. "You scared me," I said. "Did you open the gate?"

"Yeah, it's open," Xander replied slowly, his blue eyes nearly translucent in the bright sunlight and his black hair seeming even darker against the snowy background. "Why do you look like you've just seen a ghost?"

"I came out to see what direction Noah went. The trail starts here." I pointed to the footsteps, although I suspected Xander had already noticed them. "But there's blood in the snow next to Dakota's tracks."

Xander glanced at me before stooping down to get a closer look. He sighed deeply, and I could tell he didn't like the looks of it any more than I did. After a few moments, he stood and turned to me. "I'm sure he's fine. It's not that much blood. Maybe he cut himself on a rock or a branch. It's probably nothing."

I raised my eyebrows. "I know Dakota. The only time he ever came home bleeding was when that other wolf bit him.

He knows how to handle himself in the woods and he doesn't get hurt from rocks or branches."

"What are you saying?"

I stared at him, trying to figure out how to put my fears into words, when a low, powerful engine rumbled up the driveway. Xander and I turned at exactly the same moment to see a red pick-up chugging through the snow. Three snowmobiles had been secured to a flatbed trailer behind the truck. It plowed past us, the tires spinning up clouds of snow in their wake, until it stopped behind Xander's pick-up and Noah's police car.

After the engine shut off, a burly red-haired man with a matching beard and mustache hopped down from the driver's seat. He wore a heavy black snow suit and carried thick gloves in his hands.

Xander and I trudged through the snow to greet him. The door on the other side shut, and my father appeared from around the truck, a look of concern mixed with relief on his face.

"Hi, Dad," I said, searching his expression for clues of what he might be thinking.

He nodded. "Red, I'd like you to meet my daughter, Laken."

The man turned to gaze at me with soft brown eyes. Recognition swept across his face as his jaw dropped. "Well, I'll be," he muttered in amazement. "It's like I just went back in time about twenty years, Tom. She's the spitting image of Ivy."

I tossed a curious glance at my father. In all my eighteen years in Lincoln, no one had ever made that connection. And it was a good thing, too, since I had only recently learned that Ivy was my birth mother.

"Laken, this is Red McArver. We went to high school together. He knew Ivy," my father explained.

"Knew her? I had a crush on her. But she only had eyes for you." Red shifted his attention back to me. "I used to help Ivy with some of her orphaned friends." When I gave him a quizzical look, he continued. "Bears, moose, even a few owls. I enjoyed helping the animals. People were always too complicated for me. That's probably why I live alone."

"And that's why you need me to drag you out every once in a while," my father added.

"Well, it's nice to meet you, Mr. McArver," I said, stepping close enough to him to shake his hand.

"It's very nice to meet you, Laken. Your father told me a lot about you on the ride up here."

"Dad, did you tell him everything?"

My father glanced at me, his expression confident. "Yes. Even about Dakota."

When I flashed an anxious look at Red, he smiled. "I'm glad your dad told me. The only one I wanted shot down when the town held that ridiculous hunt a few weeks ago was the mayor. That wolf didn't hurt anyone, and I have a feeling any threats he made to the other girls were well deserved. Your secret is safe with me. I love the animals in these mountains, even the ones transplanted from far away."

His words comforted me a great deal, but before I had a chance to respond, I noticed Xander staring at the snowmobiles like a kid looking at his first bicycle.

Red lumbered over to the back of his trailer. "Enough small talk," he said. "Let's get these sleds fired up and move out."

Xander followed him, his eyes open wide. I walked beside him, nudging him with my elbow and grinning at him. "I think you have a little drool on your chin," I teased.

"Shut up," he quipped good-naturedly, but closed his mouth when we reached the trailer. "Hi, Mr. McArver. I'm Xander." He extended a hand out to Red as he approached him.

"Nice to meet you, son. Mind giving me a hand?" Red dropped the back gate of the trailer with a thud and hopped up onto the platform.

"No problem. Just tell me what you need me to do."

Red turned on one of the snowmobiles and started showing Xander how to maneuver it down the ramp. I went to
my father's side where he lingered in front of the truck,
scanning the surrounding forest. "If you're looking for their
tracks, they're over here," I told him, leading him to the
trail. The rumbling engines faded in the background the
closer we got to the woods. "They went that way. See?" I
pointed to the footprints.

My father stooped down, examining the tracks. He
traced his fingers over the drops of blood, a frown on his
face.

"I noticed that a few minutes ago," I said, lowering myself beside him. "It must be from Dakota."

"Well, it's not much. It's probably just a scratch. But we
should get moving. I don't like any of this." He turned toward me. "How long have you known about this?"

"Only since this morning, Dad. Noah was on the couch
when I went to bed."

"I don't mean about Noah. I mean his friend," my father
clarified.

Feeling guilty, I averted my eyes away from his stare.
"He told me about her this weekend."

"You should have told me, Laken. If someone's in trouble around here, it's my job to help them. I don't need you
kids trying to play hero. You'll only get hurt. Is that what
yesterday was all about?"

"Dad, I know how to handle myself out here."

"You might know what to do with a wolf or even a black
bear, but what about the fire yesterday? I could have lost
you."

"I'm know," I said. "I would have called you, but that
man took my phone."

"I'm getting the feeling that there's more to this than
you're telling me. But we don't have time to talk right
now." He shot me a warning look that meant I'd better be
ready to explain everything later.

Another snowmobile engine fired up behind us, sputter-

ing at first and then revving up as the motor ran for a minute. My father and I rose to our feet and wandered over to
where it sat in the driveway. The single front headlight
glared in the sunshine, the skis on each side of the front end
jutting out over the snow.

Xander stood beside it, his face lit up with excitement as
he revved the motor. "I have to get one of these!" he declared.

Red pulled the second one up behind him. "Laken, I
need your help." He motioned with his hand for me to join
him.

As I approached, he held the handlebar lever, squeezing
it every time the engine sputtered. Blue smoke rose up
around the snowmobile, dissipating in the air.

Red started to show me how to keep the engine running,
but I stopped him. "It's okay. I know what to do," I told
him. I hadn't ridden much, but I knew how snowmobiles
worked. I massaged the lever, easing up on it until the engine sounded like it would die out and then squeezing it.

Once all three snowmobiles were unloaded and warmed
up, Red shut off the engines so that we could talk. "Where
are we headed, Tom?" he asked as we gathered beside the
snowmobiles.

"That way," my father said, pointing in the direction of
the footprints leading into the woods.

"Let me take a look." Red headed over to the woods, inspecting the tracks. My father followed, leaving Xander and
I behind.

"You look way too excited about this," I commented.

"I can't believe I'm about to take a snowmobile out on a
rescue mission. This is way too cool. Are you riding with
me?"

"I don't know. That's for Red to decide. Maybe only
three of us can go. If that's the case, you might need to stay
here. After all, these are made for one rider."

"Spoilsport." He glanced away as my father and Red
headed toward us. "Leaving me here while the three of you

head out would be just plain cruel. You should ride with me. These seats look a little too small for you to ride with one of them."

I silently agreed, but Red would make the final call since the snowmobiles belonged to him.

"Okay," Red said when he and my father stopped beside us. "I only brought three helmets. Who's staying here?"

I glanced at Xander, assuming it would be him, but he shook his head. "I've got a motorcycle helmet. Will that work?" he asked, not about to let us leave him behind.

"As long as it has a face shield," Red answered.

"It does," Xander said. "I'll be right back."

As Xander ran back to the house, Red pulled three black helmets out of the back seat of his truck and gave one to my father and one to me. By the time the three of us buckled our chinstraps, Xander rushed out of his house with his motorcycle helmet. He slipped it on as he hurried through the snow like a little boy who didn't want the big boys to leave without him.

Red clamped a hand on Xander's shoulder. "You ready, son?" he asked, his voice echoing from behind his face shield.

"Absolutely."

"You and Laken take this one," Red said, pointing to the middle snowmobile. "I'll take the lead, and Tom, you take the end. You two stay between us. Ever ride one of these before?" he asked Xander.

"No, sir."

"But you've got a motorcycle I take it, so this should be a piece of cake for you. Your accelerator is here on the right." Red pointed to the handlebar lever. "Your brake is on the left one. And this—" He flipped a switch to the inside of the right handlebar. "—is your hand warmer."

"Hand warmer?" Xander repeated in awe. "Do we get butt warmers, too?"

"No, son. Pay attention." I couldn't help smiling as Red continued with his instructions. "Now here is the lock." He pointed to a red lever holding the brake in place on the left handlebar. "All you do is release this, let off the brake, and squeeze the right lever to go. The skis will turn easily on ice and snow, but if we have to cross any roads, just hold them straight because they won't turn on pavement. Think you can handle it?"

Xander nodded eagerly. "Yeah. I got this."

"Okay. You take Laken and follow me. No horsing around back there," he warned. "You break it, you buy it. These sleds are all I have. I can't afford to fix them, much less replace them."

"Yes, sir," Xander agreed. "Don't worry. I'll take good care of it."

"Good. Tom!" Red called, turning his attention to my father. "You ready?"

I looked behind us to see my father straddling the snowmobile, his gloved fingers poised on the key ready to turn it. He bobbed his helmet in agreement.

"All right. Hop on you two. Xander first."

Xander lifted his leg over the seat and reached for the handlebars. Then Red gestured for me to get on behind him. The vinyl seat didn't have much room, forcing me to squeeze in close behind Xander, my legs brushing against his as I wrapped my arms around his chest.

Red bent down to check on me. "If this is too uncomfortable, you can always wait here for us."

He obviously didn't know me that well. "No way. I'm fine, and I'm coming with you."

Red smiled. "I had a feeling you'd say that."

Xander started the engine, and the snowmobile vibrated under us as the motor warmed up again. I leaned against Xander, waiting for the journey to begin. He grabbed my hands, pulling them tighter around his chest. Then, without a warning, he disengaged the brake and the snowmobile lurched forward. The engines cutting through the morning silence, we began our trek through the snowy mountains.

Chapter 16

I clung to Xander as we traveled through the forest behind Red who plowed his snowmobile through the fresh powder, following the trail of footprints. He kept the pace steady, slowing only to safely maneuver sharp turns.

We went down the mountain first, crossing a narrow stream at the bottom. The snowmobiles splashed through the running water that hadn't frozen yet and then climbed up a steep slope on the other side. I held on to Xander to keep from slipping backward. Going downhill had been easy with gravity pushing me into him, but now I hung on, afraid I would fall off into the path of my father's snowmobile.

The forest was still and quiet, at least until the engines blasted through it. I watched the snowy landscape with a feeling of dread, worried that Dakota's injuries were worse than we thought or that Noah's friend wouldn't make it home alive. I didn't think I could handle another death. After eighteen peaceful years in this sleepy town, I'd seen enough death in the last twenty-four hours to last a lifetime.

We rode for what I estimated was about thirty minutes.

Just when it seemed like we would keep going forever, we slowed to a stop and the snowmobile engines shut off.

I raised my head from Xander's back, releasing my hold around his chest before he stood up and swung his leg over the seat. Standing in the snow, he unhooked the chinstrap to his helmet and whipped it off.

I remained on the snowmobile but removed my helmet, about to ask why we had stopped when I saw Noah up ahead.

He walked toward Red, his jeans soaking wet around his ankles and exhaustion spread across his face. I looked for Dakota as far as I could see, but the scenery of trees against the snow-covered ground was completely still.

Red jumped up from his snowmobile, pulling his helmet off when Noah approached. As I climbed off the seat, my father rushed past me, his helmet also removed. Without a word, Xander and I followed, stopping behind him when he reached Noah.

"Noah," my father said, concern in his voice. He hugged Noah before giving him a stern scolding. "What were you thinking, coming out here on your own? If you get lost or break a leg out here, I'm left without a deputy. And as the deputy, you should have told me the minute your friend went missing."

"Sorry, sir," Noah said, ducking his head and avoiding my father's stare for a moment.

"Where's Dakota?" I asked, stepping beside my father. I noticed Noah's uneasy glance toward Red and quickly explained, "It's okay. He knows."

Noah nodded. "He ran off when he heard the snowmobiles. Laken, maybe you should run ahead and try to find him."

"Is he hurt? We saw blood in the snow next to his tracks."

"It looked like something bit him on the face. I tried to get close enough to take a good look at it, but he wouldn't let me. He kept running into the woods and then coming back for me like he wanted me to follow him. As far as I can tell, it isn't bothering him."

"Okay. I'll see if I can find him." I looked at my father, and he nodded in agreement.

Leaving the four of them behind, I rushed through the snow, following Dakota's paw prints still spotted with blood. "Dakota!" I called as I wandered away from the guys. "Dakota! Come here!"

A dark shadow darted between the trees up ahead, a sharp contrast to the white scenery. Then Dakota appeared about twenty feet away from me, his chest heaving as he panted, causing his breath to puff out in a cloud. I ran toward him through the snow, lifting my feet high with each step. The cold air stung my throat and lungs, but I ignored it. When I reached him, I dropped to my knees, not caring that the snow would soak my jeans.

"Dakota! What were you thinking?" I scolded him with a relieved smile, throwing my arms around him. He smelled like a combination of wet dog and smoke. "You and Noah should have woken us up before taking off this morning." Pulling away from him, I noticed the defiance in his eyes as he shook his head. His body language the least of my concerns, I studied the bite mark just below his eye. Blood trickled down from two puncture marks, dripping onto the snow. His increased circulation from running seemed to be pushing the blood through his veins, but as Noah had mentioned, it didn't look deep or serious. And Dakota didn't even seem to notice it. The fur around his neck was wet with foam, possibly saliva, but when I ran my fingers over him, I didn't see or feel any other wounds.

Convinced that the bite on his face was his only injury, I sighed. "How did this happen? The other wolves?" I mused. "Well, the important thing is that you're okay and I found you. We'll take care of your face after we find Noah's friend. Do you know where she is?" He nodded before letting out an eager whine. Abruptly, he turned and charged away from me, kicking up snow behind him. "Dakota, wait!" I called, running after him. "Please, stop! I can't keep up!" He skidded to a halt, turned and sprinted back toward me, sliding to a stop at my feet. "We have to follow you on the snowmobiles. And don't worry about Red. You can trust him." I gestured in the direction of the guys waiting for us about fifty yards away. "Come on."

Dakota lingered where he was when I started walking away, and I turned back to see what was keeping him. He focused on something out in the distance, drawing my attention to a column of smoke rising up to the sky. I stared at it, my pulse accelerating, and I wondered if we were too late. "Oh, no. Not again," I muttered under my breath. "But how is this possible? Noah's uncle died yesterday." I looked down at Dakota who watched me. "Is she up there?"

He nodded, his expression solemn and his eyes worried.

Adrenaline shot through me, my heart racing. "We have to hurry! I can't keep up with you. Follow my tracks back to the guys."

Dakota darted past me, following my footprints in the snow. I trudged behind him as fast as I could, afraid of what we would find when we reached the source of the smoke.

By the time I returned to the snowmobiles, Dakota paced anxiously in front of the guys. "Hurry! We have to hurry!" I gasped, out of breath.

"What's going on, Laken?" Xander asked.

I stopped, bending down to rest my hands on my thighs. "There's—a—fire," I managed to get out before straightening up.

"Fire? What?" Noah shook his head, staring out into the distance.

"Laken, catch your breath. Then tell us what you saw," my father probed gently.

I turned to look behind me, but the smoke wasn't visible from here. "I saw smoke in the distance. She must be there. And Dakota was bitten by…something. This is all very wrong." I looked at Noah, meeting his worried brown eyes.

"I'm going to guess that your friend is up there. We have to hurry."

"Wait a minute," Red spoke up. "How can you be sure?"

I glanced at Noah then Xander. They understood how I knew, but I could never explain it to my father and Red, at least not now when time was running out.

"The wolf," Xander explained as Dakota continued pacing.

He ran toward us, sliding to a stop in a cloud of powder. Then he lifted his head to the sky and let out a loud howl. When he stopped, I thought I heard another howl, but it must have been my imagination. I raised my eyebrows as he whined before running off in the direction of the smoke.

"He's trying to tell us something," Xander said. "Let's go!"

He rushed back to our snowmobile and grabbed his helmet. The rest of us started to follow suit, but Red stood where he was, his jaw open in amazement. "Unbelievable," he muttered, shaking his head.

My father noticed his hesitation and called out to him. "Red, we have to go! Now! Go ahead of us after Dakota. We won't be able to keep up with passengers. We'll just follow in your tracks."

Red's attention snapped back to us. "I'm on it! I'll see you up there." Then he rushed over to his snowmobile, put his helmet on, and fired up the engine before speeding off after Dakota.

"Noah!" my father called.

Noah still stood where he'd been all this time, deep worry written across his face. Snapping out of his thoughts, he looked back at my father. "What?"

"Ride with me. We don't have an extra helmet, but I'll be careful."

"That's the last thing I care about right now," he said, running past me and Xander on his way to my father.

I reached for my helmet on the snowmobile seat and shoved it on over my hair. After fastening the chinstrap, I straddled the seat behind Xander. "Not too fast. I don't want to get dumped off this thing, okay?" I said, wrapping my arms around him.

He nodded, his helmet bobbing up and down. When he started the engine, I tightened my hold on him in the split second before the snowmobile pitched forward.

The trees rising up out of the pristine snow blurred as we flew by them. Xander wasted no time in his hurry to catch up to Red, accelerating when the trail became straight, the speed forcing him to slam on the brakes just in time to dodge a tree. I slid around on the seat, determined to hang on as long as it took to reach the smoke.

The terrain we covered from that point was mostly uphill, making it even harder to stay on. But somehow I managed, and I sighed with relief when we stopped. I didn't wait for Xander to shut off the engine before jumping up and unfastening my helmet. After yanking it off and dropping it onto the seat, I ran through the snow to reach Dakota.

Nothing could have prepared me for the scene unfolding at the peak. Dakota stood fierce and tall, his fur standing straight up on his back and his lip raised, exposing his fangs. He growled at Red who leaned against his snowmobile, his helmet discarded on the seat and a nervous look in his eyes. Behind Dakota, a line of fire about three feet high blocked the entrance to a cave.

"Easy boy," Red said, his eyes locked on Dakota. "What's going on with him, Laken? I thought we were all on the same team."

"We are. He's protecting you," I explained as Xander rushed up beside me.

"What?" Red gasped, his eyes flashing my way. "That's crazy. What about the girl we're here to find?"

"I don't know," I replied, wishing I had the answers. I glanced at Xander and he nodded, practically reading my mind.

I turned my attention to Dakota and slowly approached

him as he focused on Red, his growl continuing. When I got close to him and the fire, the intense heat overwhelmed me. The snow had melted on the ground near the cave, and reflections of the flames danced in puddles. Piles of branches and logs lined the entrance, fueling the fire and sending a plume of smoke up into the air.

"Dakota, what is it?" I tried to see what hid beyond the cackling flames, but all I saw was a black hole leading into the cave. I stepped cautiously toward it, but turned around when I heard the third snowmobile behind me.

My father quickly shut off the engine while Noah jumped up and made a beeline for the cave. He didn't get very far because Dakota charged at him, baring his teeth and snapping viciously. Noah slid to a stop, losing his balance and falling to his knees in the snow. "Laken!" he cried, his eyes begging me for help.

"Dakota!" I scolded. "What's gotten into you?" I shook my head in confusion as my father helped Noah up to his feet.

"What's going on here?" my father asked. Although he didn't say my name, he clearly directed his question at me, his eyes settling on me.

"I don't know, Dad. I think Dakota's protecting all of you."

"Then why is he letting you near the fire? Laken, this makes no sense. Get away from there and let us help." My father started to come closer, but Dakota charged at him. He stopped dead in his tracks, backing up cautiously.

"Dad, I'm fine. I just want to see what's in the cave." I held my hand up to them. "Stay there. I'll be careful, I promise."

Without another word, I turned and walked closer to the fire, my hiking boots splashing through the water. A movement in the shadows caught my eye and I squinted, trying to focus. A large shape no taller than the flames paced on the other side, moving with a stealthy stride that reminded me of Dakota.

When another movement caught my eye, I wondered if I was starting to see double. I gazed through the fire to see a pair of green eyes belonging to a light brown wolf locked on me. Its ears were pointed at me, its tongue dangling from its open mouth in the heat.

Another wolf rushed over, and I shook my head in disbelief. There really were two of them? Yet another movement in the far corner caught my eye, and I counted two more. They looked exhausted and skinny, their hips and shoulder blades poking out from under tawny brown and gray fur.

They stared at me from beyond the fire, the reflection of flames dancing in their eyes. One of them growled, and a smaller one snapped at it, causing the two wolves to break into a scuffle that ended with the smaller one yelping and slinking away.

Questions swirled through my mind. How had these wolves gotten here? I assumed Noah's uncle was to blame for this cruel torture. But why would he trap wolves in a cave behind a wall of fire? How long had they been here, and when was the last time they had eaten? Sympathy filled my heart for these animals who didn't deserve to be starved and burned alive. The probability that they were the same wolves that had chased me the night my car ran off the road in the rain mattered little to me. Whatever abuses they had endured in the past had conditioned them to fear people, giving me no leverage to communicate with them. I had to hope that I could teach them to trust me, at least long enough to get them to a safe place where they could thrive as the beautiful animals they were.

Surprisingly, the wolves' hostility began to fade. They gazed at me with a glimmer of hope in their eyes, as if they had read my mind. "We'll get you out of here, I promise," I told them.

As I contemplated my next move, a weak cough came from deep within the cave, startling me. "Hello?" called a quiet voice.

I barely heard her over the hissing flames. Raising my

eyes, I searched beyond the fire for any sign of a person, but all I saw was darkness. "Who's there?" I called.

"Help me, please." Her voice was faint, exhausted.

I craned my neck to see over the flames, my eyes adjusting to the bright light when I noticed a second line of fire behind the wolves. "Jenna?" I called. "Is that you?"

"Yes." She paused then spoke again, her voice frightened this time. "Please don't let them near me again," she begged.

"I won't. You're safe now. We're going to get you out of here."

At that moment, Dakota snarled behind me, and I whipped around to see what the commotion was about. Noah had attempted to come closer to the cave, but Dakota had planted his paws in the snow and blocked him, growling with fangs bared.

"Laken. Is that Jenna?" Noah asked.

Red and my father stared at me while Xander watched with confidence.

I nodded. "Yes. But there's a problem." I hurried through the puddles until I reached the snow and approached Dakota. All eyes stared at me, waiting.

I hesitated, trying to find the best way to explain the situation. Whatever I said would probably sound absurd and unbelievable. "Wolves," I said.

"What?" my father asked. "You can't be serious."

"It's true. I counted four of them trapped in the cave. There's another line of fire beyond them and I think Jenna's trapped on the other side."

"Why would anyone trap a girl in a cave with fire and wolves?" Red mused. "Wouldn't it have been easier to tie her up somewhere?"

"He said if she wasn't found in time, she would die," Noah said, not bothering to answer Red's question.

"Who said that?" my father asked.

"My uncle. The same man who kidnapped Xander, his father, and Laken." As soon as Noah said my name, my father glanced at me, and I remembered that he still hadn't gotten an explanation about what happened yesterday. "He was a cruel man," Noah explained. "With a very sick sense of humor. Tying up a girl and leaving her for dead wasn't his style. It's too easy, too boring."

"The man who set the cabin on fire was your uncle?" my father repeated, his eyes brimming with disappointment.

Noah nodded. "I was going to tell you once we had a moment to talk about it."

"Don't worry. You'll still get your chance," my father promised.

"So this guy's a pyromaniac?" Red observed.

"Was. And I was thinking the same thing," Xander muttered. "But I don't get it. Wolves and fire. What's the point?"

"That's easy," Noah said. "Unless he returns to keep the fires going, they'll burn out. Once the wolves get to her, she's dead. And the fire we see from the outside keeps them trapped, I'm guessing with no food. So they're probably starving and ready to rip anyone to shreds."

"Well," Xander scoffed. "Your uncle may have been a bad dude, but he certainly was creative."

"What's that supposed to mean?" Noah hissed, turning to Xander. They faced one another, staring each other down.

"Nothing," Xander replied slowly as he raised his hands. "It was just an observation."

"A girl is suffering in there, probably on the brink of death from smoke inhalation and dehydration, and you're making jokes?"

"Chill, Noah. I was just trying to lighten the mood for a moment. I would never be amused at someone's suffering," Xander stated defensively.

As Noah started to respond, I stepped in before he could get a word out. "Look, you two. You're wasting time. You'll have years to engage in your sibling rivalry after we get her out of there."

"Sibling rivalry?" my father shot out. "What?"

"They're brothers," I explained.

"Half-brothers," Xander corrected. He smiled arrogantly at his audience. "Can't you see the resemblance? But it's his fault our father died, isn't that right, Noah?"

"You know that's not true!" Noah gritted out.

Worried that any minute, one of them would take a swing at the other one, and we'd have to wrestle them off of each other while the fires continued to burn, I rushed in between them. "That's enough, you guys. Please." I looked at each of them, my eyes begging them to give it up. "There's no time for this right now."

Xander huffed as Noah backed away from him. I shook my head at them before walking back to Dakota.

My father tried to follow me, but Dakota jumped at him, his fangs bared and a low growl in his throat. "Laken, you have to call off Dakota," my father said as he stopped, helplessly watching me.

I glanced behind me at the fire and shook my head. "No," I said, turning back to them. "I have to do this. Xander's the only one who can help me."

Catching my eye, Xander slowly stepped forward, only quickening his pace when Dakota let him pass. "Laken, I think we need their help," Xander said, stopping beside me.

"No," I protested. "I need them to leave. I have to do this alone. Please send them away. They can't watch. The wolves know I want to help them."

Xander nodded and turned back to my father. "We need food and buckets. Can you go back to my house to get them? Laken and I will stay here and make sure the wolves don't get to Jenna until you get back."

"I don't know," my father said hesitantly.

"I'm not leaving without Jenna," Noah declared.

"Fine," I said. "You can stay. But Dakota won't let you near the fire."

"I don't care," Noah replied.

I dismissed him, turning my attention back to my father. "Dad, please. It's the only way. If the outside line of fire dies out first, the wolves will come after us. All they want is food."

"Okay. We'll go, but only if you promise me you'll stay out of the cave," my father said.

Before I could answer him, a loud growl rumbled from the woods. I snapped my gaze in the direction it came from to see a white wolf with blue eyes watching us from between two trees. The fur along its back standing straight up, it stalked toward us, its muscles bunched as if ready to attack.

Chapter 17

Dakota crept through the snow until he stood between us and the white wolf. He stared at it, his hackles raised and his lip curled up, revealing fangs that glinted in the sunlight.

"Great," Xander muttered under his breath. "I wonder how many other wolves are out there." He glared at Noah as if he had the answer.

I didn't say a word as I studied the white wolf. Like the others trapped in the cave, it was thin and scrawny with shoulder blades and hip bones protruding from under its fur. I wondered if this one had somehow escaped recently and if it was the one responsible for the bite wound on Dakota's face.

"Dad, we're going to need that food sooner rather than later," I said quietly.

My father nodded. "Come, on Red. Let's go." He started backing away from us in the direction of the snowmobiles.

Red stared at him in disbelief. "You're kidding, right? We can't leave them here. This doesn't look good, Tom."

"No, it doesn't," my father said before nodding at Dakota. "But this one will hold it off until we get back. Laken and the guys will be fine. Dakota won't let anything happen to them."

The concern on Red's face fading, he glanced at Dakota then at me. He thought for a moment before shaking his head. "Okay. As long as you're sure." He paused, looking at Xander. "Is your house open?"

Xander nodded. "Actually, for the first time since we moved here, it is. Take anything you can find. There are a couple chickens in the refrigerator. There might be a few steaks, too."

"We'll find them," my father assured us.

Red and my father rushed over to the snowmobiles and jumped on. After securing their helmets, they started the engines and sped away, the sound of the motors growing fainter until they disappeared down the mountain.

The fire hissed behind us and the wolves growled again. "What now?" Noah asked, looking at me, his eyebrows raised.

"She doesn't have the answer," Xander said, shooting me a knowing look. He was right, but even though I had no idea what to do next, somehow I felt like I should have the answer. "And it will probably take them about an hour to get back, so we've got some time to kill. Any ideas?"

"That's going to feel like forever," I mused. "Well, I'm just going to have to do my best." Before either of them could protest, I walked toward Dakota, my eyes never leaving the white wolf. I was prepared to turn and run the minute it charged at me, sure that Dakota would protect me if that happened. When I reached Dakota's side, I knelt down, placing my hand on his neck as the wolf continued to growl, flashing its fangs at us.

Fear lodged itself in my throat, but I refused to let it conquer me. The only wolf I had ever known was Dakota, and he'd come into our lives as a young pup. I had never approached an adult wolf that I didn't know until now. The ones behind the fire seemed like they might trust me, but I couldn't be too careful. They were hungry and desperate, and their survival instincts would kick in if they felt threatened. Now, as I faced the white wolf, I warned myself that this wouldn't be as easy as calming an injured moose or enlisting a bear's help. It might understand me, but that didn't mean I would be received kindly.

"Here goes nothing," I muttered softly. "Dakota, relax." He looked at me as if I was crazy before returning his stare to the white wolf. *'I mean it,'* I thought. *'Show it we mean no harm. It will never trust us if it thinks you'll hurt it.'* Then I looked across the blanket of snow at the wolf, hoping it was reading my thoughts. *'We're here to help. We'll get your friends out of the cave and food is on the way. You won't be hungry or mistreated again.'*

The wolf tilted its head in confusion, as if it had heard me, but didn't understand how a human could be kind. For a second, its growl faded. I took that moment as an opportunity to stand and move toward it, but I was too hasty, moving too close too fast with a false sense of security.

The wolf's growl resumed, louder this time, as it charged at me. Before Dakota could come between us, it rose up on its hind feet and knocked me to the ground.

My fall was softened by the snow, and I rolled when I landed, hiding my head under my arms. As soon as I stopped, I curled up into a fetal position, waiting for the wolf to pounce and sink its teeth into me. But I felt nothing. Hearing Dakota's growl, I looked up in time to see him leap onto the wolf. They snarled and snapped at each other, tumbling through the snow, their black and white bodies locked together. After a few seconds, a loud yelp pierced the air and Dakota emerged as the victor. The other wolf lay in a heap, whimpering. Dakota ran back to me, nudging my chest with his nose until I sat up, brushing the snow off my arms. Xander rushed over to us with Noah trailing behind him.

"Laken, what were you thinking?" Xander asked, kneeling in front of me. Noah dropped beside him, but Xander, clearly annoyed, didn't give him any room to get near me.

"I don't know. I had to try something," I explained lamely.

"I'm going to assume that you haven't had any experience with wolves other than Dakota."

I shook my head. "No. I guess a full-grown wolf is a little different than one I raised."

"You think?" Xander replied sarcastically, but with a smile.

I offered him a weak one in return then glanced at Noah, my eyes shifting to see the white wolf scramble to its feet behind him. My smile faded as it approached us, walking with a slight limp.

Noah and Xander turned, following my gaze to see the wolf a few feet away. Before it could come any closer, Dakota intercepted it, his teeth bared and a deep growl rumbling in his throat. The wolf locked its eyes on him and then dropped into the snow, rolling over and throwing its legs up in the air.

At that moment, Dakota's growl vanished.

My eyes roamed over the wolf, and I noticed right away that it was a female. Perhaps she and Dakota would learn to get along one day.

Noah turned back to me as Xander continued watching the wolf. "Now that we're safe, we need to get to Jenna out of there."

"Yes, you're right," I agreed, my thoughts returning to the matter at hand. Taking on one skinny, exhausted wolf with Dakota's help was one thing, but attempting to tame four starving wolves was a different story. I couldn't be sure that they trusted me from the moment I'd had with them earlier, but I might have a chance if I won over the white wolf. "I need a minute alone with Dakota and his new friend," I said, gesturing to Dakota who stood over her, his fur lying flat on his back as if he was willing to make amends. "Will you guys wait for me by the snowmobile?"

Xander whipped his head around upon hearing my request. "No way. We're not leaving you. You can't do this on your own."

"Well, I can't do anything with you two lurking around. If I can get her on my side, I might have a chance. Those must be her pack mates. They might trust me if she does."

"I don't know about that," Xander said. "We really should wait for your dad and Red to get back with the meat."

"No. Jenna's in there. I talked to her. We need to get her out now. I don't know how she's still alive with all that smoke, either. So we can't waste time. I'm going in." Determined to do something, I jumped up to my feet. Ignoring the snow stuck to my jeans, I glanced at the white wolf. '*Will you help? Please,*' I asked silently.

She rolled onto her belly and scrambled to her feet before trotting over to me with a slight limp to her left front paw. Circling me, she nudged my legs without a single growl. I had won her trust, and now she had mine.

With the wolf in tow, I headed back to the cave, but I didn't get very far when Xander ran after me. "Laken! What are you doing? Stop!" he called in frustration.

Hearing him, I halted and whirled around. The wolf ran toward him, growling with the fur on her back standing on edge. Fangs bared, she stared at him.

"Whoa!" he said, sliding to a stop in the snow and nearly falling to his knees. "Laken, please," he said, his voice softening. "You don't even know this girl. If she's been in there for days, surely she can wait another hour or so. Don't risk yourself."

"I can do this," I stated as Noah approached him.

"Let her go, Xander," Noah said. "I believe her."

"Oh, what do you know? You just want your friend to get out of there," Xander accused. "You don't give a damn about Laken."

"You have no idea what I care about," Noah muttered angrily as his gaze swept over me.

My eyes met his. "Thank you," I whispered before turning. The white wolf trotted beside me as I ran across the snow until we splashed through the water outside the cave. I heard Xander call my name again, but I resisted the urge to acknowledge him.

When we reached the fire, I stopped, frowning at the wolves pacing frantically behind the flames. The heat melted the snow on my jeans, and they suddenly felt heavy and wet. It gave me an idea. I turned to the wolf beside me. *'Can you distract them?'* She nodded subtly before running over to the opposite side.

As the wolves flocked to her, I jumped through the flames, feeling an intense heat around my legs for a second before landing on the other side. Without a moment of hesitation, I ran through the cave to the next line of fire and leaped over it. The second one wasn't quite as high as the first one, but I still felt the blistering heat around my ankles and calves.

Once on the other side, the first thing I did was look down to make sure my jeans and boots hadn't caught on fire. Fortunately, the melted snow and ice hadn't given the fire a chance to take a hold of me. The wolves behind me rushed to where I had just jumped from the other side, snarling and snapping. I glanced at them and then beyond the cave opening where I saw the white wolf pacing. *'Thank you!'* I thought before turning my attention to the inside of the cave.

Smoke filled the air, and I ducked down to where I could breathe. A girl barely recognizable as the pretty girl in the newspaper picture sat on the floor, her knees pulled up to her chest and her back against the rocky wall. She wore dirty, torn jeans and a white T-shirt, and her arms and legs were free of any ropes or other means to secure them.

She lifted her head, gazing at me with tired eyes. Dirt was smudged across her face, and dried blood smeared one of her arms.

Still crouching, I rushed to her side, but I wasn't sure if she really saw me through her bloodshot eyes. She looked exhausted, hungry, and dehydrated. "Jenna?" I asked, gently touching her shoulder.

She stared at me, her brown eyes barely seeming to focus. "Yes. Can you help me?" she whispered. "Who are you? How did you get in here?"

"That doesn't matter. All you need to know is that I'm getting you out of here. Can you stand?"

Before I could help her to her feet, Xander bellowed from outside the cave, his voice loud enough to be heard over the hissing fire and snarling wolves. "Laken! What's happening? If I don't hear your voice in another minute, I'm coming in!"

I turned, cupping my hands around my mouth. "I'm fine! Stay there!"

When I twisted back around to her, she stared at me, her eyes wide. "Is that—him? Don't let him in here! He's evil. He'll kill us both!"

"No, it's not. The man who did this to you is dead. He'll never hurt you again."

She gaped at me in disbelief. "He's dead? Then there's no getting out of here. If he doesn't come back to keep the fire going, the wolves will get in here. They'll kill us." She stared at the flames with tears in her eyes, trembling. "They're coming for us. I can see them. Their eyes are hungry for blood. They're going to get us."

I ran my hand along her forehead as a mother would do to calm a child. "No, they're not. Wolves don't want to eat people, trust me." *Unless they're hungry enough,* I added to myself. And this pack seemed to have reached that point.

"These wolves will," she cried. "They already got to me once. See!" She pulled up a pant leg, revealing a bloody wound on her calf where her flesh had been torn. "The man dangled me over the fire to show me what they could do to me. Why did he take me? Why would he feed me to a bunch of wolves?"

I drew in a sharp breath at the sight of her leg. I hadn't even noticed the blood that had soaked through her jeans.

At that moment, I realized she needed to get to a hospital, and soon.

"Shh," I whispered, forcing myself to sound confident. "We're going to take care of you. You're safe now. We'll get you out of here."

"We?" she asked, confused.

"Noah's here. He's waiting for you outside."

"Noah? What is he doing here?" she asked, sounding confused.

"That man was his uncle. Noah has been going out of his mind looking for you over the last few weeks. But this isn't his fault. I'll let him tell you the rest of the story after we get you to a hospital and cleaned up."

I turned around, taking a deep breath as I scanned the fire again. Beyond it, the wolves paced back and forth, their eyes nervous and hungry. The flames separating Jenna and I from the pack were starting to die out since the wood feeding them was nearly gone. As soon as a gap opened up, they would rush in and we would be cornered. My only chance to save us both was to try to talk to them and assure them that food was on the way.

If I couldn't hold them off until my father and Red returned, I feared more for Jenna than for myself. She had no strength to fight, and the scent of her blood would draw them to her right away.

Without a plan, I stood and jumped through the flames. I lost my balance when I landed, falling to the ground. As I raised my shoulders, my hands still on the ground, the four wolves stood in front of me, staring at me with their hungry eyes. Drool hung from their open mouths.

"Easy," I whispered, searching their expressions for any sign of understanding. "Please don't hurt me. I just want to help you." While I prayed that they would back off, the white wolf howled on the other side of the fire.

The wolves glanced at each other before staring at me again. "I know you don't trust people after what he did to you, but we're not like him. We're going to get you out of here. And we'll give you something to eat. You won't be hungry much longer. Trust me."

All but the largest wolf, a gray one with light brown eyes, softened their expressions, appearing to trust me. But the large one I assumed was the alpha male growled and crept toward me, sending a blast of fear through my veins as I inched backward.

With seconds to spare, Xander leaped over the fire, landing in front of the wolf. "Stay away from her!" Xander glared at the animal, a pocketknife in his hand, the orange flames reflecting on the shiny silver blade.

"Xander, no!" I screamed as he swung the knife at the wolf. I jumped up, grabbing his shoulders to pull him back, but it was too late. The wolf had already lunged at him, knocking him on top of me. Then the three of us crashed to the ground. I went down first, my head slamming into a rock. Pain shot through my skull and my vision became fuzzy for a second.

I squirmed out from under Xander as he wrestled with the wolf while the others backed up, reluctant to defend their pack mate. I rubbed my head, feeling blood under my hair. Dizzy, I scrambled to my feet, jumping away from Xander and the wolf who were locked together, the sight of them nothing more than a blur of gray fur and black clothing.

"Xander, stop! Please!"

But it was too late. He couldn't stop now even if he wanted to. He and the wolf came crashing toward me, and I shimmied out of their way just in time. They slammed up against the side wall and then dropped to the ground as the wolf yelped, his painful cry echoing through the cave.

Xander and the wolf lay in a crumpled heap, still and unmoving.

"No!" I rushed over to them as Xander uttered a low groan and rolled out from under the wolf. I helped him move to the side of the cave, noticing the blood dripping from the knife still in his hand.

As Xander caught his breath, I approached the wolf. The other three were closing in around me, their eyes worried as they nudged their companion, a bloody gash sliced across his side. I shook my head, running my fingers over the wolf's fur. "I didn't want this. None of this ever should have happened." I looked up at the wolves, suddenly scared that they would turn on me. I hoped they knew I would have stopped Xander if I'd had the chance.

The smallest and skinniest of the wolves, one with tawny brown fur and golden eyes, nudged my neck reassuringly.

Then a whimper came from the bleeding wolf, and I glanced down to see him move slightly. He raised his head, his eyes opening as he whined in pain. Relieved, I stroked his neck. "I'm not going to let you die," I whispered.

"Good. I should hope not," Xander muttered, sitting up and rubbing a hand across his forehead.

I shot him a defiant look as I stayed beside the wolf. "I wasn't talking to you. What was that, anyway?"

"What was what?"

"The knife," I huffed under my breath as if he should know what I meant.

"I wasn't about to sit back and watch a wolf tear you to pieces."

"That wouldn't have happened. I would have gotten things under control," I said, wishing I could be as confident as I sounded. In spite of being grateful that Xander had protected me, a part of me felt as though I had failed. It wasn't his fault and I didn't meant to take my frustration out on him, but at this moment, I didn't know what else to say.

"When, Laken? Before or after it ripped into you?"

A bit ashamed, I turned away from him and gave the wolf one last pat. Then I pulled up my jacket to expose my shirt and gently pressed the cloth against the open wound. As I wiped at the blood, the wolf sighed with a moan, lifting his head to look back at me.

A moment later, Noah appeared on the other side of the fire, a black bucket in his hands. He dumped snow on the flames, and it fizzled with a hissing sound. "Your dad and Red are back. We could use some help."

"They're back already?" I asked, scrambling to my feet and approaching Xander to extend a hand to him. After he reached for it, I helped him to his feet. "That was fast."

"Apparently, Red's a pretty good rider. They made it back in less than half the time it took to get up here." Noah tossed a raw chicken over the flames to the wolves who rushed at it, snapping at each other as they hoarded around it. "There. That should keep them busy for a while."

"I hope there's more than just one. They'll devour that in minutes, and we need something for this one," I said, pointing to the injured wolf still lying on the cave floor.

Xander folded his switchblade into its case with a click and shoved it in his jacket pocket. "I'll help with the buckets." Appearing somewhat groggy, he jumped through the flames and disappeared.

"Laken, there's blood in your hair," Noah said as he studied me.

I reached up to touch the cut. "I'm sure it looks worse than it is. Can you get a few more chickens?"

"Think fast." Xander appeared beside Noah, tossing me a bloody slab of raw red meat.

"Wow," I said, my eyebrows raised as I caught it. "You're giving this to the wolves?"

"Call it a peace offering." Xander flashed me a smile before disappearing again.

My father and Red appeared next, pouring snow onto the fire as I dropped beside the injured wolf.

I snatched my hands away from the meat as the wolf snapped his jaws to grab it. The wolf glanced up at me, holding the meat between his front paws and tearing into it. "Maybe now you'll trust me?" I smiled, but only until the other three wolves polished off the chicken and eyed the steak.

"Uh, guys!" I called. "We need more meat over here before these wolves attack each other."

"Got it!" Red hurled three more raw chickens over the fire like they were bowling balls. The wolves rushed to the far side of the cave and all I saw were their tails as they dug into the meat. "Laken!" he gasped, peering over the flames at me. "What in the world happened? You're bleeding!"

"What?" My father rushed over to Red's side. "Laken, I told you to wait for us."

I looked up at my father sheepishly. "I guess patience isn't one of my strong suits."

My father huffed, but let it go. "Did you find her?"

I nodded, my thoughts shifting to Jenna who still waited for us behind the second line of fire. "She's in pretty bad shape, Dad. I'd better get back to her." Before he could object, I jumped over the fire and rushed to her side.

"Help is here," I said, kneeling beside her. "We're going to get you to a hospital."

Her eyes were closed, and she didn't stir. I gently shook her shoulders and, when she didn't wake up, I picked up her wrist, breathing a sigh of relief at the feel of her pulse.

"Dad! Noah!" I cried. "I can't get her to wake up! Can you hurry, please?"

Noah blasted in through the fire, rushing over to us. "Jenna! It's me, Noah." He trailed his fingers along her cheek. "Wake up, please. I never wanted any of this to happen." He continued talking softly, but she remained still, her eyes closed.

I left Noah with her and jumped over the flames to find the bucket he had dropped. If he wasn't using it, someone should. The more of us who worked to put out the fires, the sooner we could get her to safety.

For about ten minutes, I worked beside Xander, Red, and my father, running back and forth between the snow and the fire. We had just extinguished the outside fire when the wolves finished the chicken. As soon as they saw their path to freedom, all but the injured wolf escaped, reuniting with the white wolf who had devoured an entire chicken on her own. The four of them started to leave us, but stopped, turning back to stare at Dakota. They appeared confused by Dakota who lingered with us, not interested in taking off with them. Then the injured wolf staggered out of the cave, leaving a trail of blood on the snow as he slowly made his way to the pack, a painful expression in his eyes.

As the inside fire dwindled to a few smoldering ashes, Noah carried Jenna out of the cave. Red shed his coat and slipped it around her while Noah lowered her onto Red's snowmobile. Confident that she was in good hands, I dropped the bucket I still carried and followed the trail of blood in the snow. I was worried about the injured wolf, and I didn't know how he would survive with a wound that deep. But he hadn't gotten very far. The trail of blood led me to where he had given up about twenty feet beyond the edge of the trees.

"Xander! Dad! Come quick!" I yelled, running into the woods. I dropped beside the wolf that lay in the snow, pain etched into his expression and his breathing shallow.

My father and Xander arrived in seconds with Red tagging along. They stopped a few feet away when they saw the wolf. "We need to help him," I said, glancing up, my eyes begging them to do something.

"He needs a vet," Red stated. "That cut looks like it needs stitches. Dr. Harrison can help. And she'll keep quiet about this." He looked at my father, his eyes questioning.

I followed his gaze to my father. "Please, Dad. We can't leave him here."

My father sighed. "Great. If the mayor finds out a whole pack of wolves has moved in, we're all in big trouble." He paused, looking at me, his expression softening. "Oh, all right," he said.

Red knelt beside me. "Xander, can you help?"

I jumped up and backed away, watching Xander help Red lift the wolf. Then I followed them back to the snowmobiles where they lowered him onto one of them. Xander remained at the wolf's side, holding him in place on the seat.

"I'll take the girl," Red suggested. "Laken, you and Xander take the wolf. It's going to be a rough ride back for you. You'll have to take it really slow. Think you can handle it?"

"Yes," I said.

"He's pretty heavy. I suggest you drive and let Xander hold him between you two."

I looked over at Xander, who nodded.

"The rest of us will go ahead so we can get this girl to a hospital," Red said. "As soon as we get back, I'll call Dr. Harrison and have her meet you guys at Xander's."

"Thank you, Red. For everything. We couldn't have done this without you," I said.

"It was my pleasure." He flashed me a smile before lumbering over to his snowmobile where Noah waited with Jenna in his arms.

Within seconds, the two snowmobiles started up, their engines sputtering loudly. Then they sped away, disappearing down the snow-covered mountain. The woods were silent once again as Xander climbed onto our snowmobile behind the wolf. Holding him with one hand, he reached for his helmet. When I picked up the other one, he asked, "You know how to drive one of these?"

"Yes," I replied confidently. "I've ridden before. Not much, but enough to know what to do."

"Okay. But take it slow. It's going to be a little challenging to keep this guy on the seat."

"I will. Just hold on to him."

I secured my helmet before taking my seat behind the handlebars. Then I turned the ignition key, and the engine rumbled to life. As I eased the snowmobile around a U-turn and headed down the mountain, Dakota ran ahead, taking the lead on our journey home.

Chapter 18

A brown pick-up truck was waiting for us in Xander's driveway when we returned. Sometime on the way home, Dakota disappeared into the mountains, which was probably for the best. I wasn't sure how we'd explain one wolf to the vet, let alone two. Red's truck and Noah's police car were gone, and I hoped they were almost at the hospital by now.

I parked the snowmobile as close as I could to the porch steps before shutting off the engine. As I climbed off the seat and removed my helmet, a woman I guessed to be in her forties wearing jeans and a green jacket stepped down from the driver's seat of the truck. Her long auburn hair hung from a ponytail, a tan baseball hat shielding her eyes from the sun.

Xander slipped his helmet off with one hand while holding the wolf steady with the other one.

I had felt the wolf stirring behind me a few times on the way home, but all in all, he seemed to understand that we were helping him.

"Dr. Harrison?" I asked.

"Yes," she answered as she walked around her truck and approached me.

"You got here really fast."

She smiled warmly. "Red said it was an emergency. We go way back, Red and me. He's always calling me to help the wildlife around here." Her brown eyes shifted to Xander. "What's going on here?"

"Red didn't tell you?" I asked.

She shook her head. "No. He just said I was never going to believe it, but that I would be glad he asked me to help."

"Well, it's a wolf." I watched her expression, waiting for fear to register in her eyes, but it never did.

"Hmmm," she mused, brushing past me to get a closer look at him. She ran her fingers through his fur, examining his bloody wound. "What happened to him?"

"We had a bit of a disagreement," Xander explained.

She took a deep breath. "I see," was all she said before backing up. "Can you take him inside? And I wouldn't set him down on any white carpeting if you know what I mean."

"Yes, ma'am," Xander replied with more respect than I'd ever seen him show anyone. Without another word, he lifted the wolf into his arms and carried him to the house.

I followed Dr. Harrison to the back of her truck where she opened the tailgate to the covered bed and rolled out a shelf of veterinary supplies. After preparing a needle and syringe with medicine, she stocked a carrying case with clippers, bandages and other supplies.

"Thank you for coming. This means a lot to us. I'm Laken, by the way."

She turned to me, the case of supplies in her hand. "Yes, I know. You're the wolf girl."

I felt a blush race across my face. "I guess so." It was one thing to hear the other students at school call me that with the intention of teasing me, but Dr. Harrison made it sound respectful, almost as if she envied me.

"I've always loved wolves," she said. "They're amazing

animals. It about killed me when I heard about your wolf. I'm sorry for what the mayor did. It was a real shame."

I felt a little guilty playing along when I knew that Dakota was alive and well. But I couldn't reveal the truth to anyone unless I didn't have a choice. "Thank you," I said before changing the subject. "Do you think he's going to be okay?" I nodded toward the house, indicating the injured wolf.

She sighed. "I don't know. Let's get in there and find out."

I led her across the driveway, up the front porch steps, and through the door. Xander was waiting for us in the entry hall. "Come on in," he said. "I took him down to the basement."

I raised my eyebrows at Xander, wondering how he'd managed to carry the wolf up and down stairs on his own when Red had needed his help to get the wolf on the snowmobile, but I didn't ask any questions. I was just grateful that Xander was strong enough to handle the animal on his own.

We followed Xander down the stairs to the wine cellar turned jewelry workshop. The wolf lay on the workbench, the tools and gadgets I remembered from my first visit to the cellar nowhere in sight.

"Will this work?" he asked.

"It's perfect," the vet answered, approaching the bench and placing her case next to the wolf. She sifted her fingers through his fur, studying the exposed flesh and muscle. Blood had dried on his matted fur, but the laceration was still moist.

As she reached for the needle in her carrying box, the wolf stirred, opening his eyes and jerking his head up. Alarm raced across his face and he scrambled to get up. I rushed over to him, placing my hand on his head. '*Be still,*' I thought. '*We're trying to help you, but you have to stay calm.*' His eyes remained wide with anxiety, but his body relaxed.

"Nice work," Dr. Harrison commented. "But now comes the hard part. I need to numb his side before I can start stitching him up, and it's going to sting. Think you can hold him still? If you can't, I'll have to sedate him. But I'd rather not do that if we can help it."

"I'll give it my best shot." I put my hands on each side of the wolf's face.

"Be careful, Laken," Xander said from where he leaned against a wall across the room, watching us.

"I know what I'm doing," I said. I shot him a knowing look, disappointed that he seemed to have so little confidence in me.

Dr. Harrison slid her eyes from me to Xander, and then back to me, her eyebrows raised. "Tell me when you're ready."

"Sorry," I said, shifting my attention back to the wolf. With a sigh, I gazed into his eyes. *'You're going to feel a pinch and a little burning. Stay still, okay?'* He took a deep breath, wincing when his lungs expanded. Understanding registered in his eyes, telling me it was time, and I looked at Dr. Harrison with a nod. "Go for it."

She pulled the fur back around the laceration and slowly inserted the needle. The wolf whimpered, and she stopped for a moment, glancing at me. When he remained still, she injected a little of the numbing medicine into him. Then she moved the needle to a few other places around the cut, repeating the process each time. As soon as the syringe was empty, she dropped it into the carrying case and ran a pair of clippers around the wound, brushing clumps of fur onto the floor.

Finished with the clippers, she set them down on the bench and looked over at Xander. "Can you get a bucket of warm water?"

He nodded. "Of course." Then he bolted away from the wall and up the stairs, his footsteps fading when he reached the top.

Dr. Harrison paused in her work, explaining, "It's going

to take a few minutes before the numbing medicine takes effect. So what happened out there?"

I avoided her curious gaze as I stared at the cement wall across the room. "It's a long story. But to cut to the chase, I got too close to this wolf and, when he came after me, Xander felt he needed to defend me. I didn't even know he had a knife with him." I shook my head at the memory of the cave, Jenna, the fire, and the other wolves.

"If I were in your shoes, I would have hoped my boyfriend would jump in just like he did."

"Oh, he's not my boyfriend," I said a little too quickly.

Where did that come from? Xander has been nothing but incredible to you since the Halloween dance. We hadn't had a chance to talk about our relationship, but I had to admit it had reached a point far beyond that of just friends. Perhaps my immediate protest to calling him my boyfriend was a knee-jerk reaction after weeks of fighting my feelings for him.

Dr. Harrison raised her eyebrows, seeming unconvinced. "Well, whatever he is to you, he obviously cares about you. And this wolf is going to be just fine once I get him stitched up. He might be a little sore for a while, but he's going to live."

A moment of silence fell over us before Xander emerged from the stairwell carrying a white plastic bowl of water. I hadn't even heard him coming. His jacket was gone, and his sleeves were rolled up to his elbows. "Here," he said, handing the bowl to the vet.

She motioned to the empty table space behind the wolf. "Just set it down."

He carefully placed it on the table without letting a drop splash out and returned to the wall where he'd been before leaving to get the water. Then he shoved his hands into the front pockets of his jeans, watching the vet.

I glanced at him as Dr. Harrison shuffled through the contents of her carrying box, my eyes meeting his. Noticing his icy expression filled with contempt and disappointment,

I offered him a faint smile. But his frown didn't waver, and instead, he looked away.

I would have to wait to talk to him since I couldn't exactly ask him what was wrong while Dr. Harrison worked. I shifted my gaze down, rubbing the fur between the wolf's ears as she cleaned the wound with a piece of soaking cotton, a pair of latex gloves now covering her hands. The wolf sighed and leaned his head down on the workbench, a patient look crossing over his eyes.

Dr. Harrison began stitching a few minutes later, pulling the needle up to tighten each stitch before pushing it through his flesh again. After about five minutes, she tied up the ends and cut off the excess thread. Then she applied an ointment to the wound, returning the tube to her carrying case when she finished. Snapping off the plastic gloves, she dropped them into the case. "That should do it," she announced.

I stooped down to the wolf's level, gazing into his eyes. *'She's all finished now. You might be sore once the numbing medicine wears off, but she said you'll be fine.'*

"What about the stitches?" Xander asked. "Do you have to come back to take them out or will they dissolve on their own?"

"I'll have to come back to remove them in about three weeks. In the meantime, I'd like you to keep him inside. I don't want him in the woods. He's liable to rip them open if he runs too fast. And they need to stay clean to prevent an infection. Will that be possible?"

Xander looked at me for a second before answering, "We'll figure something out. I'll do whatever it takes to help him get better."

"I know you will," she said with genuine confidence. "Well, I'd better be on my way. Can one of you walk me out? I need to leave some medicine for him." She grabbed her tote box of supplies and headed for the stairs.

"Sure." I went with her as Xander approached the workbench, hoisting the wolf up and lowering him to his feet.

Then they followed us, the wolf's nails clicking against the floor, reminding me of Dakota.

Xander lingered in the house with the wolf while I walked Dr. Harrison out to her truck. After tucking her supplies into the rollout shelf of her truck bed, she searched through several vials of medicine before selecting two pill bottles. She scribbled some instructions on a note pad, ripped off the page and handed everything to me.

"These are pain meds and an antibiotic. The pain meds can be given on an as needed basis, but the antibiotic isn't optional. Give him one pill three times a day for the next week until all of them are gone."

"Got it."

"And good luck with him. Are you going to help take care of him for the next few weeks?"

"As much as I can around my school schedule, I guess. Thanks again for coming out here."

"No problem. It was an experience. I've never treated a wolf before."

She pushed the rollout shelf into the bed and shut the tailgate. As she started to head toward the driver's seat, Xander ran out of the house.

"Dr. Harrison," he said, rushing around the truck.

She stopped and turned to him as I walked around the corner of the tailgate, wondering what he needed.

"What do I owe you?" he asked.

She shook her head. "Don't worry about it. I came up here as a favor to Red."

In spite of her response, Xander pulled a few hundred dollar bills out of his pocket. "Well, you did this for us and we appreciate it. So please take this." He handed her the cash. "For your services, and your silence."

She took the money without counting it and stuffed it into her jacket pocket. "Thank you. This is unnecessary, but appreciated." She pulled a business card out of her other pocket and handed it to him. "Call me in three weeks to arrange a time to have the stitches removed."

"Got it," Xander said before turning and walking around the truck on his way back to the house. He sailed right past me, completely ignoring me. I whipped around to follow him as Dr. Harrison hopped in behind the wheel and turned on the truck. By the time I stepped into the entry hall and shut the door behind me, neither Xander nor the wolf were anywhere to be seen. I slipped out of the jacket I had borrowed, folding it over my arms as I walked into the living room. What I saw next surprised me. Xander was kneeling beside the wolf who had curled up on Dakota's bed next to the fireplace. Neither one of them looked at me as Xander spoke quietly to him.

"Everything okay in here?" I asked.

Xander shrugged, his back still facing me. "I figured I'd better get to know my new roommate. He's all I have now."

"You still have me," I said, my voice barely louder than a whisper.

Xander rose to his feet and walked across the room, stopping in front of the couch. He scowled, a cold look in his eyes. "Do I? You made it pretty clear to the vet that I'm not your boyfriend."

I took a deep breath, suddenly realizing what was bothering him since he'd returned to the basement. "I didn't mean..." My voice trailed off as I wondered what I really had meant by that.

"You didn't mean what?"

"I don't know." I heaved a deep sigh. "Xander, these last few days, even the last few weeks, have been crazy. We've just been trying to survive. We've never even been on a real date."

He raised his eyebrows at me. "I can fix that."

"I know, and I hope you do, in time. But you have a lot to sort through right now." I paused, thinking of his father and the fact that he hadn't had a moment to grieve since yesterday. Changing the subject, I held up the pill bottles in my hand. "The vet left these. Should I leave them in the kitchen?"

He nodded.

After dropping the jacket on the back of the couch, I wandered into the kitchen. Then I placed the pill bottles on top of the instructions on the counter and returned to the living room. "He might need one of the painkillers soon." Without glancing at Xander, I approached the wolf and dropped to my knees beside him. My eyes locked with his, I explained the house rules through my thoughts. *'Xander will take good care of you. Food and water will be in the kitchen. Make sure you swallow your medicine when it's time to take it. Bathroom breaks are outside, but no running off. You need to stay in the house until your stitches come out.'* As soon as understanding registered in his tired eyes, I rose to my feet and turned to Xander.

"I'd really like to get out of these smoky clothes. Would you mind taking me home, or should I call my parents?"

He thought it over for a moment before his expression softened. "I'll get my keys."

⁄⁊⁄⁊⁄⁊

The drive back to my house was quiet. I kept trying to think of something to say, words to comfort Xander with, but I came up empty. I had never experienced the loss of a loved one like he had, and I didn't know what to say. So instead of talking, I watched the wintry landscape out the window, struck by how heavenly the snow looked as death overshadowed us.

When Xander dropped me off, I told him I would return in the evening after cleaning up, but he didn't acknowledge my promise. As soon as I hopped out of the pick-up, he sped out of the driveway, his tires burning skid marks on the pavement when he tore away.

I felt helpless as I stood on the sidewalk, staring after him. *What do you expect? You never should have told the vet he isn't your boyfriend. But since you did, you could have at least tried harder to explain it. Yes, the last few days have been a whirlwind, but he has proven over and over that he cares about you.* My inner voice left a trail of guilt in my mind, weighing on my heart when I retreated to house after the tail lights to his truck disappeared in the distance.

After showering and drying my hair, I dressed in clean jeans and a purple sweater that smelled like fabric softener. As soon as I finished packing an overnight bag, I reached for my recharged phone on the desk. Sinking into my chair, I swiped the screen and scrolled through my text messages.

Where R U? Brooke had asked.

Everything OK? had come from Ethan. *Brooke is really worried.*

I sighed, wondering what rumors were flying around school as I typed a message to Ethan. *Not sure if I'll make it to school tomorrow. Can you take notes for me and let me know what I missed?* I deliberately left out the details of the weekend and this morning.

Minutes after I sent it, he replied. *Where U been? Everyone's talking about some cabin fire you and Xander were at. Is it true Xander's dad didn't make it?*

I frowned, typing another message. *Yes, but please don't spread it around. I'll be at Xander's tonight. Call U later. Tell Brooke I'm fine. See you soon.* After sending it, I tossed my phone into my overnight bag from where I sat. Returning to school and answering the barrage of questions I would surely face seemed like a lifetime away. Right now, I only had one thing, or one person, on my mind. Xander.

After slipping into my tall black boots, I hoisted my overnight bag over my shoulder and grabbed my car keys. I hurried down the stairs, nearly crashing into my father who walked into the kitchen as I was leaving.

He looked exhausted with dark circles under his eyes, his disheveled hair and untucked shirt seeming to match his tired mood.

"Whoa," he said, immediately spying my overnight bag. "Where do you think you're going?"

"Back to Xander's," I said, hoping he wouldn't insist that I stay home.

"I'm not sure that's such a good idea. What about school?"

"School?" I gaped at him, wondering if he'd already forgotten the events of the last twenty-four hours. "Dad, don't you think—"

"I know what you're going to say. Yeah, it's been crazy lately, but you're a senior and you can't afford to fall behind. Besides, I'm worried about you. It would make your old man really happy if you stayed home for a change." He forced a faint, hopeful smile on his face.

"Dad, I'm practically a straight-A student. I can catch up. I appreciate that you're worried about me, but I'm fine. I'm just worried about Xander." The thought of not being with him tonight wrenched at my soul. No matter how hard he tried to be tough, I knew he was torn up over the loss of his father. I hated the thought of him spending the night alone in a house full of memories with the harsh reality that his father was never coming back. He may have been upset with me earlier, and perhaps I deserved it, but I was going back to him. I would be there to help him through this.

My father sighed. "How is he?"

"Not good, Dad. The only family he's ever known is gone. He's devastated, and I don't think he should be alone."

My father nodded. "Yeah. You're probably right."

"So can I go?" I asked.

He paused before saying, "Fine. One more night. But that's it. After tomorrow, it's back to your normal life. I'm only going to ask the school to excuse two days."

I smiled weakly. "Thank you. I'll ask Brooke and Ethan if I can borrow their notes, and I'll talk to all of my teachers when I get back."

"Don't make me regret this," he warned.

"I won't."

"And tell Xander I need to see him tomorrow. I've got

two bodies at the morgue and the mayor's breathing down my neck for a report."

I frowned at the thought of the mayor.

"Speaking of the mayor, how's the wolf?" my father asked.

"Dr. Harrison stitched him up. She said he's going to be fine. She was really awesome about the whole thing and promised not to tell anyone about him."

"Good. I've got enough problems right now and the last thing I need is the mayor finding out there's a pack of wolves roaming around here."

I fondly remembered the vet's kind reverence toward the wolf. "I'm pretty sure our secret is as safe with her as it is with Red. Oh, that reminds me, Red's snowmobile is still at Xander's. Do you know when he wants to pick it up?"

"I don't think he's too worried about it since the snow will probably melt soon. But I'll mention it to him when I see him next."

I turned to leave, but stopped to ask one last question. "Dad, how's Noah's friend? Is she going to be okay?"

"Looks like it. She was pretty dehydrated and the doctors said she had a bad infection in her leg, but they've got her on an IV and some strong antibiotics. Noah was with her when I left, and he was planning to stay at the hospital until her fever breaks. They're doing everything they can and, even though she's not out of the woods yet, they expect her to make a full recovery."

"That's good news. I can't begin to imagine what she went through, but I'm glad to know she'll be okay."

My father ran his hands through his hair, his expression worried. "That guy was pretty sick and twisted. I keep wondering what motivated him to torture her like that."

I glanced at him, meeting his gaze as I contemplated what to tell him. Finally, I answered, "Money, I guess. I mean, isn't that the motivation for most crimes?"

"Hmmm," was all my father said, as if not satisfied.

"Xander's father was very rich. I'm sure that had something to do with it."

"Yeah, he was. But I still don't get the connection." He shrugged. "Well, he's dead now anyway, so I guess we'll never know."

I nodded, trying not to think about what Noah's uncle might have done to Jenna and the wolves had he succeeded with his plan. At least it was all in the past now. Jenna would get better and the wolves had a long life ahead of them here in our mountains. "If we're done, I'm going to head out."

I started to turn, but stopped again when I heard my father's voice. "Your mother's still at school, but she's worried about you. You need to call her tonight, okay?"

"Can I send her a text?"

"No texts. She needs to hear your voice. She knows you're safe, but she also knows that you've been through a lot. She loves you very much, you know."

"I know. And I love her, too." It was true. I loved her just as much as I had before learning that she wasn't my birth mother. But I dreaded talking to her as much as I dreaded going back to school. They would all ask the same questions. "How are you? What happened? Are you okay?" Questions that would only conjure up the fear and pain I had felt while locked in the cabin when I just wanted to forget about it all and move on. "Okay," I reluctantly agreed. "I'll call her."

"Good. And meet me at the station tomorrow morning with Xander. Ten o'clock sharp."

"Got it." I motioned my hand up in a mock salute before turning to the closet to grab my jacket and gloves. After putting them on, I slipped out the front door.

The sun was dropping toward the mountains when I pulled up to Xander's house. Pink and purple scraped the treetops as the sun set, and shadows stretched across the driveway. I shut off the engine, apprehensive at the thought of seeing Xander again. I hated the way things had ended earlier today, and I needed to make sure he knew that I was sorry.

I reached for my overnight bag from the passenger seat and hopped out of the SUV. Then I walked to the front steps, my boots crunching in the snow.

As I approached the door, I debated whether to knock, ring the doorbell, or just walk right in. I finally chose the latter and tried the door handle, relieved when it opened.

"Xander?" I called softly, shutting the door behind me and heading into the living room, my overnight bag hanging from my shoulder.

A single lamp lit the dark room and, for the second night in a row, the fireplace was cold and empty. Xander sat on the floor, leaning against the couch with his legs stretched out under the coffee table. The wolf lay beside him, his head resting in Xander's lap.

I lowered my overnight bag to the floor and took off my jacket and gloves. After dropping them with my keys into a pile on top of my bag, I circled the couch and kneeled beside Xander on the side opposite the wolf. A large photo album took up the coffee table, a half-empty bottle of bourbon pushed off to the side of it. Xander stared at the photographs, turning the pages with one hand and holding a glass in the other.

I studied the pictures taken at the beach. In some shots, a young Caleb stood beside a tall surfboard staked into the sand, and in others, he rode the waves.

The spaces between the photographs had turned yellow over time, and I wondered how old the album was. "Is that your dad?" I asked.

"Yes," Xander said before swallowing the bourbon in his glass. Without a second to spare, he poured another drink. "He was the ultimate beach bum back in the day. I got my love of surfing from him." His eyes glued to the pictures, Xander downed the bourbon.

"Wow. It's still hard for me to imagine your dad surfing."

"He gave it up years ago. He lost interest when my grandfather passed away and he took over the family business. I was hoping he'd start to miss it once we moved here." He turned the page to more surfing pictures, but these showed a father and son.

"Is that you?" I asked, scanning them. My eyes stopped at a picture of a scrawny little boy with dark hair and baggy swim trunks sagging from his skinny waist. He smiled proudly as he stood beside a surfboard towering above him.

Xander sniffed, reaching for the bottle again. "Yeah."

I turned to him, noticing the tears rolling over his five o'clock shadow for the first time since I had arrived, and I reached out to touch his forearm. "Maybe you should slow down."

"Oh, please," he said gruffly. "Stop pretending to care. I'll drink as much as I want."

"Is that what you think? That I don't care?"

"I don't know what to think anymore." He chugged another swallow and slammed the glass down with a loud thud. I flinched and the wolf jerked his head up, alarm in his eyes.

"I'm here now, aren't I? That should tell you something. Can you at least look at me?"

He turned, staring at me with bloodshot eyes. "Is this what you want? To see how horrible this is for me?"

"No," I gasped, my eyes filling with tears. "It's killing me to watch you go through this. I want to be here for you. I know you'd do the same for me." I ran my hand up to his shoulder, fighting the urge to wrap my arms around him.

He studied me for a moment, his eyes thoughtful. Before he had a chance to reply, the wolf rose to his feet and padded through the house to the front door. When we heard a scratching sound, Xander ripped his eyes away from mine and jumped to his feet. "I need to let him out," he muttered, heading to the entry hall.

I remained where I was on the floor between the couch and the coffee table, my eyes roaming over the photo album and stopping to rest on the liquor bottle beyond it. I wondered if it would numb the growing sadness and despair in my heart.

No! I scolded myself. *Don't even think about it. Xander needs you, even if he thinks he doesn't. And you'll never be allowed back over here if Dad finds out. It's not worth it.* Forcing my attention back to the photo album, I flipped the pages for several minutes as I waited in the silence for Xander to return.

When I could no longer stand the suspense, I stood and went to the front of the house. I opened the door and looked out into the dusky night to see Xander standing at the end of the sidewalk, his back to the house as he focused on something ahead. "What's taking so long?" I asked, marching down the steps.

He turned and, without a word, gestured for me to come to him.

I hurried through the snow until I reached his side, my jaw dropping when I saw what had captured his attention. Three pairs of glowing eyes stared at us from straight ahead amidst the moonlight reflecting off the snow. Another two sets of eyes hid off to the side of the driveway. Five wolves, one of whom I recognized as Dakota, surrounded us, watching as the injured wolf nudged Xander's legs.

"What the hell is this?" Xander asked in dismay.

A smile broke out across my face. "The pack. They've come for him." I nodded toward the wolf at Xander's side. "And if he can't leave with them, they'll probably wait until he can."

"Oh, no. I agreed to one wolf. And I was okay with two, Dakota and this one. But six? That's—that's crazy!"

I chuckled softly and reached for his hand, squeezing it gently. "Don't worry. We can handle it, I promise."

Chapter 19

I let go of Xander's hand and walked toward the wolves,
ignoring the cold. Their eyes glowed, and their bodies
cast shadows over the snow. "Dakota," I said, spotting
him in the center straight ahead.

He trotted up to me as the other wolves backed away.
When he was almost within my reach, the white wolf bolted
away from the pack, pushing her way in between us. She
shot an angry look my way, growling.

"Whoa!" I gasped, stopping and throwing my hands up.
"What was that?"

Xander laughed from behind me. "Looks like you've got
some competition."

I twisted around to glare at him. "I'm glad you find this
so amusing," I muttered sarcastically. The injured wolf hovered next to him, watching the pack. Frustrated, I faced the
driveway again, glimpsing the wolves' shadows as they ran
off into the woods. Only one of them stopped, looking back
at me with soft amber eyes. Dakota. Then, with a swish of
his tail, he took off after the others.

I crossed my arms over my chest and spun around to face

Xander. "Guess you got your wish. One wolf, at least for tonight."

He shrugged, apparently noticing the disappointment in my expression. "I'm sure they'll be back when they get hungry enough."

I smiled appreciatively. "I hope you're right." Rubbing my arms, I said, "Man, it's cold tonight. Looks like the snow's going to stick around for a while. Do you mind if I stay over tonight in case Dakota comes back?" It wasn't the real reason I wanted to stay, but it was a good excuse.

"I guess not." He gestured to the porch, hesitating to return to the house until I rushed ahead of him and up the steps. The wolf followed me, and Xander brought up the rear.

Once inside, I lingered in the entry hall until Xander shut the door behind him. Things still seemed tense between us, and I struggled to find the right words to lighten the mood. After a long pause, I said, "Your gate was still open when I drove up the driveway and I wasn't sure how to close it."

"Don't worry about it. I'll take care of it tomorrow," he grumbled, brushing past me on his way back to the living room and his bottle of booze.

I shook my head before rushing after him. "Xander, please don't do this."

He stopped stiffly, whipping around, his eyes empty. "Don't do what?" Glaring at me, he closed the distance between us, pushing me as far back as I could go. When I felt the wall against my shoulders, he raised his arms to cage me in. "Don't numb myself from the pain of losing the only person who actually cared about me? Don't drown my sorrows in a bottle? Don't feel sorry for myself because the only girl I ever loved wants to stay over in case her *wolf* comes back?" Anguish rang out in his voice as he inched closer to me.

"What?" I whispered, my head spinning from his sudden outburst.

"Don't act so surprised. I already told you at the cabin.

Just before Noah's uncle torched the place. Remember?"

I nodded, my eyes locked with his. "Yes, I do. But I just figured you were spouting things out since we were about to die."

He huffed, rolling his eyes with no further explanation. Then he leaned closer to me, his hot breath grazing my face when he spoke again. "Why are you really here? I didn't ask you to come back. Dakota has been alone in these mountains his whole life. He finally has a pack. You know as well as I do that he's not coming back tonight."

I trembled, partially from his closeness and partially from my sudden fear of him. Or was I afraid of my feelings for him? Everything became a blur in that moment, and I couldn't think straight. "I don't want to leave you alone up here tonight," I admitted. "I can't. You need someone right now."

"I'm a big boy. I can take care of myself. Don't you have to be at school in the morning?"

I shook my head, not sure how to answer him. "Stop acting like this, Xander. Please. I want to be here, with you." My voice softened as I spoke, ending in a whisper.

"Prove it." His lips hovered just above mine, so close, so tempting.

I smelled the alcohol on his breath, but I didn't care. My eyelids dropped as I pressed my lips against his. He opened his mouth, kissing me urgently and deeply right away. I slid my arms up around his shoulders, pulling him toward me, but he didn't need any coaxing as he leaned in, crushing me between his chest and the wall.

My heart soared and butterflies zipped around in my stomach as he grabbed my waist and pulled my hips against him. Then he lifted me off my feet, running a hand down my thigh and hoisting it up. I wrapped my other leg around him, clinging to his shoulders as he carried me to the couch, his lips never leaving mine.

He lowered me onto the cushions, covering my body with his. Heat burned through me as his weight locked me under him. He continued kissing me, the touch of his tongue spreading fire through me.

It wasn't until his hands slipped under my sweater that reality jolted me. His fingers grazed the skin on my back, trailing a line of tingles up until he reached the band of my bra. He unhooked it with an ease that reminded me he'd done this before, probably more times than I preferred to count. My bra suddenly loosened, and I trembled, worried that he would take this further than I wanted to go, at least tonight.

My breath hitched when he touched my stomach under my sweater, and the world spun around me in a hazy blur. Anticipation sizzled through my veins, the small dose of fear worming its way into my mind not enough to curb my desire.

Then, without any warning, a wet nose smeared against my cheek. Xander must have felt it, too, because he struck out, hitting the wolf and slamming him into the coffee table. The wolf yelped upon impact.

Xander jumped up at once, sucking in a deep breath. "Oh, man!" he shot out, making me worry that he was angry at the wolf for coming between us. But Xander shifted off of me and dropped onto the floor. "I'm sorry, Blade. I didn't mean to do that. I'm sorry. Sorry, sorry, sorry," he muttered, burying his face in the wolf's fur.

I sat up, fastening my bra and adjusting it into place. "Blade?" I asked, watching them curiously.

"Yeah," Xander said, glancing my way. "I kind of came up with a name for him earlier this afternoon." He turned back to the wolf. "Sorry about that, big guy. I know it hurts. Maybe it's time for another painkiller."

Still kneeling, Xander turned to me, his expression softer than it had been all night. "I owe you an apology, too. I've been a jerk tonight."

I smiled faintly. "It's okay. You've been through a lot. And please scratch what I said about wanting to stay over in case Dakota comes back. Because that was a really dumb thing to say. I want to stay here for you, not him."

"Deal," he agreed.

"I wasn't finished. No more drinking tonight, okay?"

He nodded his head. "Done."

"And—"

"There's more?" he asked incredulously.

My smile widened as I met his gaze. "Just one more thing. It's an easy one, I promise."

"Okay," he said skeptically.

"What do you have to eat around here? I'm starving."

His apprehension faded, and he smiled with relief. "I'm sure I can come up with something." He stood up, extending his hand to me. "Truce?"

I sighed, realizing I'd never be able to stay upset with him for long. I simply couldn't resist the blue eyes and gorgeous smile I'd come to know so well. "Truce."

I reached up to take his hand. Wrapping his fingers around mine, he pulled me to my feet before we headed into the kitchen, the wolf following.

Xander flipped on the pendant lights hanging over the island as I took a seat on one of the bar stools. "So, Blade, is it?" I asked.

"Yes. I figured he should have a name if he's going to be hanging out with me for a few weeks." He went straight to the refrigerator, yanking the door open and grabbing a container of deli meat.

"What are you doing?" I asked, watching as he set the meat container on the counter and opened one of the pill bottles. He wrapped a pill in a piece of ham as Blade stared at it, drool hanging from his lips. When Xander offered it to him, he snatched it up, swallowing it whole. After Xander repeated it with a pill from the second bottle, I shook my head. "Wow," I said as the wolf swiped his tongue over his lips, savoring the ham. "You guys sure got used to each other fast this afternoon."

Xander closed the meat container while Blade disappeared around the corner on his way back to the living room. "I didn't have a lot to do," Xander said, shrugging as he returned the ham to the refrigerator. After shutting the stainless steel door, he turned to look at me from across the island. "We—I mean, I—don't have a lot of food right now. Are you okay with a frozen pizza?"

"Sure. That would be great."

He pulled a big flat box out of the freezer. After setting the oven temperature, he ripped open the package and slid the pizza onto the rack. Then he set the timer before turning his attention back to me, the empty box on the counter forgotten.

Leaning against the island, his solemn blue eyes met mine. "Did you talk to your dad before you came back tonight?"

I nodded. "Yes. He's expecting us at the station tomorrow morning at ten o'clock."

"I figured that. What else did he say?"

I stared blankly at him. "Just that—"

"Laken, I need you to know something," he interrupted, an uneasy look spreading across his face.

"Okay. What is it?" When he remained silent, I added, "You can tell me anything. What's bothering you?"

"It's going to take me a while to get through this. There's going to be ups and downs, and sometimes, my emotions may get the best of me. I want to apologize in advance for anything I might say or do."

"I think that's pretty normal after what you've been through."

"Normal or not, it doesn't make it okay. You're special and I don't want to ruin what we could have together."

"You won't," I told him with confidence.

"You seem way too sure of that."

"Why does that surprise you? Look, I'm not going to give up on you, okay?" I paused, watching his face for any sign of agreement. When a hopeful smile fluttered over his lips, I added, "Besides, I need to stay with you if that curse is real."

He nodded with anticipation in his eyes. "Yes, that's right. You need me. Now, about breaking the curse, maybe tonight would be a good time to get started."

Shaking my head, I huffed with a grin. Then I jumped off the bar stool and circled the island to where he stood. "It doesn't take much to distract you, does it?"

"Not where you're concerned." He slipped an arm around my waist, pulling me against his chest. Dipping his head toward me, he stopped just when I thought he was going to kiss me. "We're all alone here tonight, you know. You realize you're playing with fire, don't you? And I don't mean the kind of fire we were up against this morning."

"Maybe," I admitted. "But you're wrong about one thing. We're not alone, remember?"

Xander lifted his eyebrows. "The wolf? He doesn't count."

Staring at him, I let a cry for help roll out through my thoughts. As expected, the wolf charged into the kitchen, growling when he stopped a few feet away. Instantly, Xander released me and backed up.

"No fair!" he complained, holding his hands up in the air. Then he turned his attention to Blade. "Traitor! We'll see if you get another steak tomorrow."

I laughed, turning around to the wolf. "Thanks, big guy. But I'm okay. I just needed to know if you'd help me."

His growl faded, and I swore I saw him roll his eyes at me before heading back to the living room.

"Nice trick. Is that what I have to look forward to?" Xander asked.

"I don't know. I haven't decided yet," I said, a teasing tone to my voice.

"Great," he muttered before changing the subject. "So are your parents really okay with you spending the night over here? Again?"

I shrugged. "I guess. I mean, I didn't really ask permission. I'm eighteen, and they trust me. But aside from that, I think my dad's worried about you. He doesn't want you to be alone tonight, either."

"He seems like a good guy."

"He is."

"I hope I can get to know him someday. He's probably the only cop I may actually like."

"You will," I said.

"Then I guess I'd better earn his trust." He paused, a painful frown crossing over his face. "I might kick myself later for this, but you should probably lock your door tonight."

I laughed.

"What? I mean it. It's going to be a very long, cold night."

"If I thought I needed to lock my door tonight, I wouldn't be here right now."

"Didn't I once tell you that you can be naïve? Maybe I need to tell you again."

"Ha, ha, very funny." I glanced at the oven as my stomach rumbled. "How much longer on that pizza?"

Xander darted his eyes toward the oven timer. "About ten minutes."

"Good. I'm starving."

"Do you want a Diet Coke while you're waiting?"

"I'd love one." As Xander turned back to the refrigerator, I said, "You know, I hope my dad isn't the only cop you end up liking."

"What's that supposed to mean?" he asked, grabbing a glass from the cabinet and filling it with ice. When he turned to hand me the can and glass of ice, a knowing look lurked in his eyes. "You mean Noah."

"You're going to have to deal with him sooner or later," I said as I poured soda over the ice.

"Why? I don't even know the guy. It's not like we grew up together. Besides, how can we be absolutely sure he's really my brother?"

My jaw fell open. "You're joking, right? The resemblance to your father is pretty obvious. They have the same eyes and the same smile. I noticed it the first time I met your dad, I just didn't make the connection until yesterday. How much more proof do you need?"

"Okay. Maybe you're right. So we're related, biologically. But I have no loyalty to him and, clearly, he has none toward me since he tried to kill me."

"He did not try to kill you," I stated. "He did what he felt he needed to do to keep his friend alive. Don't tell him I told you this, but remember when his uncle let me go and he was supposed to take me home?"

"Yes."

"Well, I escaped into the woods. While I was hiding out, I saw his uncle lay into him. He yelled at him and took a swing at him. There's no way I believe Noah really wanted to hurt anyone if his uncle had to beat him up to get him to cooperate. Who knows how he was treated as a kid if that guy was the closest thing he ever had to a father?"

"Hmmm," Xander mused. "So what are you saying?"

"I'm saying that maybe you should give him a chance. What do you have to lose? After all, he returned your father's book."

"Something that never should have been taken in the first place," Xander grumbled.

"Noah didn't take it, so don't blame him for that. His uncle stole it from your family years ago. Look, if you're not going to get to know him for yourself, then at least do it for me. Please." I smiled softly at him until his cold exterior crumbled.

"We'll see," he said with a frown.

"Thanks," I said, assuming that was probably the closest thing to an agreement I would get out of him tonight where Noah was concerned. Then I wandered around the island and climbed back up onto the stool.

Xander opened the oven, and the scent of warm bread filled the kitchen. "Pizza looks done," he announced, grabbing a pot holder from a drawer next to the oven and pulling the pie out onto a cutting board that he placed on the stove.

"Smells good," I commented. "But anything would after today."

Xander flashed me a brief smile then reached for a knife from the butcher block and sliced the steaming pizza. When we finally sat down at the table with our plates, I realized that after the last two days of chaos, frozen pizza had never tasted better.

✁✁✁

That night, after I had my fill of pizza and called my mother as I'd promised my father, Xander and I stayed up late talking for hours. As expected, Dakota didn't return. After years of being a lone wolf, he could now be part of a pack. As much as I missed his company, I was happy for him. Besides, I now had Xander who seemed to complete me in a way Dakota never could.

When the clock struck midnight, I said good night before carrying my overnight bag upstairs to the guest bedroom. As I got ready for bed, I couldn't help remembering last night. It seemed like so long ago after the day we'd had, and yet it was just yesterday when Xander had kissed me while I wore nothing but a bath towel.

I shook my head, trying to push that memory far from my thoughts. I was exhausted and thinking about last night would surely keep me awake.

After brushing my teeth and changing into my pajamas, I turned off the lights and slipped under the covers. I had just closed my eyes, hoping to fall asleep quickly, when a light knock sounded on the door. My eyes flew open and I bolted up in bed.

"Laken," Xander called, his voice soft and hesitant. "Are you still awake?"

"Yes," I answered. "You can come in. It's open."

The knob rattled and Xander walked in now wearing a

white T-shirt and gray sweat pants, a frown lurking on his face. "I told you to lock the door."

"I don't always do what I'm told."

"I see that. I guess we have that in common." Leaving the door open, he walked across the room to the bed. When I noticed his puffy, bloodshot eyes, I wondered if he'd had more to drink since I had come upstairs. But I would have smelled it on him, and all I detected was the scent of toothpaste and soap. He sat down on the bed beside me, holding his hands up in the air. "I won't touch you, I promise."

"Under other circumstances, I'm not sure I'd like that. But thank you." I watched him, waiting for him to continue.

He scanned the room, avoiding my gaze. "I don't want to be alone tonight," he said after a long pause. "Do you mind if I sleep in here? With you." His eyes met mine as he said his last words.

"No, I don't mind," I answered softly.

I lifted the comforter up beside me and he slid underneath it. I lay down, resting my head on the pillow as I turned onto my side to face him. He was inches away, and I felt the heat from his body under the covers.

"I miss him so much," Xander said, the tear rolling down his face reflecting the moonlight. "I can go for hours and be okay, and then it hits me. He's never coming back. It's over. And there's nothing I can do to change that. I keep wishing that it was just a bad dream, that I'll wake up tomorrow and he'll be here working in the basement. But it's not a dream." When he stopped talking, I reached up to touch his shoulder. He sniffed, choking back his tears. "I never got to say goodbye to him."

"I know. That must be a terrible feeling. But instead of thinking about his death, tell me something about him. What's your favorite memory? You need to keep him alive in here—" I moved my hand down to the center of his chest. "—in your heart."

"I think my favorite memory is the day he took me out on his surfboard for the first time. I was four and all I did was ride with him, but I remember feeling so grown up."

I pictured Xander as a young child, riding the waves with his father. "When did you get your first surfboard?"

"On my fifth birthday. And I haven't stopped surfing since. Except when we moved here, of course."

"Those are good memories."

Xander smiled, his eyes dry now. "Yeah. I know I wasn't an easy kid to raise…"

I arched an eyebrow as he continued.

"But my father managed to get through the years with me. I think I aged him. I'm sure I gave him more gray hairs than he thought possible, but he always stayed calm. He had more patience than I'll ever have. I don't think I could raise a child all on my own like he did."

"Don't say that. You never know what you can do until you're faced with the situation. Look at Blade. I'm sure you never thought you'd be nursing a wolf back to health, and yet, you're doing just fine. You're a natural."

"I wouldn't be able to do it without your help. Having him housebroken in a couple minutes was pretty cool. But let's just hope I never have to raise a child on my own. I never want to put that to the test."

"No one ever does." I yawned suddenly, and my eyelids felt heavy with exhaustion.

"I'm sorry. I'm keeping you up."

"No, it's okay. This is why I'm here. To stay up and listen to stories about your dad."

"And save me from my self-destruction."

"That, too." Another yawn escaped. "Sorry."

Without another word, Xander reached for my waist and pulled me toward him. I turned over onto my other side, leaning my back against his chest and tucking my bottom into his hips. He rested his head on the same pillow as mine, rubbing my shoulder and upper arm. "This is nice," he murmured. "I could get used to this."

"Me, too," I whispered.

Then my eyes closed and I fell asleep in the warm embrace of his arms.

Chapter 20

I missed one more day of school to accompany Xander to the station where we both gave our statements for my father's report. Noah returned to work that day since Jenna's fever had broken during the night. He, too, gave a statement, identifying his uncle as the man who had kidnapped us and set fire to the cabin. I don't know what else he told my father, but whatever it was, my father believed him and didn't hold him responsible. He trusted Noah and encouraged him to put these events behind him.

My heart broke when my father pulled Xander aside to identify the remains of his dad. I wasn't allowed to go with him and, though it was probably horrible of me, I was somewhat relieved. When Xander stepped out of the room with my father, his face was ghastly white. I hugged him immediately and then took his hand to lead him out of the station. I remembered how he had been by my side every second when I thought Dakota had been killed, and I vowed to do the same for him.

Xander and I spent the rest of the day together at his house until the evening when my parents insisted I return home. I knew I needed to catch up on my homework, so I gave them no resistance. Before I left, Xander tried to assure me that he would be fine alone with Blade, but I still worried about him for the rest of the night.

I arrived at school the next day to finish out the week and, to my surprise, so did Xander. When he met me at my locker that morning, my mouth gaped open. "Hey," I said softly as I hugged him. "What are you doing here?" I asked, pulling away and gazing up at his tired blue eyes.

His black button-down shirt hung untucked over the waist of his blue jeans, his shark tooth necklace visible around his neck.

"I needed a distraction. I couldn't sit around the house all day. It's too quiet and empty, even with Blade. Besides, I figured the only way I might see you before Friday night would be to come to school."

I smiled, ignoring the stares from other students as they passed us, whispering to each other. "I didn't think you'd be coming back to school."

"Ever?"

"Well, yeah. You're not exactly eighteen. Haven't you already graduated?"

He shrugged. "Yeah. A few years ago."

"Then why come back at all?"

"I don't know. I don't have a lot to do. I probably won't need to start working for a while since dad made that last sale. I might do a little in the evenings and on weekends until school's out, but I'm not ready to isolate myself from the rest of the world yet." He smiled wickedly. "Besides, I want Marlena and her friends to see us together every day for the rest of the school year."

There was the Xander I had come to know and love. "You're terrible," I told him as I slipped out of my parka and hung it in my locker.

When I turned back to him, he reached up to touch my necklace. His fingers grazed my skin above my black sweater, sending familiar shivers through me.

"You haven't worn this in a while. I'm glad to see it back on you." He studied it thoughtfully for a moment. "There's a picture of it in the book Noah returned."

"Really? I'd love to read it someday."

"Of course. You should read it."

"And speaking of history, does this mean that you're going to help me finish our History project? I was wondering if I'd be left on my own for that." I paused then quickly added, "Not that it mattered. I could have handled it. You have much more important things going on right now."

"I wouldn't dream of deserting you," he assured me. "Besides, if I help you with that, then we get to spend more time together."

I flashed him a smile, although something pulled at me, like there was still something standing in my way of being with him. Only I couldn't quite put my finger on what it was. As he read the hesitation in my eyes and started to say something, Ethan and Brooke emerged from the crowded hallway.

"Laken! There you are!" Brooke rushed in between me and Xander to swallow me up into a big hug. "We've been so worried. I know I talked to you last night, but it's just so good to see you." She let go of me and turned to Xander. "I'm so sorry about your dad," she told him, wrapping her arms around him before he could protest.

"Thank you, Brooke."

"Yeah," Ethan added. "That's terrible." He offered Xander a handshake when Brooke backed away from him.

"Even though we never met him, we'll be at the funeral," Brooke said, sympathy shining in her blue eyes. "It's on Saturday, right?"

Xander nodded. "Thanks, guys. I'd appreciate that."

Brooke smiled at him before turning back to me. "We're going to head to homeroom. I'll talk to you later, okay?"

"Yes," I said.

"I'm just glad you're back, and in one piece," she gushed.

"Me, too."

"See you guys," Ethan said, taking Brooke's hand. As quickly as they'd arrived, they disappeared into the sea of students.

I shut my locker and hoisted my book bag strap over my shoulder. "Ready?" I asked Xander.

"Sure. Let's go." He draped an arm over my shoulders and we set off through the crowded hallway. I hoped my moment of hesitation before Brooke and Ethan had appeared would be forgotten, but I doubted it. Xander didn't miss a thing, and he certainly wouldn't forget it. At least once we got to homeroom and the bell rang, he wouldn't have an opportunity to ask me what was wrong. I would have to be more careful with my words and expressions, at least until I could figure out what was nagging at me and put it to rest.

߷

By Saturday, the snow had melted, Red had retrieved his snowmobile from Xander's driveway sometime during the week, and Blade's fur had started growing back. I didn't see Dakota all week, but Xander reported on Friday morning that he and the other wolves had come to the house the night before. He told me that he'd tossed a chicken to each one of them, teasing me that feeding the pack would make him broke someday.

The funeral for Xander's father was held at the only church in town. After a brief service for the handful of people who showed up, the casket was taken to the cemetery a few miles away.

Woods loomed beyond a black iron fence surrounding the tombstones scattered through the grass, and heavy clouds hid the tops of the tallest trees, as though death hung in the air. I stood with Xander beside the gaping hole in the ground, my heart heavy. Gathered around us were my parents, Noah, Brooke, and Ethan, their parents, and a few other people who had met Caleb in the short time he'd lived here. Everyone wore black, and I was no exception. My skirt reached my knees, cold air nipped at my legs through my stockings, and the heels to my boots sank into the ground still soft from the snowmelt. Shivering, I hugged my black coat around me and bowed my head as the minister recited a prayer.

As soon as he finished, Xander and I remained in the cemetery while everyone else weaved around the gravestones on their way back to the parking lot. I held Xander's hand in mine, squeezing it gently.

"Mind if I have a minute alone?" he asked.

"Not at all. I'll meet you in the parking lot." I released his hand and left him beside the hole in the earth. As I wound my way around the tombstones, I saw Noah lingering at the gate. He wore a dark suit and tie over a gray button-down shirt, the dark colors matching his dark expression. "Hi," I said, stopping in front of him.

"Hi. I haven't had a chance to talk to you all week." Noah nodded in Xander's direction. "How's he holding up?"

"As well as can be expected." I looked up at Noah, my gaze locking with his familiar brown eyes. At that moment, I realized what had been bothering me all week. I hadn't had a chance to talk to Noah since his uncle had blurted out that he'd fallen in love with me. And I still had feelings for him, although my feelings for Xander were stronger.

"I'd like to talk to him. I hope he knows I never wanted this. I'm very sorry for what my uncle did."

"Noah, what's done is done and there's nothing you can do to bring Caleb back. You have to stop beating yourself up. No one blames you. At least I don't."

"Thanks. I just wish I'd had a chance to get to know him. He was my father, too. All my life, I wanted nothing more than to have a father. It's the only reason I agreed to move here. So that I could meet him. But just when I was ready to introduce myself to him, Jenna disappeared. I couldn't do anything then, at least not without risking her life."

"How's she doing?"

"She's good." Noah smiled. "She wants to see you. Her memory of the morning we found her is still a little foggy since she was so exhausted, but she keeps asking me why I let a girl jump through fire into a den of wolves."

"What did you tell her?"

"Just that the girl who found her had everything under control."

"I hope you also told her that you left that morning on your own to rescue her."

He glanced down at the ground before lifting his gaze to me. "She doesn't need to know that."

"Is it true? What your uncle said?" I blurted out before I could stop myself. I knew a funeral wasn't the best place to ask about his feelings, but I wasn't sure when I'd get another chance. I had to ask. I needed to know, and soon.

"What are you talking about?"

"He said, 'I never told you to fall in love with her.'"

"You picked up on that?"

"Yes, I did. So is it true? Did you?"

Noah shifted his uneasy eyes at me and, in that moment of silence, I knew the answer. "Would it matter if I said yes?" he asked.

Tears brimmed in my eyes. "You should have told me. So all that time after you disappeared, you still cared?"

He nodded. "Yes."

"And what about now?"

"I don't think it would change anything," he said, dodging my question.

I watched his solemn expression, wondering how different things might have turned out if he'd told me the truth instead of pushing me away.

"So I guess you're with Xander now," he said.

Nodding, I focused on the woods in the distance. "It kind of just happened," I explained lamely. "I didn't really plan it."

"I see the way you look at him. The way you act when he's around. He means a lot to you, doesn't he?"

"Yes, he does," I admitted. *In spite of his mood swings, drinking, and arrogance.*

"Well, I wish you the best." Noah started to turn and leave, but I grabbed his hand. He stopped, looking at me curiously.

I released my hold on him when I was sure he wouldn't walk away. "Wait. This isn't goodbye."

"Then what is it?"

"I don't know. Do we have to figure it out now? Can we be friends?"

"I'm not sure that's possible."

"We don't have a choice. If I stay with Xander and you get to know him as your brother, we're going to run into each other. We might as well make the best of it. Isn't that what you want? To know your brother?"

"Of course, it is. I'm just not sure he wants that, too." He glanced across the cemetery at Xander.

"Give him some time. He'll come around eventually. So what are your plans now? Are you going back to Pittsburgh?"

Noah shook his head with a faint smile. "No. I live here now. And I like it here. Your dad's been good to me, so I want to stay. I don't have anything to go back to anyway, except my mom, who is really pissed that Efren's plan failed miserably."

"What about Jenna? Will she go back?"

"I'm not sure. I was going to try to talk her into staying. The ski season is just around the corner, and I'm sure she could get a job at a restaurant in town."

"I think she really likes you."

Noah nodded. "I know."

"Maybe that's a good thing."

He shrugged. "Maybe. We'll see. Anything's possible, I guess."

"You've got that right. Anything is possible." I stepped

closer to him, throwing my arms around his shoulders for a brief moment before releasing him and backing up.

"I'd better get back to the hospital. See you around." Without waiting for a response, he walked away.

I watched him head through the parking lot to his car and drive away. When I turned around to look for Xander, he stood right in front of me, a scowl on his face and his blood-shot eyes dry and puffy.

"There you are. Ready to go?" I asked him.

"Ready as I'll ever be," he grumbled, brushing past me toward the parking lot now empty except for his pick-up truck.

"Hey, wait," I said, confused. I ran as best as I could in my skirt to catch up with him. "Xander, wait up! What's that all about?"

He skidded to a halt, whipping around to face me. "Why did you wait for me, anyway? Why didn't you just go with Noah? He's the one you've wanted all along. And from the way he just looked at you, I'd say he wants you, too. So what's stopping you?"

My eyes clouded over with fresh tears. "Xander, don't do this, please. Not now."

"Look, I know something's been bothering you. You deny to the vet that I'm your boyfriend, and every time I think it's me you want, I can tell you're not sure. It's him, isn't it? It's always been him."

"No!" I cried, shaking my head. "You've got it completely wrong."

"Do I? Then what was that hug all about?"

"You're not jealous, are you?"

"Damn right, I am."

"You have absolutely nothing to be jealous about. I needed to talk to him. I didn't feel like things ever really ended between us. I mean, it felt like we left things hanging in mid-air."

"And now? He wants you back, doesn't he?"

I dropped my gaze, realizing that Xander spoke the truth.

When I looked back up at him, I didn't have a chance to explain.

"Then what are you still doing here?" He shook his head and started walking toward the truck. "Come on. I'll take you home." He motioned to the truck before heading to the driver's side of the cab.

With a frown, I hurried over to the passenger side and managed to climb into the seat by balancing on my toes. As he drove me home in silence, I tried to think of something to say. I wanted to comfort him, to tell him that I had just explained to Noah that Xander was the one I wanted, but I couldn't find it in my heart to forgive him for his stubborn jealousy. What kind of relationship could we have if he didn't trust me?

When he dropped me off, he didn't even say goodbye. I climbed out of the truck on my own and rushed into the house. Then I flew up to my room before my parents saw me and buried my face in my pillow as the tears burst from my eyes.

છ૭છ૭

I spent the rest of the night at home. I sat with my parents for dinner, but I only picked at my food. My appetite was nonexistent, and all I could think about was Xander. Xander and his dark mood swings, his stubborn jealousy, and his arrogance. Xander and his sexy blue eyes, his thick dark hair, and his tanned muscular chest. Xander and his drinking to cope with the loss of his father. Even though today had ended badly between us, I didn't want him to suffer through the night alone after his father's funeral.

As soon as dinner ended, I rushed back up to my room to call him, but all I got was voice mail. "Hi, Xander, it's me, Laken," I said after the beep. "I hate the way things ended today. I need to talk to you. Call me when you get this, okay?"

Without giving him even a minute to call me back, I sent him a text. *Just left you a voice mail. Call me.* I wanted to say so much more, to tell him that I missed him and I was worried about him, but I forced myself to keep it short and simple.

He never returned my call or my text. I pined away through the night with a book, but I couldn't concentrate and the words flew by in a blur as I turned each page. By the time I put the book down and turned off the bedside lamp, I couldn't even remember what it was about.

Not surprisingly, I tossed and turned for hours, finally falling asleep long after midnight. When I woke up, bright sunlight streamed in through the window above my desk. It was another sunny but cold November day. As I turned onto my side and stared at the sliver of blue sky I could see from the angle of the window, I realized what I needed to do. I sat up, pushed the comforter off to the side and raced into my bathroom to take a hot shower.

Forty minutes later, dressed in jeans, tall black boots, and a red sweater, I grabbed my phone and car keys and hurried down the stairs, thankful that my parents weren't up yet. There was no doubt in my mind that they would want to know where I was going at eight-thirty on a Sunday morning. The last thing I needed was to have to explain anything about Xander. He was so complicated that sometimes I didn't understand him myself.

Without bothering to grab a coat, I ran out the front door and raced down the sidewalk to the Explorer. After jumping into the driver's seat, I started the engine and backed out of the driveway. As soon as I shifted out of reverse, I slammed my foot down on the accelerator, tearing away from the house.

The woods were still and quiet when I pulled into Xander's driveway and parked next to his pick-up. After turning off the Explorer, I stepped out of the truck and slid my phone into my back pocket. With my keys in one hand, I shut the door as quietly as I could and walked to the back of the truck. I stopped, studying the front porch of Xander's log house, not sure if he was even awake. As I forced myself to put one foot in front of the other, the door opened and the wolf appeared. He wandered down the steps, acknowledging me with a quick glance before trotting off toward the woods.

Then Xander emerged in the doorway, his face bent as he focused on his phone. He seemed oblivious to the cold in a black T-shirt and blue jeans, his right sleeve cutting across his tattoo. I continued walking toward the front porch, but he didn't seem to notice me.

Before I could say a word, I felt a vibration coming from my back pocket. When I stopped and reached for my phone, Xander looked up, his expression softening as he watched me. I smiled at him, but remained quiet and swiped my phone to see that I had a new text message. From Xander. I quickly read the two words he'd just sent. *I'm sorry.*

I slipped the phone back into my pocket and raised my eyes to him. Nervous, I bit down on my lip, my pulse quickening. "I'm sorry, too," I said before racing up the porch steps.

He caught me when I reached the top, pulling me into his arms and locking his lips down on mine. He slid a hand down my back to my waist as I raised my arms around his shoulders, sifting my fingers through his hair. Shuddering, he pulled me closer to him, his tongue grazing mine and his chest pressing against me. There was no mistaking the familiar tingling shot that through my veins from his touch.

After a minute, he lifted his lips from mine. "Do you realize these last eighteen hours have been the longest of my entire life?" he asked.

I smiled, and joy swelled in my heart. "Xander, I'm sorry I didn't do a better job explaining what happened with Noah yesterday."

He pressed a finger to my lips. "Shh. Don't apologize, because even if you had tried, I probably wouldn't have listened."

"But you have to know that yesterday, after the funeral, I told Noah that I chose you. You're the one I want." I stared at him, swallowing nervously. "And you have no idea how much that terrifies me."

"What does?"

"You," I declared, my eyes not wavering. "But I've made up my mind. In fact, I think it's been you all along, ever since the first day of school."

Xander smiled. "What took you so long to admit it?"

"Oh, I don't know. I guess I needed a bad guy to kidnap us and practically kill us to realize it." I paused, hesitant to ask the question on the tip of my tongue. "So, are we okay now?"

He nodded. "Yes. But I'm the one who should apologize for giving you the silent treatment yesterday and then not calling you back. Do you forgive me?"

"I may need a little more convincing," I teased, expecting another sexy, steamy kiss. Instead, he broke away from me and hurried back into the house.

I frowned, wondering what was so important that he had left me standing alone on the front porch. I was about to follow him when I heard soft footsteps behind me, and I turned to see a pair of honey colored eyes watching me. "Dakota!" I ran down the steps and dropped to my knees on the sidewalk as he bounded over, nearly knocking me to the ground. I laughed as he slopped wet kisses all over my neck.

His tail wagged when I stroked his neck. "Where've you been?" I asked. "I miss you!"

While I spoke, the other four wolves led by the white one emerged from the woods. Dakota glanced at them before turning back to me, the guilt in his expression telling me that he had found his place in a pack. And that was where he belonged.

"You have new friends. I get it. It's okay, Dakota. I'm happy for you. Just promise me you'll keep yourself, and all of them, safe and out of trouble. Nobody can know about you or any of them." He gave me a subtle nod. "And don't stay away too long. Come back whenever you can. I'm sure I'll be here a lot." I threw my arms around his neck, burying my face in his fur for a moment. "I'll miss you, Dakota," I whispered. "It won't be the same without you, but I am happy for you."

I stood and watched with new tears in my eyes as he and the other wolves disappeared into the woods.

I took a deep breath, composing myself before turning around. Blade appeared at my side, trotting ahead of me to the front porch. I followed him up the steps and into the house, looking for Xander but finding the kitchen and family room empty. Then I headed back to the entry hall, nearly running into him when I turned the corner. He held a large manila envelope in his hand.

"I was looking for this. It came in the mail last week and I couldn't remember where I put it. Here." He handed it to me.

It had already been opened, and I reached into it to pull out an airline envelope. "What's this?" I asked, my eyebrows raised.

"You'll see. Read it."

I tucked the manila envelope under my arm and opened the ticket. As I read the itinerary, my mouth dropped open. "Hawaii?"

Xander smiled. "For New Year's. I know it's about six weeks away, but now you have something to look forward to. If you say yes, that is."

"Hawaii?" I repeated, shaking my head in dismay. "Xander, I don't know if I can accept this."

"Of course, you can. You've shown me your world, and now it's time for me to show you mine. I'm taking you to Hawaii for your first surfing lesson."

I stared at him for a minute before rereading the ticket in my hand. "Wow. I don't know what to say. I'm going to have to ask my parents, though. What if they don't let me go?"

"If they're nervous about you going on a trip with your boyfriend, then I guess I'll have to arrange for them to come with us."

When I didn't answer him, still surprised by his gesture, he placed his hand on mine. "Well? Do you want to go? If you don't say yes, I don't know what I'm going to do. The airfare is nonrefundable."

I dropped the ticket back into the manila envelope and launched myself at him, throwing my arms around his shoulders. "Yes," I murmured with a smile. "Of course, I want to go."

Xander kissed me again before raising his head with a sly grin. Then, in true Xander fashion, he asked, "So, how soon do I get to take you bikini shopping?"

Epilogue

I had never seen so much blue in my life. From where I lay on the surfboard as I paddled out to sea, everything was blue—starting with the ocean and ending with the clear sky above. They met somewhere on the horizon, but I couldn't tell exactly where. The warm sun kissed my skin as water droplets rolled down my arms, still slippery with sunscreen. As Xander had promised, the tropical Hawaiian sun was a welcome change from the snow and ice covering the entire state of New Hampshire right now.

"Okay! That's far enough!" Xander called from behind me.

I paddled with one arm to swing the board around and faced the beach. Behind it, a rocky cliff rose up to the sky with a scattering of green bushes here and there. Xander sat upright on his surfboard about halfway between me and the shoreline, his wet hair flopping over his forehead and his tanned chest glistening in the sunlight. Even from a distance, the sight of his toned abdomen and strong arms caused a flutter to race through me.

"Paddle toward me. When I say now, get up just like you practiced on the beach," he instructed, his voice loud enough to be heard over the crashing waves.

I did as he said, moving my arms on both sides of the

board while the current propelled it toward the shore. When a wave broke under the board, I knew it wouldn't be long. My muscles bunched, I was ready to spring to my feet. As the next wave rushed up behind me, he yelled, "Now!"

I leaned my weight on my hands, jumped to my feet, and slowly stood up. Holding my arms out, my knees bent, I rode the wave all the way in, a smile plastered on my face. As soon as the board lost momentum, I dropped down to lay on top of it.

Xander paddled over to me, sitting up on his board as soon as he reached me. "That was great! You're a natural. How did it feel?"

I sat up and dangled my feet in the water. The strap to my new white bikini top slipped off my shoulder and I reached up to push it back into place.

"Lame," I stated, shaking my head. "What's up with these waves? They're too small. I want to ride the big waves like the ones you see in the movies. Can we go to another beach?" I should have known something was up when Xander brought me to a deserted beach. The island had been packed with tourists when we had arrived. Surely, the beaches with the good waves were bursting with surfers.

Xander laughed. "Not so fast. You need to learn to balance and get a little confidence. That's not going to happen if you're getting bashed in by rough surf."

I huffed, pouting. "Well, you're no fun."

A sly smile crept onto his face. "You want fun? I'll show you fun!" He lunged at me, grabbing me in his arms and sending us both crashing into the ocean. My board flipped when I fell off, and Xander pulled me under, his strong arms holding me tight.

We surfaced seconds later, standing on the sandy bottom with the water reaching our shoulders. My hair hung against my back and water droplets clung to my eyelashes. Xander held me in his arms, his hands exploring my back, my hips, and the sensitive skin along my sides.

I was painfully aware that all I wore was the skimpy bikini he had helped me pick out at an island surf store yesterday.

"Hey!" I said, gently slapping his shoulder. "This isn't part of the lesson."

"I can't help it if I can't concentrate with you in that bikini," he said with a sparkle in his eyes.

"Then why did you convince me to buy it?"

"Because it's white and I was hoping it would be seethrough."

I groaned. "Is this what I have to look forward to?"

"If you mean having a guy who can't think of anything other than getting his hands on you all the time, then yes."

I couldn't help smiling. It wasn't a totally bad thing, and I had to admit I enjoyed the attention. "Maybe we should get back to the lesson." As I spoke, Xander's eyes shifted away, looking beyond me out at the ocean. I heard a strange splash that didn't match the rhythm of the waves and I looked curiously at Xander. "What was that?"

"We're not alone. Turn around."

"What in the world?" I spun around in time to see two rounded fins cutting through the surface about twenty feet away. Then another dolphin surfaced, puffing out of its blowhole before diving below the surface. Bewildered, I glanced back at Xander before breaking away from him. Diving head first into the water, I swam out toward the dolphins.

Once I reached the area where they had surfaced, I treaded water and spun around, searching for them.

"Laken!" Xander called. "What are you doing?"

I waved to him. "Just wait there. I want to try something."

"Be careful, please! Those are wild animals." He shook his head, muttering to himself as if he had just remembered who he was talking to.

Moments later, a dolphin surfaced a few feet in front of me, peering at me curiously. Then another one, and another one, and soon I counted six dolphins swimming nearby. As they came closer, I held out my hand. One of them stopped, lifting its head and nose out of the water. It inched closer to me until I could stroke its smooth head. "Hi, there," I said softly, not sure if it could hear me over the waves crashing against the shore.

As quickly as the magical moment began, the dolphins dove under the water, kicking up their tails with a splash and disappearing deep under the surface. I turned to see Xander swimming toward me. "You scared them away," I complained when he reached me.

"I had to. It's illegal to get close to them. I don't want you to get arrested on your first trip here."

"How could that happen? There's nobody in sight."

"Okay, okay. It made me nervous. I didn't want to see you get hurt," he admitted.

"I have a pet wolf and I've talked to bears." I laughed. "You sure you can handle being with me?"

It was his turn to laugh. "I guess it's going to take some getting used to. Life with you is going to be an adventure."

I smiled at him, looking at the reflection of the ocean in his clear blue eyes. At that moment, I could honestly say I had never been happier. I had found that one special person to share my life with, something that some people searched for their whole lives and never found. I was truly, undeniably in love with him. And as if that wasn't enough, I could be myself with him. I no longer had to hide my deepest secret. "That's right. Are you ready?"

"I hope so."

"Good." I flashed him a sparkling smile. "Now, I think it's time to catch another wave." I started to swim away, but he caught me.

"Not so fast!" was all he said before pulling me against him and kissing me under the Hawaiian sun.

ACKNOWLEDGEMENTS

This section is starting to sound like a broken record. It gets harder to know what to say since I've written four acknowledgements in less than a year. Like the last book, I want to start this section by thanking my readers. Those of you who have taken a chance on my books mean the world to me! Thank you for your messages and feedback. Nothing makes me happier than to hear from someone who enjoyed my story!

To my family for all the support. Every one of you has played a role in this series from my son who inspired the first scene to my brother who actually got the tattoo that Xander has. Thank you for bearing with me over the years. I know I've driven many of you crazy by dragging my dreams and stories on vacation and to holidays since I have to take advantage of any free time I get. I mean it when I say you're all part of the team and any success this book series has is a testament to all of us.

To my niece, Macie, for reading this story in rough draft and believing in me even when I had such a long way to go. To Veronica for reading this third book long before it made its way to the final edits and giving me encouragement.

To my publisher, Black Opal Books, and the editors, Lauri, Faith and Joyce. Thank you for all of your support and taking a chance on my story. I have learned a lot from all of you!

To Jenn Gibson for the beautiful covers. I said it the last few times, and I'll say it again. Thank you for your hard work and dedication. Your work is amazing! I appreciate everything you have done for me!

Lastly, to my family, coworkers, and friends as well as everyone mentioned above. Thank you for listening and supporting me. It's been an incredible journey and it wouldn't be nearly as special if I didn't have all of you to share it with!

About the Author

Tonya Royston currently lives in northern Virginia with her husband, son, two dogs, and two horses. Although she dreamed of writing novels at a young age, she was diverted away from that path years ago and built a successful career as a contracts manager for a defense contractor in the Washington, DC area. She resurrected her dream of writing in 2013 and hasn't stopped since the first words of *The Sunset Trilogy* were unleashed.

When she isn't writing, Royston spends time with her family. She enjoys skiing, horseback riding and anything else that involves the outdoors.

More information about Royston and her upcoming endeavors can be found at www.tonyaroyston.com.

Made in the USA
Middletown, DE
03 August 2016